Parasite Eve

by Hideaki Sena

Translated by Tyran Grillo

VERTICAL.

Published by Vertical, Inc., New York.

Originally published in Japanese as *Parasaito Ibu* by Kadokawa Shoten, Tokyo, 1995.

Notes courtesy of Prof. Shigeo Ohta translated selectively
from the Kadokawa paperback edition.

ISBN 1-932234-19-5

Manufactured in the United States of America

First American Edition

Vertical, Inc.

www.vertical-inc.com

CONTENTS

Prologue

Everything vanished suddenly before her eyes.

Kiyomi Nagashima had no idea what had happened. The houses she passed every day were reflected in the windshield only a moment ago. Just ahead, the street took its familiar slope downward and bore slightly to the right, where a traffic light had just changed to yellow, before vision failed her.

Kiyomi tried to blink, but her sight did not return. No matter how much effort she put into it, nothing appeared. They had all gone away: the white sedan driving in front of her; the tail light of the bus waiting at its stop; the cluster of high school girls hastening along the sidewalk. Kiyomi looked down in her confusion to check the steering wheel. Then, she was truly shocked. The steering wheel was gone. In fact, she did not even know where her hands were. She could not feel the seat belt around her waist nor her foot on the gas pedal, for neither was where it was supposed to be. There was only darkness fanning out, continuing endlessly in all directions.

There was a churning around her, and she was floating in a warm, viscous liquid. She was naked. Her clothes had vanished without her ever noticing.

That dream again.

That dream she had once a year, on Christmas Eve, in which she felt herself writhing in some pitch-dark world without beginning or end. She'd always had that strange dream. This was the dream, and she was now entering into it again. But she did not know why she was having it just now. Like the stars' orbits, the dream always came to her with regulated precision. She never dreamt it on any other night but Christmas and had certainly never entered into it while she was awake.

Her body was changing profoundly. She lost all feeling in her arms and legs. Maybe they'd actually vanished. Head, torso, and hips gone, a body long and narrow like a worm's, she felt herself to be. Kiyomi shook and slithered ahead through the slightly sticky blackness.

What is this place? It was a question she had asked many times before. Her body seemed to recall this place, yet no matter how much she tried, Kiyomi her-

Prologue

self could not remember. Once, in some far-off place, Kiyomi was just like this, not understanding anything, just squirming and swimming. That much was true. Had it been yesterday, a recent year, or in the more distant past? She could not tell. To begin with, it was not clear that time flowed in this vast gloom.

Kiyomi felt her body changing again. Something small divided slowly deep inside of her. At the same time, she felt a gentle constriction in her very center, and the ends of her body flowed quietly in opposing directions.

She was becoming two.

It was a strangely tranquil feeling. Time seemed to pass so gently, slowly.

Where am I? When is this? What am I? Such mundane concerns no longer mattered. She wanted only to remain floating like this in the dark.

She gradually split in half. There was no pain. Rather, she was insensate and that was bliss. Everything sedate. No turmoil. Dividing like it was natural. Calm. All was calm.

Kiyomi let all her nerves relax as she slowly surrendered herself to the flow…

Her vision was then completely restored just as unexpectedly as it had abandoned her. She clearly saw now her own two hands grasping the steering wheel. Kiyomi blinked, then looked straight ahead.

She was heading straight into a telephone pole.

PART ONE
Development

Parasite Eve

1

Until the phone rang that morning, it was the beginning of an average, uneventful day for Toshiaki Nagashima.

At 8:20 am Toshiaki parked his car at the School of Pharmaceutical Sciences. The lot was still more than half empty. Briefcase in hand, he got out of the car and locked it. He looked up indifferently at the Pharmaceutical Center. Rising six stories high, the building was steeped in somber gray beneath the cloudy sky.

In the entrance lobby, Toshiaki changed into a pair of sterile sandals, then took the elevator to the fifth floor. Double doors opened to reveal a corridor extending in both directions. Far back to the right was the lecture hall where he taught his course on Advanced Methods in Biofunctional Sciences. It appeared that most of the students and other staff members had yet to arrive, for not a sound could be heard. However, late mornings were not unusual. The other organic science courses were quite different, entire staffs assembling and seminars beginning at 8 am. Toshiaki's course was an exception in that they wasted no time on finding fault with their students' time management skills. Instead, he and his colleagues stressed that what mattered was for the students to conduct their experiments and present the data.

As a mere research associate, Toshiaki made an effort to arrive by 8:30, but this was not a commitment required of him.

He opened the door to Lab 2, which housed his desk, turned on the light, and entered. After hanging his coat, he placed his briefcase next to the bookshelf. Two chemical agent order forms had been written up and left for him on the desk by his students the night before: specifically, requests for the restriction enzymes *Eco*R I and *Bam*H I. Toshiaki attached the forms together with a paper clip and pinned them to the desk-side wall.

Looking over the notes he'd made the day before, he began to prepare for his experiment. First he left the lab and keyed open a door just down the hall which led into the Cultivation Room. The room's interior was imbued with a ultraviolet sterilizing light, which he switched to an ordinary fluorescent light as he stepped inside. He took two plastic culture flasks from the incubator and placed them under a microscope. He adjusted the focus and peered through the lenses, gazing at the cells at the other end. After ensuring he was satisfied with their condition, he returned the cells to the incubator, then removed a few implements from the autoclave and placed them into the clean bench.

Toshiaki returned to his lab and removed several testing chemicals from the refrigerator. Just then, Sachiko Asakura, a second-year master's student he had been mentoring, walked in.

"Good mor-ning," she enunciated pleasantly as she entered.

Toshiaki returned the greeting like an echo.

Asakura put her coat away, revealing a figure shrouded in a white summer sweater and jeans. She had her long hair tied behind her back. Removing her sweater, she donned a white lab coat.

At nearly 5'9", Asakura was quite tall for a woman, shorter than Toshiaki by only an inch or so. When she passed by, she acknowledged him with a smile and a small bow. Asakura's height was greatly accentuated in her long coat, and it was always pleasant to watch her stately figure as it fluttered about the lab during an experiment.

Toshiaki informed her he would be in the Cultivation Room and, with that, left the lab.

Once the clean bench preparations were complete, he removed the culture flasks and commenced his work. The cells he was using, known as NIH3T3, were relatively common. He had, however, introduced retinoid receptor genes into the cells of one of the flasks. Two days before, he'd placed each respective cell culture into a new flask and bred them; then, the following day, he'd added a dose of β-oxidation enzymes into the indicator solutions. Today, he planned on collecting mitochondrial data from both cultures. His expectation was that the activity of the β-oxidation enzymes would be higher for the cells receiving the gene transfer than for the control cells.

Just when he began the procedure, there was a phone call.

Toshiaki heard the lab phone, but his hands were occupied and Asakura was over there in the lab. He assumed she would take the call. After three rings, she seemed to have picked up the receiver; for a dozen seconds, the morning's peace was restored. But soon there was the sudden echo of rushed footsteps. Toshiaki continued working, wondering what was the hurry. Not knowing why, he chanced a glance at the wall clock. The hands indicated exactly 9:00 am.

The lab door burst open.

"Dr. Nagashima, you have an urgent phone call."

As he lifted his gaze slowly, he saw Asakura's face in the doorway, her mouth trembling slightly.

"It's from the hospital. Y-your wife. She's been in an accident."

"What?"

With that he rose.

Development

2

The streets around the University Hospital were congested, rows of outpatient cars spilling over onto the public roadways. Unable to suppress his mounting impatience, Toshiaki sounded his horn furiously.

The person on the phone had been a staff member from the emergency ward. Kiyomi was driving her car, he said, when for some reason she veered off a turn, crashing straight into a telephone pole. Considering how bad the wreck was, he doubted she had even tried the brakes. Kiyomi had suffered a potentially fatal impact to the head. Toshiaki asked about the location of the accident, only to discover that it was a main drag he used too. It was an easy road to speed on, but its unobstructed view made it anything but dangerous.

"Dammit!" he shouted, turning the steering wheel sharply as he peeled out from the middle lane and made a U-turn. Car horns blared everywhere like pigs, but he paid no attention to them. He circled around to the hospital's back entrance, skidded into a parking area reserved for personnel, and dashed inside through a loading bay. On the way he managed to grab hold of a passing nurse to ask where the emergency ward was.

The hallway felt endless as Toshiaki ran with all the speed he could muster, his leather shoes making skittish sounds upon the linoleum floor. His lips shaped Kiyomi's name in a continuous murmur. He turned right at the next passageway, nearly knocking over an elderly woman in his haste. Noticing her at the last moment, he jerked his body around to avoid her and continued hurriedly down the corridor. He refused to believe it. What had gone wrong? Hadn't Kiyomi smiled that morning like always? Toshiaki thought of breakfast. They ate fried eggs with fish and miso soup with tofu. Not that there was anything unusual about it. It was as common a breakfast as one could imagine, a meal that implied she meant to continue their life just so. This was all too sudden.

They'd left together that morning. Kiyomi was going to the post office and took her own car. She had just gotten the car, a used compact, six months ago because she needed it for shopping. She liked cute things and was attracted to its red color.

"Excuse me, but are you Kiyomi Nagashima's family?"

Toshiaki caught his breath. An aging nurse had come running up and was peering into his face.

Toshiaki cleared his throat, swallowed, and forced out an affirmative reply.

"Kiyomi-san is in critical condition," the nurse explained. "It appears she sustained a strong impact to the head from the accident. When she was carried here, she was already hemorrhaging badly and not breathing."

Toshiaki walked past her and sat himself down on a couch in the hallway. He gazed at the nurse's face in blank amazement, unable to wrap his mind around what she had just said.

"Can you save her?"

"We've taken her straight into the operating room for emergency treatment. Her condition is serious... I would advise that you summon her relatives."

Toshiaki groaned.

Kiyomi's parents came at once. Her father managed a surgical clinic in an old housing district nearby and lived right next to his workplace, only a few miles from the University Hospital.

Both their faces were pale. Kiyomi's father asked Toshiaki how she was holding up. When he learned of her critical state, he gulped, closed his eyes, and slumped onto the couch.

Kiyomi's mother, normally the epitome of unwavering composure, was badly disheveled. Concealing her face behind a handkerchief, she showered the nearby nurse with cries of anguish. Toshiaki stared blankly at the hunched figure of his mother-in-law. He hadn't expected this. He realized with a jolt that Kiyomi's parents were human beings after all.

When he was invited to Kiyomi's house for the first time, Toshiaki's impression was of a peaceful, elegantly dressed family, smiling, sipping tea, enjoying each other's company surrounded by high-class furniture. Her father was an easygoing and reliable man and her mother, while reserved, wore an inextinguishable smile. He had always thought them perfect, like a family one might see on TV. He could hardly picture the couple before him now as the comfortably tranquil pair they always presented themselves to be. Theirs now was a show of raw emotion.

"Calm down," Toshiaki's father-in-law chided his wife, but he was unable to mask the trembling in his voice. She turned around with a start, her eyes wide open. Then, letting out a great sob, she leaned her body brokenly into her husband's.

It was well past noon, but they had no appetite. They relocated to the waiting room at the nurse's suggestion and sat down, staring absentmindedly at the clock. The nurse came occasionally to update them. By applying massage, they had been able to restore Kiyomi's respiratory function, but she was lapsing into gasping fits and was now on a respirator. After undergoing some CT scans, she had been moved to the Intensive Care Unit.

After thirty long minutes, a doctor finally came in. They all rose from the couch. The man wore glasses and had a certain aura of frailty. He was still young, probably in his early 30's. But his facial features were chiselled, and his eyes gentle. Toshiaki had a good feeling about him. The doctor introduced himself as a brain surgery specialist. He turned his face almost defiantly towards them and explained everything in the most sincere tone.

"Kiyomi-san was suffering from a serious cerebral hemorrhage. As soon as she was brought to our ward, we operated on her brain and attempted to resuscitate her heart and lungs. She's breathing now with the aid of a mechanical respirator; she has lost the capacity to breathe on her own. We will continue to medicate her with heart stimulants and keep a close eye on her. However, she is in a deep coma right now. It's extremely regrettable for me to have to tell you this, but she is heading toward brain death..."

Kiyomi's mother hid her face to smother the pain-stricken voice that escaped from her mouth as a strange *ah*.

Toshiaki did not know how to respond. Terms like "mechanical respirator," "deep coma," and "brain death" coiled into a vortex in his head. He could hardly believe that his beloved wife was being described in such terms.

Suddenly, Toshiaki sensed heat. He looked up. His body felt hot, like it was on fire. The room hadn't gotten any warmer. It felt more like he'd ignited from within. The temperature shot up. Unsure what was going on, Toshiaki looked around him, but his vision clouded with crimson and was soon gone. He opened his mouth to scream, but only a dry rasp came from his throat. The back of his throat had vaporized. Flames would rise from his fingertips at any moment. He was going to burn, he thought. He was about to start burning.

"What will happen to her?"

The heat left him. His mother-in-law was interrogating the doctor.

"We are monitoring her brain waves, blood pressure, and heart rate. If the blood flow to her brain stops, she will start losing brain cells. We are performing CT scans to monitor the situation. After reviewing the results, we will examine whether brain death has occurred."

Toshiaki could hardly tell where the doctor's voice was coming from. He blinked. He saw a hand. It was his left hand. He tried closing and opening it and saw that his fingers were moving. They did not flare up as he half-feared.

By the time he came to his senses again, Kiyomi's mother had drawn near to her husband, and the doctor was informing them that the first brain-death examination might have to be conducted that evening. Toshiaki felt dizzy and sat on the couch, still reeling from his hallucination. There was a throbbing in his temples.

"Are you okay?" said the doctor.

Toshiaki waved him away.

Kiyomi was going to die.

He felt deceived. Everything seemed to be happening in some distant world. His entire body was still flushed. *What was that anyway?* he wondered amidst the banging in his head. *What on earth was that heat?*

Development

3

At 6 pm the three of them were allowed into the ICU.

When they entered the room, they were instructed to change into pale green sterilized gowns and hats and to wear special masks. In addition, they had to sanitize their hands and feet. As for Toshiaki, he was already familiar with this type of procedure, having performed many experiments on animals in which prevention of infection, and therefore the wearing of such garments, came with the territory. But he never imagined he would be wearing them in a hospital setting. Because Kiyomi's father was a surgeon by profession, he became a respectable figure in this attire. Only Kiyomi's mother, visibly annoyed by the sensation of the roughhewn gown against her skin, was unaccustomed to it.

It was an unexpectedly large room. There were a number of stretchers lined against the wall and half as many machines used for blood transfusions. Two small monitors were installed in the wall from which countless tubes and wires extended. In spite of all the technology, most of the other beds were unoccupied, giving the room a dormant atmosphere.

Kiyomi was lying down on the second nearest bed. Tubes had been inserted into her nostrils. Toshiaki followed them with his eyes. They ran from her nose into a bucket-shaped object and continued from there into a white machine that had several manual controls and a meter with a needle, which quivered left and right within its prescribed arc. It wasn't a large machine, but every time the needle jumped, a hissing sound issued. This was the respirator, according to the doctor. The wall monitors were both aglow with Kiyomi's brain wave activity.

They all gathered around and gazed upon her. Her head was shaven and wrapped in cloth and bandages, but the rest of her was covered with a simple sheet and no other injuries could be spotted. Aside from the scars on her head, she looked completely unscathed.

After leaving the room, the doctor led the way to his office. He offered them a seat and sat down at his desk. Films of Kiyomi's CT scans had been posted to a

light box on the wall. As he showed them the brain wave data, the doctor began
to explain more about her condition. Brain death, he said, was an irreversible
state that occurred when the brain stem was deprived of blood and ceased to
function. This was distinct from a "vegetative state" where the brain stem was still
functional. The hospital was required to verify any potential patient's condition
with an officially sanctioned examination in accordance with Welfare Ministry
standards. Additional brain wave response inspections, along with more CT
scans, were also available at their hospital.

"These are the results of the first exam, conducted at five o'clock."

The doctor handed them a spreadsheet which contained the results of
Kiyomi's auditory brain stem response, pupillary dilation, and respiratory tests.
The doctor explained each in detail. He emphasized that there were no noticeable changes in her brain wave activity in the face of stimuli and that she was not
breathing on her own. If she were taken off her respirator, she would cease to
breathe, her heart would fail, and her temperature would plummet.

On the right side of the form was a blank chart in which the second examination's results, to be conducted the following afternoon, were to be recorded.

"We will see if the second test yields the same results. By that time, over six
hours will have passed since the first, and this is how we ensure that no mistake
is being made."

Toshiaki was only half listening to the doctor's words. He could not dispel
Kiyomi's peaceful expression from his mind.

"We will leave her as she is for now, on the respirator. I would recommend
that you discuss, as a family, the issue of when to take her off it. Until then, you
have my word that we will do anything in our power to sustain her. We will keep
her on a nutrient-rich IV and periodically shift her lying position so she won't
develop bed sores. Please understand, though, that while she may be breathing,
Kiyomi-san is already, in fact, dead..."

They all returned later that evening to the ICU and sat at Kiyomi's bedside.
Her father had begun to regain some emotional stability by now, while her moth-

er was still unable to make sense of things, overwhelmed as she was by her tears. The day's hardships had etched weary circles under her eyes. She laid herself down, completely exhausted. Kiyomi's father, realizing the day had been too much on his wife, thought it better to return home and left with her in his arms.

Toshiaki was unable to sleep and stayed behind.

At around 10 that evening, a nurse came in to give Kiyomi's body a rubdown with a hot towel. The petite nurse exuded nothing but sweetness. Still in her early twenties, she possessed a genuine sincerity and the special attention she afforded to Kiyomi struck a chord in Toshiaki's heart.

As he helped the nurse with her work, Toshiaki again felt the warmth of Kiyomi's skin. A few beads of perspiration dotted her back and saliva had welled up in her mouth. Her skin was still firm, cheeks flushed with a pale rouge. Toshiaki had never seen a so-called "vegetable," but as he looked upon Kiyomi's body it was impossible for him to distinguish her from that harsh term.

"Please talk to your wife," the nurse said with a smile as she went about emptying Kiyomi's bedpan. "It'll cheer her up."

Toshiaki did not doubt the nurse's advice and so he held Kiyomi's hand, talking to her continually throughout the night. He told her about his day, shared memories, and talked about the things he loved most about her. He felt a warmth from her palm passing into him. Her chest rose and fell regularly as the hiss of the respirator echoed through the ICU.

Toshiaki went to the university early the next morning, overcome by a sudden desire to be alone. He drove slowly through the streets which now seemed to him devoid of shadow and form. A faint mist hovered around the campus grounds. As Toshiaki inhaled damp air into his lungs, he walked into the building and went straight to his lab. It was still early, so there was no one else around. He sat down at his desk and leaned back in the chair, letting out a deep breath. Outside the window, the pale houses along the road blurred far into the distant haze.

The image of Kiyomi's comatose face wavered in his mind.

Toshiaki had witnessed the death of loved ones more than he would have liked, whether from terminal illness or simply old age. He could honestly say he was capable of understanding death. That is, until he saw his wife's body lying motionless on a hospital stretcher. Any previously held notions of mortality no longer applied.

But was she really dead?

In Toshiaki's delusional state, pessimism encountered the warmth lingering in his hands from the night before in subtle billows of conflict.

His knowledge of the controversy surrounding brain death had been gleaned from television, newspapers, and further from various educational materials and medical journals. If anything, Toshiaki's attitude was affirmative. Brain death was to him a scientific matter that was unfairly subjected to sentimental arguments. When there were patients who needed organ transplants in order to survive, why, he wondered, should people hesitate to have replacements extracted from brain-dead donors?

He gnawed his lip at the thought of taking organs from Kiyomi's living body.

Toshiaki conducted dissections on rats and mice nearly every day, yet he was far from accustomed to it. It always made him terribly uncomfortable to imagine doing likewise to a human being. In his mind, the image of an anesthetized lab rat with its stomach cut open overlapped with that of Kiyomi's nude figure, the rat's liver and kidneys distorting into her abdomen...

Kidneys.

Toshiaki shut his eyes.

Kiyomi had registered as a kidney donor last year. It all came back to him quite clearly now.

Toshiaki thought organ transplantations were something to be lauded. It would be wonderful, of course, if Kiyomi's kidneys could be of any use. Yet, because she was still warm with life and her heart going strong, he could not let himself be reconciled to the idea of extracting her kidneys. He simply didn't feel that his wife was dead. He was confident that she could go on and live.

He opened his eyes. The mist had already dispelled outside and the buildings along the streets now greeted the dawn, scintillating blindingly in the morning sun. A crow's cry could be heard in the distance. A new day was beginning. For most, it would be like any other. For Toshiaki, it would become the day in which the reality of his wife's accident would leave behind its first indelible traces.

He needed to move around. But before returning to the hospital, he walked over to the Cultivation Room to check his cell cultures once more. He would replace them with a new batch if they had stabilized.

He inspected his flasks under the microscope. There was nothing particularly in need of his attention. He gazed vacantly at his hybridoma and cancer cell cultures. Then, without warning, an idea came to him.

Toshiaki took his eyes from the lenses and peered at the red indicator solution inside the flask. A voice filled with wonder escaped from his lips.

"Oh, Kiyomi..."

His heart was racing. He sprung from his chair. The idea spread swiftly through his mind. As he staggered away, he could not take his eyes from the flasks upon the table.

Kiyomi's body undoubtedly suffered extreme brain trauma. Still, when he held her hand, he knew life continued to emanate from her.

Not *everything* in her had died.

His eyes still glued to the flasks, Toshiaki clenched his fists and shouted at the ceiling.

In his excitement, the hospital was much too far away...

He slammed on the gas pedal and changed gears hastily, muttering Kiyomi's name under his breath. There was so much to do. He had to see what Kiyomi's parents thought about offering up her kidneys, reestablish his connections with an old surgeon friend, and ultimately gain the doctor's approval for his plan. He was sure of achieving this all without a hitch. Kiyomi was still alive. Knowing this for sure, tears began to flow from his eyes.

Parasite Eve

From now on, my dear, we'll always be together...
So did his heart cry out.

Development

4

Toshiaki and his father-in-law watched intently as the second examination was carried out. The doctor in charge, whom they had met only yesterday, divided his duties with another. Toshiaki had prepared himself for some grandiose procedure, but in actuality, all they did was place headphones on her and poke her skin to see whether or not she responded to stimuli. Kiyomi's brain waves remained even. The head doctor recorded the results on the chart. Toshiaki mused about how unscientific their methods were.

All findings were negative. When he was done, the doctor handed over the form and gave a look that seemed to implore acknowledgment. Toshiaki compared the chart to Kiyomi's face, then returned it to the doctor with a single nod. The doctor accepted the form, signed his name on the top, and stamped it.

"Kiyomi-san has been judged to be brain dead."

"Yes."

Toshiaki knew he could have said something more appropriate and was amazed by his own vapid response.

"Well then, please step into my office for a moment," the doctor said, and led them in.

A woman was waiting inside. Upon noticing them, she stood up from her chair and bowed politely. Toshiaki returned the gesture vaguely.

"This is our transplant coordinator, Azusa Odagiri," stated the doctor by way of introduction. "It has been brought to my attention that Kiyomi-san is a registered kidney donor, so I took the liberty of inviting her here."

Odagiri handed them her business card. This suit-clad woman looked younger than Toshiaki and gave the impression of a capable professional. Her piercing eyes contrasted with the gentle curve of her cheek lines, and this imbalance helped give her an air of being approachable. Her expression promised honesty and intelligence. She bowed slightly again and said how pleased she was to meet them.

A recipient's transplant procedure could only be consummated when a donor was present. The only available donors, excluding those still living and depending on the type of treatment needed, were usually patients diagnosed with brain death or heart failure. ER doctors needed to stay focused on their own tasks, so it was undesirable for them to push to perform these operations. On the other hand, if a transplant surgeon approached the patient's family directly for the organs, it invariably ended in hurt feelings. To mediate between transplant and emergency medicine, someone had to deal specifically with all these issues. This was where the transplant coordinator, Odagiri, came in. Hers was a job which spanned many areas and, because of the doctors' overbearing schedules, meticulous familial consolation and care were upheld as the most important of her duties.

Toshiaki and his in-laws seated themselves on the couch and faced her.

"I will get right to the point here. With Kiyomi's kidneys, we could save the lives of two dialysis patients. CRF, or chronic renal failure, is a condition that can afflict even the very young. Unfortunately, there is no cure. All they can do is clean out the body through dialysis treatment. But because of the time factors involved, it's nearly impossible for such patients to lead an active social life, and they are under strict dietary restrictions as well. With a transplant of just one kidney, such a patient could begin to live normally. I can assure you that these kidneys would by no means be wasted."

Toshiaki listened to this earnest appeal and spoke up to discuss details.

"I understand perfectly well that Kiyomi's kidneys could save the lives of others and I'd like to donate them for that purpose. It was her wish to register in the first place and I think we should respect it, so please do what you feel is best in this situation. I only ask that you remove nothing more. I don't know if Kiyomi would have approved of any further extractions. I would never dream of doing anything without her prior consideration."

He felt they were conversing like actors in a play. After speaking his mind, he awaited the reaction of his father-in-law, who closed his eyes and managed to nod once in approval.

"I am truly grateful for your willingness to go through with this. I cannot thank you enough." Odagiri bowed her head deeply in gratitude. "I will help you through the entire process to the best of my ability."

Toshiaki carefully filled in the transplant consent form that Odagiri presented. In the center of this thin sheet was written:

I hereby consent to the surgical removal of the following organs and tissues:

from the body of the patient for the purpose of transplantation.

This dry sentence had been printed in the middle of the form. In the blank spaces above it, Toshiaki entered in his wife's name, address, date of birth, and sex. Then, gathering all of his strength, he circled the word "kidneys." At that point he inhaled deeply and, before exhaling, entered in the current date, his surname as the consenting party, address, and relation to the donor.

"I'll also need your seal here."

Odagiri pointed to a spot at the bottom with a long white finger.

Toshiaki took out his personal seal from his front pocket. With great tact, Odagiri removed a red ink pad from her purse and placed it in front of him. Toshiaki pushed down hard on the seal with a slight wriggling motion, affixing it to the form. His name stamp "Nagashima" stood out vividly, almost to the point of lewdness. He averted his eyes for a moment and wondered if he was making the best choice. He had just officially sanctioned the removal of organs from the woman he loved more than anyone. Such a serious decision made by merely signing a single sheet of paper...but this was the right thing to do.

Toshiaki shook his head. It was late in the game to be having such qualms. Hadn't he decided that this would extend her life? Didn't this have to be done so that he could be with her always? Kiyomi was not only what was on the outside, but rather, *every living cell in her body* was Kiyomi. And he had to make her his.

Toshiaki needed to make his move.

Just then, a sort of fever seized him. It was the same heat that had visited him when the doctor had told him about Kiyomi's condition. His head began to spin.

As they were leaving the office, Toshiaki edged stealthily past his father-in-law over to the doctor and spoke in a hushed voice.

"I actually have a request concerning Kiyomi."

"Yes?"

"Please, just hear me out, and this is to be confidential between us... I want something in exchange for offering her kidneys."

"Exchange? What..."

The doctor eyed him suspiciously. Toshiaki placed his trembling arm around the doctor's back as if restraining him, and whispered:

"Give me Kiyomi's liver... I want to use it for a primary culture."

Development

5

Upon finishing his ward duties, Kunio Shinohara returned to the Department of Surgery on the fifth floor of the Clinical Research Center. He rode the elevator down, proceeded right, and opened the office door. As he massaged his shoulder, he crossed the lifeless room over to his desk. When he passed the experimentation table, he cast a glance at the digital clock resting upon it. It indicated 5:30.

On his desk were two memos left by his secretary. They concerned his request for a copy of a medical article (alas, it couldn't be found) and a visit from a pharmaceutical company's marketing representative. Shinohara took a small note pad from the chest pocket of his white coat and tossed it onto the desk. He massaged his shoulder again, trying to loosen the stiffness that had knotted itself there during the course of the day. These actions had become frequent and involuntary for him. He mumbled out loud that the distance from the ward to his office was just impossible. Hearing himself, he looked around embarrassedly.

It was rare for no one else to be here. Usually at least one of his younger research students was around. Maybe they had gone out to eat a little earlier than usual.

He poured some instant coffee into a mug and sat down at his desk before opening his address book to scribble in some additional plans. As he was doing so, the telephone rang. It wasn't an internal call. The low electronic tremolo indicated an outside caller. Shinohara stood up and walked over to the phone, cup in hand. He then took a sip of his coffee, picked up the receiver, and answered.

"Hello, Surgery Department."

"This is Nagashima...from the School of Pharmaceutical..."

"What? Is that you, Nagashima?"

A smile came to Shinohara's face as he nodded to the voice on the other end. Shinohara's relationship with Toshiaki began when he took the same pharmaceuticals seminar to complete his Ph.D. Simply passing the state exams didn't mean a medical school graduate could get a Ph.D. He had to remain at the dispensary for a standard period, writing articles and passing tests. In those days, the 29-year-old Shinohara placed the utmost priority in getting his Ph.D. Drowning under the extra work requested of him by his seniors, he managed to continue cultivating cells. Shinohara's dissertation topic was cancer gene production in liver cells. To study this, he collected cells from extracted rat livers, carried out primary cultures, then took healthy liver cells and added cancer-inducing drugs to observe the formation of proteins. The focus was almost banal, but back then the particular protein byproduct had yet to be researched extensively and was good for a doctoral thesis. The associate professor of Toshiaki's seminar had developed a detector for the protein.

Toshiaki himself was still a graduate student then. Cancer cells had not been his area, but he carried out daily primary cultures on rat liver cells, excelling greatly in the skills involved. Shinohara learned these techniques well from him, staying on for two years as a research student before returning to the medical department to obtain his doctorate a year later. He continued his friendship with Toshiaki, with whom he occasionally went out drinking. Despite being separated a little by age, they enjoyed each other's company as equals.

As Shinohara pressed the receiver to his ear, he downed a mouthful of coffee. Boy, not tonight, he thought amusedly at first; yet right away he realized that something was not quite right. A voice was groaning across the wires. Shinohara furrowed his brow, wondering if some lines had come crossed, and tried pushing down on the cradle a few times. Something was wrong. Toshiaki hadn't spoken a word since announcing himself. White steam rose from Shinohara's coffee cup, engraving helical spirals into the air. Unable to endure the silence any longer, Shinohara opened his mouth to say something, when a low voice came from the receiver's depths.

"Kiyomi is dead."

Shinohara shivered. He looked unconsciously around the empty room. The fluorescent light flickered, then regained radiance, casting its usual shadows on the floor, each particle of light falling like rain.

"What?"

Shinohara surprised himself with the volume of his voice. Two minute globules of his saliva traced arcs in the air before descending out of sight.

"But Kiyomi lives."

"Hey, back up..."

"Extract Kiyomi's liver cells for me. I'm not a doctor, so I'd never be able to handle it. But I can count on you, right?"

"Kiyomi? What happened to her?"

"I'm coming there right now. You'll do this for me?"

"What are you talking about? Where are you right now?"

"I'll be there soon."

And with that the line went dead.

Shinohara stood in place for a while, grasping the receiver tightly. Frozen in bewilderment, he was unable to make heads or tails of this. The only thing he could say for sure was that his old pal was not himself.

He thought of Toshiaki's last statement, *I'll be there soon*, and frantically looked about the room. Did he mean to this office? He had called from an outside line. Where was Toshiaki now?

Just then, not even one minute after the call, the door opened behind him. Startled, Shinohara looked over his shoulder. Toshiaki was standing there, a faint smile upon his face.

The cup slipped from Shinohara's hand and shattered into pieces.

6

Mariko Anzai was in her room, poring over the math homework spread out across her desk. She was singing along to a tape of her favorite pop singer that a friend from school had made for her. Her assignment was surprisingly difficult for a change, but since this was her favorite subject, she was up to the challenge. Just when she had figured out the problem she was working on, the phone rang.

"Alright, alright..." she muttered, receiving the interruption with mild irritation. She stood up and went out into the hallway.

The clock showed 8:20. Outside her own room, the house felt all too cold and silent. Her father had yet to return home from work, but these days it was not unusual for him to be out until 11:00. Since becoming the head of his department, it was always like that. He was quick to attribute his lateness to his busy schedule, but Mariko knew the real reason. *You just don't want to look at me more than you have to.*

The phone's ringing threaded into the patter of her slippers on the hallway floor. These seemed to be the only two sounds in the house. She picked up the receiver unceremoniously.

"Hello?"

"Good evening. My name is Odagiri. I am a transplant coordinator. I must apologize for the unexpected call, but is Shigenori Anzai at home?"

Mariko held her breath and looked reflexively at her left wrist. The sleeve of her sweatshirt was rolled up, exposing the IV hole to which her eyes were drawn. Further up along her arm was another hole concealed beneath the sleeve, and both began to tingle.

"Dad hasn't come back from work yet..." she replied unsteadily and with an uncomfortable smile.

"Is this Mariko by any chance?"

"Um, yes...this is Mariko."

"Ah, good. Actually, I'm calling because a donor for your kidney transplant has been found and I wanted to pass along the good news."

Her heart skipped a beat. *A kidney transplant...* The words ran along her spine and pocked her skin with goose flesh.

When Mariko's first kidney transplant failed, her father was insistent about registering her on a waiting list for kidneys from nonliving donors. Only a year and a half had passed since then. She was amazed that an organ had surfaced so soon. Mariko retraced her memories of the past eighteen months...

"Suitable nonliving donors are rare, which means we'll just have to be patient and wait."

This is what a doctor named Yoshizumi had told her with a pat on her head. But to Mariko, still in elementary school at the time, these words were meaningless. She never planned on going through a second transplant. She'd only heeded her father's request to save his face.

When her father heard Yoshizumi's words, he asked the doctor uneasily, "Wait? For how long?"

"I can't say for sure. At the larger metropolitan area hospitals, over ten transplants from cadavers are performed every year, but that's because Tokyo itself produces a relatively ample supply of donors. Hereabouts, we carry out only a procedure or two a year. There are also those who are 'brain dead' but the idea of extracting organs from them doesn't sit well with most of society, at least here in Japan. So all we can do is wait for a kidney from a heart failure patient. We need the freshest organ possible, but the way things are now, many obstacles stand in our way that significantly narrow down the number of available kidneys. Compatibility is also a concern. There's a waiting list, but it has an order that must be strictly adhered to out of fairness to all potential recipients. If a suitable kidney is found in another region, it's possible to have it shipped here. Even so, it's not so uncommon for patients to wait five, even ten years."

"Ten years..."

Mariko could still remember clearly her father's hopeless expression at that moment.

"Wouldn't it be wonderful if we could do it right this time..." Yoshizumi said with a hint of bitterness.

Mariko simply looked downward, biting her lip.

She was sure they blamed her. They thought the operation had failed because she wouldn't listen. They all acted nice towards her, but actually hated her so much they wanted to hit her. What did they know, anyway?

"Have you gotten sick at all recently? A cold, maybe?" said the woman on the phone, yanking Mariko from her unpleasant reverie. Mariko curtly replied that she had not come down with anything. She pressed her left hand to her chest, trying as much as she could to calm the heartbeat rising inside of her. *Am I really going to have another transplant?* This time, it would not be her father's kidney as before, but one from a complete stranger's lifeless body. The idea sank into her guts like a stone into water.

Images of the fish she dissected in a science class experiment and of a cat run over in the street came to her mind. The organ of a dead human being, a *corpse's* kidney, was going to be placed into her body. A dreadfully cold sensation ran through her.

No way.

I don't want a transplant!

Unaware of Mariko's pained thoughts, Odagiri continued in her fast-talking manner.

"Do you know what time your father will return from work?"

"W-well...he's always late, so..."

"When he gets home, please tell him to call me as soon as possible, okay? If you can, call him right now. Ask him whether or not you want to proceed with the operation. If we don't hear back from you soon enough, we'll be forced to go down the waiting list. So please. The sooner the better."

By the time Shigenori Anzai returned home, it was past eleven. His section was preparing for the release of next year's word processor models. He had been incredibly busy these past few weeks, unable even to enjoy his days off. Work had become exactly the bad habit he always imagined it would.

He opened the front door in a weary daze and noticed the hall light was off. Thinking it curious, he flipped it on and looked down. Mariko's shoes were on the floor, so he knew she was home. Ordinarily, she would have left the light on for him.

After loosening his necktie, Anzai went into the kitchen and grabbed some cold cut ham and a can of beer from the refrigerator. Taking the ham between his teeth, he opened the door to the living room, sat on the floor, and clicked on the television. An airplane crash in South America was being discussed on the late night news.

As he watched images of the accident, he thought about how seldom he saw his daughter these days. She was probably still awake, but then, he no longer did such things like go to her room and say hi. They were both busy in the mornings, too, and hardly exchanged a word. They ate their meals separately, something that had already become normal for them. Things would probably stay this way until Mariko went off to college. Anzai guzzled down his beer.

The news ended about 20 minutes later. He needed to take a look at some files, so he switched off the television and stretched.

"Dad," Mariko suddenly called from behind him. Anzai turned around quickly to see her standing there in her pajamas. Her eyes looked a bit swollen.

"What is it? Something wrong?"

Mariko was silent for a long while. Her cryptic attitude irritated him a little.

"You had dinner, right?" he said. "Still hungry? You shouldn't keep eating so late, you know."

"...a while ago, there was a call..."

Picking up on her tenseness, Anzai put his beer on the table and stood up.

"A phone call...? From the hospital you mean? Was it the doctor?"

"No...it was the transplant co-something."

Transplant. Anzai stiffened.

"What did they want? Did you listen to what they had to say? When did they call?"

"Around 8:30…"

"Why didn't you tell me sooner?!"

Anzai clicked his tongue at her, then ran to the phone. He got the number from her and dialed it. Had their turn come? There was no other explanation. So why, he wondered, had Mariko been so hesitant to tell him? Soon, a voice came from the other end.

"Should we plan on proceeding with the transplant?"

"Of course, by all means!" Anzai said excitedly. The coordinator began by briefly laying out the most immediate concerns. She wanted Mariko to come to the hospital as soon as possible. If the results of her examinations checked out, all they would have to do was wait for the donor's heart to stop.

With immeasurable gratitude in his voice, Anzai thanked her and hung up.

"Mariko, you're getting a transplant! I never thought they'd find one this soon. You'll be able to eat tasty meals again!"

He looked at Mariko with a smile, but she was trembling with a pale face that was far from rejoicing. She shook her head from side to side. Anzai swallowed back his joy and extended a hand towards her.

"What is it Mariko? They're going to fix everything. Aren't you happy?"

"…no," she said wearily.

Why was she being so disagreeable?

"What's with you tonight? Everything's going to be fine now. You were so happy the first time, weren't you?"

Mariko shook off her father's hand.

"No! I don't want a transplant!"

Anzai approached her, but she only turned away, tears in her eyes. She began heaving up sobs. The sudden good news must have confused her. He had no idea how to calm her.

"Mariko."

With knees shaking, she stepped back to the wall and screamed, "I'm not Frankenstein's monster! I don't want to become a monster!"

Development

Dr. Takashi Yoshizumi was contacted by Odagiri at 11:30 pm with news of a donor from the university hospital. Yoshizumi, who had just been looking over all the patients' data spread out over his desk, sat upright at the word "donor."

"She's a 25-year-old woman, brain dead from an intracerebral hemorrhage. I met with her family this afternoon and we have their consent."

Nodding to the coordinator's every point, Yoshizumi jotted down a more abbreviated form of what she said in a memo pad. Azusa Odagiri had assumed her position as coordinator just last year, yet she was already known for her meticulousness and her skill with donor families. In recent cases Yoshizumi had handled, he owed much to Odagiri for her sound dealings, which had enabled successful operations.

Yoshizumi worked at the City Central Hospital, the main institution for kidney transplants in the region. When the families of brain-dead patients offered for the deceased's organs to be donated, an attending physician made a call to the CCH. The transplant coordinator then met with the family personally to explain the details of the transplant process. If they accepted her proposal, she obtained their signatures on consent forms. The procedure was, in effect, no different for patients who had registered at organ banks, because no transplantation could really be performed against a bereaved family's wishes.

"We have a candidate recipient. I'll wire the data over to you."

Yoshizumi nodded in approval and pushed the startup button on his PC.

Now that the information was being transferred, preparations were already half-finished. At the CCH, recipients were usually chosen after the following steps. First, a sample of the donor's blood was extracted and sent to the lab to check its ABO and HLA types. A routine test was also made for diseases like AIDS. With this data in hand, the coordinator began the selection process.

At the CCH, designated the regional center for kidney transplants, there were data on file from many patients hoping for an organ. These included name, date of birth, nature of compatibility, as well as histories of blood transfusions, transplants, and dialysis. In the region alone, approximately 600 people were on the waiting list for kidneys of the dead. The first to be chosen were those whose blood types most closely matched the available donor. Then, from within that group, candidates were ranked by HLA compatibility. Since there were two kidneys for every donor, two different recipients were usually chosen.

It was customary for one of them to come from Yoshizumi's hospital, partly because it handled coordination duties. His hospital's two most highly compatible patients were summoned for tests, and the more suitable one ultimately underwent the operation. If it looked like there were no viable candidates in the local region at all, they would search via the national hub of kidney transplants, Sakura National Hospital in Chiba, to ship the kidneys to some other part of the country. When the transportation of the organ could not be executed swiftly, however, chances were that the kidney would not take. The organ lost its freshness and weakened if it took too long to ship. It wasn't without reason that recipients were selected first by region.

Yoshizumi cradled the receiver on his shoulder and began typing. The coordinator's data appeared on screen: a list of prospective recipients, ranked from highest to lowest by compatibility. He scrolled down, briefly surveying the entire list.

"Number 1, Mariko Anzai, and Number 2, Matsuzo Iwata, are the prospective candidates. Ms. Anzai will be under your care."

Yoshizumi had heard that name somewhere before. He wrinkled his forehead, then gasped in surprise. After taking a moment to collect himself, he scrolled up and peered closely at Number 1. Mariko Anzai. Yes, he knew that name. She was 14 years old and had already had one transplant, at the CCH transplantation division. Yoshizumi looked at Mariko's HLA type. It was consistent with the donor's. Zero mismatches.

Mariko Anzai.

There was no mistaking it now.

Development

It was the same girl Yoshizumi had operated on two years before.

She had received her father's kidney, but the transpalnt had failed. The operation itself was a success, and no serious rejection symptoms had appeared. Yet, the kidney did not assimilate with her body and finally had to be extracted. Yoshizumi bit his lower lip. He had much to regret about the case.

HLA, or Human Leukocyte Antigen, is a genetic marker found on the surface of human cells. The HLA of pathogenic cells differs from one's own. When illness attacks, unrecognized HLA types are regarded as intruders and subsequently destroyed as a natural immune system response. Because HLA is also found on the surface of transplanted organ cells, the organ is incompatible whenever its antigen type differs from the recipient's. For this reason, transplants between people of similar HLA types are preferred. Only, unlike the simple ABO blood types, HLA types are quite complex. There are six classes of HLA: A, B, C, DR, DQ, and DP, and each encompasses ten or more subclasses. In transplant medicine, the most advanced analysis compares A, B, and DR types. Each of these three antigen classes is inherited, one from each parent. In other words, three classes and six pairs of antigens can be analyzed. The abundance of antigen classes, however, was a troublesome factor. Finding a donor with a six-fold match was not easy. Even between siblings, the chances of full compatibility were only one in four, and the probability of perfect compatibility with someone outside of the family was less than one in ten thousand. Because of this, many transplants were performed despite one or even two mismatches. This, however, meant that the organ had a higher chance of being rejected.

In Anzai's case, the transplant had taken place between father and daughter, and tissue compatibility was high. It should have been a successful transplant. Yet, it failed, and the reason was that Yoshizumi and his team had failed to gain the trust of Mariko Anzai.

Yoshizumi breathed in deeply. He gazed upon Mariko's name at the top of the display and pressed his fingertips around his temples to interrupt the unpleasant memories bubbling up in his head. He told himself to concentrate on the work at hand and spoke to Odagiri, who was waiting patiently.

"So Mariko Anzai has no mismatches."

"Correct," she replied. "There are no other donors in this area with such perfect compatibility. Please take some time to review the data."

It was true. None with just one mismatch, either. There were, however, five candidates with two mismatches. One of them, the third name on the list, had been selected as the other candidate for this donor's kidneys. He was 51 years old, had a five-year dialysis history, and was currently under care in a neighboring prefecture. A woman who was number 2 on the list couldn't be reached.

An estimated 20,000 people in all of Japan were registered for kidney transplants. Yet, within that group, the annual number who actually received organs hovered at around 200. Then there were the dialysis patients, who numbered 120,000 nationwide. The consideration awarded to transplants for patients with chronic renal failure was too small. Compared to Europe and America, Japan was known for having an extremely high dialysis patient-to-transplant operation ratio. By no means did this indicate that Japan's medical techniques were behind the times. Instead, it was public unease about regarding brain death as actual death that was the primary source of hesitation, for doctors and patients alike, to promote such procedures. Praying for a new kidney, patients were forced to deal with a long life of dialysis, a process both physically and financially straining, while those fortunate enough to receive a kidney were able to enjoy a normal social life.

"One more thing. Just in case candidate Number 1 can't accept the kidney, it's been decided that Number 5 will also come to the hospital for testing," said Odagiri. "She is 36 years old with two mismatches and a three-and-a-half year dialysis history."

"Got it."

He printed out the charts for the two main candidates. In the instance that Mariko had contracted some serious illness, the 36 year-old woman would take her place on the selection ladder.

Yoshizumi compared schedules with the coordinator and solidified their arrangements. He was to perform the extraction first, at the university hospital. He would then pass one of the kidneys along to Odagiri, who would then ship it to the neighboring prefecture, while Yoshizumi brought the other to the CCH to conduct an immediate transplant. Odagiri planned everything in great detail. Time between the extraction and the transplant was critical. Once the donor's heart stopped they would be running on a tight schedule. It was the coordinator's responsibility to make sure all the surgeons, assistants, nurses, and recipients were on the same page.

When all preliminaries had been exhausted, Yoshizumi thanked her and hung up.

It seemed that Yoshizumi's chance at self-redemption had come at last.

Mariko Anzai. I'll save the kid if it's the last thing I do.

8

Just two days after the consent forms were signed, Kiyomi's heart rate began its inevitable decline. Her breathing maintained a certain regularity, if only through the respirator. However, her body's faculties were finally reaching their limits. Her vital signs were falling.

"We've arranged for the transplantation unit from the City Central Hospital to come here this evening," the doctor said to Toshiaki. "Once Kiyomi's heart stops, we'll need to extract her kidneys promptly. We need to prepare her femoral artery beforehand. For this purpose, we'll be conducting a simple operation tonight. After her heart stops, a cannula will be inserted into the artery to cool her kidneys."

The securing of the arteries was soon completed. When Toshiaki returned to the ICU, he saw that Kiyomi's thigh was marked for insertion of the cannula. Her medication had been stopped, but her blood pressure remained steady, wavering around 100. The doctor explained they would likely need to wait until morning. *And Kiyomi's warmth will last only just as long*, thought Toshiaki absently. Moment by moment, her body was changing into a mere object for donation. Unable to shake the reality of it from his mind, Toshiaki spent the night at his wife's bedside.

At 10 pm the nurse came in as usual. She emptied Kiyomi's bed pan, swabbed her nostrils and the inside of her mouth, wiped the perspiration from her back with a towel, and changed her body position to prevent bed sores. She did all of this without the faintest sign of annoyance. In fact, she sometimes cast a sympathetic smile at Toshiaki as she worked.

Toshiaki had never been seriously ill. He had, of course, spoken with many medical practitioners throughout his career, but realized that he knew nothing, until now, of the actual work that doctors and nurses did.

"I'm truly grateful," Toshiaki said, bowing his head. "I think Kiyomi is, too, for all you've done for her."

The nurse stopped what she was doing and said, smiling, "I'm happy to hear that. I'm sorry we weren't able to help her."

"It's okay," he countered, flushed. "You did everything you could. All of you."

The nurse's smile turned ambiguous. She looked away from him as she resumed her duties.

"Working in the ICU, sometimes I just don't know," she said timidly, almost to herself. "You can give your all to the patients. They still die almost every day. What are we doing here? It's just too depressing sometimes. ICU nurses quit much faster than in other departments. Still…" Her words cut off there as she finished with the cleaning. She put Kiyomi's clothing back on and turned around to face Toshiaki, hands at her sides.

"When people say nice things to you, it makes you want to go on."

With that, she exited the ICU.

9

Kiyomi remained in quiet stasis until morning. Soon after the minute hand ticked past noon, her blood pressure began to drop rapidly. By 1:00 pm it had fallen below 95 and, an hour later, was below 80. The ICU soon became a swarm of doctors and nurses as they bustled in and out, driving Toshiaki and his father-in-law into the corner of the room. It was such a marked contrast to the quiet that followed the brain-death examination.

"The CCH transplant team will be arriving at two thirty," said one of the doctors, looking at his wrist watch. "They'll start by inserting a catheter. The extraction will begin once she loses her pulse."

"May we be present when she passes on?"

The doctor nodded.

"You'll have five minutes to say your farewells, after which Kiyomi will be brought to the OR."

The hissing of the respirator was inaudible in all the commotion. Kiyomi's blood pressure was now down to 75.

Yoshizumi, accompanied by Odagiri and two staff members, entered the university hospital. They brought with them a minimal, but essential array of surgical equipment and perfusion containers for Kiyomi's kidneys. This being a university hospital, there was plenty of technology at their disposal, but Yoshizumi never forgot to have his own by his side for an extraction. Because speed was so imperative, it only made sense to use his own familiar tools.

After exchanging greetings with the hospital staff, Yoshizumi left Odagiri in the waiting room and went into the ICU to check on the donor. Her blood pressure was nearing 65 and her heart rate was down to 30 beats per minute. Once her blood pressure fell below 50, circulation would no longer be complete, and cells in her extremities would begin to decay. Since the donor's family had consented to the procedure, the catheter was going to be inserted into her femoral artery now so that they would be ready when the pressure fell below 50. The head doctor showed the donor's data to Yoshizumi for confirmation. Odagiri was then informed via intercom that the catheter was being inserted.

Fifteen minutes later, Yoshizumi and his assistants prepared the perfusion equipment. They spread the donor's legs slightly and placed the machinery between her feet. One of the assistants soon began to adjust the equipment settings while another disinfected the area around her thighs, whereupon a silicon double balloon-tip catheter was readied. When sterilization was complete, Yoshizumi looked at the donor, standing at her left side, and patiently confirmed that the femoral artery and vein were well secured. After a quick glance to see that his team was on full standby, he inserted the balloon-tip catheter into the donor.

He carefully advanced the catheter until the balloon arrived at the right spot. Yoshizumi indicated his approval to the assistants with a single nod and told them exactly what to do. They connected a perfusion pump to the end of the catheter. He then guided the catheter into the femoral vein and had it connected as well. All preparatory steps were now complete. Her blood pressure was at 62, and her heart rate had fallen further.

Yoshizumi and his crew temporarily exited the ICU to wait it out. Noticing the family, he signaled for them to be let in and headed to the doctor's office. He hadn't met the family yet, and it was indeed his belief that he should keep a low profile with them. For the bereaved, a transplant surgeon was no better than a hyena snatching away the body of a relative. He did plan to meet with them just once, before the actual operation, but it was the coordinator's task to intermediate between them. No need to risk upsetting the family. Yoshizumi sipped some coffee in the office, reclined on the couch, and looked up at the ceiling.

Mariko Anzai's face came to him.

SHE sensed the change.

Kiyomi Nagashima's body was crossing over to Death. After the accident, her metamor-

phosis had proceeded slowly but surely. Now it was accelerating. Kiyomi was dying; her body was losing warmth, and it would stiffen first, and eventually dissolve. Her brain had already begun its deterioration. Hormonal discharges would soon stop. Blood flow was weakening. Cells were rupturing and crudely spewing their contents.

Everything was proceeding according to plan.

Robbing Kiyomi of her vision was the easy part. A little trick on her optical nerves was all it took. In that small window of opportunity, She induced Kiyomi's hands to turn the wheel off course. Her primary concern was ensuring that the accident didn't damage Kiyomi's body too much. It had to be brain death. If, by the miniscule chance, she'd ruptured any internal organs by hitting her abdomen instead of her head, there would be no talk of kidney transplants. At the moment of collision, She gauged the most precise timing to apply the brakes. She held back Kiyomi's abdomen with all Her strength to prevent it from lurching forward, fixing both of her hands on the steering wheel to protect against peripheral injury. Kiyomi's forehead struck the steering wheel. She could tell skull fragments had pierced the brain. Everytime She thought of that moment, She felt a shiver of excitement. Kiyomi would die, but She would live. Forever.

Kiyomi's kidneys were to be transplanted into two patients. Ideally, at least one of them would be female and the process would be complete. Toshiaki would perform the primary culture as planned. She'd already induced such thoughts in him without his knowing.

Toshiaki.

She imagined his figure and Her body twisted slightly. It was almost time. Her entire being trembled. She remembered Toshiaki's voice, his expressions, the warmth of his body. She'd been waiting for a man like him. He was the only human being who could appreciate and understand who She truly was. She refused to let go of such perfection.

She would become one with him.

An acrid excitement sent Her into convulsions. And as Kiyomi's blood pressure made its rapid decline, She surrendered Herself to the afterglow of Her bliss.

When Yoshizumi and staff received word that blood pressure had dropped to 50, they returned to the ICU once again. An hour had lapsed since the catheter insertion. The assistants set up a number of Ringer's solution bottles, to which perista pumps were connected. After ensuring that the catheter was in position, Yoshizumi inflated its two balloons with clean air to intercept blood flow.

At Yoshizumi's signal, his assistants ran the pump. Cold perfusate passed through the catheter at a precisely calculated rate. Yoshizumi placed his hands on the side of the donor's chest to verify that it was flowing properly.

The human body has a main abdominal artery and vein through which a great amount of blood flows. The arteries which supply blood to the kidneys extend from this main artery. Similarly, the kidney veins are linked to the abdominal vein. The abdominal artery and vein each fork out in the lower abdominal region and continue into both legs. The balloon-tip catheter had been inserted up through this lower arterial branch to reach the kidney extension, and the balloons then inflated to interrupt blood flow in the abdominal artery. At this point, a coolant, or perfusate, was sent through the catheter tube. There were minute holes in the tube between the balloons so that the perfusate could seep through into the abdominal artery. Since the artery was blocked above and below by the balloons, the perfusate flowed directly into the kidneys. The donor's kidneys were swiftly cooled and simultaneously flushed of blood. After the perfusate passed through, it traveled into the kidney veins and on to the lower abdominal vein, where it was recovered by the perfusion device and sent back in.

The fresher the kidney, the better. Compared to kidneys extracted from brain-dead donors, heart-failure donor's organs were inevitably less viable given the period of blood deprivation. To save the kidneys from such damage, it had become standard procedure to introduce a perfusate through the artery to rapidly cool the kidneys upon heart failure. Cooling them before they were extracted improved their chance of staying alive in their recipients. With the donor's family's consent, it was even possible to begin the procedure prior to heart failure.

One of the assistants reported the perfusion rate at regular intervals while another monitored the donor's heart rate. Her skin turned pale and cold from lack of blood flow. It was 40 minutes since the perfusion began. Her heart stuttered, reducing her pulse to a hush.

"Please call in the family," Yoshizumi said to the patient's doctor and nurse. "This will be their last chance to see her alive."

At twenty minutes past five, the nurse came into the waiting room to call Toshiaki and Kiyomi's parents. She informed them of the situation and brought them back to the ICU.

When they walked into the room, Toshiaki was astonished at the dramatic change in Kiyomi. Unable to tear his eyes away, he gazed steadily at her face and approached her slowly with the doctor. With every step, her face grew more and more distinct. He looked around and stopped at the left side of the stretcher. His mother-in-law was sobbing behind him.

"Kiyomi's vital signs are indicated here, but as it is now her pulse is erratic and nearly unverifiable," the doctor said as he pointed to the screen at Kiyomi's bedside. "The respirator is still running, but she barely has any heartbeat and her blood pressure has fallen sharply. Her skin, as you can see, is getting very cold."

Kiyomi's face was so white it was nearly translucent, her lips like two flower petals glazed with frost. It looked like a clear stream was flowing inside her body. Lashes extended from closed eyelids like crystals, casting short, thin shadows upon her skin. Without thinking, Toshiaki extended a hand towards her cheek. The moment his fingertips made contact, a numb sensation shot through his arm to the back of his head, not unlike the time he had accidentally touched dry ice: a pain that flickered between coldness and heat. He gasped and his hand trembled. He stroked Kiyomi's cheek calmly with his index and middle fingers, continuing down along her neck, then stopped at her white chest where the veins showed. Though obscured by her garment, he could tell clearly that Kiyomi's nipples were erect. Toshiaki took his hand away and wrapped his fingertips in his other hand to warm them. A cool sensation seemed to linger there.

Toshiaki's heart leapt with a great *THUMP* that broke into its steady rhythm. Feeling as though he were suffocating, he placed a hand upon his chest. *THUMP*.

Development

As if to mock his nerves' autonomy, his heart leapt again. He felt hot.

"We will now stop the respirator, if we may," the doctor stated.

Hand still clutching his chest, Toshiaki gazed at Kiyomi and took a deep breath, his lungs swelling unsteadily as they filled with air. *Kiyomi's body is being destroyed*, he thought. The doctor flipped the respirator switch. The machine, which until then had been keeping rhythm like a metronome, stopped in an unfinished hiss, and several seconds later, let out a languid *ssss*. The movement in Kiyomi's chest abated. The doctor glanced at his wristwatch and said quietly, "Official time of death is 5:31 pm."

Kiyomi's father inhaled audibly.

THUMP. Toshiaki's heart cried out yet again. It was such an enormous wave of sound, he wondered why no one else in the room could hear it. Maybe Kiyomi was sending the last of her life energy into him, almost as if he had caught her final heartbeat. She seemed to be telling him: *I don't want to die.*

"After the extraction, she will be transferred to the morgue for a post-mortem inspection," said the doctor before encouraging them to leave the room.

Toshiaki and his in-laws exited the ICU. Three men who looked to be doctors were standing in the hallway. The coordinator was behind them, holding a large box and giving instructions. One of the men, who looked to be the leader of the three, noticed Toshiaki and Kiyomi's parents and approached them. He looked to be about 40 years of age, but a certain pride in his face made him appear younger. He bowed his head simply and stated his name.

"I'm Takashi Yoshizumi, from the transplantation staff at the City Central Hospital. I've been placed in charge of both the kidney extraction and transplant. We're about to begin the surgery. Please forgive me for being so brief."

"I see. Good luck."

Toshiaki extended his right hand and exchanged a handshake with this man called Yoshizumi, who was studying Toshiaki's face as if shocked at something.

"What is it?"

"Nothing...excuse me."

Yoshizumi bowed once again and, seeming to shield his eyes, left together with the coordinator and the two other men into the prep room.

After a while, Kiyomi's stretcher was wheeled back into the OR.

"Please stay in the waiting room," a nurse called to them.

Kiyomi's parents entered the narrow waiting room and collapsed onto the couch. Seeing this, Toshiaki went down the hallway to find a phone.

"Kiyomi...hold on just a little longer," he murmured, recalling the image of her stark white cheek. Soon, he would take her to a warm place where he could tend to her always. He would raise her. *Kiyomi, I will never part from you.*

Mariko was wheeled along on a stretcher. Shigenori Anzai followed along, holding the hand of his anesthesized daughter.

"I'm sorry sir, but you cannot pass beyond this point," informed one of the nurses, placing a hand on his arm, as they reached the OR. The young doctor pushing the stretcher opened the door. Anzai was not allowed so much as a peek inside as Mariko's body was wheeled in.

"Please leave everything to us," said the doctor before ducking out of sight.

Anzai gazed at his palm, where Mariko's hand had been only a moment before, and instinctively made a fist to keep her warmth there.

"Mr. Anzai, calm yourself. Everything's going to be fine. Please rest over here," a nurse said, and led him into the waiting room. She sat him down upon a couch, then brought him some coffee from a vending machine. She handed Anzai the hot paper cup, which he grasped with both hands. His thoughts were churning over the events of the night before.

Soon after talking with the coordinator, he'd arranged for a taxi to take them to the hospital. Mariko threw such a tantrum the entire ride over, he feared she'd have an actual fit. When they arrived, she calmed herself somewhat, but cried for what seemed forever. She was never so emotional during the last transplant.

Mariko was moved immediately into the ICU for testing. After verifying her dialysis data and checking her blood pressure and potassium count, she was subjected to dialysis and transfusions. She was screened thoroughly for infectious diseases. They seemed to assume that the thought of undergoing an operation was making her nervous. By the time she was informed about the details of the operation and asked to give her approval, she seemed an empty husk.

"You're still okay with this?" asked Yoshizumi. Anzai naturally agreed. Yoshizumi then peered into Mariko's face. "And you, Mariko?" he asked.

"Is that person really dead?" she responded despairingly.

Yoshizumi understood what she was getting at and explained that the donor was brain dead. There was no chance of her coming back to life.

The tests confirmed Mariko's eligibility. They had prepared all last evening for today's procedure by shaving off any body hair around her abdomen and covering her with a sterilized sheet from the waist down to prevent razor burn infections. They also prescribed immuno-suppressants. Anzai spent the entire night sitting in a chair at her bedside.

Odagiri was a very perceptive woman. She understood Mariko's nervousness and fitful anger and talked with her throughout the night. Anzai was still concerned, but everyone was handling the situation with great patience.

They received word at 1:30 pm that the transplant would begin. When Yoshizumi came to Mariko's bedside to relate the information, her eyes widened in fear, to such an extent that Anzai feared they would pop right out of her head. Her lips quivered. Her teeth chattered.

"Don't be afraid, it's just like before. Everything will work out fine, I promise," Yoshizumi said gently and gave Mariko a pat on the head.

She'd opened her eyes wide again and asked the same question, still rigid from fright. "Is the person giving me this kidney really dead? Is she really, *truly* dead? Won't she come back?"

Yoshizumi was gone now. He was at the UH…to get Anzai's daughter a kidney from a "truly" dead person.

Anzai looked up at the nurse's face. She returned his gaze with compassion. He glanced absentmindedly at the clock behind her. It was 5:35.

10

Bringing one assistant with him, Yoshizumi went into the dressing room and changed into a green surgical outfit. Although he was accustomed to wearing it, it always felt crude when he put it on. He then entered the washroom nearby. Yoshizumi stood in front of the two stainless steel sinks that lined the wall and stared at his own face in the mirror, covered in mask and surgical hat.

He and the assistant opened the sink plugs, washing their arms with filtered water. Next, they put a disinfectant solution into their palms and smeared it thoroughly over their arms. They then each took a scourer in their hands and scrubbed vigorously. After working up a fine lather, they rinsed it off with the shower nozzles and cleaned their fingertips and nails with a small brush. This process was repeated three times.

Proper hygiene and a sterile environment were always necessary for any operation, but one had to be particularly attentive to these issues in transplant surgery. A transplant recipient's immunity had to be regulated in order to stave off rejection of the new organ. While this did increase the chances of success, the treatment severely weakened the recipient's resistance to bacterial infection. If the new kidney became infected, the patient could actually die. The surgeons therefore took the utmost care in the pre-op disinfection procedures.

They entered the OR, put on gowns handed to them by a specialized nurse, and slipped on latex gloves. Yoshizumi flexed his fingers a few times to stretch out the gloves until they fit comfortably.

Yet another assistant was busy disinfecting the donor's skin. Only her abdomen was left exposed, draped on all sides by sterile green cloth. More than just covering the body, the cloth served to prevent any lingering bodily bacteria from infecting the operating field, and to keep the surgeon's focus from straying. The green color dampened the visual impact of blood.

Yoshizumi walked around the body and positioned himself at its left. The first assistant came over and stood opposite. Yoshizumi exchanged a glance with him, then surveyed the room, checking to see that everyone else was ready.

"Seventeen minutes since heart failure," Yoshizumi heard the nurse announce.

"Alright, let's begin."

A scalpel was passed into Yoshizumi's dexterous right hand.

From a round hole opened in the cover sheets, the body's abdomen shone under the lights. Yoshizumi placed his hands upon it and made the careful first incision. Blood oozed out vividly from his precise line. He secured the slit with forceps to stop any further arterial leakage. He spread open the incision by hand and, pulling the outer layers, cut through the peritoneum. He clamped a number of smaller forceps into the body cavity. Blood from numerous veins still permeated the area, but time was scarce and he could not afford to stop all of it. Yoshizumi staunched the blood as best he could and sped up the incision until the digestive organs were exposed. He lifted the upper part of the liver with a spatula-like tool to see more clearly inside, then passed the device over to his assistant.

Yoshizumi immediately recalled the face of the donor's husband. He could not drive it from his head. There was something very peculiar about him. The man's eyes were vague, yet somehow alive with conviction, trembling as if possessed. And when he shook his hand, Yoshizumi almost called out involuntarily, for it felt like plunging into boiling water. He had feigned calmness, despite wanting nothing more at that moment than to break away from him.

Yoshizumi shook his head once again. He forcibly erased Toshiaki from his mind to focus on the operating table. There were much more important things in need of his immediate attention.

Many think that the kidneys are in the vicinity of the waist, but they are actually higher, located just behind the bottom-most rib of the rib cage. In order to reach the kidneys, internal organs such as the stomach and pancreas had to be systematically moved out of the way.

He tied off all visible arteries in the colon and pancreas area and cut them away. The assistant sucked out the contents of the stomach through a tube. When everything looked clean, Yoshizumi severed the esophagus. At this point, almost every digestive organ in the upper body was cleared. His goal was now within close reach. Had Yoshizumi been extracting a kidney from a living person, he could not be so careless, but dealing now as he was with a dead body, an abbreviation of time necessitated this indifferent handling. Again, the nurse dictated time since heart failure.

"Twenty-three minutes."

Yoshizumi and his assistant removed digestive organs from the peritoneal cavity, turning them over and placing them on a tray between the donor's legs. On top of the green cover sheets, these organs took on the appearance of some morbid exhibition. Since all peripherals had now been removed, only the kidneys remained. The assistant widened the incision with his hands to give a better view for Yoshizumi. The neatly hollowed space allowed for more room in which to work. He could see both kidneys perfectly now. They were a neat pink color and glittered with reflected light. Yoshizumi was pleased at their excellent condition.

With such an unobstructed view, he easily located the aorta abdominalis into which the balloon-tip catheter had been inserted. The swollen balloons were at exactly the correct junction, indicating that perfusion had been a complete success. He looked down to find the ureter, a minute threadlike tube running from the kidney to the bladder. In order to ensure an easy extraction, Yoshizumi peeled away the surrounding tissue, then severed the ureter near the ileum, leaving only the kidney veins and arteries to be cut. If these incisions were miscalculated, it would impede the transplant later on. Yoshizumi could no longer be so haphazard. He progressed cautiously as he peeled away extraneous blood vessels.

"Thirty minutes."

When extracting both kidneys, they were not severed and taken out one at a time, but were removed simultaneously, with the blood vessels between them still attached. Only then were they separated.

Yoshizumi ordered that preparations be made for transport. After both kidneys had been extracted, they would be separated so that one could be delivered

Development

to the CCH.

Upon checking to see that the assistants had set up the storage device, which contained extracellular fluid, he cut off the upper portions of the lower kidney arteries and motioned that the perfusate now be stopped. He then promptly cut the aorta abdominalis. The assistant held both kidneys gently and shifted them over to a lower area. A nurse supported the assistant, keeping close watch on the delicate blood vessel tips. The two kidneys were now attached only to the arteries and veins stretching from the lumber artery. Yoshizumi cut these now.

OK, he thought to himself.

The first assistant scooped up the kidneys and placed them into a stainless steel tray.

"Thirty-six minutes," the nurse stated.

"We're separating the kidneys. Get the coordinator in here."

The nurse ran out of the room. Yoshizumi took the two lumps sitting on the tray into his hands and examined them carefully, checking the arrangement and length of each blood vessel with scrupulous care. Every kidney's anatomy varied subtly depending on the person. At times, the shape of the blood vessels did not quite match up. A close inspection was imperative at this point to ensure a smooth transplant.

Yoshizumi carefully separated the two precious organs. Odagiri entered in an operating gown and with a shipping bag, from which a container was quickly removed.

"Take the right one," he said. "It looks fine, and it should do just fine. It has a healthy ureter, artery and vein all intact."

"Time?"

"Thirty-eight minutes," the nurse responded.

"Got it." Odagiri timed her watch while Yoshizumi placed the kidney into the container. She picked up the bag and left the room after a brief thank you. She was now responsible for the organ until it reached the neighboring prefecture. A two-hour drive awaited her.

Without even waiting for Odagiri's departure, the first assistant began setting up the cold storage container for the other kidney. He ran a perfusate through the kidney and watched as the meter sprang to life. He adjusted the pressure until the meter indicated 50.

"Forty minutes," the nurse announced.

"There, it's done."

However, the procedure was only half finished. Yoshizumi now had to return to the CCH and perform Mariko's transplant. They immediately rounded up all of their equipment and exited the OR.

Yoshizumi gave a quick word to the head doctor. "We have one more procedure to attend to. We're heading back to the central hospital now. Thank you for all your help."

The doctor responded vaguely. Yoshizumi turned around and was about to go meet up with his assistants when the doctor muttered something under his breath. "Why the liver...?"

"Hm?"

Not grasping the doctor's meaning, Yoshizumi stopped in his tracks and turned back, looking questioningly at the doctor, whose brow was furrowed.

"It's the donor's family," said the doctor, sounding perplexed. "Her husband from the School of Pharmaceutical Sciences, to be more exact. He requested that we remove the donor's liver as well...he wants her liver cells."

"What for?" Yoshizumi's eyes widened. He could not even begin to fathom such a request.

"Dr. Yoshizumi!" his two assistants called, waiting impatiently outside the door. He looked back and forth between them and the doctor, whom he wished to hear out in more detail, but there was simply no time to do so.

"If you'll excuse me," Yoshizumi said and took off.

Development

11

Soon after the kidney extraction, Kunio Shinohara commenced perfusion of the liver.

Toshiaki had called him around two o'clock to say that Kiyomi's operation was soon approaching, and Shinohara had been standing by in his office after finishing his usual business. In order to obtain liver cells with high viability, they could not afford to waste a second. Shinohara had made various preparations in advance so that he could leave for the OR at any moment. He had also caught hold of one of his medical students and primed him for assistance.

He was contacted again by Toshiaki at 5:50 when the extraction was underway. Shinohara, along with the student, brought everything to the hospital. He placed cultivation liquid into an incubator, setting it to 37° C. He put on an operating gown and awaited word that the transplant crew had completed their operation. Shinohara then entered the OR at 6:15. He laid out a plan of action to his student, allowing him to ready the perfusion equipment and HEPES buffer solution.

Kiyomi's abdomen was left open. The liver shone with a tan color and looked to be in good condition. It appeared to have no imperfections of any kind. The transplant team had been very expeditious. It would be easy, he thought, to procure viable, fresh cells. He felt strangely moved by the thought that Toshiaki's wife had been beautiful down to her liver.

He wiped the area around the organ with care and judged arterial elasticity by pushing with his fingertips. Meanwhile, his student led a tube from the buffer, passed it through a pump, and attached it to a polyethylene cannula. After clamping back the liver artery, Shinohara cut away the hepatic vein on the left side and swiftly inserted the cannula. The student flipped on the pump switch. Blood flushed out from the left side of the liver; it gradually turned a yellow ochre, the organ's actual color. The student confirmed the flow rate as adequate and the buffer was circulated for twenty minutes.

Primary cultures on liver cells were a standard procedure in modern-day laboratories all around the world. Liver cells were extracted and cultured, then subjected to drugs and the changes observed to investigate their various regenerative mechanisms. However, procuring cells from living people was difficult unless you had ties to clinical medicine, so the many researchers, like Toshiaki Nagashima, who worked in pharmaceuticals used raw materials from rats. Though they were good to work with, rat liver cells were of a slightly different structure than human cells, especially in the arrangement of their enzymes.

Currently, the most popular way to get liver cells of high viability was to take them from transplant organ donors. The quality of the cells differed according to age, so in most cases donors from about age 18 to 30 were preferred. Many of the donors selected were those who had died in car accidents. They differed from patients who'd died of illness in that they had not been receiving any drugs for treatment. There were no worries as to the effects of such drugs on the liver.

The perfusion was running smoothly. Shinohara's assistant removed a second buffer from the incubator, into which he had mixed a collagenase and sodium chloride solution. The perfusion solution was then exchanged with this mixture. They waited for yet another twenty minutes. The collagenase would ease the unbinding of the liver cells.

Shinohara gazed somewhat hesitantly upon the innards taken from Kiyomi's covered body. The sheets did nothing to hide her delicate curves. He thought back to the wedding two years ago between Toshiaki and the corpse that now lay before him. As the best man, Shinohara, who wasn't used to giving speeches, spoke nervously in front of the entire gathering. Kiyomi had just turned 23, but her carefree expression and the innocent look in her eyes had been more that of a high school student. When he complimented her on being such a ravishing bride, this corpse had blushed and looked over bashfully to Toshiaki. How had things been going for them? Shinohara couldn't seem to recall any details.

The left side of the liver now appeared nominal. He pushed around gently.

Development

It felt soft to the touch, indicating that the collagenase had done its job. Shinohara checked his stopwatch. The perfusion period was complete. As he prepared some Leibovitz solution, he told his student to inform Toshiaki, who was waiting outside, that it would only be a little longer. Shinohara cut off the left side of the liver with a scalpel. After checking its weight, he transferred it into the temperature-controlled Leibovitz solution. When he shook the flask lightly, the liver sample broke up slowly. Some more shaking would do it. The rest was lab work.

Before leaving the OR, Shinohara capped the flask to prevent bacteria from getting in. Toshiaki, who was leaning against the wall in the hallway, snapped to attention like a rubber band and ran up to Shinohara. His face was jaundiced and lifeless, but as soon as he recognized what was in Shinohara's hand his bloodshot eyes livened up immediately. He sighed with joy.

"Everything went well," said Shinohara as coolly as possible. "I haven't washed it yet, though. Be gentle when running it in the centrifuge. About 50 G's should do it. And be sure to dispose of any debris that seeps through the gauze. I assume you know all this already, but I just want to make sure…"

"Yes, of course."

Toshiaki plucked the flask from Shinohara's hand and placed it into an ice box. He grasped it like some sacred object and thanked Shinohara earnestly as he made to leave. He would now return to the lab to purify the cells. Was he deceiving Kiyomi's parents by doing this? Toshiaki kept close watch over the box, an overt obsession in his tear-stricken eyes. No matter how Shinohara looked at it, these were not the actions of a sound human being, and he suddenly regretted what he had done. He tried to convince himself that he had not just taken a vital organ out of his friend's dead wife, that he had not yielded to Toshiaki's insane desire.

"Nagashima, you sure you're okay? Is that all you need?"

Toshiaki stopped. He turned around slowly and glared back at Shinohara, then spoke in a low voice.

"Why wouldn't I be okay?"

"Don't you feel like you're doing something weird here? Are you just going to leave her folks behind? How about her remains? Shouldn't you want to be with her right now?"

"Her remains? What are you talking about?"

He seemed taken aback by the question. Shinohara felt cold. Toshiaki's face slowly changed in appearance as he gazed pitiably upon the box clutched at his side. His harried expression was gone. Toshiaki stroked the box quietly and there was a disturbing gleam in his eyes.

"I'll be back in three hours," Toshiaki said. "But please, don't be mistaken. Kiyomi isn't dead yet."

He left Shinohara to stand there by himself with only the sound of hurried footsteps fading along the wintry hallway of the ICU.

Development

12

Yoshizumi rushed to the CCH via ambulance. The kidney transport cooler clattered as the vehicle swerved left and right throughout its 30-minute journey.

Before such advanced containers were invented, kidneys were toted in cold storage boxes. In principle, these more primitive containers differed little from the coolers we bring to the beach. Time was precious and, in those days, the chances of a successful transplant were relatively low. The perfusion methods in current use were a significant improvement. Not only was the organ's structure kept intact, but its freshness was also better preserved.

Yoshizumi was sitting on a padded seat, arms folded and eyes closed. In transplantation medicine, such moments were the only opportunities for respite. Because the hospital was within city limits, the transportation time was fairly short, but airplanes were used in cases when kidneys needed to be sent in from other prefectures. A two-hour trip in the sky was like an oasis in an otherwise arid landscape of stress. There was no point being on the edge during the transportation stage. It was better to rest one's mind in these blessed intervals so that no mistakes would be made during the operation itself.

Organ extraction from brain-dead patients had yet to be wholly accepted in Japan. Consequently, transplant doctors were forced to wait until the donor's heart stopped and an investigation into the cause of death was completed before the actual operation could be performed. Such organs were naturally more susceptible, but this could not be helped. Only when brain death was recognized legally, thought Yoshizumi, would the percentage of successful kidney transplants rise to a more reasonable rate. The organs would be generally fresher, and, more importantly, there would be more donors. This would lessen the chances of recipients requiring long-distance donations.

Until just a few years ago, Yoshizumi and his fellow staff had even gone through the trouble of obtaining kidneys from America by air. Though problems of morality were imposed upon the medical community when trying to extract organs from brain-dead patients in Japan, they were able to find some of the organs they needed overseas. At that time, Yoshizumi thought Japanese society odd for being so sensitive about Japanese donors when it quietly accepted organs from the States. At any rate, the results were not good because of the lengthy transportation time. The recipients, waiting for their urine to flow, would fret, panic, and weep when it did not. All recipients believed that a rosy life awaited them once they got their transplants. They never suspected that the operation might end in failure. Yoshizumi's heart sank whenever he had to inform a recipient about a malfunctioning kidney in need of extraction. Some recipients would ask for another transplant, and some of them would indeed get another kidney and be cleared from the hardships of dialysis. Others would shake their heads and say they never wanted to go through another transplant.

The face of a former patient came to his mind. A single woman in her thirties, she stood before him, her hair loose and unkempt. She spoke with a hint of scorn as a wary smile rose to her lips. "I've had enough, doctor," she told him. "It's not like I'm getting any younger. I won't be able to get any good jobs now, and I've already given up on having children. I'm fine with dialysis. I don't need this false hope anymore. You keep telling me someday I'll be able to eat whatever I want again and even travel abroad. Don't mislead me with your lies. Do you have any idea how I felt when you told me it had to be removed? I wish I'd never heard of transplants. If I knew only about dialysis, I wouldn't have had to go through *that*. Enough, doctor. I'm too tired…"

The ambulance turned a sharp curve. His eyes still closed, he took a deep breath. He knew this curve well. It belonged to the road leading to the hospital.

A completely naked Mariko lay face up on the operating table covered by a cloth. Her body was still innocent and childlike and had changed little from two years ago. The anesthesia tube extended from her face into a machine. The anesthesiologist stood by to keep a close eye on things.

Nearly everything was prepared before Yoshizumi's return and Mariko's body was now thoroughly cleansed. In a sterilized room, the only sources of bacteria were human beings themselves, so hygiene was especially important. It was necessary to disinfect the recipient's skin assiduously before the operation. The assistants had applied an antibacterial solution with a brush, similar in shape to a scourer one might use to clean the dishes, scrubbing Mariko's lower abdomen and thighs. Any bodily hair, such as pubic hair, hindered the operation, and had been shaved off the day before. And, because bacteria could infect razor nicks, her lower body had been protected throughout the night and day with a sterile towel.

Yoshizumi stood to Mariko's left. Joining him also were two anesthesiologists, three surgical assistants, and two nurses. The walls were a light green and exuded a most inorganic feel. Excepting the large equipment and the operating table, the room was bare and looked more spacious than necessary. The doctors wore green surgical gowns similar in color to the cover sheet that draped the lower half of Mariko's body. Amid this sea of green, her abdomen stood out in bizarre contrast.

Yoshizumi looked up at the shadowless lights in the ceiling: six ball-shaped bulbs arranged in a circle, an additional one nestled in their center. The lighting in an OR was usually arrayed under an umbrella-like frame, but this OR, designed especially for transplantation surgery, had a special ventilation system to keep it germ-free, and the lights had been designed to impede the flow of air as little as possible. They looked just like the bottom of a flying saucer and gave a clear definition to everything in the room, from the outlines of all the equipment to the doctors' expressions and color of a patient's organs.

Bubbles of disinfectant solution scintillated on Mariko's skin. One of the surgical assistants inserted a catheter into her bladder to clean it out. This rinsing, too, had to occur in a germ-free state.

"Present time is 6:47 pm. It has been 76 minutes since heart stoppage and 40 minutes since the kidney extraction."

"OK. Let's begin."

Parasite Eve

With the catheter left in place, Yoshizumi set to make the first incision. He made a mark from the left side of her torso to just above her genitals and cut along this line with a standard scalpel. At this point he switched to an electric scalpel, which he would be using for the duration of the procedure. He cut through the rectus fascia, exposing the external obliques and rectus sheath. The obliques were located on either side of the abdomen and were red in color, while the sheath was white. Yoshizumi carefully ran the electric scalpel along the area where these two joined. Next, he opened the edge of the rectus sheath, then slowly cut the secondary layer underneath it. Mariko's first transplant two years ago had been to the right-hand side. This time, it would be her left.

A transplanted kidney was not actually situated in its natural location, but slightly lower, closer to the pelvis. The kidney was therefore connected not to the aorta abdominalis or vena cava inferior, but instead routed to the internal iliac artery and vein. This lower spot wasn't hindered by other organs and permitted a speedy operation.

Yoshizumi carefully peeled off the peritoneum, exposing the gastroepiploic vessels. One by one, he bound the lymph nodes that ran along the bottom of these vessels and clamped them off to prevent unwanted excretions from saturating the operating field. Next, the inner iliac artery and vein were both severed in advance to avoid veinal thrombosis during attachment. Yoshizumi also clamped back the inner iliac artery with forceps and cut off a moderate amount of its remaining length. Using an injection needle, he cleansed the inside of the artery with heparin to avoid clotting.

Yoshizumi took a breath and checked the placement of his incisions. With the cavity held open by silver forceps, numerous bindings were visible. Forceps clamped vessels shut. An assistant wiped away the blood left inside. The field was clear. He could see the ilium's blood vessels very well now and there was no evidence of hemorrhaging. Now, he could finally attach the kidney into Mariko's body.

At that moment, Yoshizumi suddenly felt hot.

Development

Startled, he lifted his face. The assistants around him continued working as if nothing were wrong. He looked around the room, but no one else seemed to notice.

Then, the assistant across from him interrupted with a suspicious glance.

"Is something wrong?"

"No..."Yoshizumi muttered from under his mask.

The heat continued. As he tried to get his bearings, he sought the source of the sensation. He was perspiring heavily, but the air felt the same. The heat was all inside him. A nurse wiped his forehead. He was sweating.

Before long, the heat subsided and he was back to normal. The assistants checked on him once more to make sure he was still up to the task. He assured them with a raised hand and returned his attention to the operating table.

What was that? he thought. It wasn't a dizzy spell, the heat didn't assail just his head, but his entire body. Just when he'd pictured the donor's kidney. Now he remembered how hot the donor's husband's hand had seemed when he'd shaken it. Had the man been prey to a similar bout? *What's going on here?* Yoshizumi found it hard to keep his focus on the operation for some time.

The kidney was still set in its container. While transporting it to the CCH, any changes in the kidney's perfusion status or mass were recorded by the machine. Yoshizumi had already examined these readings before beginning the operation to see that there were no anomalies. He asked for the current stats just to make sure. The perfusion volume was at a viable 117 ml per minute.

Yoshizumi and his assistants took the kidney from the container and started on the blood vessels. First, Mariko's inner iliac artery had to be attached to the kidney artery. The procedure required the utmost care. Working closely together with the first assistant, who stood across from him on the other side of the patient, Yoshizumi joined the blood vessels at their severed ends with two strands of surgical thread. These held the arteries together while they performed a more complete suture, rotating the operating table to provide the best angle at each point. None of the vessels in the kidney had hardened, so there was no fear that the inner membrane would peel off. When this was finally done, an assistant slowly lowered the kidney into the body cavity. An involuntary sigh of relief escaped Yoshizumi.

The position of Mariko's pelvic vein matched up well with the kidney's. Yoshizumi checked to see that the vessels weren't twisted or folded in any way, and picked a spot where they would join. First applying a couple of forceps just below it, he opened a hole in the patient's vein. After cleansing the inside of the vessel, he and his assistant passed the needle back and forth once again to complete the procedure.

He signaled with his eye to the assistant, who nodded and began removing the forceps, first from the outer iliac artery, then moving on to those near the vein tips, and finally to the main arterial clamp.

As blood flowed into the kidney, some seeped out of the needle hole where the renal artery had been joined, but it soon stopped after some pressure was applied. The transplanted kidney accepted Mariko's blood and everyone watched as it reddened and regained surface tension. Yoshizumi rubbed it to encourage circulation. He had witnessed this scene numerous times in his career, but never had he seen such dramatic revival. The organ appeared literally to be coming back to life in Mariko's body.

Just then, urine spurted from the ureter. An assistant hurriedly picked it up with a forcep and caught the urine in a saucer. This type of discharge was common enough with transplants from living donors and usually came a few minutes after the blood vessels were connected. It almost never occurred, however, with kidneys of a lower viability. Yoshizumi, who had performed nothing but kidney transplants at the CCH, had never seen such a healthy discharge in an organ from a dead donor. He had no doubts that this transplant would be a complete success.

Just then.

He looked up with a jolt.

Again. That heat.

He could hear his own pulse throbbing in his ears. Something was manipulating his heart. The heat. It felt like he was on fire.

Yoshizumi started to pant. Everyone appeared blissfully unaffected as before and he tolerated his agony alone with all his might. *What the hell is this?* he thought to himself. Of course he had no answer. *Why?* The heat returned just after blood began flowing through the kidney. *It's almost as if...*

Thinking that much, he shot a gaze at the kidney.

He refused to believe it. He denied even entertaining the possibility. It was madness. He shook his head. He couldn't afford to lose it just yet. The operation wasn't quite over; the ureter still had to be sewn in.

He took a few deep breaths and at last the feverish attack subsided, but some of the heat remained, tingling inside like an afterglow. Yoshizumi tried his best to mask this change in himself and set out on the remaining leg of the operation.

He first shifted a few clamps to see the bladder more clearly and cut it open vertically right at its center. Then he sucked out the salt solution used earlier for cleansing, to see inside.

The bladder was a soft, white organ located behind the pubic bone. One ureter already entered into it from the recipient's own kidney on the reverse side. The opening of the ureter was clearly visible through the incision in the bladder. To create a new ureter hole right next to it, Yoshizumi and an assistant held up the membrane with a surgical splint. He dug into the mucous tissue with the electric scalpel, without driving all the way through. The hole had to be at a slant; if it was perpendicular, the urine would leak. Yoshizumi placed the tips of a pair of right-angle forceps into the opening and slowly peeled away the mucous membrane, after which he switched to a pair with longer ends to ease out a diagonal tunnel. He now pierced the hole with his scalpel and exposed the forcep's tips on the other side of the bladder.

The remaining length of the ureter from the extracted kidney was more than sufficient. Yoshizumi paid special attention not to twist it with his forceps as he led it into the bladder. After tucking it in to a proper length, he cut off the excess.

Next came the joining of the ureteral opening. He turned around the lining of the ureter and, spreading it open within the bladder, sewed it with thread. Yoshizumi placed his forceps into the new ureteral opening to confirm that it had spread out. Sometimes it was sewn partially to the back lining by mistake. He inserted a thin tube inside the ureter and it passed through smoothly.

Good. He breathed relief. The kidney was attached to the recipient. Now, all that was left was to close up the body. He wanted to get this over with.

He sutured up the bladder lining and moved the clamps upward to make a final check on the kidney and take a biopsy sample. He would have to create a slice specimen for later analysis. They checked that there was no blood leakage and washed the area with salt solution. A suction tube was placed in the area around the kidney and bladder so that its other end would stick out of the body. Then they proceeded to sew the muscles back together.

"10:36 pm. Time since extraction is four hours, twenty-nine minutes."

All the incisions sewn shut, the doctors and nurses breathed a collective sigh, Yoshizumi included. He glanced at the suture. The kidney was now completely embedded.

What was it with this kidney? Yoshizumi was unable to take his eyes away from the sutures. The heat had weakened and was now only a faint glow. The beating of his heart flooded his ears. All he could think was that the kidney now in Mariko's body was jerking his heart around and burning him from the inside.

Mariko was to be moved to the main ward, where she would be kept under close observation for a few days for possible infections and sudden rejection symptoms. Yoshizumi remained aloof, avoiding the usual string of duties, while they readied for her transport.

He felt the remaining heat smoldering within his body. He also felt a little dizzy but couldn't rest yet. Though he would have to keep a close eye on Mariko's condition, he wanted nothing more now than to get as far away from the kidney as possible. Proximity to it would bring no good. Yoshizumi found this feeling impossible to shake. His heart was pounding vigorously, as if it was laughing at him about his feeling.

Development

13

The Pharmaceuticals building rose into an evening sky tinted in navy blue. Atop a hill just a few miles away a television tower radiated color like a brocade, and the light was illuminating the very heavens. The digital clock in the dashboard read 7:54. Some people were still working, as indicated by the windows lit up irregularly along the side of the building. The light was on in the Biofunctionals classroom too; many of the students were probably still in. Toshiaki parked his car at the main entrance and ran inside with the ice box.

Without bothering to change into his sandals, he rushed into the elevator lobby and pressed the button impatiently. The elevator stopped unexpectedly at the fourth floor. Someone had probably locked it there to transfer some equipment. Toshiaki clicked his tongue and pounded the button with his fist, then just made a break for the stairs. The sloshing inside the cooler told him the ice was melting. On the way up he ran into someone on a stair landing, spilling water out onto the floor. He hastily opened the box and checked its contents. The flask was safe. Whoever he had run into said something to him, but he ignored it and scaled the remaining steps.

"Doctor!"

Sachiko Asakura's voice echoed loudly in the hall when he reached the Cultivation Room. She was wearing a lab coat and cradled a bag of Eppendorf tubes in her hands. She opened her eyes wide and looked back and forth between the ice box and Toshiaki's face.

"I need to use the Cultivation Room," Toshiaki said as he tried freeing himself from Asakura's gaze. She was in his way.

"What's going on? Is your wife…?"

"Won't you just get out of my way?! There's something I need to do."

"What happened? First we don't hear from you at all, and now you want to conduct some experiment… I was so worried, and so was everyone else."

"Listen, Asakura…"

"If there is anything we can do to help, don't hesitate to..."

"You're in my way!! Move!!" Toshiaki screamed. Shocked at his behavior, Asakura cowered back and cleared his path as he made way for the Cultivation Room.

The room wallowed in the blue of the sterilizing light. Toshiaki threw the switch to turn on the fluorescent lights, put on a pair of sandals near the entrance, and went inside.

He immediately turned on the centrifuge and the clean bench. The sound of air being drawn into the latter filled the room. After opening the gas jet valves, he turned on the clean bench burner.

Toshiaki removed his flask from the ice box and checked its condition again. He put the flask into the bench, then pulled up his sleeves and disinfected both arms with ethanol. After roiling up the flask's contents with a stirrer, he poured the liquid into multiple tubes through gauze, and placed the tubes into the centrifuge. Discarding the supernatant, he suspended the liquid in a buffer solution, and ran the tubes again through the centrifuge. He repeated this three times. Lastly, he suspended the solution again on a culture medium and drew some of it into a special tube with a pipettman. Then he jumped up from the bench and ran over to the inverted microscope. He placed one drop of the solution onto a glass slide that had a measure and placed a cover slide over it. Setting the controls with a shaky hand, he peered into the lenses.

Globules of cells shone with a pale yellow hue. Toshiaki let out a voice filled with awe. The cells showed a fine shape and were shiny. If they had been half-dead, they wouldn't have glittered so.

Toshiaki mixed the cells with a trypan blue solution to determine viability and cell count. There were hardly any dead cells, which would have turned blue. Approximately 8×10^7 cells per gram of liver, with a viability of 90%. Superb.

Toshiaki returned to the clean bench, quickly poured the cells into culture flasks, and placed them into an incubator set at 37° C. He mixed the remaining cells into a preservation liquid, placed them into a blood serum tube, wrapped the tube

Development

in cotton, then stored it in a freezer at -80° C. Having finished that, he took a deep breath. The hum of the centrifuge's motor reverberated faintly in the room.

Toshiaki removed a flask from the incubator and placed it under the microscope. He swallowed in anticipation and placed his eyes to the lenses. Kiyomi's liver cells were glowing against an orange background.

For a long time, Toshiaki could not tear his eyes from their play of light and shadow. It was beautiful. *What cells could be more beautiful than these?* he thought. They were large and spherical like pearls and emanated such a magnificent light that he almost felt dizzy. Without realizing it, Toshiaki was uttering Kiyomi's name in a delirious murmur. Though unfortunately her body had been harmed, these cells were a testament to her preservation. Her kidneys had been sacrificed for unknown recipients, whose transplant surgeries were certainly well under way by this point. And by a similar act of offering, her liver was now in his possession, resplendent before his eyes. Reduced as she was to individual cells, Kiyomi was still beautiful. She was still alive. These cells must not die… It was Toshiaki's duty to prolong their heritage; he refused to lose any more of her. A hot shiver rippled through his body.

He made a gulping sound as he swallowed again. Unable to endure it any longer, he let out a sigh saturated with ecstasy.

14

SHE was content, with Her new surroundings.

A comfortable place where She had complete freedom. Temperate air engulfed Her; a source of gradual energy. She was well aware of the great potential which lay in Her hands.

When he looked upon Her, She felt an intense excitement. Of course, he couldn't hold Her close just yet. Nothing could be done about that now. But She planned on revealing Her splendrous figure to him soon enough.

It did not elude Her, Toshiaki's enraptured voice, as he peered upon Her from above. Her entire body trembled, swimming around contentedly in cytosol.

She'd made the right choice. She'd been waiting an eternity for this day to arrive. At last, She was truly appreciated, for here was a man who made a genuine effort to understand Her.

Toshiaki Nagashima. He and I would be so perfect together.

Until now, such men had passed through Her life as mediators...mere stepping stones to keep Her alive until today. Those before him were all so foolish, though they never doubted their own greatness. Scoffing at them, She'd remained outwardly silent.

But She would hide no longer.

She'd devised many plans for Her happiness over the long years. While pretending to yield to these men, She had positioned strength at crucial points, someday to manipulate their very cores. The men did not know this.

The first man ever to know what I have done and who I am — probably this Toshiaki Nagashima will be the one. She thought this.

She remembered Toshiaki's eyes and felt warm all over, felt a quickening of all Her functions. This feeling...She didn't remember ever experiencing it until She met him. She did not know what it was. But the woman called Kiyomi tasted it when she was loved by Toshiaki, this She knew.

And now She Herself was feeling it.

Did this mean: She and Toshiaki loved each other?

Maybe. But She could not explain why She had become capable of this sensation.

Development

But this is evolution, She told Herself.

This was simply Her way of acclimating to Her new environment. She had evolved, once again.

Toshiaki had to be used, further. He would grant Her every desire. From now on, it will no longer just be creating copies of Herself...

He will give Me a daughter.

She multiplied fully into the space around Her. There was ample space.

Doing this brought Her great delight. However, this alone would not satisfy Her. Everything up to this point had been mere preparation.

As She continued to multiply, She occasionally had a dream. It was the life of a woman named Kiyomi, whom She had observed for 25 years. One by one, She dug up memories that had lodged deep within Kiyomi. In comparison with the ocean of time She'd spent waiting, the shallow years of Kiyomi's existence were but a few solemn waves. Because this was true, She could evoke Kiyoki's memories with great clarity.

It was fun rummaging around in Kiyomi's being. For it meant also to remember Toshiaki.

Quietly, but steadily, She replicated Herself, as She dreamed...

PART TWO
Symbiosis

Parasite Eve

1

Kiyomi Kataoka loved her birthday.

Whenever the day came near, everything from school to streets took on a new vitality. She was greeted with joyful laughter and song wherever she went. She loved all of it. Not everyone was excited for her sake, of course, but she liked to think that all the people in the world were enjoying themselves on her account. It was the time of year when shopping districts resounded with the familiar lilt of "Rudolph the Red-Nosed Reindeer" and "Jingle Bells," and smiles graced the faces of all who walked the streets. It was truly the best day of the year.

When Christmas approached, she and her parents decorated a real tree in their living room. From the time she was in kindergarten, they had spruced up the house together every year. Kiyomi always had the honor of plugging in the cord to set the tree aglow, but only after making sure the room was as dark as possible. The large tree would scintillate with blues and reds and, as she watched the lights reflecting off the wallpaper, Kiyomi thought of how wonderful it was to have a birthday on Christmas Eve.

During grade school, she invited her friends every year to her birthday party. Her mother did most of the cooking, but Kiyomi also helped out with the smaller things. Cooking with her mother was always fun. After the food was ready, her friends came over and wished her a happy birthday as they walked through the door.

They all arrived with presents in hand and Kiyomi delighted in seeing them pile up under the Christmas tree. They then gathered around the large dining table to eat, play games, and sing songs. Kiyomi usually played "Silent Night," which she had learned from her piano teacher. After her friends returned home, she received presents from her parents, usually books and stuffed animals.

"You know, Kiyomi, you were born exactly at this time," said her mother as she glanced at the clock on Kiyomi's tenth birthday.

Her father was sitting on the couch, smoking a pipe. He looked at Kiyomi and smiled warmly. He said:

"It was nine o'clock when I heard your cry. It was such a lovely cry…full of strength. And your mother was crying too, from joy. It was a cloudless night. At midnight, I looked out the window; the hospital was on a hilltop, so the entire town was spread out below me. I could see the stars so clearly. That's when I decided to name you Kiyomi."

The characters of her name meant "holy" and "beauty."

Stuffed animals clutched at her side, Kiyomi waited for Santa Claus to come. But eventually she succumbed to sleep.

She had a dream that night, as she did every year.

A dark place. A low rumbling, resounding without pause. A stream slowly enveloped her body, clouding her perception of up and down. She surrendered to the current, feeling herself floating upon it. Enveloped by a womb-like warmth, time could not be felt here. Kiyomi tried to imagine where she might be; she felt mysteriously at home. *I've been here before…long ago.* But she could not remember where "here" was. All was dark, and there was nothing, in this dream that was like a dream…

When she opened her eyes the next morning, a pile of Christmas presents, rivaling the amount she had received for her birthday the night before, was stacked neatly at her bedside.

Kiyomi tried asking her parents once.

"Does Santa make you dream?" Her parents exchanged confused glances, but listened intently as she told them everything about the dream. When she expressed a feeling of having been there before, they groaned with surprise and admiration. She asked them, "You know the place?"

Her mother smiled gently and embraced her.

"I think I do, sweetie. You were probably in my tummy."

"In your tummy?"

"That's where you came from. I'm sure you were just remembering the feeling of being inside me."

"Is it dark in there?"

"Yes, it's dark and warm, and it feels like you're floating in a bath."

"Hm…"

"I've never had that kind of dream. You must have a good memory."

"Don't other people dream about it too?"

"I doubt it. Everyone usually forgets about it."

After that her parents started discussing difficult things that Kiyomi didn't understand, like "intrauterine education" and "memory formation." While Kiyomi accepted her mother's explanations, she did not feel her curiosity had been sated. The landscape of which she dreamt was something far more ancient. She understood that it was indeed a place she'd seen before her own birth, but it wasn't in such a recent past. It was far more remote, far away.

Symbiosis

2

The sunlight was unmerciful.

Sachiko Asakura shielded her eyes with her hands and looked towards the sky. Cotton-like clouds drifted swiftly from right to left across the blue expanse. The jet stream was swift that day, but standing as she was far below, upon asphalt, Asakura could only feel the intense, steady heat filling the stagnant air. Feeling the effects of the summer weather most acutely in her black one-piece suit, she wiped off beads of sweat from the nape of her neck with a handkerchief. She ran into the shade, fleeing from the sunlight.

The funeral service was just ending. Asakura, along with other students and staff members, had come to Toshiaki's home to help with the service. The undertakers and relatives had everything under control, but she had insisted on helping out with the reception. The coffin was to be carried out soon and she had just taken a step outside to make sure the hearse had arrived.

Toshiaki lived in a government condo. The ashen walls were cracked here and there, giving them a feeling of antiquity. Twenty-four families lived in his four-story wing. Toshiaki had shared a happy life on the third floor with his now deceased wife. This was the first time Asakura had ever seen his place. The area had probably been little more than a field of rice paddies once upon a time. Now it was host to a cluster of homes and had the air of a declining residential district.

The parking lot was packed with cars, with just enough space to pass between them. Every vehicle shimmered with distorted heat trails; grazing them carelessly would surely have burned the skin. The narrow street in front of the complex was also subdued, as still and silent as the woman towards whom its paved lines led all who were gathering here today. The occasional echo of a motorbike engine from the distance was the only sound to be heard. All of a sudden, a gloom fell upon everything. When Asakura looked upwards, she saw that new clouds had rolled in to cover the sun. She took one step forward, pulling away from the apartment wall. At that precise moment, the light returned, glaring up her surroundings anew. She squinted into the glare.

"Finally the first floor," said a voice, followed by a rattling sound. When Asakura turned around, a group of men carrying Kiyomi's coffin were edging their way down the stairs. The concrete steps were narrow, flaked with peeling paint, and the men were having trouble turning the coffin on a stair landing. Toshiaki led the procession, holding a mortuary tablet in his hands. At his side were Kiyomi's parents, with a photo of the deceased.

Someone from the undertaker wove the hearse through the crowd of parked cars and backed it up carefully to the side of the building. The back door was opened. A few grunts later, the coffin was loaded inside. Asakura watched silently in the background.

Once the coffin was in place, the mourners all gathered in a semicircle around it. Seeing that final blessings were about to be given, Asakura hurried over to meet up with the others, standing modestly behind them. Because of her height, she could see Toshiaki's face clearly in the center of the congregation.

"I want to thank you all for coming today..." he began in a tone that was plain, almost disturbingly so. There was no cadence in his voice, like he was just going through the motions. The only one unable to control her tears was Kiyomi's mother. She was petite, and her hair had luster. A few wrinkles were carved into her forehead and around her mouth, but she looked surprisingly childlike; she must have been adorable as a young girl. Kiyomi's father, on the other hand, had the air of a distinguished man in the prime of his life. He listened patiently to Toshiaki's words with eyes and head cast downward. But his shoulders sometimes trembled, betraying the sadness he was unable to contain. Toshiaki's flat voice, only the more unfitting in contrast, gave off the unreality of a shimmer at the bottom of a cascade of sunlight.

Toshiaki's look during this entire ordeal kept nagging at Asakura. The darkly clad man who sat near the altar during the ceremony was not the man she knew as mentor and role model. His features used to be gentle, taking on a penetrating look whenever it came to research. This was not the Toshiaki she saw every day in the lab. His face was pale, offset by dark patches under his eyes. Sometimes his back teeth chattered like he was having chills, and his fingers twitched slightly. She'd seen him like this for the first time the night before, when she and her classmates had come to see how he was holding up. He'd changed so much that for a moment she couldn't speak.

A large black-and-white photograph of Kiyomi adorned the altar, and the picture showed the smiling face of a woman who still possessed a child's innocence. Asakura had met her only once; Toshiaki had brought along his wife for last month's open session of the School of Pharmaceutical Sciences. Asakura recalled her charming smile and how, though Kiyomi had to be a few years older than her, she'd actually looked younger, thanks probably to her features. Asakura had felt flustered; even the woman's name, Kiyomi, was pretty.

She'd stolen glances at Kiyomi's face from a distance as the beauty lay in her coffin. Apparently Kiyomi had hit her head in a car accident, hence the white cloth covering her skull. This gave her a slightly different impression but did little to taint her attractiveness. Her face was made up and her lips were frozen in a faint smile. Her white cheeks, so pale they appeared translucent, were of fine complexion, and at one point Asakura could barely suppress a sudden strange urge to touch them.

Throughout the entire ceremony, Toshiaki kept looking at her photo, only half-listening to condolences. For the most part, he looked vacant, but sometimes cast the photo a smile like he'd just remembered to. Asakura had noticed a similar expression on him the night before. It was so tranquil that it terrified her. She'd had to look away, like she'd unwittingly taken a peek at some secret between the man and the deceased.

Toshiaki resumed his speech, during which Kiyomi's name was intoned innumerable times. The sunlight beat down harshly and everyone was getting tired. Some continuously wiped their foreheads with handkerchiefs, but most just stood in place, waiting patiently for him to finish.

Toshiaki had changed completely. After Kiyomi's death, his soul seemed to be in turmoil. Helping out with the funeral, Asakura felt that this was a man she didn't know and was unable to say a word to him. She was only feeling more perplexed. It was like that when he made his sudden appearance at the lab a few nights before. He just shouted at her when she was trying to express her worries, then set himself to work at the clean bench, clearly possessed. Afterwards, he went back to the hospital without a word. As he left, his countenance was one of dreamy intoxication. While he was gone, Asakura secretly peered into the incubator to see what he had been doing. A new culture flask and a six-well plate were left inside. On the lid, the word "Eve" was scribbled in Toshiaki's handwriting. She didn't know anyone by that name. Gently removing the flask, she observed it under the microscope and saw the shapes of healthy cells but could not identify them. She did not understand why Toshiaki had yelled at her just to perform a routine cellular procedure. Feeling very uncomfortable about it all, she'd hastily returned the flask to the incubator, placing it as close to its original position as possible, a little scared she'd be found out.

Toshiaki's tone changed subtly as he came to his closing statements.

"Kiyomi will now be carried out of our lives...but this does not mean she is dead. Kiyomi's kidneys have been transplanted into two patients. Let us never forget that she thrives within them."

Under his plain delivery, Toshiaki appeared to be hiding a faint excitement. There was a certain force in his words that one didn't associate with eulogies, and Asakura didn't miss the grin that crossed his features. Toshiaki thirstily licked his lips in between words. As she watched this, Asakura's mouth went dry, too. The scattering sunlight covered everything in a bleary whiteness, and the mourners were sweating like dogs by now, but they all remained quiet, eyes cast downward to the asphalt. Only Toshiaki's face was raised. Asakura, who was getting really nervous, couldn't tear her gaze away from it until he closed his salutation:

"Kiyomi will live on."

When she came to her senses, people were already making to leave. Toshiaki and several relatives separated into two cars and pulled out onto the street. The others gathered in the shade of the entrance to bid them farewell from there.

Symbiosis

The hearse left, followed by the black sedan that Toshiaki had climbed into. Emitting low engine rumbles, the vehicles turned at the intersection. A cool glint flashed off the black body of the hearse just before it disappeared from view.

Everyone stood there for some time.

"We will now prepare to receive the ashes," said a man, who appeared to be a relative, provoking sounds of relief from the small crowd. The man returned to the apartment steps and the rest followed suit. Asakura trailed behind.

"The husband was a bit strange, don't you think?"

When Asakura heard this, she looked up, startled at such a direct comment. Two middle-aged women were talking in front of her. They appeared to be relatives or close acquaintances, but their indifferent gossip indicated otherwise.

"'Kiyomi will live on.' Gives you the creeps, doesn't it?"

They probably thought they were taking care not to be overheard, but their high-pitched half-whispers were all too audible to Asakura. She felt uncomfortable and wanted to get away, but the pair's conversation crept into her ears as if she were their designated audience.

"He was pretty weird during the wake, too. I guess he was just devastated by the suddenness of it all. Must be having a hard time accepting it."

"Well, apparently he's been acting like this for a while. I heard that for a while there, Kiyomi was, you know, brain-dead."

"I had no idea… Ugh, I hope I never end up that way."

"Me neither. You know, he allowed kidney transplants… They say he's been acting odd ever since."

"How could he let them do that? I mean, he let them take out his wife's kidneys? Didn't he feel bad?"

"Exactly. Why mangle her body like that? I bet he thought letting them go ahead made him look good."

Asakura could not endure this any longer. She felt sick in her stomach and clambered up the stairs to get away from them. Pushing aside the two, who kept rattling on, she raced up with a sort of desperation.

3

Mariko was bedridden after the operation, only faintly conscious and still under the watchful eyes of the staff. In her daze, she couldn't even make out how she lay. It felt a lot like putting on glasses when you didn't need them.

Waking up from anesthesia the day before, Mariko had found herself in a sickroom with fluorescent lighting in the ashen ceiling. She realized she was no longer in the OR, which gave her some relief. A masked nurse came over to her, peered into her face, and called for the doctor.

The nurse's voice resounded in Mariko's ears, making her wince. Forehead throbbed, vision quickly melted. The ceiling faded out of focus, then vanished from sight.

"You can relax, okay? The operation is over," said a man's voice from some-where, but it only became part of the growing pain in her skull.

She dropped off to sleep for a few hours afterwards. When she opened her eyes again, two nurses were on either side of her. One of them noticed Mariko trying to lift her head.

"Easy does it. You're still recovering, dear. Sleep some more," she said. Surely enough, when Mariko tried moving her head, it ached intensely. She laid her head back on the pillow in defeat. She felt hot and dizzy like she had a terrible cold.

Something was sticking into her groin. When she opened her eyes, she saw a nurse fiddling with a tube. Mariko moved her waist a little and felt that the tube led into her body. Somewhat embarrassed by this realization, she turned her face aside. She then became aware of another one in the left side of her chest. She knew all about these tubes, as they had been used to remove bodily fluids after her previous transplant. The other nurse took her arm and put something black around it. Mariko's arm began to throb with a strong pulse.

"I'm just taking your blood pressure, okay?" said a tiny voice.

The two nurses continued their examination. Mariko closed her eyes and let them do their work. She felt something strange below her navel on the left side, and thought she might try to touch it, but could not since the nurse was still taking her pulse. She wondered if it was her newly acquired kidney.

The kidney.

Mariko opened her eyes wide.

At last she sobered to the reality of her transplant and a flood of memories washed across her mind: the sudden phone call during the night, the hospital, the tests, the blood transfusion, listening to the doctors and nurses as they explained everything to her...

Mariko gathered all her might to speak, but her voice emerged only as a hoarse and barely audible whisper. The nurse stopped and cocked her head.

"Person who gave me," Mariko repeated desperately.

"What? Who?"

The two nurses looked at each other, unable to understand her question.

"The person...who gave me...the kidney. What happened. Where..."

"...ah."

One of them nodded and smiled at Mariko.

"No need to worry about that, okay, dear? The operation went very well. Your donor must be very happy about it right now in heaven. In fact, the person who gave you your kidney says you have to get better as soon as possible."

"No," Mariko complained. "Tell me please... Was this person really dead? Did this person really *want* to give me a kidney?"

The nurses looked upset. They smiled uncomfortably and tried to smooth things over.

"Alright now. Let's just calm down, okay? You're still feverish from the operation, so..."

Mariko shook off the nurse's hands and screamed as loud as she could, but an explosion of dizziness swarmed in her head and she shut her eyes. Her voice fell to a rasp that she herself couldn't hear.

When she opened her eyes again, her father was at her side. A difficult expression was on his face.

"Everything's fine. The operation went well."

She forced a smile. He looked a little uncomfortable in his germ-free attire. She could not see his mouth, but his eyes darted around in discomfort, their focus clearly averted from her. She took a deep breath and closed her eyes.

"You're running a fever of about 100° F, which is fairly normal after transplant surgery. We've given you some medication to make it go down," said Yoshizumi, who'd entered the room along with her father. This doctor was the last person Mariko wanted to see right now. She clamped shut her eyelids even tighter.

The nurses took turns throughout the day to stay with Mariko and monitor her condition. They took blood pressure and urine samples every hour and regulated her transfusions. On the verge of sleep at almost every moment, she entrusted her body to them. Yoshizumi came in to check her data and talk with her. Mariko did not remember it, he said, but after the operation, she was given a radioisotope-tagged drug and a renogram. These checked whether blood was flowing properly in her newly transplanted kidney. He told her gently that there were no indications of ATN or any infections but that the catheters and drainage tubes would have to be left in just a little longer. Mariko closed her eyes again and pretended not to listen.

Her room was single occupancy, not too large. The doorway was concelaed by a protruding section of the wall, behind which there seemed to be some kind of basin for washing hands and gargling. Before people came in, there was always the sound of splashing water.

Mariko was fed through a mouth tube. She could not even begin to describe the flavor of the thing, but it was actually tolerable.

"You'll only have to put up with this a little more, then you'll be able to eat tasty stuff again!" a nurse encouraged her. Mariko nodded vaguely. She then recalled an exchange between her and Dr. Yoshizumi from two years ago.

..."So I can eat oranges again?"

Mariko was in such good spirits then she was almost embarrassed with herself. She asked about all the edible things she could think of.

"And apples? And potato chips? I can have as much miso soup as I want? And ice cream? Even chocolate?"...

Mariko felt herself urinating intermittently. Because of the catheter, she did not experience the usual discomfort of a full bladder. Instead, her urethra became warm, the catheter felt different, and she could tell that urine was coming out. When she was aware of it, it was all she could think of. It was an odd sensation. For a year and a half, she had never urinated, undergoing three dialyses per week instead. She had trouble remembering what it was like to go to the bathroom or to have the urge to do so.

She had an intermittent dream in which she was sleeping, indeed, in a hospital bed. Details were hard to make out in the dark room. The door was closed and she had no clue as to what lay on the other side. A pale light shone from the crack underneath it. At least the hallway lights were on. She had to think for a moment about where she was and why she was there before soon remembering being in recovery from transplant surgery. She felt paralyzed, only able to move her hands. She touched around her abdomen gently. Something was palpitating inside her body. Distinct from her heartbeat, something with a life that wasn't Mariko was pulsing on its own. She felt around more carefully, trying her best to guess what it might be. Whatever it was, it seemed to be struggling to get out of her body.

At that moment she heard a flabby sound. *Flap...*

She opened her eyes and looked around. Nothing felt out of the ordinary. And just when she was ready to pass it off as a trick of the ears...: *Flap.*

It came from beyond the door, like the echo of vinyl slippers shuffling along the corridor. Thinking it was just somebody coming to her room, she exhaled in relief, but an instant later knew that wasn't it. The hairs all over her body stood on end. The pace was too slow for a person walking.

And again. *Flap...* Her hands on her pulsing lower abdomen, Mariko locked her gaze firmly upon the door. The thing inside her seemed to be beating faster now. *Flap.* Slowly, the sound was drawing near. A cold shiver swept through her. She could hear nothing else, not the wind, not the cars and motorbikes in the street. Only the footsteps and the beating in her body. The footsteps were now just outside the door.

FLAP.

And that was when she'd wake up.

A worried nurse tried to comfort her and wiped the perspiration from her forehead. But upon waking up, unable to separate dream from reality, Mariko would scream. By midnight her temperature had risen far past 100° F. While she fought the fever, she had the same dream over and over.

On the second day of recovery, she was allowed to sit up just a little. The upper half of the bed was jacked up thirty degrees. Yoshizumi came in with some nurses early that morning to collect more samples. Mariko noted her father's presence as well.

"Everything okay? I heard you had a bad dream last night," Dr. Yoshizumi asked smiling, taking her pulse. That grin, practically pasted onto him, frightened Mariko. *He's never forgiven me for it*, she thought, and turned away from him.

"Mariko. Talk to me please?"

Yoshizumi would not shut up. He treated her like a child half her age and it made her nauseous. She was still in grade school when she had her first transplant and maybe back then it was okay to treat her like a kid. But she was in middle school now and Yoshizumi didn't seem to notice.

"You still have a bit of a fever, hm?" Unable to get any sort of response from her, Yoshizumi may as well have been talking to himself. "You also have a little blood in your pee. We totaled the protein count yesterday at a whopping 2.7 grams. That's not good, but it won't stay that way. Don't worry, it's quite normal right after a transplant. And I expect your fever will have gone down by tomorrow. What matters is that you're peeing. You know, that pretty much means the operation was a success. No signs of infection, either."

Yoshizumi's voice rang in her ears, and scenes from after her first transplant came back to her. Yoshizumi's expression when he began suspecting that she'd failed to take her meds. The look in her father's eyes. Mariko closed her eyes and shook her head but was unable to rid those looks from her mind. She couldn't stand it any longer.

She was screaming, "You want this transplant to fail, don't you!"

Yoshizumi drew back in shock. The nurses and Mariko's father stood completely motionless with eyes wide open, unsure of how to react.

"What are you saying…"

"I know you do!" Mariko screamed, interrupting him. "You think it's my fault it didn't work the last time. You think I'm a bad girl, so you want this transplant to fail too!"

"Mariko, stop! Please…" said her father, visibly upset. But she could not suppress her rage. She was no longer in control of the words spilling from her mouth. Yoshizumi tried to touch her, to which she objected loudly and started weeping. The nurses were equally overwhelmed. One of them took Mariko's hand, trying her best to appease her. Mariko pried it away from her grasp.

At that moment the drainage tube in her side twisted and pain shot through her entire body. She cried out and buried her face in the pillow. She realized what she'd been doing, and her anger subsided.

While she lay quietly, her back and waist began to hurt. At her request the nurse shifted her body, but the pain didn't recede. Her perceptions grew dim from the fever and the searing pain in her back. Simply keeping her eyes open was becoming impossible without discomfort.

Mariko dreamt again that night. She was sleeping in the same dark room and the footsteps returned on cue. Slowly but surely, they were approaching her door. Her eyes were glued to the light leaking from under it.

Why did the sound frighten her so much?

She kept telling herself it was just a nurse making her rounds, but this did not shake the uneasiness that gripped her heart. Someone was coming and it was no nurse or doctor. This was something, she thought, far more *scary*.

Two things were beating so fast in her body that it was hard for her to breathe: one, her heart racing with fright; the other, something less familiar that was clearly enjoying itself, quivering excitedly in her abdomen every time the sound drew closer. Both seemed to pound in her head and ears, and her entire body was hot. Her chest and her abdomen, running away each with their wild beat, threatened to tear her asunder at any moment.

Flap.

The shadow of a figure entered the glow under the door. Mariko let out a voiceless scream. For a moment the shadow stood motionless outside her door. Then, with a light *flap*, it turned toward the door. Mariko's heart nearly jumped from her body, and the thing that dwelled in her abdomen squirmed around ecstatically. Her waist rumbled, making the bed creak. Her back was drenched with sweat.

Mariko's eyes were fixed on the door. And she was aghast.

For the knob was turning, ever so slightly. Silently, and so slowly you could hardly tell it was moving at all, the knob was turning. Whatever was on the other side was trying to get in.

THUMP.

Mariko's abdomen leapt up. The bed bounced and her body was in the air for a second. *The kidney*, she thought. The new kidney was trying to come out of her. Choked with fear, Mariko still could not take her eyes from the door knob. She finally realized who was coming for her. She despaired. Her heart, which had been beating so wildly, fell silent.

The door began to open. Light poured in through the crack.

Mariko screamed, and woke up.

Symbiosis

4

Toshiaki resumed his duties the day after the funeral. As always, he parked his car in the college parking lot at 8:20 and was in his lab by 8:30.

No one else was in yet this morning. He turned on the light and walked over to his desk, now overflowing with a week's worth of leaflets and pamphlets from various companies extolling their new products. He'd usually, at least, skim through the English-language catalogues of cloning vectors and cytokines, but he was hardly in the mood right now and placed them in a rack at the side of his desk. He heard a clanging noise and the door opened. He looked up and turned around.

Asakura put her hand over her mouth as she saw him, her body straightening from surprise.

For a while, neither could speak, and the awkwardness was quite something. Asakura moved her mouth like a dying fish as she searched for words, while her eyes darted nervously about the room.

Toshiaki managed a smile and raised his hand in greeting.

"...morning."

Asakura started, but the tension was now gone.

"Good morning!" she said with a smile and a bow.

The awkwardness faded. Toshiaki apologized for the inconvenience of his absence and thanked Asakura for her help at the funeral.

"Please, think nothing of it," she said.

"How are the data coming along?"

Asakura's face beamed when she heard these words, and she nodded.

In most science departments, undergraduates were assigned to staff members and conducted experiments on their own in their instructors' field, and the School of Pharmaceutical Sciences was no exception. Ten seniors were assigned every year to Toshiaki's Biofunctional Pharmaceuticals course. Aside from the professor, the staff included an associate professor, an assistant professor, and two research associates, who were each charged with certain students. Toshiaki had taken two under his wing this year. Having already completed their first term exams, they were now able to devote themselves to lab work. However, they both hoped to enter the graduate program and would be taking a vacation, once August came around, to prepare for their entrance exams at the end of the month.

Asakura had gone through all this and was part of the graduate program now. Toshiaki had mentored her throughout her senior year, and she had continued with the same concentration, with him, for her master's. Now in her second year, she would be graduating soon; in fact, she'd already secured employment at a leading pharmaceutical firm. All she needed to do now was assemble her data for her master's thesis.

"The MOM19 level has increased, as you expected," explained Asakura as she showed Toshiaki a printout of the previous week's results. During her senior year and her first master's year, there was still something rickety about the experiments she set up, but her intuition and versatility were now those of a real researcher. Her explanations were concise, yet thorough, and Toshiaki understood her perfectly.

"Also, the cells you'd transfected were growing fast, so I had to transpose them. I mean the ones you introduced the retinoid receptors into."

Asakura stated these words without fanfare, but they gave Toshiaki chills.

Did she know about the other cells? He studied her face assiduously for signs as he nodded. Just then, the door opened and in walked one of his seniors, who was quite taken aback at Toshiaki's unexpected return.

"Good morning," said Toshiaki gently and began talking with the student, missing his chance to probe what Asakura knew about the cells.

Perhaps because Toshiaki had been able to talk with Asakura, he was able to greet the other staff members without much awkwardness. They all bowed and uttered condolences to him, but things didn't get too soppy.

Symbiosis

"You shouldn't return to work so soon. Take a break," Mutsuo Ishihara, the professor, told him. Toshiaki thanked him but turned down the offer.

"To be honest, I was actually getting more depressed being away from my work."

Ishihara raised an eyebrow.

"I see," he said worriedly. "Just don't overdo it."

That night, after the staff had gone home, Toshiaki stepped into the Cultivation Room with a feigned nonchalance and opened the incubator. He took out the stainless steel sheet from inside. There appeared to be no change in Kiyomi's cell flasks from the night before. He gazed at the word "Eve" written on the lid; he'd chosen this name because Kiyomi's birthday fell on Christmas Eve.

After performing the primary culture on her liver cells, he had come here every night to look at them. At two or three in the morning, after all the students would have left, he came to "meet" with the cells, not even turning on the lights, making sure nobody caught on to his secret visits. Bathed in the pale glow of the clean bench, Toshiaki would put his eyes up to the microscope and peer at the cells.

He imagined that Kiyomi would have been frightened by a figure hunched over a microscope in a gloomy room during the dead of night. She had always been very sensitive, looking away during the murder scenes of TV dramas, calling for his help whenever she needed to get rid of an insect in the house. He had never been able to describe his experiments to her in detail. Even after they married, for some time Kiyomi innocently kept asking him about his research. He gladly informed her about the more general findings of his work, but took care to avoid talking about dissecting rats, cultivating cancer cells and bacteria, and such matters. He knew not to, after the mention of a routine mouse injection had been enough to frighten her. Toshiaki also made sure no odors from the lab animals lingered on his clothing when he got home.

But now Kiyomi herself was in a culture flask. Even on the night of the wake, after gazing upon her face one last time, he had come here to observe Eve. On that night, Toshiaki was seized by strange delusions that Kiyomi had divided and disseminated.

She was surely more than just a corpse and the cells now in his possession. Each of her kidneys now thrived in other people.

"I'm sorry but you can't meet them," he'd been told over the phone the day before.

He'd held the receiver, just sitting still for several seconds, before he could plead again.

"Why not? Please. Just once."

But the woman on the phone told him that the patients' privacy had to be respected and that any such action would be an intrusion.

Toshiaki had called the City Central Hospital after struggling in vain not to. He simply couldn't resist after he'd read the letter from the transplant coordinator, Odagiri. The letter was very polite. It explained that Kiyomi's kidneys had been transplanted into two recipients and that one of them was a 14-year-old girl. It spoke of her favorable recovery and expressed a deep gratitude on behalf of everyone involved. At the end of the letter, a postscript said to contact her should there be anything they could do for him.

Kiyomi's kidneys were still alive, resuscitated in other bodies. Toshiaki's heart ached at the thought. He wanted to meet these people desperately. If anything, he hoped to find traces of Kiyomi in those who harbored her gifts.

In the end, he could do nothing but hang up the phone in defeat.

Of course, the hospital's response made perfect sense. If the donor's family were allowed to meet the recipient, unpleasant arguments of a financial nature could easily arise. If the organ in question was ultimately rejected by the recipient's body, the result could be no little hurt on both sides. By keeping the two parties ignorant of the other's identity, it was ensured that their lives would be lived without any unnecessary trauma. Though Toshiaki found no fault with this reasoning, he refused to abandon the notion altogether.

Symbiosis

He wanted so much to *feel* Kiyomi's existence, despite her body having already been reduced to ashes. All he could do now to satisfy his desire was to look at her liver cells. Ever since the coffin was carried away, his apartment had become dark and terribly cold, enshrouded though it was in the brightness of early summer.

Toshiaki had returned to his lab duties with these thoughts swimming in his head. If he went back to work, he could meet with Kiyomi anytime and not have to resort to lurking in the university halls under cover of night. He could spend more time with her.

Toshiaki removed another flask from the incubator and placed it under the microscope. He then turned on the lamp switch and drew his eyes close to the lenses.

As he turned a small wheel with the middle finger of his left hand to bring the image into focus, Kiyomi's cells emerged in full clarity. They had grown protrusions and looked like stars, adhering to the bottom of the flask. In this one area alone, about ten-odd cells covered the bottom completely. Toshiaki moved the stand, shifting the field of view left and right to check the other cells. He had added a number of growth factors to the solution for the primary culture, and Eve looked alive, very much so.

After looking at the cells for a while, Toshiaki noticed something strange. He squinted.

The cells had increased in number.

Unlike cancer cells, normal liver cells did not multiply all that much. A built-in control system made sure that they divided only when, and as much as, necessary. Cancer cells were precisely those that weren't subject to this control. When cultivating cancer cells, adding a serum, their nutrient, was enough to have them multiply up to the brim of a flask over the course of just a few days. In order to continue with the cultivation, one actually had to remove the cells from the flask and to redeposit just a portion of them. Meanwhile, in order to cultivate liver cells, which had weak self-replicating capabilities to begin with, one had to introduce growth inducers to the solution, in addition to the serum, to make sure the cells didn't die. Even then, liver cells never divided and proliferated vigorously like cancer cells. In fact, they usually died out after a few weeks.

But these cells were different.

Cell coverage was dense, but far from uniform, gathered in some places like little archipelagos and only sparsely in others, a pattern that arose only when cells were multiplying. Toshiaki had been careless not to see it until now. Their growth rate must have been increasing with each passing day. He suspected for a moment that perhaps they were fibroblasts that had been mixed in, but when he examined the cell's shapes he confirmed that it was indeed the liver cells.

Toshiaki checked each flask and plate. All showed similar signs of growth. The plate wells were already overcrowded, so much so that if he didn't transpose them, the cells would begin to die.

This was getting interesting.

Eve consisted of normal liver cells but was growing at the rate of cancer cells. There was a small possibility that the presence of cancer-related genes was causing this anomaly, but Toshiaki had no reason to suspect that Kiyomi had been suffering from liver cancer. It looked like he had in his possession an extremely rare cell type. Some unique mutation, the likes of which had never been reported before, was transpiring within these cells. Establishing lines of these could not be that hard, either.

Toshiaki flicked on the clean bench lamp and ignited the gas burners. He took some trypsin and a culture medium from the refrigerator. He tossed a 15 cc tube, still in its wrapper, on the bench. Finally he placed a cell plate on the bench with care.

He sat in front of the bench and began gathering the cells. They would have to be cloned. His obsession with Eve was only growing stronger now that it promised to aid his research on mitochondria. Countless questions swarmed in his head. Had the mitochondrial form in these cells changed with this metamorphosis? Were β-oxidation enzymes being induced? How about the formation of retinoid receptors? If the mitochondria had indeed changed, was it in fact responsible for the cellular reproduction? If so, how, why?

Kiyomi's face floated before his eyes. She was smiling, so cheerfully. Her large eyes, her gently curving eyebrows, her lips that shone with a rosy hue, without the aid of rouge, those soft cheeks, all were set aglow by her smile. Toshiaki loved her smile. He could almost hear her pleasant, rolling voice.

He recalled the first time they met. Kiyomi, not used to drinking, was flushed from the beer she'd had, but this detracted nothing from the loveliness of her laugh. Toshiaki talked too volubly about his research, but she listened with interest. Her curiosity didn't abate even after they started going out. Toshiaki was touched by her sincere desire to know more about him, though it seemed she also concealed a certain jealousy towards his work. She sounded lonely when he was delayed by his experiments late into the night. He was sympathetic to her complaints, but was also vexed that he couldn't convey to her that his love for her and his love for research were two completely different dimensions of his life. It was not a matter of choosing one over the other. To him, research was a necessity, but Kiyomi never seemed willing to grasp that.

But the two had become one now. Toshiaki felt strangely elated. Studying these cells was, at one and the same time, spending quality time with her.

As he continued with the limiting dilution of the cells, he felt a slight fever rise in him. He felt that Kiyomi was calling out to his body. Despite not being able to meet the recipients, he *did* have these cells. Working with them, he could connect with Kiyomi.

He had to nurture the cells with care. He would prolong their life, as much as possible, and produce significant data. He knew this would have made Kiyomi glad, too. He'd come home late so often, even after they were married, and couldn't give her all the attention she deserved. He would now make up for it by pouring all of that lost love into Eve.

With a firm resolve, he reached for the next plate.

5

Kiyomi's friends were always impressed that her parents were both doctors. Whenever they came over to her house, they could not help but notice its spaciousness and well-decorated interior. A grand piano stood in the living room, as well as a wooden book case that housed a charming assortment of music boxes and French dolls. Kiyomi's mother enjoyed baking and usually made cake or cookies for her and her friends.

"We've only got an apartment. My father's always complaining he doesn't have enough money 'cuz he's a high school teacher," said Chika in a bright voice, despite the mouthful of freshly baked cookie. Denying any possession of such riches, Kiyomi replied modestly that Chika had plenty going for her, all the games she had, not to mention an older brother to keep her company at home.

"Oh, he's a pain. He's so uncool," Chika retorted, shaking her head dramatically. Then she laughed and said Kiyomi's house was the best.

Kiyomi had many friends and enjoyed her time with everyone. She had been close to most of them since grade school. But because she and Chika were in the same homeroom class for their first two years of middle school, they had become especially good friends and spent much of their free time together. They differed in character and taste, yet this only served to augment their friendship. Chika often described Kiyomi's lavish household, to use a vocab word she had learned in history class, as "bourgeois." Kiyomi understood Chika's praise to be genuine at bottom, so she didn't mind at all.

Kiyomi inherited her mother's hobbies and had recently begun to pursue an interest in baking, occasionally making cakes together with her mother. She was also fond of doll-making. For her birthday the year before, she'd received an *Anne of Green Gables* book from her father and had fallen in love with it. She now owned the entire series and had reread them from cover to cover a number of times.

"Kiyomi, you're such a lady, everything you do. 'Course, if I grew up like you, I'd be baking fancy cookies too," Chika said heartily.

Symbiosis

After finishing their cookies, they sipped orange juice from straws.

"I would love to be more like you, Chika." Kiyomi was thinking of Chika's fifty meter dash in gym class that day. Though Chika was short, she had the right reflexes and excelled in short distance running, for which she held the top honor in her class. She'd participated in city meets, and she was always the star on Sports Day. For the relay run, she easily beat out boys from the other classes. Her figure stood out quite noticeably on the track.

"Nah, I suck. Look at my legs, they're getting fat. None of the cute guys'll even get near me!" said Chika sarcastically and smiled.

"Don't be silly. You're adorable, Chika...I'm sure you'll find someone who appreciates you."

"You're just saying that. 'Sides, if you looked up 'adorable' in the dictionary, your picture'd be right there next to it." Chika laughed as she said this, but then her expression grew serious. She leaned in closer.

"What's wrong?" asked Kiyomi, somewhat unnerved.

"A question for the witness. This'll go on record, so you must answer honestly. You do have the right to remain silent."

"What is it, Chika?"

"What's your type?"

"Huh?"

It was such a sudden question that Kiyomi did not know how to answer. She looked around bashfully, then gazed directly at Chika's face. Chika's eyes took on a mischievous look; the straight line of her lips twisted and broke into laughter.

"You're too much, Kiyomi." Chika held her belly and continued laughing. "Is it that hard to answer?"

"Hey..."

"I could see you ending up with someone like your dad," she said, at last suppressing her snickering.

"You think?"

"Definitely. He seems like someone you can really count on. They say if you have a father like that, you end up with pretty high standards."

"I never thought about it..."

"Your family's like a TV show, anyway. You've got your quiet father, gentle mother, and the little princess. Everything you need for the perfect drama."

"Don't say things like that...it's embarrassing." Kiyomi's face turned red and she hid it behind both hands. She tried to change the subject.

"Well, enough about me. What about you? You haven't told me what your type is."

"Me? Hm..."

She grew serious again, folded her arms, and tilted her head. Her emotions always changed so quickly. Kiyomi was more reserved in character and was envious of Chika's outgoing nature.

Chika thought about it for a good thirty seconds. Then, a smile rose to her lips.

"Someone who will think of me forever."

"Yeah."

Kiyomi nodded, a smile upon her face as well.

Kiyomi's grades were in good standing and she was an active member of the brass band. She was accepted into a prep school without even attending cram-school classes. The high school was considered one of the best in her prefecture, with a lot of the graduates going on to college. Meanwhile, Chika's diligent study in her final year of middle school paid off and she was accepted into the same high school as Kiyomi. Chika always wore a cheerful smile in the company of others, showing no signs of stress, but Kiyomi suspected that she was secretly a very hard worker.

The high school placed as much emphasis on extracurricular activities as on academics, and most students picked up something. Chika did what she was best at and joined the track and field club, while Kiyomi joined a chamber ensemble.

High school life was as enjoyable as they could have imagined. Kiyomi liked to read in the time between classes and after-school activities. After finishing *The Tale of Genji*, she started on *Anne of Green Gables* in the English original.

The seasons passed by quickly. Nevertheless, somewhere in her heart, Kiyomi felt like high school life was all she would ever know; hence her exclamation of surprise one day during the summer of her second year when the teacher handed out a college selection form to the class.

Later that day after practice, Kiyomi was putting her things away when Chika dropped by the practice room. She was carrying her backpack and duffel bag in one hand. As she stood in front of the doorway, peeping into the room, she gently waved her free hand. Her hair was a bit wet from the shower she had taken after track. Kiyomi smiled and waved back, signaling with a finger to wait a moment. When most of the band members had left, Chika stepped into the quiet practice room and sat next to Kiyomi, who was cleaning her instrument.

Watching Kiyomi's fingers detachedly, Chika asked, "So what do you think you'll do, Kiyomi?"

"I don't know."

Kiyomi shook her head. The still warm sunlight poured in through the window, illuminating her hands as she wiped fingerprints from her trumpet with a small cloth. The heat had been quite intense throughout the day, but remained now only in scattered places as a languid afterglow. It was already 6:30 and, before they knew it, the voices echoing from the basketball team in the rear gymnasium had faded away.

They hopped on their bikes and took the road home together, riding side by side. The streets were unusually inactive, not a single soul in sight. The girls, too, were silent. Kiyomi began to feel uncomfortable, pedaling her bicycle faster to keep up with Chika.

Kiyomi broke the silence at last.

"So, we were just starting to get used to high school and now we have to decide what to do with our lives. It's too much to handle right now. I can't even think beyond band practice, you know?"

But Chika simply pedaled, staring off wordlessly into the distance before them. Kiyomi studied her profile. Before long, they had passed the street and reached a paved road which ran straight through a rice paddy. The failing heat of the rays was pursued by twilight and their surroundings became steeped in deep blue. The brightness of a single star twinkled from a gap in the clouds. Chika replied at last.

"I want to become a doctor," she mumbled.

Surprised, Kiyomi looked at Chika, whose eyes remained fixed on the sky spread out above them.

Chika's mother had passed away that spring. Kiyomi did not understand the details very well, but knew that there had been something wrong with her heart. The days of nursing and the funeral itself must have been hard on Chika, but she'd never once shown a depressed face to Kiyomi. She continued to smile and joke around in her usual manner and remained the person Kiyomi could always talk to. Yet, Kiyomi had been unable to read what had been transpiring in her best friend's mind.

Kiyomi had trouble falling asleep that night.

What did she want to be? She could not picture herself finding a job and earning a salary. She would probably attend college but had no clear ideas as to what she would major in. She had plenty of time and she could decide once she was in college; that had been the extent of her thinking.

Chika's comment that day struck at her heart. Chika seemed to know what she wanted to be, at least. Kiyomi didn't. Chika had taken a step ahead and was pulling away from her.

Kiyomi fantasized about what shape her life would take. Who would she marry? What would her children be like? How would she die? She lay in bed with her eyes open, staring at the dark ceiling with a contemplation that was fragmentary at best. The fluorescent light dangling from above began to spin around slowly. She had no idea if she was awake or dreaming. Countless doubts arose, overflowing and spilling over one another inside her head.

Symbiosis

6

"How are you feeling?" Yoshizumi said to Mariko and flashed a smile.

Five days had passed since the operation, and everything was going smoothly. Two days ago they had removed the upper drainage tube from her kidney and today the urinary catheter. The bladder tube was still in place, but would be removed tomorrow.

Barely glancing at Yoshizumi's face, Mariko looked away.

Didn't think so... Trying not to betray his disappointment, Yoshizumi said, "It seems your fever's gone down, and so has your CRP value. Don't you feel better? You're still slightly anemic, so let's adjust your transfusion level."

He then explained the test results in a way Mariko would understand. If she knew about her condition fully, he thought, she would have a much more positive attitude towards the treatment this time around. She should also be relieved to learn that there were no symptoms of organ rejection or serious infections.

The real transplation treatment didn't begin until after the operation. In the case of kidney transplants, the surgery itself was relatively simple, something any trained surgeon could perform. The problem was what happened afterwards.

A transplanted organ was a foreign body and inevitably elicited resistance from the recipient's immune system. It was to minimize this that HLA compatibility checks were made. Yet, immuno-suppressants were always necessary, and the dual use of prednine, an adrenal steroid, and azathioprine used to be common. The success rate for transplants shot up, however, with the development of more effective suppressants like cyclosporin and FK506. Because these drugs are reno-toxic, today they are used only in conjunction with other drugs. Based on clinical data, Yoshizumi's group favored a three-drug combo consisting of a minimum of cyclosporin, some adrenal steroid, and mizoribine, an antiobiotic. Since this wasn't Mariko's first transplant, she'd been prescribed a relatively small volume. Suppressing the immune system helped the new kidney survive but made the patient vulnerable to infections, a potentially lethal outcome given the lowered barriers. This was the crux of a transplant procedure, which was often compared to tightrope walking. The patient had to be kept under close watch for signs of organ rejection on the one hand and infections on the other. Yoshizumi was painfully aware that transplants were the work not of the surgeon alone but of the nurses, clinical technicians, and pharmacists who had to stay in close touch during the post-op period.

Mariko was still turned away. Yoshizumi cast a backwards glance at her father, but he, too, looked away.

Yoshizumi sighed in his heart.

Mariko was clearly not in the mood for small talk. She had been acting this way with her father and the nurses as well. It seemed she wanted to forget, even deny, that the transplant had ever occurred.

In the eyes of a young patient, parents and doctors were dignified, powerful figures and therefore understandably intimidating. Yoshizumi remembered having similar instances with other transplant patients under his care. However, in Mariko's case, he suspected there were other issues. He had no idea why she was so adamantly opposed to the transplant, even after the fact.

Maybe I failed the last time because I couldn't figure out why. At a loss, Yoshizumi shook his head to dispel his self-doubt.

"You should be able to stand up and move around a bit the day after tomorrow. You'll get to eat some real food then, too," he said and patted Mariko on the head. The nurse at his side smiled reassuringly. But Mariko still made no effort to look in their direction. As if to shut out the existence of Yoshizumi's hand, her head lolled lifelessly under his touch. Yoshizumi removed his hand.

It was quite a different story after her first operation, when Mariko looked gratefully at Yoshizumi with tears in her eyes and thanked him countless times. He had smiled in return and patted her head as he'd done now.

Until her first transplant, Mariko underwent dialysis for about one year. After that, her father offered his own kidney, to which Yoshizumi gratefully obliged.

When Mariko first appeared before them, the cherry blossoms were in full bloom. They all watched from the waiting room window as petals fell plaintively in the courtyard. Mariko was charmed by the pink scenery fluttering outside, as if seeing it for the first time.

She had just started sixth grade. She wore a white top with a green skirt and sported a bobbed hair style. Her large, round eyes were wide with joy. She listened closely to what Yoshizumi had to say and even laughed at his jokes. Her cheeks were still slightly swollen, making her all the more charming. She had hardly grown at all in the preceding two years. Even in class, she was usually moved up to the front during gym or morning assembly, a fact that made her feel a little uncomfortable.

There were a number of orientation sessions with patients before the actual transplant took place. They were informed in detail about the types of treatments they could receive, the pros and cons of each, the truths of the operation itself, and how they were to carry on with their lives after recovery. Their goal was to alleviate any misconceptions or anxieties born of ignorance. Nurses also carried out a similar duty, but in Mariko's case Yoshizumi had taken it upon himself to provide any and all explanations.

Mariko listened to his words enthusiastically, but was devastated to learn that she had to continue taking immuno-suppressants even after the operation. Nevertheless, she accepted it soon enough.

"So how long do I have to take them?" implored the young Mariko, staring at Yoshizumi intently.

"For as long as you live," he answered, not taking his eyes away from hers.

"Always...until I die?"

"Yes, but I know you can do it."

Mariko covered her eyes and was silent for a long while. She seemed to be thinking seriously about what this meant. She then looked up, her lips tightly sealed, and nodded firmly.

She progressed well for a number of days following the operation. She was beside herself with joy and spoke to everyone smiling, exhibiting a happiness and talkative disposition typical of successful patients. This was usually a result of being released from dialysis and was in proportion to how much the patient had hated it. Still, Yoshizumi didn't feel bad seeing her so happy. The dialysis experience must have been hard on her, and she genuinely seemed to appreciate having a new kidney. She seemed simply moved that she was urinating again, and when he visited her a week after the operation, she cried out and buried her face in his white coat with tears of gratitude, he patting her head.

Even after Mariko left the hospital, Yoshizumi met with her several times for checkups. Her face had rounded a bit, a side effect from the steroids he prescribed, but she was as darling as ever. She was delighted to be eating the same school lunch as everybody else, freed from her strict diet. She repeated over and over how good her meals tasted, how happy she was that she'd had a transplant.

"Doctor, I'm all healed now, I'm not sick anymore, right?" Mariko interrupted their conversation one day, smiling broadly, peering into his eyes.

For a moment Yoshizumi was silent, not taking her meaning.

"You can live normally now like everybody, so in that sense you're cured. But with transplants, you can't let down your guard. You're still taking the immunosuppressants, right? You absolutely mustn't forget to take them. Without them, even a successfully transplanted kidney will stop working. You must promise me that you'll always take your medicines. Can you promise me?"

"…yes," she nodded.

Yes. She'd nodded. She did nod…

And yet she would return to the operating room only four months later.

"We haven't discovered any pathogens yet," said Yoshizumi as he walked Anzai out of Mariko's room now. He invited Anzai into his office to tell him about her post-op condition. Yoshizumi offered him a seat.

"Our nurses have been taking samples of Mariko's fluids and sending them for analysis. We haven't found anything, so I wouldn't worry."

Anzai looked relieved and wiped the sweat from his brow.

"But as long as we're here, there's an issue I feel I must address..." he said gravely. "Just why is Mariko acting that way?"

Anzai looked downward.

"Mr. Anzai?" he asked again.

"I...don't know," he responded. Yoshizumi's silence urged him to continue. "Ever since the first transplant failed, I haven't been able to tell a single thing she's thinking. She's kept her emotions hidden from me all this time. I'm beginning to wonder if this is all my fault..."

"Did Mariko not want this transplant?"

"That's not the case!" Anzai looked up to say, but his voice was shaking.

Yoshizumi tried to wear a warm smile. "Please tell me the truth, Mr. Anzai. I realize a parent such as yourself has only his child's best interests in mind and naturally wanted this operation... But Mariko didn't, did she?"

"No," Anzai confessed, his head drooping. "I don't know what to say, after all you've done for her. It was the same when the coordinator called. Mariko kept it from me at first. I was surprised to learn we'd been contacted about a transplant. And when I returned the call to give the go ahead, Mariko was so furious that she was spasming... She was abnormal."

"Abnormal...?"

"She yelled, 'I'm not a monster'..."

Yoshizumi didn't know what to make of this and changed the subject. "She's been having constant nightmares since the operation. Any idea?"

"None." Anzai shook his head in despair.

"I think she's afraid of something. She might have developed a bad image of transplants. So she didn't want one and is having nightmares now. She wasn't this way the first time. It's as though it's not being operated on that she hates, but transplants and transplant doctors like me. Any idea why she feels this way?"

"I'm sorry, but I really have no clue." Anzai could only hang his head in shame. He seemed to be pleading for an answer himself.

Yoshizumi felt much sympathy for the man. He said gently, "I've been informed that the other recipient's been diagnosed with accelerating rejection."

"Accelerating?"

"It can occur anytime from twenty-four hours to a week after the operation when the recipient turns out to have had an antibody against the donor's antigen. He's being treated as we speak."

Anzai was speechless.

"Thankfully, Mariko's condition is stable. But I can't predict how it will turn out in the long run. I will, of course, do anything in my power. If she has no will to get better, though, we could lose her to an infection. We have to get her to open up to us."

"...how wonderful that would be..." Anzai assented feebly.

Symbiosis

7

Toshiaki sat before a co-focal laser scanning microscope and entered his calibrations with an external computer mouse. After staining the Eve 1 cultivation with Lodamine 123 stain, he placed its flask onto the platform inside the machine.

Toshiaki had cloned Eve in the past few days. The batch that displayed the strongest propagative abilities he named "Eve 1," allowing it to multiply for experimental use. The laser microscope had just been installed in the joint lab on the second floor this past spring. It was an ACAS ULTIMA, the newest model. A rather large piece of equipment, it took up the space of an entire business desk. An inverted microscope was fitted on the left side while the right was furnished with a command monitor that displayed all the data. Behind it was the laser tube. The central computer itself was located underneath the desk.

Toshiaki examined Eve 1's mitochondrial structure. The Lodamine 123 stain caused the mitochondria to glow with a distinct fluorescence that made them more visible. The laser activated a fluorescent agent that emitted photons of certain wavelengths. These passed through an optic cleansing filter and clearly outlined the shape of each mitochondrion. The most remarkable feature of the ACAS ULTIMA was that any part of a cell could be isolated. Cells themselves had a thickness and weight to them and one could not completely lay out their structural details using standard microscopic technology. Gathering information through the latter therefore had its limitations. But with this machine, one could cut many tens of layers from top to bottom of any cell and view images of individual sections on the monitor. After this, the image data were rendered into a three-dimensional model of the cell. This device exhibited unsurpassed accuracy in the research of nerve cells and others requiring 3-D constructive analysis.

Toshiaki clicked to start the program. Mitochondria appeared in succession as slender green shapes, scattered here and there against the black background of the screen.

When he was finished looking over the data, he entered a series of commands into the computer and a 3-D blot graph appeared. At that moment, Toshiaki simply couldn't contain the sudden exhalation that left his lungs. These mitochondria were unlike any he had ever seen before. They were expansive and fused together in a vast, advanced network, as if energy superhighways had been built between them.

He felt a thrill of hope throbbing in his heart. He selected other cells inside the flask and performed similar scans to identical results. A radical change had occurred in Eve 1's mitochondria.

Toshiaki printed out his findings and shut down the machine, then returned to his lab on the fifth floor to check how many stained Eve 1 cells were left by using the flow cytometer, a device which measured the intensity of fluorescence in cellular material through a process known as a histogram.

He collected cells from the flask and placed them into a centrifuge. After purifying them with a buffer, Toshiaki took the cells and returned to the joint lab once again. He turned on the flow cytometer. A moment later, the previous images reappeared on the monitor. He put in a new set of parameters.

Toshiaki hooked up a nozzle from under the machine to the tube. The cells were then sucked into the cytometer and sent to a laser apparatus. Because the collection tube was so thin, cells passed through it in a linear fashion and were hit by a laser one at a time to detect their fluorescing properties, the levels of which were dependent on the amount of agent used. This machine differed from the microscope in that it calculated the degree of stain in each cell individually, plotting their distinctive features on a graph.

Toshiaki set the tube in place and clicked on the word "GO" above the image. At once, countless dots appeared on the monitor, each denoting a single cell. Toshiaki focused on the histogram to the right as its line graph moved in short spurts.

"My God..."

The intensity was off the charts. Beyond comprehension. The mitochondria in each cell of Eve 1 were indeed increasing and their forms undergoing dramatic changes. The mechanisms which normally governed them were causing anomalies via excessive mitochondrial production. Toshiaki knew of no research having ever reported anything remotely like this. "Astounding" was the only word he could think of to describe it. That the cells had acquired some strange propagative capability suggested a sudden change in gene-linking proteins. There was a high possibility that this was influenced by the mitochondria within the cells themselves.

Toshiaki was shaking with excitement. Something new and unknown had awakened in Kiyomi.

He printed out these results immediately and ran back to his lab, where Asakura was performing a DNA extraction.

"Asakura, come here for a moment."

Toshiaki grabbed her and rushed her to the Cultivation Room. He showed her the Eve 1 flasks in the incubator. She eyed them with suspicion.

"Can you extract the mRNA from these cells for me?" Toshiaki placed a flask under the microscope and urged her to look. "I want to determine the induction of beta oxidation enzymes in a Northern blot."

"…these cells, what are they?" Asakura asked as she took her eyes from the lenses, clearly shaken from what she saw. Toshiaki lied, explaining he had received them as a laboratory sample from another university. Asakura's face did not indicate acceptance, but she pried no further into the matter, choosing instead to nod her head in resignation.

That evening, Toshiaki dreamt about something other than Kiyomi for the first time in a long while. He was back to grade school days, sitting on his bedroom floor in knee-highs and a T-shirt, working on a toy model. An electric fan blew cool air onto Toshiaki's back at regular intervals. Wind chimes echoed faintly outside and sweat dotted his forehead from the hot summer day.

Unlike his peers, Toshiaki preferred to stay at home all day reading books and sharpening his engineering skills. He enjoyed educational magazines, had a particular fascination for dinosaurs, loved zoos and museums.

The end of summer vacation was already approaching. His father had taken him to a science museum earlier that day, where Toshiaki spotted an unusual plastic model on display at the gift shop. A group of life science researchers had created a robot which mimicked the movements of a crab, manipulated freely by remote control. A plastic model version was soon merchandised, eventually finding its way to the display window which graced Toshiaki's curious eyes. Seeing how much his son was drawn to it, Toshiaki's father bought it for him and he began putting it together the moment he was home.

The model had very few parts, so assembly was effortless. When he switched on the remote, its joints began moving and large claws swayed back and forth, feeling their way around. To his young eyes, the crab appeared to be truly yearning for the ocean. With quiet awe, he pressed another button on the remote. The legs moved in alternating motions, propelling the crab sideways just like its natural counterparts. More than ecstatic, he made his new creation walk all around the house.

Toshiaki was startled when he realized that the crab's movements were being driven by uncomplicated mechanical parts. A single small motor gave it life. He wondered if all creatures were so simple, but knew this was impossible. He remembered raising tadpoles some years before, when he watched with great anticipation as they sprouted hind and front legs from nowhere then lost their tails. Robotics would never be able to replicate such mystery.

A revolving lantern turned slowly in the corner of his room. He had made it during his free time last summer with veneer and cellophane from the stationery store. At night, Toshiaki took it out onto the verandah. He lit a candle inside and the paper propeller on top turned slowly, making the cellophane cylinder spin. It changed to purple in the darkness, then to red and green, quietly turning around and around...

Before long his dream flashed to middle school, then to high school, when

Symbiosis

Toshiaki learned that all living organisms were governed by their DNA. He was impressed by the perfection of this system. Why did existence have the ability to design such a beautiful code? And how could such a simple structure account for the endless diversity of life forms?

Again, the dream switched scenes. Toshiaki was now in his lab, but it was very outdated, not even the most basic equipment to be found.

A conversation from his senior year at college followed:

"I think you should concentrate on studying mitochondria," said Professor Ishihara to a still young Toshiaki overflowing with vitality. The professor had just been appointed to the School of Pharmaceutical Sciences the year before and was searching for a new research topic. "These days, there are few researchers, if any, who are really thinking about extranuclear genetics. Sooner or later, nobody will be able to talk about the essence of human life without some understanding of it. We tend to forget there is also a society among cells on par with the center we consider so superior. If any one part of that microcosm becomes dysfunctional, the whole thing's a goner. I believe it's our duty to look at the whole picture. What do you think, Nagashima? Would you be willing to give it a shot? I'd like you to come up with some ideas."

Toshiaki was immediately taken with the plan. Here was an unknown world of knowledge, far exceeding anything he had learned in biochemistry and genetics, just waiting to be explored. He felt the sheer thrill of breaking new ground.

Mitochondria revolved noiselessly, much like the handmade lantern in his room, countless specimens coiled around one another in large clusters. They floated in space, turning without end. Toshiaki watched them in his dream. Discernible only as opaque shapes, they blocked the sun. He was lifted from solid earth and struggled not to be swallowed up by the darkness.

Eve 1's analysis was proceeding smoothly.

Toshiaki hardly noticed the time passing by. It was already August and the hot days pressed on. Leaves from the trees and shrubs surrounding the school complex glittered intensely like thousands of small mirrors in the sunlight, shooting through the glass of the lab window and bathing the room in a bright haze. In the poorly air-conditioned Pharmaceuticals building, most activities had come to a halt. Toshiaki's course was as inactive as the others were busy and all signs of stress were beginning to fade now that the seniors were all on break studying for their graduate entrance exams. Only Toshiaki and Asakura stayed behind, though their motives for doing so were totally unrelated. Shut up in this small, sweltering room, he was absorbed in Eve 1's data, instructing Asakura as needed.

According to the Northern blot results and RT-PCR data, the β-oxidation enzymes in Eve 1 had worked remarkably well.

"I've never seen anything like this before," Asakura said upon completing the experiment, barely able to hide her excitement. "The clofibrate enhancement is incredible. There's a peculiar band here that has appeared in all of them. It's almost as if these cells are developing into something else entirely."

Asakura pointed to the large, dark band on the data film image which indicated a dramatic increase in the enzyme's messenger RNA.

"The clofibrate...?" Toshiaki muttered, looking into Asakura's face. "Let's try checking all retinoid receptor levels. Then, we'll add clofibrate to the culture medium and see what happens. Check the mitochondrial growth rate alongside the import experiment and carefully record any changes. By the way, Asakura, be sure to let me know if you plan on taking a vacation this summer."

"Nope." Asakura smiled a bit, inclining her head. "I graduate this year, so...I plan on continuing my experiments without pause."

"In that case, you can help me speed up this project. I think you'll be well prepared for the conference in September, anyway, seeing as you're almost ready to collect all your findings."

"Definitely," Asakura said with a prompt nod.

Toshiaki had added a peroxisome proliferator, or extract, into the Eve 1 culture flask. The extract, of which clofibrate was a representative example, was a substance that caused an organelle in cells called a peroxisome to multiply. At the same time, however, peroxisome proliferators also induced β-oxidation enzymes within mitochondria, a process which changed their overall shape and composition. Toshiaki had intentionally encouraged this mutation by introducing the extract.

The results were just as he expected. Eve 1's mitochondria were showing great expansion due to the clofibrate, and the enzyme formation was immense. Enzymatic movement to mitochondria was manifestly bolstered. Later, he would have to look at the induction mechanism in greater detail on the genetic level. Toshiaki was sure that the mitochondrial induction mechanism would become clear thanks to Eve 1.

"It's here!"

Toshiaki removed a stack of magazines from their green mail bag with intense enthusiasm.

As he pulled them out, the word *nature* emerged, followed by *INTERNATIONAL WEEKLY JOURNAL OF SCIENCE*. Asakura peered patiently over Toshiaki's shoulder, mad with anticipation. Toshiaki removed the rest of the magazines, almost ripping the bag in his haste. The photography which graced the cover of *Nature* sparkled in his eyes. On the front were titles of featured articles. "Science in Mexico" was printed in large letters, but underneath them, in smaller type, were the words: "Approaches to mitochondrial biogenesis."

Toshiaki swiftly turned to the table of contents, tracing his finger along the page until he reached "LETTERS TO NATURE." There were two articles on mitochondrial interaction. He found the page number for the second and flipped to it.

"We did it!" shouted Asakura.

Toshiaki's mind burned with a single thought: *My own work has appeared in Nature!* His and Asakura's names were printed alongside Professor Ishihara's. They were already expecting the journal's arrival this week, but to actually see and hold it in their hands was a different thrill altogether. Toshiaki had submitted the article the year before, but only now had Part 1 finally come to print. Asakura's voice was filled with sheer excitement as she looked it over.

Their work had been included as part of a small feature. It was no longer Toshiaki's only area of concentration, however. As he continued to find more conclusive data on Eve 1, the results of his research were sure to have an impact upon the world. Everything about Eve 1 was too good to be true. This would someday place him among the highest, most elite circles in the world of science.

Toshiaki flinched from a sudden explosion outside. The smell of powder drifted into the building.

A large fireworks show was being held at the river nearby. The Pharmaceuticals building was the perfect place to enjoy the display. That night, Toshiaki, Asakura, and other staff members and students all went together onto the roof.

The enormous fireworks exploded in chrysanthemum-like shapes against a cloudless night sky. They were so close, it seemed one could touch them just by extending a hand overhead. In a single moment, jewels of light filled their vision, spreading outward as each fizzled into darkness. They could almost feel the glittering, fiery dust pouring down from the heavens, streaking their faces with vibrant colors. Asakura opened her eyes widely, gazing upon the full expanse of the sky. The fireworks changed colors rapidly, from shades of red to vibrant greens. Her cheeks changed color with each new flash as flowers and waterfalls danced in the sky.

She and Toshiaki each opened a can of beer together and drank them down as they savored this aptly timed spectacle. Asakura's eyes scintillated. She drew near to Toshiaki and spoke to him. He smiled and nodded in return. The smell of smoke saturated the air, but he was not bothered by it, because these fireworks were blessing their published work. It was also more secretly a celebration of his rapid progress with Kiyomi's cells. Toshiaki's only regret was that he could not share this happiness with Kiyomi. He wished so much to show *Nature* to Kiyomi, and to see these fireworks reflected in her proud eyes. The beating of his heart entwined in painful harmony with the rhythm of the bright display, sending ripples of energy trembling along his skin.

Symbiosis

8

Kiyomi was accepted into a local university. She had always done well studying on her own and her entrance exam came and went without stress, despite not having gone through the usual summer prep courses, cram schooling, or private tutors that plagued many of her peers. Even when she went out with her parents the day the results were announced to find her name on the bulletin among those accepted into the English Literature Department, her happiness was shallow at best.

She questioned whether this was really the right path for her and still worried herself about it after the opening ceremony. Kiyomi had only picked English because of an interest in the language and her fondness for reading. But once classes began and she made friends with a few classmates, she appreciated college life much more than she expected.

One night, a party was held for incoming students. It was there where she had beer for the first time. By high school, most of her friends were already drinking alcohol, but Kiyomi always abstained. The beer was bitter to her, but she liked the taste of it. All of the mentors at the party were likable and made her laugh. Before she knew it, she was feeling a little buzzed.

The party was now well under way, and everyone was mingling. Kiyomi went around to socialize with a few upperclassmen for as long as she was able to. Just when Kiyomi was ending a conversation with an older female student, she paused for a moment and broke off the conversation. It was then that she noticed a composed young man sitting next to her. He too looked to have just finished a conversation with someone and was drinking his beer with a faint smile on his lips. Their eyes met and, with an unpracticed hand, Kiyomi lifted her can and offered some of her beer into his empty glass. She poured it in too straight, turning more than half of it to foam, and bowed her head in apology. He told her to think nothing of it and sipped off some of the froth with a laugh. That is when she asked him:

"So what department are you in?"

"Pharmaceutical Sciences," he answered.

"Oh? So you learn about drugs? How to make cold medicines, that sort of thing?"

He smiled bitterly at the questions he had heard many times before and took a swig of beer.

"Well, that's how it started out, but these days it's a bit different. When I was younger, I always thought it was just studying to be a pharmacist."

Kiyomi nodded. She remembered there being many girls among her high school classmates who, when considering easy jobs, had been encouraged to become hospital pharmacists.

"But the School of Pharmaceutical Sciences is really wide-ranging. Sure, you can become a pharmacist, but you can also do more fundamental research. It's a mixed bag, really. Everything from medicine and physical science, to agriculture and engineering. So even within the department there's a lot to choose from. Some people do organic synthesis, others measure and analyze, for example, certain components of blood. Then there are those whose work is not directly related to medicine. Others culture all kinds of cells and study the effects of cancer on DNA replication. It's a small department, but a unique one, so it's hard for outsiders to really get the gist of it. But 'true' pharmaceutical science is a combination of all these things and more, I think."

The young man told her about the various kinds of research being conducted in each course within the school. She chimed in now and then, listening intently all the while. He broke down his explanations of the seemingly difficult mechanisms of cells and genes. Though Kiyomi's knowledge only went as far as what she had learned in high school biology, she clearly followed what he was saying.

"That's wonderful. That you get to study it, I mean. You really seem to know a lot."

"Nah, I just started my first year in the master's program. I've still got a long way to go."

Symbiosis

He scratched his head bashfully. Kiyomi assumed he was around 22 or 23 years old, if he was just beginning his master's. She understood now why he'd given off an impression of being mature.

"I'm even thinking of going for a Ph.D., as long as I'm able to. But if I was going to do that, this would probably be my last time showing up at a party," he said jokingly.

Kiyomi was deeply impressed. She had been such a passive listener in her classes, but here was a student already doing his own research and even had the willpower to pursue a Ph.D.

"So…what exactly are you doing research on?" In spite of a fear that his answer would be too technical to understand, she asked anyway in an effort to keep the conversation going.

"Mitochondria."

THUMP.

As soon as she heard his answer, Kiyomi's heart leapt. She let out a yell and pressed a hand to her chest.

"…something wrong?"

He looked doubtfully into her face.

"No…it's nothing."

She forced a smile and clung to her chest.

What was that? Kiyomi focused her attention on her body's interior. All she could sense was her own heartbeat. The odd, single thump had come and gone.

She turned her head a little to the side and thought to herself, *Maybe I'm just a little drunk is all*, then smiled again to ease his concern.

"Really, I'm fine. Please, continue."

The young man seemed unconvinced, but soon he was telling her all about his research.

"Mitochondria are usually mentioned briefly in junior high and high school textbooks, so you've probably heard of them before. Basically, they're necessary components of cells that create energy."

"Yeah, I know that much."

"When fats and sugars are drawn into the cell, they undergo a conversion process and are changed into acetyl-CoA in mitochondria. There, the 'citric acid cycle' leads to the formation of adenosine triphosphate, or ATP. It's this ATP that the body uses in various ways as energy."

"I understand…I think," Kiyomi said, nodding slightly. She had apparently retained more than she thought.

"My research focuses on why such a conversion occurs in mitochondria in the first place. The process requires a lot of enzymes, and mitochondria are packed with them. Here we run into a problem. We're usually taught that only the nuclei of cells contain genes, but you might be surprised to know that mitochondria also have their own DNA, though it's a very small amount in comparison. But this genetic material doesn't have the info for the enzymes necessary to convert fats and sugars. The genes only code enzymes for the electron transport system needed for making ATP, and just some of those enzymes at that. So where are the genes for the conversion enzymes? They're all in the nucleus. In other words, the nucleus controls the production of enzymes. When the nucleus needs energy, it sends out a command. The more enzymes you have, the more conversions you get. Now, enzymes are usually produced by ribosomes in the cytosol, after which they must find their way into the mitochondria. But how do they get inside at all? Since enzymes are proteins, they can't just pass through the fatty mitochondrial membrane. Also, how does the nucleus know it needs energy? How does it signal that enzymes have to be produced? And stepping back for the big picture, how does the nucleus control mitochondria anyway? Mitochondria must have originally carried the genes for the enzymes. How did the nucleus just pull those mitochondrial genes into itself? It's so mysterious. At least, I think so."

Kiyomi was completely overwhelmed. She had known what mitochondria were, but she'd never had any reason to think about them so extensively. They were certainly mysterious, as he had said. She was now aware of just how much was still unknown about our biology and that there were people actually trying to bring clarity to all of this.

Thinking he may have been too long-winded, the young man smiled wryly and ended there. He then looked at the glass in her hands and reciprocated her earlier favor by pouring some beer into it. There was only a little left in the bottle, so he dumped the rest into his own glass.

"So, what's your name?"

"Kiyomi Kataoka."

"Well, Kiyomi, pleasure to meet you. My name's Toshiaki Nagashima."

They both smiled and lifted their glasses to drink up.

9

As Anzai walked out of the room, he looked at his daughter once more.

"I'll be back...I'm just going to talk with the doctor for a little while."

Mariko was turned the other way, her mouth shut tightly in defiance. Anzai understood from her body language that she wanted nothing to do with him. He cast a glance at the floor and left.

While walking along the white hallway which ran straight through the ward, he thought about the operation.

Ten days now, and still Mariko was making no efforts to talk to him, nor to anyone else for that matter. The only time she spoke was when they were checking up on her, and even then she answered only bluntly and without eye contact.

Apparently she had had another bad dream the night before. Her loud screams had been audible even in the hallway. The nurse assigned to her that night tried to shake her out of it, but Mariko appeared lost between dream and reality. Despite all of this, when Yoshizumi asked if anything was wrong, she said nothing and turned away as always.

Before he knew it, Anzai was in the lobby. He pressed the down button and waited for the elevator to arrive.

He had spoken to Yoshizumi many times throughout this entire ordeal. They inevitably talked mostly about Mariko's practically autistic behavior.

Yoshizumi made it clear he was having a very difficult time with her and complained of the indifference that had been absent in the little girl he had treated two years ago.

No matter how much he tried, Anzai could not figure out why she was shutting herself off from everyone.

The doors opened in front of him. Anzai entered the elevator without paying much attention and pressed the button for the first floor. The doors closed, followed by a gentle sensation of decent. The ventilation fan hummed quietly above his head.

Symbiosis

When first informed of his daughter's renal insufficiency, Anzai knew nothing about the condition. It was the winter of her fourth-grade year. When Mariko was wheeled out from the waiting room, the attending physician had a pitiful look in his eyes and gave Anzai the bad news.

"To put it more technically, she is suffering from glomerular nephritis. In your daughter's case, the inflammation has been progressing slowly for some time now. As it is, her urinary lining has become compacted. If we don't act soon, her kidney will malfunction, blocking her urinary production altogether. Please take a look at this data. We tested her glomerular filtration rate, abbreviated here on the chart as GFR, and blood urea nitrogen levels, BUN. From this information, we were able to make a fairly confident diagnosis. She is already starting to show some common signs, such as swelling, breathing abnormalities, and nervousness."

Frightened, Anzai fell silent, then said, "Is there a cure?"

"I'm sorry, but no." He was unnerved by the doctor's sudden bluntness. "There is currently no established cure for chronic renal failure. Medications and surgery are no use. The cells themselves just stop working."

"So, what should we do?"

"The only option right now is dialysis treatment. People like her actually get along fairly well with it. We just hook up a machine that does the work of the kidneys, expelling used-up matter from the body. I will set you up with the best dialysis treatment center in the area. They've handled plenty of cases, so you'll be in good hands."

Anzai hardly noticed when the elevator reached the first floor. He got off and went into the lobby. The air conditioning was overpowered by hot air coming from the entranceway. He wiped the perspiration from the back of his neck and crossed over to the building where Yoshizumi's office was located.

Anzai lamented the fact that he and Mariko had hardly talked at all these past few years. His time was currently consumed with product development, and he felt that his work was vital. He would be pushing into his fifties this year. At any rate, if he didn't work there, he'd have achieved nothing in his life.

In truth, his lack of interaction with Mariko was not a recent development. It had been this way ever since he joined the company. Work was really his only occupation. That was not to say he never found the time to marry, though he hardly ever opened up much to women. He met his future wife when he was 33. Even after they were wed and Mariko was born, Anzai never made an effort to come home early. On most Sundays, too, he was out on business and hardly spent any time with his wife and daughter.

Immediately after buying their first house, his wife died of an illness, leaving their large two-floor house as a monument to loneliness. Mariko came to spend much of her time alone.

She was usually in bed by the time he got back. After waking her up in the mornings, he would rush off to the bus stop. Her affliction had therefore gone unnoticed much longer than it should have.

The hospital was well-accommodated with dialysis equipment of all kinds. Anzai stared in wonder when he and Mariko were first shown through the facilities. There were at least fifty beds spread out in a large room, nearly all of which were occupied with patients. Dialysis machines were set up at every bedside, a sight that made him queasy. Everyone was lying around languidly with tubes in their arms. While many were looking intently through magazines and comic books, others, like the person next to Anzai reading tabloids, were simply idling the time away. And weaving among them like white threads were the nurses. Anzai was informed that nearly three hundred people were receiving dialysis treatment there.

The patients varied in age. There were a few children Anzai thought to be even younger than Mariko and many who looked to be in their 70's. There was also a man his own age. Maybe it was the fluorescent lights, but most of them seemed to have sickly complexions. And despite the very modern machinery, everything seemed somehow run down.

It was not long before Mariko had to begin dialysis herself. The doctor said she would need to undergo surgery to have a shunt made for her. To enable dialysis, a tube had to be hooked up to a vein in the arm, and to facilitate this an artery was joined to the vein to widen it. Mariko would get an internal shunt. It was hard to make one for children, but it didn't get infected easily and therefore lasted longer.

Two weeks after the operation, Mariko's dialysis began. Three times a week, directly after school, she spent four to five hours in a hospital bed for the procedure, after which she took the last bus to return home by ten. This continued for six months. In that whole time, Anzai visited the hospital only a few times. Mariko spent more than enough time in bed alone, gazing absent-mindedly out the window. She sometimes had bad reactions to the treatment, which usually resulted in seizures. *It couldn't have been easy on her*, thought Anzai. When he recalled the figure of his sleeping daughter, he felt a twinge of pity. What crossed her mind as she watched her blood flow into the bedside monitor, the slowly turning blood pump and the long, thin dialyzer leading back to her arm? Only now did he wonder what she had gone through. At the time of the actual treatment, such things had hardly even crossed his mind.

"Please think of this as a temporary measure," the doctor had said. "In the case of young children with kidney failure who have to go through long periods of dialysis, side effects are not uncommon. The biggest concern is a stunting of body growth. Kidneys do have a role in physical development, and a failed kidney will hinder it. Growing taller means a lot to children. Were Mariko to continue dialysis like this, she might become deeply concerned about her height. Prolonged treatment would inhibit bone growth and have possibly adverse effects on her reproductive system as well."

"But what other options do we have...?"

"Transplantation is of course the best way to go. Would you like us to look into it for you?"

Despite the doctor's earnest offer, Anzai had been unable to get a handle on his emotions at that moment.

The most logical thing to do was to submit to the knife and offer one of his own kidneys. And yet, the idea frightened him. He was concerned for his own well-being and conferred with the doctor at great length about his hesitations.

Whenever Anzai went out drinking with his colleagues, their conversations always seemed to return to the topic of his daughter's condition. Anzai would answer only vaguely and try to change the subject, but since everyone was usually drunk, they were persistent. Organ transplantation was a hot topic in the news at that time.

"Must be a beautiful thing they share, those parents who give organs to their own kids, wouldn't you say?" his superior slurred one time. "In other countries, they take organs from dead bodies and transplant them into the living. That's just barbaric if you ask me. Then again, we handle everything much more delicately here in Japan anyway. Hey Anzai, what if you gave one of your kidneys to your daughter? You've got two of 'em, you know. You'd get along fine with one. How can you just stand by when she's in so much pain? Your wife is dead, so you're all she can depend on. That's what I'd call real love."

Though an affable smile came to Anzai's face, he was trying with all his might to quell the anger boiling up inside of him.

In reality, these were just the ramblings of someone who didn't have a child with kidney problems. Was he saying that Anzai was inhumane for not wanting to give up an organ? Did parents have an obligation, even in body, to their children? Was it his duty as a parent to make an unconditional sacrifice? Surgery was a horrible thought for anyone, and if he could find a path to avoid it, he would take it. Did that go against the love between parent and child? He almost voiced his opposition aloud, but instead tightened the grip around his glass and listened to what his colleagues had to say.

When he came to his senses, Anzai found himself at Yoshizumi's office. He shook his head once and cooled his heated thoughts before knocking on the door.

Symbiosis

10

The sound of boiling water filled the air. Asakura placed a sample tube into it, then set the timer. At last, she was close to finishing a day-long experiment. She sighed and looked around the room.

She was on the second floor of the Radioisotope Research Building. The room was used exclusively for the treatment of low level radioactive matter. She was the only one there, her surroundings having fallen into quietude hours before. It was past 10:30. Today marked the middle of summer vacation. Asakura smiled to herself. When no one was around like this, working through her experiments became a completely private endeavor.

She had come to campus early that morning to start importing proteins into Eve 1's mitochondria, having no time to concentrate on anything else. Before she knew it, day had turned into night. Considering she had taken no breaks since starting the experiment, she was very grateful to be nearing its completion.

Eve 1 really is intriguing, she thought as she stared blankly at the bubbles rising in the simmering water. In the two years since joining the course, she had worked with numerous kinds of specimens, but never had she seen anything so inexplicable.

Eve 1 was still propagating. Since Toshiaki had introduced a clofibrate subjected to BSA conjugate, the cells were dividing at a rate faster than common cancer cells. He told her that Eve 1 had been sampled from a human liver, but this did not fit in with the sheer greed with which they evolved.

Asakura had tried asking Toshiaki where exactly he procured the cells. Undoubtedly, Eve 1 had come from the ice box he was carrying that night on the stairs. He always managed to weasel his way out of answering the question every time it was posed. Asakura secretly tried looking them up in a cell bank catalog, but there was nothing registered under the name "Eve," nor anything that even resembled it. When she came up empty-handed, she figured it was a type of cell not named by anyone yet. In other words, the cells had not in fact been distributed from any other research facility. Toshiaki had christened the cells himself.

This may have explained the secrecy, but still she could not help wondering where they had originated.

Toshiaki had been looking after his wife. Or so she'd heard. He couldn't have had the time to be contacting other universities for laboratory samples.

This left her with only one logical explanation.

Asakura shivered at the thought.

She couldn't imagine Toshiaki Nagashima would ever do that. She'd always felt grateful towards him. It was thanks to him that she was able to tackle every experiment presented to her over the past two and a half years.

When Asakura began her senior year and enrolled in the Biofunctional Pharmaceuticals course, it wasn't for any particular reason. Thinking of it now, it was nearly impossible for third-year students to fully grasp the experiments they were conducting in their classes. They chose courses purely out of careerist motives or which were reputed to be easy.

Asakura, too, had no burning desire to get into any particular classes. But it was a hands-on lab session hosted by the Biofunctional Pharmaceuticals seminar course where she learned to truly enjoy the lab for the first time. In that experiment, she extracted plasmid DNA samples from *E. coli*, into which she inserted some genes. Until then, she had always thought of DNA as being mystical and sublime, yet here she was extracting it through surprisingly simple means. Though she initially had many fears about manually "cutting and pasting" DNA, she came to know the pure joy of actually accomplishing it. She shared this sense of wonder with a teacher who happened to be nearby at the time. The teacher smiled gently and said, "That's exactly what we want you to see. It's the whole reason we do this."

That teacher was, of course, Toshiaki.

At the post-session get-together, which was held in the Biofunctional Pharmaceuticals seminar room, her seat was, by chance, right next to his. She learned from him that his course studied mitochondria.

Symbiosis

Only then did she think to join it. *There* was a place where she could perform fascinating experiments and acquire valuable skills along the way.

Her wish came true and, as fate would have it, she would conduct experiments under Toshiaki's tutelage. Asakura still remembered the excitement she felt when she received official word. She felt more than fortunate to be learning from someone like him. He was the type who had broad interests and therefore possessed a wide variety of technical knowledge. Because of this, she was able to experience firsthand a whole range of experimental situations. He taught her nearly all the methods he thought necessary for the field of biochemistry.

She soon learned to enjoy the scientific process, especially when her work pleased her mentor with good results. She was always amazed at his scrutiny. When interesting findings presented themselves, not only did he form a relevant hypothesis every time, but also devised a way to test it immediately. Asakura was often drawn into long discussions, at which times Toshiaki's face was radiant. Overwhelmed though she was, she tried to catch up with him and read many an article. She decided to stay on for two more years after graduating simply because working with Toshiaki was such a joy.

Asakura had never imagined that she'd enroll in a master's program. Of course, she loved her science classes in high school, but she never once pictured herself in a white lab coat working on isotopes late into the night.

Her height had been the cause of many playground insults when she began to grow rapidly in fifth grade. She was soon the tallest of her class, and the boys looked curiously small to her.

About halfway through her middle school years, some boys finally sprouted up and outgrew her, but she still stood out among the girls. She joined the volleyball club, where her height was much appreciated. Extracurricular activities were a positive outlet for her; they provided an arena where her sense of dedication could flourish.

In high school, she started to worry about her tallness.

Her growth had only begun to slow down when she reached 5'8", but compared to those around her she was still quite tall. Her female friends expressed envy, and, though she smiled it away, inside she was a sack of sighs. She dated a few boys during her freshman year, but she could never get over her always being the taller one.

She also had difficulty trying to buy clothes that fit her, and finding stores that carried her shoe size was far from easy. So many times she had found clothing with just the kind of design she liked, but had to give up because it did not fit her. Whenever she was not in her school uniform, she usually resorted to shirts and jeans.

At school, she was sometimes the target of boys' teasing. Many of them were her friends, so the harassment was likely intended as nothing more than playful jabs, but regardless, she took it to heart because they were so persistent.

Asakura had no boyfriends in college. This did not make her feel lonely, however. Still, she sometimes asked herself if her self-consciousness about her height was making her squeamish with the opposite sex. Maybe this habit of working so late every day was a weak way to deny that it was just so.

The piercing beep of the electric timer brought her back to reality. It was time to stop the boiling. She smacked her forehead for being so careless and removed the sample to put it on ice.

She set up some acrylamide gel in an electrophoresis machine. The top surface of the gel was segmented like teeth and pre-coated with a refined plastic. As soon as the Eve 1 sample was cooled off, she began applying it cautiously into each gap using a pipettman.

After portioning out everything that she needed, she flipped on the power supply switch. A dial spun around and settled as she set it at 20 mA. Right away, powder-like bubbles began to rise from within the immersion tub.

"Finally," Asakura said as she stretched. The immersion process would take close to three hours. She was free to do whatever she wished in the meantime.

It was just past eleven. If she stayed here and read, she was bound to fall asleep. She thought it might be best to go home for a while and take a bath.

Symbiosis

She left the isotope ward and returned to her office. Taking her bag from her locker and turning off the lights, she went out into the hallway and locked the room.

It was about time she started preparing for her speech. She was to give an oral presentation at the annual meeting of the Japanese Biochemical Society in September. Toshiaki and a fellow colleague, along with a few students, had been invited to present their work. Asakura was nearly finished with the research she needed to complete for the meeting, with only two or three experiments remaining to be done.

She wondered just how long Toshiaki would continue to analyze Eve 1. She was suspicious. The conference should have been his first priority right now.

As the lights had already been shut off, the corridor was dark, giving her an eerie feeling as she walked down its length. A lukewarm draft blew uncomfortably past her cheek. Her sandals made unsettling echoes as they slid along the floor, their sounds seeming to hang in the thickly saturated air behind her.

Asakura could not stop thinking about how bizarre those cells were. Not only were they abnormal, it was almost as if they emanated some tangible force.

She honestly wanted nothing more to do with them, but could not very well say so to Toshiaki. Though she had obediently worked on the experiments so far, it did not stop her from being gripped by a certain fear now and then.

Ever since she was little, Asakura sometimes had moments where she knew that she would be sick the next day, or get the feeling that they would lose a volleyball match. While they were trifles, these brief flashes of intuition affected her deeply. They always made the hair on her neck stand on end with an almost painful itch.

It was this same sensation now, growing stronger with each day working on those cells.

Asakura understood Eve 1 not by observation, but by intuition.

It horrified her. It would not normally have bothered her so much, were she not constantly working late nights with no one else around. In the lab she could distract herself with the radio, but music was not allowed in the isotope room. Maybe that was why she felt so vulnerable today.

She prayed that Toshiaki would soon relieve her of any further work on the cells, but her wish was not likely to be granted any time soon. His attachment to Eve 1 was unnatural. Ever since Eve 1 yielded such intriguing information, his attitude had become quite cheerful. Compared to the days after his wife's accident, he certainly seemed to have regained his former self. But that changed as soon as he began working on Eve 1. He would then take on the look of an obsessed man. Asakura was afraid to speak to him at such times, which made things even more difficult since she was dying to ask him all about Eve 1.

Toshiaki did more than keep the cells alive. They were actually growing. It was as if they were...

Asakura held her shoulders.

It was as if they were happy.

Nonsense, she thought, forcing herself to deny what was already clear to her. As she started up the stairs, her feet instinctively picked up speed. She kept telling herself that it was nothing, that she was worrying too much. But she ran as fast as she could, wanting more than anything to get home.

Symbiosis

11

"We all have countless parasites living inside us," the stately professor began his lecture.

A large paper sign hanging in front of the stage read: "BIOFUNCTIONAL PHARMACEUTICALS COURSE, PROFESSOR MUTSUO ISHIHARA." He was a man in his early fifties. His hair was graying, but his voice had vigor.

Despite being a lecture hall, the rectangular room seated only 150 people and was much smaller compared to the liberal arts auditoriums, which typically accommodated over 300 students. Because the number of students in the School of Pharmaceutical Sciences during any given year tended to be small, this space was more than sufficient. Kiyomi took a seat closer to the back where the stairs ascended and looked down at the seats below. There were least 50 people in attendance, half of whom were probably pharmaceuticals students. There may have been a few from other departments like herself, but she suspected that nearly everyone there was actually enrolled in the Biofunctional Pharmaceuticals course. There were some auditors who were in their fifties and sixties, but no one in their teens.

One of the auditorium windows had been left open to let in the breeze. A cool draft flowed past her cheek and the sound of rustling leaves wafted gently towards her like ripples upon water. She glanced outside at the fresh green foliage sparkling in the sunlight.

Kiyomi was now in her third year of college. Her freshman and sophomore years had gone by in the blink of an eye. She had been very active so far, taking notes in every class, continuing with brass ensemble practice, helping manage the annual music festival, comparing notes with friends and trying her best not to miss a test. She even managed to relax now and then by going on group trips and ski weekends with classmates.

"So, are you getting an internship next year or what?"

She'd had a sudden wake up call when a friend blurted out this question one day. Kiyomi realized she still had no idea what she wanted to do with her life. She had somehow completely glossed over the uncertainty which troubled her so much in high school. Now that college was half over, she knew this was the time to make decisions about her future. Even so, she had yet to feel motivated.

It was only June, but the days were warm. Refreshing summerly winds shook the branches of the shading trees and her white shirt fluttered. The skies were constantly overcast through fall and winter, but now they had cleared up beautifully, drenching the buildings and pavement with much needed sunlight.

Kiyomi was taking this opportunity to attend a public lecture being offered at the School of Pharmaceutical Sciences. Every year on the second Sunday of June, the school's faculty held free educational lectures open to the public in an attempt to dispel misconceptions about their field. The school's chair and profs would outline their research in some detail; this year, they were also going to discuss the basics of medicinal plants and devote some time to charged issues like drug side-effects and the AIDS virus. The spacious medicinal plant green house, located at the rear of the building, was also opened to the public. Visitors were invited to have a small picnic outside. The event had been popular for quite some time, but Kiyomi had never joined in the festivities until a classmate invited her along.

The day was graced with a clear blue sky and gorgeous weather. Kiyomi took the bus with her friend and arrived at the School of Pharmaceutical Sciences around 9:30 in the morning. Kiyomi's university was typical in that it catered to many personal and academic interests, but it was best known for its various stellar scientific departments. The School of Medical Sciences and its affiliated hospitals were in the northern part of the city, the School of Agriculture was right near the subway station, and the School of Engineering was up in the mountains. The Pharmaceutical Sciences building sat atop a small hill, a five-minute walk from the School of Liberal Arts. When they got off at the bus stop they had a pleasant view of the streets spread out below. Maybe Kiyomi was imagining it, but the breeze seemed cooler up here.

Symbiosis

There would be one lecture in the morning and three in the afternoon, each lasting an hour and a half. In the interim, everyone was encouraged to see and explore the greenhouse. The morning lecture was to begin at 10 o'clock. Kiyomi went into the lobby, where an exhibit about Chinese herbal medicine was on display, and looked over the list of lecture topics. The first was entitled "Drug Manufacturing: Chemistry and Pharmacology" and looked to be a talk about the development of pharmaceutical products. Thinking this would be a little over her head, she looked slowly down the list to the afternoon schedule. She read, "The Benefits of Chinese Medicine," and "What is Gene Therapy?" …

Then, the last topic caught her eye:

"Symbiosis with Mitochondria: The Evolution of Cellular Society."

THUMP, went her heart.

She clutched her chest at this unexpected reaction. More than a heartbeat, it felt like a cry for help. Her breathing quickened. Her head was on fire. Her hands twitched with the aftereffects of the shock. She held her chest tighter to stop it. A single bead of sweat trickled from her temple down her cheek. She could not tear her eyes away from the words on the poster.

Kiyomi clenched her teeth and inhaled as deeply as she could. The strange beat was long gone, and in its place was her regular pulse, pumping blood.

Yet she was unable to move for a while. Another drop of sweat flowed down her face, following the same trail as its predecessor before falling to the floor.

"What's wrong, Kiyomi?"

Her friend looked worriedly into Kiyomi's face. She shook her head and said it was nothing, then looked up and tried to smile, but managed only a twitch of the lips.

"Really, I'm fine. Let's go in." Her companion looked worried, but nodded reluctantly and followed her outside.

Just before leaving the lobby, Kiyomi looked back at the poster once again. *Why?* she wondered. She'd felt the irregular beat when she'd seen the words.

Was this what they called arrhythmia? She shivered at the thought. *Symbiosis with Mitochondria.* Her body had somehow reacted to that strange lecture title.

Her logical self told her something was wrong, yet she was strangely capti-
vated by the prospect of hearing the lecture. She might be at the greenhouse
while the talks on Chinese medicine and genetic healing were underway, but the
final presentation she didn't dare to miss.

At last, the time came.

It was at this point that her friend needed to leave. She had a part-time job
as a private tutor and had a five o'clock appointment to make. But Kiyomi would
not miss this lecture.

A screen was being lowered behind the podium and next to it was a sign with
the lecture topic written in large letters. Although they spelled out the same
words that had affected her so deeply earlier, Kiyomi had no reaction to seeing
them now. This did not, of course, change the fact that they *had* affected her. She
wanted so much to understand her reaction and had a feeling that the answer
somehow resided in this lecture.

Professor Ishihara, after explaining common parasites such as round worms,
began to explain exactly what symbiosis was, using intestinal microbes as an
example.

"Just like parasites, microbes thrive in our intestines, living off the nourishment we provide to them as hosts. But they also help us utilize vitamin K and
provide many other valuable functions unknown to many of us. This relationship
by which two distinct life forms not only coexist, but also profit from their
mutual bond, is called 'symbiosis.' These exemplary microbes are therefore not
just parasites, so to speak, but are indeed necessary components of our biology.
Judging from this, one might wonder if our symbiosis is restricted only to such
microbes. Of course, that is not the case. Which brings us now to the subject of
today's lecture: namely mitochondria. I am sure you've all at least encountered
the word in junior high, but we have come to learn that mitochondria, too, are
parasites. They are not insects, so it may seem a bit strange to call them 'parasites.' However, they are the same in that they exist in all human beings by means

of a symbiotic relationship. And from research conducted on mitochondria, we have discovered many interesting things about them. In my lecture, I will be utilizing what scientists have concluded through research to explain this symbiosis."

At this point, Professor Ishihara took a breath and gave a signal to the slide assistant. The slide projector fan began to spin and the auditorium lights were turned off. Kiyomi looked behind her to see who had pressed the switch, but could see nothing, her eyes still adjusting to the darkness.

At that moment, a familiar face entered the corner of her vision.

It belonged to a young man sitting three rows behind her. She focused on him, straining to get a better look, but could not quite identify him in such a dark room. He seemed to notice her as well. Kiyomi felt a little embarrassed and turned quickly back around.

A large diagram of a cell shone on the screen.

"This is a simple drawing of a human cell," Professor Ishihara explained. Using a laser pointer, he continued. "This area in the very center is the nucleus. It is where chromosomes are contained and is filled with all kinds of genetic information. And this oval-shaped area here represents a mitochondrion. It has both an outer and an inner membrane. The inner membrane is folded like so. Now, this diagram is basically the same one you would remember from your textbooks, and, as such, is probably familiar to most of you as shown here, but this does not mean they have this shape in reality. Their structure is actually quite different than what you might think. Next slide, please."

As soon as the image changed, faint murmurs of surprise rose from the audience.

"This is mitochondria's true form."

The screen's black background now framed a large picture of a cell. Inside them were what appeared to be countless green-colored threads. All of them lined diagonally upward, they seemed ready to wave forth. There was a gaping black hole in the center where the nucleus would have been. Kiyomi figured that mitochondria had been somehow stained, then photographed through a microscope to obtain this image. Each cell was crowded with hundreds, even thousands of them, beautiful like folds of velvet. Kiyomi's preconceptions about them were totally wiped away by the splendor before her eyes.

THUMP.

Her heart again.

THUMP.

This was it. Kiyomi realized it now. This was what her heart had reacted to. Her heart thrilled to mitochondria.

But why?

Kiyomi's eyes were riveted to the screen, her breath short. She stared intently at the large image before her, forgetting everything else around her. A few more pictures of stained mitochondria were shown. Some green, some blue, they swelled beyond the screen, twisting, dissolving, breaking away, changing into variant forms. She was fascinated by their structure. Their wriggling, winding forms resembled intestinal bacteria, and she understood why the professor was comparing them to parasites.

He said there was DNA in mitochondria, that this DNA differed from DNA in the nucleus, and pointed out that mitochondria were proven to be the descendants of what were once parasitic bacteria. Ishihara also explained in detail that long ago, back when we were still delicate single-celled organisms, mitochondria invaded us, and have since thrived in symbiosis.

"At this point I'd like to talk a little about the history of cell development. Life is first thought to have appeared on this planet around 3.8 billion years ago. The first life forms were simple, pliant membranes containing DNA that dwelled near underwater volcanoes on the ocean floor, receiving nourishment in the form of hydrogen sulfide. At this time there was still almost no oxygen in the earth's atmosphere. However, 2.5 billion years ago, these first life forms evolved into so-called cyanobacteria, a rudimentary form of chloroplasts. They created sugars from photosynthesis and were the first organisms to, in essence, 'breathe' oxygen. Cyanobacteria multiplied at an extraordinary rate and spread through-

Symbiosis

out all the world's oceans. Because of this, oxygen levels rose both in the water and the air. But the old type of bacteria which lived off of sulfuric gases began to suffer. Unlike us, they were actually threatened by the growing presence of oxygen in the sea. The world had become the domain of cyanobacteria, leaving their less evolved counterparts no other choice but to limit their quiet existence to their beloved sulfur-rich areas. It was at this point that aerobic bacteria came into the picture. As I said before, the ocean was teeming with oxygen created by cyanobacteria. What aerobic bacteria did was find a way to make use of this oxygen; they became the early ancestors of mitochondria as we know them today. By utilizing the oxygen around them, aerobic bacteria were able to produce energy far beyond the capacity of normal bacteria. The purpose of that energy? Mobility. These bacteria were the first to actually swim around in the sea. And then, 1.5 million years later, a most amazing event occurred when aerobic bacteria entered the bodies of our distant ancestral life forms, who were barely surviving near volcanoes. It is possible they originally wanted to consume us, but chose instead to make their home inside of us. From that moment on, our relationship with mitochondria began."

A photograph of a single mitochondrion appeared, this one taken through an electron microscope. Situated in the middle of the screen, it was constricted in its center, about to divide. There was a small black mass inside of it which appeared to be pulling into two halves as well. Ishihara pointed this out as DNA. Mitochondrial division and multiplication happened inside the cell. The DNA was distributed among the new mitochondria. In all this, mitochondria seemed no different from, precisely, bacteria. Kiyomi thought to herself, *Mitochondria are alive and they're multiplying inside of my body right now.*

"Now what would you say if I told you it is because of mitochondria that we are all here today? As I said before, our earliest ancestors lived in a symbiotic relationship with mitochondria and were able to produce vast amounts of energy. They became aerobic, which in turn gave them the advantage of volition. From this they were able to take sustenance by their own means, instead of hav-

ing literally to wait for it to float by. Using their own energy, they could go looking for it themselves. Now here, our ancestors acquired a new level of intelligence, namely the capacity to capture prey by any and all means necessary. They
figured out how to most efficiently obtain their food. Nerve connections responsible for conceptualization and instinct began to develop, and, before long, they
acquired a rather advanced way of thinking.

"We must not forget that, around the same time, mitochondria were not the
only living matter to be incorporated into cellular life forms, but that some cells
also combined with cyanobacteria. And what happened to them, you might ask?
They became self-sustaining organisms that required only sunlight for survival,
without needing to go through all the trouble of searching for food. All they had
to do was to maximize their surface area to catch as much sunlight as possible. I
am sure you have figured out by now that these became plants. Though this
explanation may be a bit diluted, now you know the basic difference between
plants and animals. We can say with relative surety that our ability to move and
think as we do is solely the result of our symbiosis with mitochondria."

The professor then began explaining the evolution of all living things as he
pointed to a map outlining just that. At the base of the diagram was a thick trunk
labeled "Our Ancestral Life Forms" which joined up with another trunk labeled
"Mitochondria." From there, they separated into three paths: "Plants," "Animals,"
and "Fungi." Halfway up, the "Plants" branch merged into one line with
"Chloroplasts," itself extending from the "Cyanobacteria" trunk. Kiyomi thought
the "Mitochondria" trunk looked the most robust in the diagram.

The image on the screen returned to the previous photograph of mitochondria, and Ishihara continued.

"However, as they are now, mitochondria do not have the ability to multiply
at will. To this very day, we have no idea exactly how mitochondria divide. What
we have concluded, through extensive research, is that they are somehow controlled by genes in the nucleus. When mitochondria first parasitized our cellular
ancestors, they must have had an inherent genetic code which told them to prop-

agate. But soon, mitochondria inserted this code into the nuclear genes of their hosts. And so now mitochondria have only a fraction of their original genetic code left. The processes by which mitochondria divide, as well as the creation of the proteins that comprise them, all begin with the nucleus. Mitochondria therefore put their all into producing energy. From their point of view, they have it pretty easy, considering that the nucleus does all the hard work. The sugars and fats needed to make energy are provided by the host cell. Things aren't bad for the host cell either because, supplied the materials, mitochondria create high-quality energy that the host could never generate on its own. In short, mitochondria have sustained an excellent symbiotic relationship with their hosts' cells since long ago, much in the same way that we do with intestinal microbes."

At this point, Ishihara paused to take a sip of water.

Kiyomi's heart was beating so fast, it was about to jump out of her chest. She had been too enraptured to notice that she was panting like a dog, her mouth hanging wide open. She became aware of herself when the professor stopped. She was surprised at her behavior and swallowed back her saliva with a gulp. Her heart pounded away like there was no tomorrow. Having no other way out, her breath escaped audibly from her nose in a steady rhythm. Kiyomi was ashamed. She covered her face with her hands, trying to quiet herself as much as she could. She shut her eyes and took a deep breath.

She was confused. Why did she have such an interest in all of this? Why was she so enchanted by it? These were questions for which she had no answers. Kiyomi's forehead was dotted with sweat, as were her chest and inner thighs. Her dress clung to her skin. She wiped her forehead with the back of her hand, where the sticky sensation remained.

Kiyomi opened her eyes, removed a handkerchief from her pocket, and dabbed her neck and forehead. When she looked back to the screen, Ishihara was discussing mitochondrial DNA, explaining how it brought about abnormalities associated with the aging process. This had to do with something called active oxygen. The genetic mutations in mitochondria, he explained, were responsible for many diseases. He then moved on to the inheritance of mitochondrial genes by our descendants.

"Mitochondrial genes are interesting in that they are passed along by the mother. At the time of conception, mitochondria in the sperm enter into the egg as well, but in most cases this paternal DNA does not multiply in a fertilized egg. Because only maternal DNA reproduces, the mitochondria of any given child are nearly identical to that of its mother. As a result, the genes are ultimately passed down matrilineally. Even so, diseases caused by mitochondrial genes are not all inherited from the mother's side. This is a mystery not even current research has been able to clarify. We have only recently come to know that the genes are not passed on entirely maternally. This is a rather complicated issue, so let us move on."

The rate of pictures decreased, changing to brightly colored graphs and various other diagrams. These images looked to have been rendered by computer, and did not excite Kiyomi as much as the microscope photography. The professor continued talking about mitochondrial genes for five minutes. In the meantime, Kiyomi's heartbeat slowed down from its violent pounding to a more subdued pace before eventually returning to normal.

She breathed a sigh of relief and sat upright, trying her best to concentrate on Ishihara's lecture as he moved on to the next subtopic.

"...We have all experienced stress, whether with the people we encounter in school, at home, or in the workplace. Ours has been called the most stressful age in the history of civilization, but I believe stress is simply inevitable, once we have the very act of sharing our lives with those around us. This is very much similar to the relationship between mitochondria and their host cells. When two different entities live in a sealed environment, stress is created. In fact, as stress is exerted upon the cells, so-called 'stress proteins' are activated within them. These proteins allow the symbiosis between mitochondria and the nucleus run smoothly."

Ishihara proceeded to explain, with the use of simple visuals, that there were various types of stress proteins within cells, that one of their jobs was to move enzymes into mitochondria, and that when stress proteins died off, this resulted in mitochondrial mutations.

Kiyomi's heart was now perfectly at ease. She looked at her hands, only to find they were knotted tightly, the only indication of the agitation she'd experienced. She opened and closed them a few times to loosen them up and smiled to herself.

Just then, the screen changed yet again, and a large bar graph appeared. Ishihara explained these were the results of their lab experiment. They had examined the degree to which enzymes were still transferred into mitochondria when stress proteins were systematically affected. The horizontal axis named the various stress proteins, from which extended bars of varying heights.

"From this we can see that when some of the stress proteins decay, mitochondria become unable to produce enzymes sufficiently. This lack of mitochondrial function appears to be linked to many diseases."

Kiyomi was staring at the screen, following the bright red dot of Ishihara's laser pointer. After he had finished and told the assistant to move on to the next slide, Kiyomi happened to notice something small written in Roman alphabets in the bottom right hand corner.

Her chest popped: WHUPP!

It came so abruptly that she let out a small cry and pitched herself forward. The slide projector clicked again and another bar graph appeared on the screen. Kiyomi ran her eyes frantically from corner to corner and found the same letters written there. Again, her heart erupted. Professor Ishihara went on, but Kiyomi could no longer hear what he was saying. Again, the click of the projector. Again, the screen changed to another bar graph. Surely enough, the same letters on the bottom right hand corner. Three times, this intense jolt swept through her. Her body lurched audibly off her seat. She felt everyone's eyes on her, but could make out none of them in her daze. Her heart was going to explode. Kiyomi clutched her chest in a desperate attempt to calm herself. She opened her mouth and tried to speak, but only a painful wheeze escaped. Her breaths grew shorter by the moment. Her face was on fire, her heart was thundering. Somewhere in the jumble of her mind, she tried frantically to rationalize what was happening to her. The fine-printed lettering on the screen. Kiyomi had not even read it all. In a brief moment of lucidity, she strained to remember what it said. Everything was turning foggy. Someone ran up to her. She remembered now. The words floated into her mind's eye as clearly as the pulse throbbing inside her brain:

Nagashima, T. et al, *J. Biol. Chem.*, 266, 3266, 1991.

There was something familiar there, something in that name. T. *Thump*. To-shi-a-ki. Yes, that was it. *Thump*. TOSHIAKI NAGASHIMA. *Thump*. She had heard that name before. She knew him from somewhere. Of course, she thought, he's the one I met when I first came to college... Thump, THUMP, **THUMP**.

"Are you okay?"

A voice from afar. Someone was trying to lift her. Kiyomi saw the person's face just before dizziness overwhelmed her. Ah, it's him...

At the same time, she heard a different voice from deep inside her heart.

<HE IS THE ONE.>

A massive convulsion racked her entire body. She buried her face in the stranger's arm, entrusting her shivering body to him. Kiyomi lost consciousness before she could ask:

Who...

Symbiosis

12

Mariko had been up and about for a week now. Her body was weary from sleeping so much and her legs were a bit wobbly. Still, it was better than having to endure being bedridden any longer.

From her bed, she had seen only white walls and the machinery that surrounded her, but now she could walk over to the windows and gaze out into the courtyard. Leaves and branches were vibrant with lush green. She looked upon them intently, almost breaking a sweat imagining the heat that awaited her outside.

She had only recently been given more freedom in where she could go. Whereas before she had to remain in her room, she could now wander through the ward. And starting tomorrow, she would be able to go to the hospital store, and even take showers. Doctor Yoshizumi and the nurses were all exceedingly glad that her recovery was going so smoothly, but she was indifferent to what she thought to be a false play of emotions. Everyone was trying so desperately to understand what she was going through. Being constantly surrounded by so much anxiety made her even more depressed.

Her father came to visit her at night.

He was in his usual suit and tie. *Isn't he hot in those clothes?* she wondered. They probably had good air-conditioning at work. With a feeble smile, he raised a hand to her in greeting.

"How are you feeling?"

Always that line. Always asking something he could tell just by a single look. Mariko sighed.

"Can I get you anything? I can get you a book or something if you want."

She knew he was forcing his smile. She was getting annoyed.

"Can I have some money then?"

"What did you say?"

Her father was somewhat taken aback by her sudden request, as it was the most substantial thing she had said to him in weeks.

"Money. They said I can go to the hospital store tomorrow. I'll just buy something myself."

Her father grew quiet and, for a long while, neither said anything.

At last, a humming sound broke the silence, a car in the distance or noise from the ventilation. When it ended, Anzai sighed.

"Mariko," he said. "Why are you being so stubborn? Tell me. Please?"

Silence.

"You were so happy the first time, weren't you? I thought you were glad to be out of the hospital and back in school. Why are you so unhappy this time? Do you just hate transplants? Did you like dialysis better? What is it? Say something."

Silence.

"Mariko…"

She wondered how much longer she could keep her mouth shut. Anzai was at a loss for words and gave up. They heard the hum again.

Mariko simply did not understand anymore. Why had her father wanted to give her a kidney so badly?

"…Dad?"

Her father looked up.

"Dad, did you really want to give me your kidney?"

"What are you saying?"

He was clearly upset, but she could not take it back now.

She glared at him. It was her father this time who averted his eyes.

"You really didn't mind doing that? Weren't you just annoyed that I was sick? If mom were still alive, wouldn't you have wanted her to give up her kidney instead? On top of that, it was my fault it f-"

"Stop it!"

The sound of a slap shot through the air.

Slowly, but surely, her cheek began to swell with pain. For a good while, Mariko could not process what had happened.

When she looked at her father, he was shaking, looking at the floor. Hidden as it was in shadow, she could not see his face very well, but he seemed to be choking down some harsh words.

After some time, he left, and Mariko stared for a long time up at the dark ceiling. Occasionally, the humming noise came faintly to her ears. Listening to it, she thought it sounded like magma shifting deep within the earth.

"Mariko has come back to us from the hospital today," her homeroom teacher had announced her return, as Mariko stood in front of the whole class.

All eyes in the room were locked upon her. The kids in the front row were staring, and the boys in the back were craning their necks just to get a better view.

"Mariko here has just been through transplant surgery. She received a kidney from her father. For a long time, she has been unable to play any serious sports, but from now on I think she will be joining you for lunch and after-school activities. I want you all to get her filled in on what she missed while she was in the hospital, and to offer your help whenever she needs it."

Mariko felt slightly embarrassed and kept her head down. But in her heart, she was elated to be back. She could finally be with her friends again.

Something flickered in the corner of her eye. Mariko turned to see a friend grinning, flashing a small peace sign at her and mouthing the syllables:

"Con-grats!"

Mariko flashed back the sign, briefly so the teacher wouldn't notice.

School was just like always and her peers treated her no differently than before. Her classes had gone a little further ahead since the last time she was there. She was a bit lost in math and science at first, but her friends drilled her on the new material and helped get her back up to speed. Before long, Mariko's life was back to the way it used to be before dialysis. She was glad to be on an even footing again with everyone else.

She was held back only from P.E. It had been decided that there was no need to rush her back into it. They'd wait and see for a while.

At the time, they were practicing swimming in gym class. Mariko sat at the pool's edge to admire everyone's vigor, which sometimes sent water splashing playfully in her direction.

As she watched her classmates take turns practicing their crawl strokes, Mariko felt a dull pain in her lower abdomen. When she pressed her hand gently upon it, it felt like she had a tumor inside of her.

The operation scar was clearly visible on her side. Her tendons had stiffened around the sutures and little bumps were raised up along the scar. It twisted around like a centipede whenever she turned her waist. She did not much care for this little memento, since it was a permanent reminder that her father's kidney lay embedded just beneath it. Some time had passed since the transplant, but she still felt a certain incompatibility. Usually it did not bother her so much, but during gym, when she watched the swimmers' bodies with their unblemished sides, she was soberly reminded of her own imperfection. Once she was conscious of it, a series of traumatic hospital memories always came back to her against all will.

One time, she felt the kidney moving during swim practice, and the sensation refused to go away even after the class had ended. She wondered, *Why does it hurt so much?*

Maybe it's because my dad's kidney doesn't belong in me?

The thought gave her the chills.

What if I get sick again? What if this kidney fails, too? I'll probably have to go back on dialysis, and I won't be free like this ever again.

She did not have to think of these things. There was no reason for any of it to happen. Every time she fell into these reveries, her pessimism snowballed. Her father had already given her one kidney. If this one failed, she could not get another one.

Or that was what she'd thought.

Her turn for a donated organ would not come anytime soon, Doctor Yoshizumi had told her. She would have to wait a long time before a donor of her type would appear. That's why they'd registered her right away. She couldn't tell her father she didn't want a second transplant, he'd yell at her. That was the only reason why she let them go through the motions, as far as she was concerned.

Mariko couldn't decide if she wanted another transplant. She tried her best not to think about it. When, during her resumed dialysis sessions, she imagined undergoing another transplant operation, she felt a painful tightening in her chest. She would close her eyes and clench her teeth: all the tasty dishes she'd been able to eat again, all the fun she'd been able to have. The thoughts came pouring to her and she didn't know what to think anymore. She could only wonder why she'd done what she'd done.

When had it all begun? Mariko searched her memories. *When?*

Splashing water. It sounded familiar. Swimming class, she wondered? No, that wasn't it. Voices echoed from memory, growing louder. They began as a stirring, then changed into cheers. Again, splashing water. There was yelling, which grew louder and louder, threatening to burst her ear drums.

In a flash, the scene folded out before her.

There was a bright blue sky. A single cloud floated across it, as if reflected upon water.

The cheering enveloped her. She stood up along with everyone else and gave her own cry of encouragement. The sound of splashing water threaded itself through all the shouting and into her ears. Yes, that was it. The day of the intramural swimming tournament.

After the individual events were done, it came time for the relay race. Three boys and three girls from every sixth-grade class in a 25-meter relay. Not only was it the last tournament of grade school, but the last race as well. This raised the excitement to a fevered pitch.

By the time the fourth swimmer jumped into the pool, Mariko's class was in second place. The leading class was five meters ahead, but there was still enough time to turn things around. Everyone was swimming their best that day. Mariko and her classmates gripped the pool's edge, leaning over as they rooted their team on, forgetting that they were getting drenched.

The fourth swimmer in Mariko's class touched the wall just a few seconds short of the first place team. Not a moment later, a huge amount of water sprayed up into the air as the fifth swimmer jumped into the pool.

She was the last girl on the team. After staying underwater for five meters, she rose back up to the surface. When she was visible again, there were only three meters between her and first place.

"Let's go!" shouted Mariko in unison with the friend next to her.

But the distance between them didn't shrink any farther as the two maintained their interval for twenty meters. The anchors for each class were preparing for the change-off. Mariko's friend nudged her with an elbow.

"Hey look, Mariko. Aoyama is anchor for Class 1."

Mariko did a double take.

It was him, all right. Sporting a dark tan, perhaps from practicing at the pool on Sundays too, he was standing on the diving board, shouting and beckoning his teammate on as she swam towards him. That was when Mariko's kidney began to ache. She frowned and pressed a hand to her side. She'd all but forgotten about her transplant until she'd seen Aoyama's suntanned figure just now. Her heart was racing. She tried to shake off the pain, raised her voice along with the crowd, then looked to see which place Class 1 was in. She started. Third place.

Two big splashes filled the air, one right after the other, as anchors from the first place team and Mariko's team plunged in. The cheering became even more frantic.

"Just a little more!" shouted Aoyama. He was leaning out over the end of the diving board, only one or two meters remaining before his teammate would touch the edge of the pool.

The first place swimmer and Mariko's classmate surfaced. They both took a breath and made their first stroke at the very same moment, with the same three meters still separating them.

Symbiosis

Mariko could not take her eyes off Aoyama. She knew that cheering for her class was more important right now, but all she could do was to stare at him as he called out from the diving board.

His teammate touched.

A moment later, Aoyama jumped in, flying farther into the air than Mariko had ever seen anyone do before. He painted a beautiful line above the pool, and from his finger tips to his feet, cut into the water with the utmost precision.

Mariko heard no splash from his dive.

And in fact, all of the sounds around her had disappeared. Her own voice, her friends, the screaming of the crowd…all was hushed, as if frozen in time. It was like suddenly being in a silent film.

Aoyama surfaced. He turned his head to the side, took a breath, and plunged his left hand thumb first into the water to propel himself forward.

Mariko then saw that the feet of her team anchor were in line with Aoyama's outstretched fingertips. Aoyama was gaining.

Her throat was sore from shouting so much, but she cheered on. She kept hollering even though she could not hear herself.

She had no idea who she was rooting for. She wanted to support her class, but her eyes were locked on Aoyama. As they approached the goal, Aoyama and Mariko's teammate were head to head. Aoyama turned his face to breathe.

Mariko felt their eyes meet.

She gasped. Her kidney ached. She fell silent and just gazed at Aoyama.

The first place anchor touched the wall, followed soon after by second and third. The pool darkened for a moment as clouds covered the sun overhead.

Aoyama had won by a fraction of a second.

Suddenly, the roar of the crowd returned. The noise crashed into her ears like an avalanche. Everyone threw up their arms and yelled as loud as they could. Her friend hopped over to her.

"We still made third place, Mariko!"

She rejoined the cheering with a smile upon her face.

149

Parasite Eve

Aoyama was president of his class. He was a little on the light side, but excelled at sports. He was pretty articulate and was always quick to make people laugh. Mariko had never been in the same class with him, but had been interested in him ever since fifth grade.

She never spoke to him, since he was usually found to be chatting animatedly with the throng of girls that seemed to follow him everywhere.

She felt they wouldn't get along anyway.

Being the sporty type that he was, Aoyama probably liked cheerful, athletic girls, Mariko had always assumed. She'd been in bad shape from dialysis, and now, she'd just had transplant surgery. And while she'd probably be able to do gym again someday, she couldn't be termed healthy at a stretch. She was short, and she had that scar on her side. She had to take drugs every day, like some sick person. It was hopeless.

Even so, she asked Doctor Yoshizumi if she was okay now.

She wanted him to tell her she was cured for life, but his answer was quite the opposite. If she forgot to take her medicines at all, her new organ would be rejected. Under no circumstances could she treat her situation casually.

Mariko simply nodded at the doctor's words. She knew he was telling the truth.

Why did she have to get kidney failure in the first place? She never hated her body so much as now.

She wondered how things might have been if she hadn't gotten sick. She'd have been able to play sports…

Still, she was happy enough to chance upon him in the hallway. After class, she would go out of her way to walk past his homeroom and peek inside to get a look at him, even though it was in the opposite direction from where her locker was. After she passed by his classroom, she would turn around and go down the hall, taking the roundabout way, walking an entire lap through the school building. Whenever Aoyama was not there, she would act cool and continue walking. But if he was there, she could barely contain her happiness, and her steps would lag.

That was her mistake.

With summer vacation over and two weeks into September, everyone was just coming out of their hot weather daze.

Classes were done for the day, and Mariko went over to look at Aoyama as usual. She craned her neck and scanned the classroom's interior.

He was not there today.

She was about to continue on in disappointment when she heard a voice address her.

"What'cha doing there, Mariko?"

She stopped dead in her tracks.

When she looked in again, she saw two boys sitting on desks. They had huge grins on their faces. There were hardly any other students in the room.

"Why'ja always take a peek?"

She had shared a class with these two the year before. They were known for sticking their noses where they did not belong and being pushy towards girls. Mariko and her friends disliked them.

"So what if I did?" she shot back in a callous tone in an attempt to hide her embarrassment.

But this only encouraged the pair. One of them cut to the point.

"Oooh, I get it. You like Aoyama. That's why you're always hangin' around here after class."

They'd figured her out.

Mariko felt her face turn completely red. She wanted to say something, but just stood there stuttering.

"Too bad, you just missed him. You know, he told us puffy-faced chicks aren't his type anyway."

The two started laughing.

Mariko turned back on her heel, wanting to get out of there as quickly as possible, but just as she was about to run away, she heard those dreadful words.

"Hey, I heard you got a kidney from your dad?"

Her legs froze.

"Awww, it went breaky, so you had to get help from your daddy? How cuuute."

Why were they saying these things to her? It had nothing to do with Aoyama. If only she could cover her ears and block their words. Her body had frozen and she couldn't move a finger. She wanted nothing more than to disappear at that moment.

But the boys went on.

"She's just like that Frankenstein monster, don't you think?" one of them said to the other.

"She wants to live, even if it means taking someone else's kidney. Aww, what a greedy little girl."

"What a freak. I bet her body's all patched up."

"Wonder if she can even take a piss."

Their guffaws rang in her head like horrid bells. She wanted so much to tell them to stop, to say that she wasn't a monster, that she wasn't put together from dead people like that creation of Dr. Frankenstein. But nothing came out.

"Stop it you guys!"

A voice cried out and, the moment she heard it, Mariko fell forward as the tension in her body snapped. Her head made an awful sound against the hallway tile. As she tried clearing her blurred vision, she saw a group of girls quarreling with the boys, but could not make out who they were.

She ran away. A voice called out from behind her, "Mariko, wait!" but she ignored it. The distance to her locker had never felt so long. She changed her shoes hastily and ran home with all her might, not stopping once on the way. By the time she got to her house, she was short of breath. Her side was in terrible pain, her surroundings distorted through tears.

When she walked in the door, she immediately removed all of her immuno-suppressants from their pouch, tore open the packages, and threw the multicolored capsules and pills into the toilet. She pushed down on the handle and watched as they swirled around and flowed down the pipe out of sight, leaving only a gurgling sound in their wake.

I'm not a monster.

Mariko crouched in front of the toilet bowl, buried her face between her knees and cried there in the bathroom, her body convulsing in unison with her sobs.

It was not long before rejection set in.

Mariko was taken to the ICU right away. She clearly remembered Doctor Yoshizumi's expression of disbelief that day.

"Why didn't you take your medicines?" he asked, but the question fell on deaf ears.

"I did take them."

Yoshizumi was unconvinced.

"If you had, then you wouldn't be here right now."

"I took them just like you said."

"You shouldn't lie, Mariko. You're not well. Why did you do this? Didn't I tell you to take your meds every day? Didn't I warn you?"

Yoshizumi's voice was tinged with despair. He'd probably tried his best not to sound that way, but Mariko didn't miss the tone.

"We're going to have to take it out now."

After all they'd gone through, it had come to this.

Yoshizumi, Mariko, and her father discussed a plan of action, though Yoshizumi did most of the talking. He sat in front of Mariko's bed, looking at her pitifully, more, it seemed to her, for his own sake than hers. Her father reacted to each of the doctor's words with utter disbelief.

I ruined my father's kidney, Mariko thought. She was afraid to imagine what he must have been thinking, but she couldn't keep terrible guesses from running rampant in her brain.

Her father was naturally upset. His own child had rejected a most selfless sacrifice. She had been on her way to a normal life again, but had thrown away her only chance to get there, through her own negligence. Mariko was sure her father thought she was beyond saving.

Yoshizumi must have shared the sentiment. After all the hardships they faced, and despite having gone through all the necessary steps, she had repaid their diligent work with intolerable foolishness. Mariko was sure the doctor thought she was hopeless.

She was sure.

Mariko closed her eyes. The faint humming sound had faded into silence.

Hot air from outside permeated the hospital room, making it difficult for her to fall asleep. The bed creaked faintly as she turned onto her side.

She thought of school.

She had no desire to return there. The laughter of those two boys was still trapped in her ears. If she did go back, it was only a matter of time before she became an object of ridicule again. It was an unbearable thought. If this was how people were going to treat her, then living a life of dialysis was, to her, the more favorable option.

The next morning, a nurse came in carrying a white bag filled with packages of immuno-suppressants.

Mariko wondered what would happen if she didn't take them. She would only need to pretend to swallow them and hide them in the back of her mouth. Then, when the nurse was not looking, she could spit them out and stuff them under her pillow. No one would suspect a thing.

Then again, the doctor was sure to notice something eventually.

In the heat, her thoughts soon grew vague and disjointed. As she drifted between wakefulness and sleep, she imagined scenes from the near future when this transplant would end in failure.

Just then, she heard an indistinct noise.

Symbiosis

Her ears perked up in alarm. She stopped breathing and listened for nearly a minute, but heard nothing.

Just a figment of her imagination.

She breathed a sigh of relief and looked at the window. A street light threw jet black lines on her face mimicking the blind that was lowered between them.

She always had the same dream here of some unknown entity walking slowly with determined footsteps, her room as its goal. She wouldn't be able to run away. Her body was always paralyzed, her heart pounding close to bursting. And then her kidney would announce itself by moving around, enthralled by the strange presence approaching her door.

The footsteps always stopped just outside the hospital room. Before long, the doorknob would begin to turn.

She always woke up just as the door was about to open.

But Mariko knew who the footsteps belonged to.

The donor.

The corpse from whom she had stolen a vital organ had come to reclaim it.

She was reminded of a strange little comic book she once read long before her kidney problems even began. A friend had bought it for her. Mariko didn't remember the author's name or the title and could only vaguely recall the story, but she still remembered clearly the shock of reading it. It had made her afraid to even go to the bathroom alone.

The story centered around a young girl who was paralyzed after falling down a flight of stairs. All the doctors judged her dead from the fall. Even though she was fully conscious and aware of her surroundings, her total lack of bodily control hindered her from telling them that she was still alive.

The girl was brought into the operating room and designated as a heart donor. She tried desperately to make everyone notice she was alive, to no avail, and had to watch as her heart was cut out.

But after the girl was buried, her grudge became insatiable. Wanting nothing more than to take back what was rightfully hers, she resurrected herself from the grave.

After that, Mariko remembered only that at the end of the story, the zombie girl tracked down the recipient and gouged out her heart.

The girl was drawn with horrifying features and the image had always stuck in the back of Mariko's mind. When she'd first heard about the kidney donation, the comic was the first thing that had come to her mind.

She still had no idea what kind of person her donor had been. Though she asked the nurse about it repeatedly, she was always given the same indirect answer.

Maybe her donor actually wasn't dead. Maybe she was still conscious like the girl in the comic and wanted somehow to let Mariko know she was alive. Doctor Yoshizumi had gone ahead with the operation in spite of her terrible helplessness, and had taken the kidney, leaving the donor no choice but to wander in search of vengeance.

The footsteps in her dream could belong to no one else. Sooner or later, the zombie would come to seize its kidney from Mariko's body. It would tear open a hole in her side and run away with the prize in its hands and malicious words upon its lips. Someday, the door would open.

Then she would die a horrible, bloody death on that very bed.

Symbiosis

13

The hot days pressed on, but Toshiaki continued to work without pause. The ventilation system in his office left something to be desired, while the air conditioning in the cultivation and machinery rooms gave him new reason to be conducting experiments. It certainly beat out lazing away in his sauna-like apartment.

Eve 1's replication had gone on uninhibited. Since adding clofibrate, a peroxisome proliferator, the speed of division had risen.

Eve 1 had clearly taken well to the induction. Even so, Toshiaki's curiosity was far from satisfied. Clofibrate was just one peroxisome proliferator, and other variants could yield an even higher rate of division.

Toshiaki took out all the available peroxisome proliferators from the refrigerator and added a sample of Eve 1 to each. He also tried adding retinoic acid and various other growth factors. An article had linked the induction of beta enzymes in mitochondria by peroxisome to the fact that peroxisome attached to retinoid receptors, a DNA-binding protein that also perhaps coded enzymes.

Toshiaki gauged the intake of tritium-labelled thymidine to measure any potential increase in Eve 1's propagative capacity.

The results surpassed his expectations. Multiplication was exponentially higher with a simultaneous medication of retinoic acid and peroxisome. The printout showed figures beyond anything Toshiaki had ever seen before.

"Um, doctor…" came a voice unexpectedly from behind him. He looked up from the data on his desk to see Asakura standing there.

"What is it?" he answered, at last remembering she was still there.

Asakura hid her face a little, seemingly at a loss for words. She was not her usual confident self. After being urged a few times, she finally got to the point.

"I thought I might work on preparing for my speech."

"Oh…of course."

"And so I was thinking I'd like to take a break from Eve 1, for a little while at least, and resume with the experiments I was working on before…"

Toshiaki was so engrossed in Eve 1 that he had forgotten all about her presentation.

The Japanese Biochemical Society met once every year. It was a large-scale event that allowed Japan's biochemists and molecular biologists to gather under one roof and share the fruits of their research. This time it was being held in September near the university. It was customary for a few people from their seminar course to make an appearance every year and talk about biofunctional pharmaceuticals. One objective of the program was to have every master's student give a speech at least once while still enrolled. Doctoral students had ample opportunity to write articles and present at conferences, but the only chance for undergraduate and master's students to give any sort of scholarly presentation in front of a crowd was at graduation. An academic conference was therefore the perfect opportunity to give them such experience. In addition, it trained them to form logical ideas and to learn how to convey them to others. It undoubtedly felt good for the students to share the knowledge they had worked so hard to attain, but it was also a stressful event that they were often never completely primed for.

This was to be Asakura's first conference and she wanted to be ready, yet she still did not know which slides to use or how to structure her presentation. Toshiaki should have been more attentive, but he'd neglected her for his own obsessions.

"Yes...of course. I'm sorry, let's interrupt the Eve 1 analysis for a while."

At those words, an expression of relief came to Asakura's face.

Toshiaki checked to see that her slide data were all in order. She would need to include blotting graphs, so he arranged to teach her the following day how to use the scanner.

That night, just before he was about to leave for home, Toshiaki checked on Eve 1. Asakura was conducting an absorbency test in the mechanical room.

Though he told her he would stop analyzing Eve 1, Toshiaki secretly decided to continue with it on his own. For the time being, he wanted to see what exactly he had accomplished by adding peroxisome proliferators and retinoic acids.

He plucked a culture flask from the incubator and placed it under the microscope. As he adjusted the lenses and peered through, the shapes of lively cells came into focus.

For the time being, the miracle shown in Eve 1 was far more important to him than anything being announced at any academic gathering. Toshiaki was also on the bill, but the data he was presenting was already six months old, a far cry from his Eve 1 findings. Generally, the application deadline to participate in the meeting was about half a year before the day it was held. The theme of one's speech needed to be sent along with the form, and no matter how much viable data arose afterwards, one was not allowed to include them in the presentation unless they had a direct bearing on the submitted theme. A last-minute change was out of the question. However, Toshiaki was now driven by a strong impulse to report this year on Eve 1. If he were to reveal the information he had gathered over the past weeks, there was no telling how dramatic the response would be.

This was first-rate material. It would be a blast of a wake-up call to all mitochondrial researchers. Research institutes from all around the world would request that samples of Eve 1 be provided to them. Kiyomi's cells would live on everywhere. Just the thought of it made him ecstatic.

At the base of the flask, Eve 1 had formed numerous colonies. This despite the fact that he had taken care to leave only a thin layer the night before. His eyes widened at the unbelievable rate of propagation. He had to put the proliferation regimen at that of cancer cells or even lower, or else Eve 1 would fill a flask in just a day. Thankfully, he'd started out with a small sample and there had been no adverse effects, unless this was just another sign of the cells' strength. Toshiaki looked at the colony in the center.

At that moment, he heard a sound.

At first, he thought it was a fly buzzing around. It sounded like it was coming from overhead, but he also felt it beneath the floor.

Before long, it increased in volume. Surprised, Toshiaki removed his eyes from the microscope and looked around him. The drone grew even louder, and he knew it was coming from somewhere nearby. There was a definite power in it. It rose, then softened, inscribing waves into the air. His body began to resonate. It was as if the very electrons inside of him were being stimulated.

He gazed at the flask on the microscope stage. The cultivation liquid was rippling inside the flask. Where the microscope's light illuminated it, orange-colored rings welled up, spread out, then diffused. Toshiaki gulped. The noise became louder still. Ripples hit the walls of the flask and formed complex crest patterns, one after another.

It's Eve 1, he shouted in his heart, *Eve 1 is breathing!*

He put his eyes back to the lenses.

The colony was pulsating.

With a *thump*, its surface rose and fell. It was swelling and contracting, like a heart.

It was as though the colony had become a collective life form. In the short while he'd taken his eyes off, it had even grown, the cells multiplying and spreading out so that the entire lens field was now filled by the colony. With every writhing thump, the field vibrated. It was a little while before Toshiaki could accept the fact that the cells were causing the waves in the cultivation field and were also responsible for the sound.

He was enchanted by the display. He had never seen anything like it before. It was like looking at a new life form.

But that wasn't the end of it.

Toshiaki gulped down his breath. The colony was rising up in the center like a mountain. Two rounded areas began to cave in on either side a little above this peak. Further down, a single horizontal crack appeared. The cells on the upper end of the colony started changing form rapidly, becoming thin like fibroblasts. They started lining up in one direction.

"Holy..." Toshiaki moaned.

Symbiosis

What was appearing there was a human face.

The entire colony was working together to form a face. Two eyes, a nose, a mouth, and then hair were rendered. The cells were not done yet. They continued to divide and multiply, and the face progressed from a roughhewn image to one with a mannequin-like delicacy. There was no mistaking it, a human face that Toshiaki had seen before was emerging in fine relief.

"What the…"

Kiyomi.

It was Kiyomi's face. And it was looking directly at him. The cells had revived every detail, down to her pupils and fleshy lips, nothing changed from when she was alive.

The cells ceased, leaving a perfect replica of her face at the bottom of the flask. Toshiaki gazed fixedly upon it. His throat was dry.

The mouth moved.

Kiyomi's lips and tongue moved to form four distinct syllables in succession.

A much different sound echoed from the flask. No. Toshiaki was unsure if he had actually heard it or not. Perhaps it had resonated inside of him. Either way, he understood.

<TO-SHI-A-KI>

That was what it had said.

"Kiyomi!" he yelled out.

He was not insane. This was Kiyomi. She had come back to him. He called out to her in desperation.

"Kiyomi! It's me! I can hear you Kiyomi! Can you hear my voice?!"

He heard a sound at the Cultivation Room door. Toshiaki looked up quickly to glimpse a shadow in the frosted glass.

Someone was watching him.

Had his voice been heard?

He sprang to the door and looked into the hallway, but no one was there. Whoever it was had run away.

Asakura? Perhaps, but he didn't go out into the hallway to check.

He returned to the microscope, but now all he could see were the small colonies from before. No matter how much he strained his eyes, he could see nothing even resembling Kiyomi's face. Silence returned. All evidence of what had just transpired was gone.

Toshiaki stood there for a long while in amazement.

Symbiosis

14

"Are you okay?" came Toshiaki's voice, prompting Kiyomi back to her senses.

She awoke to find herself lying on a couch. There was a blackboard above her and a large bookshelf against the opposite wall lined neatly with hardcover volumes with English titles. It looked like a classroom at the university, but when she saw there was no equipment of any kind, figured it was a faculty lounge.

Kiyomi gave an affirmatory nod and stood up. She then remembered what happened and immediately placed a hand on her chest. She remained in this position for a while, checking her heartbeat, and felt its usual, quiet, regular activity. Feeling relieved, she composed herself and sat down on the couch. Soon, a young man stood up next to her and peered worriedly into her face.

"Are you sure you're okay?"

"Yes, um…I'm fine. I'm so sorry to trouble you," she said, bowing her head lightly.

"Well, I'd still take it easy for a while, just to be safe." He scratched his head a little. "This is our seminar room. It's Sunday, so no one will bother us here. Can I get you some water or anything?"

"If it's not too much trouble…I'll have a glass of water."

"Sure, no problem at all. Wait here, I'll be right back."

He smiled gently, to put her at ease, then left.

The room was blanketed in silence. Kiyomi bent down her head, sighed in relief, and fixed her collar.

The young man's face floated in her vision like an afterimage.

It was the face she had noticed behind her in the lecture hall right before the slides began. The face she had seen just before she fainted.

She remembered falling into his arms and the warmth in her cheeks.

Kiyomi thought of the letters on the screen. She searched her memory for what they said. A person's name. She closed her eyes and tried calling them back from memory. Naga…?Yes, Nagashima. That was the name, or something like it.

Startled, Kiyomi opened her eyes and looked up. I'm such an idiot, she thought, at last recalling who the young man was.

He came back into the room with a mug in one hand.

"Here you go," he said with a smile and handed it to her. She leaned forward and put it to her lips. Iced oolong tea flowed soothingly down her throat.

"Um, thank you. Mr. Nagashima...right? Sorry if I'm mixing you up with someone else."

For a moment, Toshiaki made to speak, then stared at her face. She knew he was going to ask how she knew his name.

"We met once, two years ago." She smiled as cheerfully as she could. "At the orientation party. You probably don't remember me. I was just a freshman then. My name is Kiyomi Kataoka."

Toshiaki looked to be at a loss before a broad smile came to his face.

"Ahaaa...I remember now."

They then talked for about half an hour. He apologized for not remembering her. She had thought him to be very calm and collected then, and now, talking with him again after such a long time, this impression grew even stronger. Back then, he'd said he was a first year master's student, so she was not surprised to learn that he had graduated already and was now working on his Ph.D. Kiyomi made no efforts to hide her respect. He's so different from me, she thought. He knows exactly what he wants to do with his life. Toshiaki explained with a laugh how obsessed he was with his work. She thought it was wonderful when he smiled like that...

She probably would have talked with him more had Ishihara not interrupted them. He had just come back from finishing his presentation. Upon recognizing Kiyomi, he spoke to her in an almost melodramatic way.

"Are you okay, young lady? You really gave us quite a scare back there."

Kiyomi apologized for the inconvenience and bowed her head. The professor talked to her with a paternal solicitousness, asking if she had ever had such a fit before, and recommended that she have a doctor take a look at her. She answered all of his questions until he was satisfied.

"Nagashima, take her home, will you? Just so she'll have someone with her in case she has a relapse."

As she got into the passenger's seat, Kiyomi thanked Toshiaki numerous times for the ride.

"Now stop apologizing, I'm running out of rejoinders," he said with an embarrassed smile. Kiyomi apologized. He started to laugh. She laughed as well.

The following Sunday, they went out together for lunch and afterwards for a drive. They exchanged phone numbers.

Kiyomi called him the next day. The day after that, Toshiaki called her late in the evening.

From that moment on, their relationship was sealed.

Toshiaki was busy with his experiments for school and, even though they met on Sundays, he wasn't able to spend all day with her. Since he dealt constantly with cells and animals, he could not afford to take an entire day off. Nevertheless, he managed his time to accommodate her as much as possible. When he was working on an experiment and had free time only in the evening, they would rent a video to watch together. Regardless of his hectic schedule, Toshiaki could not get her out of his mind, and he came to like her more and more.

Kiyomi wanted to know everything about him. For the most part ignorant about the details of his research, she usually asked about it whenever there was a break in the conversation. Toshiaki's face practically lit up as he told her about his work in his eager, accessible way. His eyes were so lively when discussing his research. Kiyomi was in love with his passion. It was amazing being with a man so devoted to his pursuits.

"Because I provided that data to Professor Ishihara."

Kiyomi had asked Toshiaki why she'd seen his name on the slides that open-house day.

"I got some useful data when I was still a master's student, and the prof told me I should write an article. I knew I'd be going on to get my Ph.D., so I suppose that drove me too. It was hard since I had to write it all in English, but it ended up being included in a pretty good publication, *The Journal of Biological Chemistry*."

"Is it famous?"

"It's first-rate, actually. It contains biochemistry-related articles and it's read worldwide. The slides you saw were included in my article. You might know this already, but scientific journals are divided into two types: those with articles and those with commentaries and more general information. You've probably seen magazines like *Newton*, right?"

"Sure."

"Those are the more general ones, but they aren't usually considered quote-unqoute science. They're just designed to enlighten the general reader. The other more technical ones devote their pages to reporting new discoveries made by working scientists. Researchers from all backgrounds read these journals and contribute articles on their own findings. Usually they have to write them in English. These journals also have panels of respected professors. The committees read our submissions and decide what is fit to be published. If it's not up to par, they send it back and tell us to rewrite it."

"How did yours turn out?"

"Well, I did this one experiment that wasn't as complete as it could've been. I was told that if I fleshed out my results, then everything would be fine. So I reworked it. They published it verbatim. I actually have a copy right here."

Toshiaki handed her a pamphlet, every page of which was filled with finely printed English, accompanied by various diagrams. From what she saw flipping through the pages, it looked like very dense reading, unsuitable for skimming over. Kiyomi expressed a heartfelt admiration towards Toshiaki for having accomplished this much.

"You have to write more articles, right?"

"Well, to complete my Ph.D., I need to do three articles in English. My seminar prof included my name in one of his recent articles, so all I need is one more."

"Will it be put out in this journal again?"

"No, you can't get published in a journal of this stature too many times. I want my work printed in an even higher-ranking one."

"Higher?"

"Scientific publications have different standards and some are more influential than others. I think about the level of my research and decide where best to contribute it. Each journal also has its own theme. Some deal with a broad overview of science, others specialize in unorthodox areas. Some have nothing to do with my own research. The ones with the most prestige are *Nature*, published in the UK, and the American *Science*. It's almost impossible to get published in those two. The next ones down the list, for the field of biochemistry at least, would have to be *Cell* and *The Journal of Biological Chemistry*."

"Then this article must really be something!"

"I should hope so. But it's not like I did it all on my own. I couldn't have done it without my professor's help. Also, an acquaintance of his is on the review panel, and I think that helped too..."

Good-natured Toshiaki could never boast without qualifying his own achievements. Kiyomi liked the way he smiled bashfully as he did so.

The third or fourth time they kissed, Toshiaki's tongue slid into her mouth. It felt so good she felt feverish. She could tell her heartbeat had quickened, too. Toshiaki's hand softly alighted on her bosom over her blouse. She was afraid he'd learn how aroused she was. Nevertheless, she responded by meeting his tongue with hers. She'd never felt such joy. He's the one, she thought. He's the one I've been

WAITING FOR.>

Kiyomi pulled herself away.

"What's wrong?" asked Toshiaki suspiciously.

"...I thought I heard a voice."

"A voice?"

<HE IS THE ONE I'VE BEEN WAITING FOR.>

"There it is again!" she screamed.

Toshiaki held and calmed her, telling her there was no voice.

She listened closely as she shivered in Toshiaki's arms, but could hear nothing anymore.

"You're just imagining things," said Toshiaki while stroking her hair, but she was sure she'd heard it. It was the same voice she'd heard just before fainting in the lecture hall. It was high-pitched, but neither male nor female, and seemed to come from nowhere.

Toshiaki assured her everything was okay and placed a gentle kiss upon her cheek. Her heart had settled, but she was still trembling.

"Something bothering you?"

At the sound of Toshiaki's voice, Kiyomi came to her senses. He was sitting opposite her for breakfast.

"Nothing," she said with a smile.

It was the first time she stayed with him until morning. She'd been very tense from the beginning, but Toshiaki had treated her with utmost gentleness. Her body had been on fire, so shy she'd felt; her chest had hardly been able to contain the wild beating of her heart. But he'd whispered in her ear that she was beautiful, and that had made her happy.

Symbiosis

15

After receiving word from the nurse that Mariko's urinary output was decreasing, Yoshizumi went to check on her.

She had gained some weight, and, according to the examination results, her blood creatinine and BUN levels were on the rise. Yoshizumi prayed that things would work out this time.

He came into the room to find the young girl lying on her bed. Her face was warm from a slight fever. Yoshizumi raised her a hand in greeting, but the gesture was ignored. He flashed a pained smile to the nurse and sat down at Mariko's side.

"So you're having trouble going to the bathroom? Is there anything else bothering you?"

"...dunno," she answered, facing the other way.

She had at last been responding to him the past few days. That said, she answered only bluntly, but for Yoshizumi it was a relative improvement. Maybe allowing her to walk around in the courtyard had lifted her spirits enough to instill some self-confidence.

Her recovery was going smoothly. Any signs of infection or refusal had yet to appear. Beginning this week, the amount of adrenal steroids in the immuno-suppressant solution had been reduced, and she had also been allowed outdoors. Her chances of developing infections from outside contaminants were negligible by now. If things continued this way, she could be released from the hospital soon. Any signs of organ rejection, however, would prolong her stay.

Yoshizumi lightly disregarded her succinct 'dunno.' She was probably telling the truth. Patient awareness of the first stages of rejection was vague. Fever and weariness were common, but these were often the result of the patient's restricted water intake, so the situation had to be dealt with carefully.

"I just want to do a few more tests. There's still a possibility your new kidney could be rejected, but all signs so far point to a swift recovery."

Upon Yoshizumi's mention of the word 'rejected,' Mariko nearly jumped out of her skin, though her expression didn't change.

"We'll postpone your going out into the garden for a while, okay? I'd like to do an ultrasonic wave test on you. You remember we did that the first time?"

Silence.

"We'll just be listening to your blood flow. It only takes a minute or two. It won't hurt at all, I promise. We'll take a look at the results and judge from there."

Mariko gave a wordless nod as a signal of consent. Upon seeing that, Yoshizumi told the nurse to prepare the Doppler meter. With this machine, they would be able to tell if the transplanted kidney was hypertrophic or if blood flow was inadequate. Because this method was easily administered right there in the sick room, Yoshizumi used it whenever possible.

He entrusted the nurse to handle things, smiled once more at Mariko, and left the room. Strolling down the long hallway towards the elevator lobby, he watched the daylight pour in through the windows, casting sunny rectangles across the floor.

Does Mariko's condition indicate organ rejection. Yoshizumi turned the question over in his mind as he walked. He was still unsure after viewing the results so far. Organ rejection was becoming more and more infrequent in recent years thanks to the advancements in immuno-suppressants. But there was a trade-off in that the new drug cyclosporin's toxicity was rather hard to gauge.

There was no denying cyclosporin's efficacy. It was a necessary part of Mariko's treatment. But cyclosporin had the drawback of being reno-toxic if too much of it accumulated in the blood stream. At the City Central Hospital, blood samples were taken every morning to monitor the extant level of the drug. Intake was then adjusted to avoid the triggering of any side-effects.

The results of Mariko's monitoring were sent daily from the lab to Yoshizumi's office. From what he had seen already, her cyclosporin level was not rising dramatically, but he had a feeling that her blood creatinine was. It could have meant either rejection or kidney poisoning, but from Yoshizumi's experience, he felt the former was more likely in this case.

Why would rejection be setting in now?

Yoshizumi felt cheated. No. He was only being pessimistic because things had gone almost too smoothly.

He was overwhelmed by doubt.

Remembering that Mariko had stopped taking her medicines the first time, he stopped dead in his tracks.

Could she be throwing away her drugs again?

Nonsense.

He shook his head. The presence of the immuno-suppressants had been confirmed in the test results.

He resumed his stride, head lowered in shame for having doubted her even a little. He wondered if he had ever expressed suspicion towards her without even knowing it. Maybe she was sensitive about this. It would certainly explain her hostility towards him.

Maybe that was why she was so reluctant to open up to him.

Yoshizumi took a deep breath and pressed the elevator button.

The results of the wave test were finished and reported back to Yoshizumi. As he suspected, there was a noticeable decline in blood flow. He decided to take a needle biopsy from her kidney and scheduled a time with the nurse.

Mariko was brought into the OR. Yoshizumi soon followed after disinfecting himself in the scrub room.

The procedure was over in a few minutes, the sample then passed off to an assistant.

"Send this to the Biopsy Department for me. I want an immunofluorescence examination, light micrograph, and electron micrograph. How long will it take?"

"With the light micrograph, twenty minutes."

"Okay, let's hope for the best."

But as Yoshizumi exited the OR and stood by in the office, he could not control the anxiety welling up inside him.

Would Mariko's kidney give out on him again?

Would it need to be removed after all they had done?

Were this a typical case, Yoshizumi would not have given it a second thought, and he was surprised at his own reluctance to do so if necessary.

When Mariko's organ rejection had set in, she had been immediately rushed to the hospital. Her father had found her at home alone in terrible pain.

Yoshizumi had been taken by surprise. Since leaving the hospital, she had been taking medications and coming in for periodic checkups to make sure her new organ was being accepted.

When Mariko was brought into the ICU, Yoshizumi was shocked to find that the presence of immuno-suppressants in her blood had decreased. Acute rejection. He took drastic measures and immediately gave her an injection of OKT-3, but it was too late. Mariko received an emergency blood transfusion and dialysis, but her kidney had already become a threat to her very health. There was no choice but to extract it.

Nothing was more depressing than extracting a transplanted organ. It meant reversing all the effort put into the treatment for many months by an entire staff. In fact, the patient's perceived quality of life would be lower than before the transplant. It was usually the surgeon who knew the positions of the blood vessels from the first op who was tasked with the extraction procedure. Preparing for it was, for Yoshizumi, the greatest possible humiliation.

On the day of the extraction, it was drizzling outside. Yoshizumi watched it from his office window, regretting that he had not brought an umbrella with him. The gray sky seemed to see right through his heart.

The extraction was performed in the same operating room as the transplant. The only difference was that Mariko already had a scar on her lower right abdomen. Yoshizumi reopened it with an electric scalpel.

He was relieved to find that the transplanted kidney had not adhered to any of the surrounding anatomy. Six months had passed since Mariko's transplant. Her rejection was not a gradual process and all signs pointed to acute kidney failure. In cases of chronic rejection, inflammation often occurred which bonded the organ strongly to the abdominal wall, making it impossible to peel away all of the blood vessels without damaging them. In Mariko's case, Yoshizumi would have no such problems.

From beginning to end, the operation was plagued by an oppressive atmosphere. Even when connecting the blood vessels with nylon thread, Yoshizumi was unable to allay his nerves. He knew it was a procedure which required precision, and he did not think himself fit to be extracting Mariko's transplanted kidney...

The test results were in. Yoshizumi confirmed that the kidney had been rejected again. Though the rejection was still slight, there was a large amount of PMN leukocytes in the capillaries and some thrombosis in the narrow renal artery. In the case of cyclosporin poisoning, there were usually minute glasslike grains in the arteries. Mariko's sample exhibited no such formation.

He prescribed Methylprednisolone. Had Mariko's condition been more severe, he would have used OKT-3, but he saw no reason for it here. He would check up on her after three days of this treatment, then draw a conclusion, observing her closely for one week thereafter.

Yoshizumi finished his instructions, took a breath, and swallowed some coffee. He went back to his desk and gazed absentmindedly at the white steam rising from the cup.

Mariko was a completely different person after the extraction.

She lapsed into the deepest depression. Patients whose kidneys did not take were rarely in good spirits. At first, Yoshizumi thought that Mariko was so closed because the transplant had failed. And so, when he recommended that she and her father register for the waiting list, he thought he was doing her a favor. He told them about a new method called CAPD, hoping to alleviate, if only a little, the pressures of returning to a life of dialysis.

However, when he thought about it now, Mariko's state of mind was more complex than that.

At the time, Yoshizumi never figured out why Mariko did not take her medicines. Some children did, of course, forget. There were various reasons for this. Sometimes it was in defiance of adults, others disliked the facial swelling which often occurred as a side-effect, and still others simply stayed over at their friends' or went on trips without telling their parents. Also, many decided that, since they felt so good after the operation, it was okay not to take them.

Yoshizumi honestly did not understand children's feelings very well. He had never quite figured out how to interact with them. He thought maybe it was because he had no children of his own.

Soon after he began his career, Yoshizumi married one of his former class-mates. Because both of them worked at the hospital, they had no time to raise children. Some years after they married, when they were finally able to make time for themselves, Yoshizumi discovered that his sperm was abnormal and that he was incapable of making any woman pregnant.

When Yoshizumi gave her the news, his wife, who'd always said that work came first and that they could have children later on, looked away from him, but not before he'd caught a brief but unmistakable look of contempt in her eyes.

He ought to have paid more attention to Mariko's state of mind. He regret-ted it though it was too late. He should have talked with her more.

It had looked like she'd gotten out of her depression. She'd listened to Yoshizumi and Anzai and even agreed to registering for another transplant. Yoshizumi had assumed she'd gotten over the trauma of extraction.

How wrong he'd been.

Coping with her now, he understood that she was far from over it. It wasn't because of the extraction itself two years ago that she was depressed. She was tormented about something else unknown to Yoshizumi. Whatever it was, she was keeping it to herself. She'd only been pretending to be okay, fooling all the grown-ups around her. Yoshizumi hadn't been able to see it.

Maybe it was already too late.

Maybe he was past the point of ever being able to win her confidence.

No, thought Yoshizumi.

Symbiosis

If he couldn't win the patient's trust, then he should retire from transplant medicine.

He had to talk with Mariko more.

That evening, Yoshizumi went to see her again.

She was lying in her bed with an IV tube in her arm, staring at the ceiling in solitude.

She seemed surprised at his visit. Her reaction was to be expected. Unless it was urgent business, he would normally not make an appearance except during scheduled patient rounds.

"What's wrong? Are you upset because you can't go out?"

She turned away without answering. Yoshizumi paid no attention and sat down in the chair at her bedside.

"The rejection is still very slight right now," he continued. "If you just take your medications, you'll be fine. There's no need to worry."

"..."

"It's okay. Things will calm down in no time. I'm sure of it. Soon, you'll be able to go home and eat whatever you like."

"..."

"By the way..." Yoshizumi hesitated for a moment before asking what had been burning in his mind. "Won't you tell me what happened after your first transplant?"

He saw her shoulders move somewhat at the question. He went on.

"You never told me that anything was troubling you... I never asked, and I'm sorry. There must have been some reason you didn't take your meds?"

"......"

"Won't you talk to me about it?"

Mariko was silent, but she was clearly agitated.

Without saying another word, Yoshizumi waited a long while for her to speak up. The silence was almost palpable, drifting down slowly from the ceiling like snow, embedding itself in Mariko's bed sheets.

"Doctor, I'm sleepy..." she said at last.

"I see..."

Yoshizumi stood up. He'd gotten a pulse at least. Unlike before, she was making an attempt, however slight, to be communicable.

"Don't worry about a thing, okay? We'll make it all better," he said, and left the room.

The following evening, Yoshizumi again looked over the biopsy results. He compared the data from the frozen samples, examined with an electron microscope, to the absorbency test results.

"This is a bit strange," said the lab technician.

Yoshizumi, cradling the phone, was looking at a film brought to him by a nurse from the lab, to which the technician's comment had been attached, prompting him to inquire into the matter.

"Given that the rejection is so slight, there are no immediate concerns. But something worries me." The technician lowered his voice in an evasive tone. "I've never seen anything like this."

Having already noticed the abnormal shapes on the film, Yoshizumi understood what the technician was talking about.

"You carried out the procedure without difficulty, I assume?"

Glitches in setting up a tissue sample could yield images that were contrary to fact. He suspected it may have been an error in the dying technique.

But once he knew no mistakes had been made, he had no other explanation.

He removed the first biopsy results from the filing cabinet and looked them over once more. Yoshizumi started. There was clearly something there. He was careless not to have seen it before.

The mitochondria in her kidney cells were deformed.

They were several times larger than normal and had fused in small sac-like nets across every cell.

Symbiosis

He, too, had never seen anything even remotely like it.

He had a bad feeling about this and threw the film onto the desk. He gulped down a mouthful of coffee.

Certainly mitochondrial expansion was known to occur from cyclosporin use. Yoshizumi had also heard that the ethacrynic acid in oral diuretics sometimes caused a mutation in mitochondrial structure. However, considering the small amount of cyclosporin he had administered so far, this was highly unlikely.

If anything, this was evidence of cyclosporin's toxicity. But could there be another reason? If the kidney had been abnormal from the beginning, why had it functioned properly until now?

He then remembered that inexplicable heat he felt during the transplant procedure when he touched the kidney. His heart had been strangely excited by the contact. The kidney had seemed, almost, to be working his heart.

Maybe there was a connection.

Yoshizumi felt goose bumps rise along his skin. He had to keep this from Mariko. But what was he going to do about this anyway? He could only hope that no ill came of this development. These mitochondria probably had nothing to do with the rejection symptoms. The kidney had been functional until now, and it could still take.

Staring at the film upon the desk, Yoshizumi prayed it would.

Parasite Eve

16

SHE remembered clearly the first time She became one with Toshiaki. When he entered Kiyomi's body, her face tightened as she stifled her cries. She, on the other hand, shivered with the pleasure of anticipation and plunged into a state of inordinate excitement.

Kiyomi sensed Her excitement. No wonder, since She thrived in the major nodes of Kiyomi's brain and nervous system. Kiyomi's nerves, her spine, and her synapses were all crucial for conveying information to her brain. Over the years and months, She had come to dominate all of Her host's organs so that they could no longer manage even the simplest functions without Her. When She was excited, so were Kiyomi's brain cells; the result of a spectacular burst of neurotransmitters between her synapses. No wonder Kiyomi was ecstatic. Her special stimulation was one that put others' joy to shame. And so Kiyomi soon forgot the pain and devoted herself to the act. And She, too, surrendered to the pleasure that Toshiaki gave. Oh, this Kiyomi, whose first time it was, how loudly she did moan, how gamely she quivered, how she passed out at the end!

Making love with Toshiaki was pure bliss. Recalling the instances from Kiyomi's memory, She relished them. Toshiaki's skill wasn't honed, sometimes he was even puerile. Even so, She felt a most supreme happiness being loved by Toshiaki, and controlled Kiyomi's body from within to receive his love as often as possible.

She transfigured Kiyomi's body in various ways to make it more desirable to him. As time went by, She gradually altered Kiyomi's face into one that Toshiaki would be most fond of. She reworked Kiyomi's nervous system to accommodate Toshiaki's transgressions. Kiyomi never knew why she experienced things so intensely. But for Her, Kiyomi's nerve structure was laughably simplistic and easy to manipulate. Kiyomi was so innocent in her purity, it was pitiable. To the end, she was unaware that the joy by which her own body was possessed was something not her own. But for Her to receive Her joy, and to capture Toshiaki's heart, it was necessary that Kiyomi feel what She felt. She couldn't afford to let him abandon her. He was just the man She'd been searching for. She needed to focus Toshiaki's love.

On Kiyomi...

And then on Her.

Symbiosis

Her body fluttered with joy. Soon. Perfection was within reach.

Though She could manipulate a host's cellular reproduction, it was difficult to maintain the structural changes. The forms She created tended to break down easily. She had to work on the genomic level.

Fortunately, there were sufficient tools here to perform genetic mutations. Right beyond the door was a clean bench where a bluish UV lamp was probably shining. Various carcinogens were lying in the office beyond. With a little hike, it was even possible to get irradiated. There was no shortage of catalysts, either.

She let loose now and unleashed her power to multiply.

Asakura looked away from the monitor with a sigh of exhaustion.

She had shut off the air conditioning a while ago, so the room was silent, save for the refrigerator which interjected with an occasional hum.

She stood up from her chair and stretched. It was already close to midnight. Toshiaki had left for home three hours ago. She could hear other footsteps around the time he left, but now there was only silence. She was likely the only one left in the building.

She took a plastic bottle of iced tea from the refrigerator and poured some into a mug with a gurgle that sounded strangely loud to her in this quietude. She brought the rim of the cup to her lips and took a mouthful. The sensation of cool tea in her throat helped to ease her fatigue.

She was still making slide diagrams for the annual meeting. Though she had drawn up some charts before for her senior thesis, she was still not fully accustomed to the whole process. No matter what she did, it took an immense amount of time. She watched the monitor, moving the mouse around. In what felt like a moment, two hours had flown by, and she'd finished only one diagram.

With cup in hand, Asakura returned to her desk and studied the image glowing on the monitor. She had taken her time with it, initially unsure of how to combine it with the other pictures she had scanned. She'd regretted not having asked Toshiaki while he was still around. Looking at the finished diagram, though, she was quite proud of it.

The lab really had an atmosphere all its own this time of night. Asakura took another sip of tea. By day it was just like any other lab. When evening fell, however, its mood changed. Maybe it was from shadows cast by the fluorescent lights, but the unusual shapes of the equipment on the experimentation table were much more vivid, somehow lurid. The contrast of the antiquated desk with the much newer machinery added to the ambience of strangeness. A most eerie place for a stranger to get lost in.

Maybe I should stop for today and go home.

At this thought, a chill ran up her spine, settling at the base of her head. The downy hairs on her nape tingled and stood up on end.

She turned around full circle, her eyes flitting across the room. The air was stagnant. Not even a draft. Her tingling had a different cause.

Nothing in the lab was different. Only silence, populated by her and the shadows on the floor. Everything was cold and lifeless.

The tingling was almost intolerable, turning into sharp pain. Asakura put her cup on the desk and pressed a hand to her neck. The pain began to spread.

Her entire body was shaking and she felt weak at the knees.

That name came to mind.

Eve 1.

Eve 1 is the cause of this.

A dragging noise.

Something was moving. She called out, but heard only hoarse air escaping her lungs.

She wanted to run away, but her feet were stuck to the floor. It was hard for her even to move her eyes. She strained her ears and gazed at the wall. On the other side of it was the Cultivation Room.

She heard the noise again, more clearly this time. It had come from the Cultivation Room. Something was moving around in there.

Eve 1's name rang in her head like a siren, lighting up in pure red. Still, it made no logical sense that Eve 1 would be making any noise at all. Right now, Eve 1 was in the culture flasks, which were themselves in the incubator. There was simply no reason for the noise, not to mention the movement.

At that moment, she heard a moist, formless sound, like a large damp mass falling to the floor.

Asakura gasped in surprise. Her knees began to shake. She was planted firmly in her chair. She jerked her knees inward. Just then, her fingertips touched the cup, knocking it over. A piercing shatter. Droplets of tea and ceramic fragments flew into her face. Pain swelled in her cheeks.

SHE stopped, upon noticing the noise.

Someone was here.

She'd been sure no one was left in the laboratory. It couldn't be Toshiaki. He'd gone home.

She searched Her memory. The figure of a tall woman came to mind. It was her.

She'd failed to sense the signs. She was never curious about bodies other than Toshiaki's. It couldn't be helped now.

No more noises. Maybe the woman had left...or maybe she was unable to move, shivering in fear.

What should She do with her?

She saw no reason to hesitate. She would need to reveal Herself sooner or later. Besides, the woman was alone. Toshiaki was Her ally now. She could finish off this woman's dreams once and for all.

No. If She did that, she could make noise and bring attention. But there was another way.

She shook Her entire body. Then, She started slowly towards the door.

Asakura breathed in sharply upon hearing the noise again.

She dropped to the floor, trembling as she looked around from beneath the desk. For the next minute or so, nothing could be heard, and she was at last able to calm herself. Just when she was ready to pass it off as a trick of the ears, the sound returned like a dragging mop.

"No..."

Large drops of perspiration fell nervously from the tip of her chin, soaking into the front of her shirt. The inside of her skull was hot as fire. While her head seemed to be boiling, her skin, coated with sweat, felt icy cold.

Sounds of splashing. Moving. Plops, like bubbles bursting.

Asakura imagined a slimy glob of garbage coated with mold, a rotting viscous mass mottled green and brown and black, and nearly threw up.

A dull scraping. Wet thumping.

The door. It was trying to open the Cultivation Room door. Asakura had locked it after Toshiaki had left.

There came then the sickening sound of thick fluid squeezing through a narrow hole, mixed in with a gurgling like a stopped-up drain. Bile rose to the back of Asakura's throat. The thing was trying to crawl through under the door. Asakura swallowed back the sour stench in her mouth with her saliva. A moment later, coldness swept over her, and her teeth began to chatter.

Flump... Flump... Again. She could hear the dragging noise clearly this time. It had made it into the hallway.

She could not stop her teeth from chattering. *I should be quiet. I can't let it know I'm here.* Asakura put a hand to her mouth, trying her best to silence herself. The chattering of her teeth echoed in her skull.

Ftup!

"Aa...!"

Something had hit the door.

There were two doors into the lab, one on her side and another farther back. Both led into the hallway. Whatever was making the noise was trying to get in through the door closer to the Cultivation Room. The refrigerator let out a hum. The sudden noise made her cry out again. She covered her mouth. Too late. Her voice could easily be heard from the hallway.

Symbiosis

Asakura's eyes clouded over and she lost sight of her surroundings. Both the lab doors were closed, but they weren't locked. This thing would have no trouble getting in. Once the knob turned, it would only be a matter of moments before...

She held her breath.

The knob was turning. Asakura was frozen stiff. She thought she should run to the door and lock it, but she couldn't move a muscle.

And then, the door opened.

She heard a distinct squishing sound.

If only I could run, she thought. From where she was squatted, she could not see the open door at all; her view was blocked by an experimentation table. She looked at the other door, but her direct path to it was impeded by a large desk. Even so, it was probably no more than ten steps away. The distance felt way too far.

Without warning, her vision went completely dark.

For a moment, she was unsure as to what had happened. But then, she saw two pale, flickering lights: the lamp on her desk and the standby light of her Mac. Everything else was swallowed in blackness. She could no longer see the desk, equipment, or even the nearest door.

It had turned off the lights.

There was a switch near the other door. Asakura gasped again upon realizing what this meant.

This thing knew that if a switch was flipped, the lights would turn off.

It knew that if it turned the knob, the door would open.

...It had intelligence.

She refused to believe it.

At that moment, a pale yellow light appeared from near the door.

Since the experimentation table was still in her way, she could not make out what was happening. A light tapping. Something being moved.

It had opened the refrigerator.

She heard agent vials being taken out. It was searching for something.

A sign saying "RUN!" was flashing inside Asakura's head. She got on all fours and moved her hands and feet in desperation. Her heart was shooting ahead but her body wasn't following. She managed somehow to crawl on all fours to a position where she could see the entire refrigerator. The door was half-open. The thing was on the other side, rummaging through the shelves, making sick, sticky noises now and then. It seemed not to notice her. Asakura could not see the thing, nor did she particularly want to.

She turned an angle and crawled gradually to the door. Just a little more, and she would reach it. And when she did, all she had to do was get up, open it, and run at full speed. If she could just reach it with her hand, she would be saved. Her heart pounded furiously.

Suddenly, there was a scraping sound, and an intense pain shot through her knee.

Asakura screamed and held her kneecap. Something had stuck into it. She tried pulling it out, but cut her fingertips trying to do so. Her palm become wet with blood. Tears flowed from her eyes and she cursed herself upon realizing her own carelessness. The cup. She had crawled onto a fragment of it.

Whatever this thing was, it moved with agility. It fell to the floor. It was on to her escape.

Asakura's heart froze. As it moved towards her, she could make out a few details. Almost all of it was completely opaque, but what she did see looked like a heap of flesh.

"No," she said with tears in her eyes. But it continued its approach. There was a sound like that of tentacles wriggling along the floor and bubbles popping like crushed tomatoes. The whole circus was coming her way.

"Please, stop…"

Asakura appealed desperately. She tried to crawl away and escape, but when she moved, the violent pain in her knee forced her to the floor with a thud.

Lying on her belly, she screamed as she stretched out her arms and dragged herself forward. It was almost upon her. Tears flowing down her cheeks, mucus dripping from her nose, she tried to push up with her elbows, but her body would not budge at all. She cried out in despair. Her knee throbbed in pain. Hands were sticky with sweat and blood.

Something warm and slippery touched one of her ankles.

It then grasped firmly and pulled.

Asakura reached out a hand. Her fingertips met the edge of a sink. She curled four fingers around it with all her might. The creature pulled her leg without mercy. The joints in her fingers reached the threshold of pain. Asakura screamed. She reached out her other hand, but it touched nothing. The thing pulled harder. Her index finger let go. She screamed out repeatedly for it to stop, but it pulled even harder. Its grip moved up to her shin. Her leg bones creaked from the pressure. Her middle finger popped out of its socket. Only her ring finger and her little finger were still barely holding on, but felt like they'd be ripped from her hand at any moment. The creature took hold of Asakura's other ankle, then pulled her with a sudden jerk.

The two fingers cracked and she let go of the sink.

As she was pulled away, the cup shard imbedded in her knee screeched across the floor.

The creature came down on her back with all its weight. A sticky solution clung to her. The peculiar odor of culture medium, sweet, powdery, invaded her nostrils. She tried to shove the thing away, but she could not get a grip on it. Her arms simply slipped into the thing and got stuck there.

The thing turned her around so that she was lying face up. She kicked her feet, but it was useless. She was completely restrained.

She cried out desperately for help, but a moment later her voice was stifled when something came into her mouth. She clenched her teeth in resistance, but her jaws were soon wrenched open. The sticky thing coated her tongue and teeth. Her face still turned upward, Asakura vomited. What was in her stomach shot up with great force and came showering down on her own face. Bathing in the half-digested food, what was in her mouth started to swell and to fill her throat.

17

December 24th had come at last.

Before making dinner preparations, Kiyomi arranged some holly and paper flowers around the living room. And while the space near the television was small, she managed to set up a tree in it. She adorned its branches with cotton in imitation of snow, hung miniature toys, and draped it with ornamental bulbs. She even renewed the dining table by replacing the tablecloth with lace, finishing it off with a polished candlestick in its center. Kiyomi looked around the room, which she had given a holiday air in not even an hour's time, pleased with her work.

She had lived with Toshiaki in this one bedroom apartment since they were married. Still, she never passed up on the Christmas decorations. Toshiaki made a big deal out of it at first. Considering they did not even have any children, he was not into the whole decorating thing. But Kiyomi would not be swayed. She had always celebrated the holiday this way, because for her it was not only about Christmas, but her birthday as well.

On a whim, she turned to the window. She ran to it in anticipation and drew the curtain, opening the misted pane slightly. White crystals danced in the evening air.

Kiyomi sighed joyfully, leaned forward, and gazed around the neighborhood.

Everything outside was already faintly dusted. The powdery snow descended gently, yet steadily from the sky. She could not see too far into the darkness, but where the light from her window shone, she clearly made out each individual snowflake.

A white Christmas!

She was elated and hummed "Silent Night", one of the first songs she ever learned on the piano, to herself.

It was getting late when Toshiaki called. The cake was done and dinner was

Symbiosis

all ready. Kiyomi pressed the receiver to her ear and sighed in disappointment as she cast a sideways glance to the pot of stew she had made especially for the occasion. Toshiaki said that one of his senior students had failed an experiment and needed to be brought back up to speed. Toshiaki would be staying to keep an eye on him while he redid the procedure.

"Does it have to be today?" she implored.

"We've already started using the sample. If we don't do it now, it'll go bad."

"I see..."

He apologized profusely. Kiyomi restrained herself and said, in a cheerful voice, not to worry. But she felt lonely. Toshiaki had done the same thing last year. She wanted him to dismiss his work for just one day and come home. It was her birthday, after all. Maybe that was a selfish wish, but it was the truth. Trying to estimate how much longer he would be tied up, Toshiaki began to describe the procedures that had to be conducted.

"Anyway, I need to extract a rat liver and homogenize it for a mitochondrial blot..."

The moment Kiyomi heard those words, her chest leapt.

<TOSHIAKI.>

Kiyomi gasped. Her ears rang loudly, vision turned red. Her entire body reacted as if scalding water were being poured all over it.

"What's wrong?"

A moment later, she came to her senses. A bit shaken, she put the receiver back to her ear and smoothed over the interruption. She told him it was nothing, saying she had only noticed the snowfall and gone to see it.

She stood motionless for a long while, sweat building up in her armpits. Now a sudden coldness was making her shiver.

These reactions were getting stronger. It had accelerated ever since she married Toshiaki, but lately it was particularly severe.

Just hearing the word "mitochondria" set her heart racing. Up until the beginning of their marriage, she often wanted to know all about Toshiaki, and

187

even asked him about his experiments. In these past few months, however, she had stopped speaking of his research altogether. The fits were becoming violent and unbearable. Something unknown to her was responding to all of that. A voice from within.

The voice's master was ecstatic upon hearing of Toshiaki's work, tearing around elatedly inside of her. She felt it with this phone call as well. She thought to tell Toshiaki to hurry home, but the voice in her head seemed to want him to continue with the experiment.

Kiyomi had no control over herself anymore.

Toshiaki ended up coming home around eleven. He apologized for being so late, then looked around the room and smiled with wonder at the decorations.

Kiyomi lit the candle and the tree and then laid out the dinner. Toshiaki expressed his delight. She was still unhappy that he'd come home so late, but his efforts now to liven up the occasion by being talkative pleased her very much.

After dinner, Kiyomi brought out a cake. She came up with a special frosting design every year. This time, she had made snow-covered trees and a small wafer house at the center. She thought she'd done a pretty good job.

As the candle burned low and the room darkened, they ate cake and drank champagne. Toshiaki took out a package from his bag, her birthday present, and handed it to her. She opened it to find a cute watch.

It was past 2 am when they went into their bedroom.

As they turned out the lights, Toshiaki leaned over and kissed her softly. The moment his lips touched hers, a pleasant sensation ran along her spine.

Kiyomi sighed in spite of herself. She lost all feeling in her legs and surrendered. It was such an amazing excitement, she thought she would melt.

She soon realized that her tongue was venturing out aggressively. Though the rest of her body was limp, her tongue seemed to have a mind of its own. No. She could not believe it. It couldn't be. There was no strength in her hands and feet. She was just standing there, held in Toshiaki's arms. Even so, her tongue continued in rapture, curling around his own in hunger, and gliding along the back of his teeth. This wasn't happening.

Suddenly, she was overcome with intense drowsiness, ready to fall into darkness at any moment. She'd have fallen into the abyss if Toshiaki hadn't been holding her. She let her head fall back. Yet the tip of her tongue still writhed around in search of sustenance. What was this? Toshiaki placed a kiss upon her neck. A violent flash behind her eyelids. Sleep assailed upon her without mercy. She shook her head helplessly to drive it away. What was going on?

Just before all her senses seemed to twist ominously, a voice echoed across her brain.

<TO-SHI-A-KI>

She opened her eyes instantly. The drowsiness withdrew a little, but only for a moment. Returning with full force, it drew a thick curtain over her consciousness. No. Kiyomi shook her head again, struggling to keep her eyes open. It was the same voice as before. *Make it stop!* She called to Toshiaki for help, but her voice only turned into a deafening roar in her head.

<TO-SHI-A-KI>

Who are you? Her heart began beating like a drum. She gasped for breath. She had never felt anything so excruciating. Her body spasmed. She was crumbling. Sleep kept crashing in like a tidal wave, and she just barely withstood the onslaught again and again. Every time her mind receded, the voice's master pushed up from inside her. It was full of joy, calling out Toshiaki's name. Kiyomi was anxious. It was as if the voice's master was making love to her husband; if she fell asleep, it would rise to the surface of her body and mingle lustfully with him. It was going to steal him from her. She desperately fought to keep herself awake. She managed to come afloat a few times, but soon sank into the bottom of the dark.

Someone was speaking. A loud voice that seemed to echo throughout the room. Was it hers or the other's? She sensed in it a profound delight. She could not tell what she was doing now...only that her body was in chaos, jostled about in the shadows of roaring waves.

When Kiyomi came to, everything was quiet.

She was dreaming.

It was the same strange dream she had every Christmas Eve. A dream about her distant memories of wandering in darkness.

But the dream had evolved. Kiyomi noticed elements that were different from the vision she had every year.

She felt herself moving all around. Her vision was vague, making it impossible to distinguish up from down. And yet, she could feel, upon her skin, the current changing direction, moment by moment. She was moving fast. Her strength surged and she felt like she could go anywhere, traversing unimaginable distances. She realized she was happy about this.

She had no idea how much time had passed. There was suddenly an odd turbulence in the current washing over her body. Something was close to her. It was large and clumsy in its movements, wriggling and swaying uncertainly.

She remembered it. She had come across it many times. Some of those times, she had attacked it. It punctured easily, but on occasion it captured her.

As she grew conscious of it, a new impulse arose in her without warning. She had no idea what it was, where it came from, or what it was trying to tell her. Before she could even notice she'd burrowed into the other thing.

It seemed surprised. But when she shared her power with it, it accepted their coexistence. Inside it was comfortable. Maybe she'd found her eternal nest.

In her dream, Kiyomi wondered what this feeling was, what it could possibly mean.

But she didn't know.

She didn't know what to make of any of this.

Symbiosis

18

"First up's you, Asakura."

Asakura stepped up to Toshiaki, who passed her a pointer. She proceeded to the screen, manuscript in her right hand and the pointer in her left.

Toshiaki spoke as he pressed the switch on his stopwatch.

"Yes. Our first presenter is Sachiko Asakura, whose topic will be 'The use of retinoid receptors in the gene induction of *2,4-dienoyl-CoA reductase* unsaturated fatty acid beta oxidation enzymes.' Asakura?"

"Thank you, slide please."

There was a soft click and a diagram appeared on the projection screen. Glancing at her manuscript, she began.

"I have come today to report that we have successfully introduced clofibrate in rat livers and generated unsaturated fatty acid beta oxidation enzymes in their mitochondria. By activating nuclear receptor proteins with peroxisome prolifer-ators, we have established that retinoid receptors are a vital component in the induction of these beta oxidation enzymes. For this experiment, we investigated '2, 4-dienoyl-CoA reductase,' enzymes necessary for the beta oxidation of unsat-urated fatty acids. We cloned their genes and found that these genes are governed by retinoid receptors. This is what I will be discussing today. Next slide, please."

With another click, the screen changed.

Toshiaki listened attentively, glancing now and then at the stopwatch face. All the professors and most of the staff and students of their course were gathered in the small seminar room. Though the fans were on, the curtains had been closed and the lights turned off for the slides. The crowd made the room feel much more claustrophobic than usual.

It was five days before the conference. Thinking it would make things easier on the presenters if they practiced their speeches at least once beforehand, the professors had called for a mock session. Assembling slides at the last minute was bound to cause mishaps; writing up the presentations well in advance and giving a trial run, on the other hand, helped reduce the stress for the first-timers.

Asakura had completed her slide diagrams much more quickly than Toshiaki had anticipated. Perhaps she'd slaved at it and worked late hours; but no, this did not begin to explain the speed with which she'd finished them. When asked how she'd pulled it off, she simply smiled and didn't answer.

In any case, she seemed well-prepared for her presentation, which put Toshiaki at ease. Asakura had certainly been hustling more than ever, coming to the classroom early in the mornings and working fervently until late at night without showing any signs of tiring. She'd made Toshiaki wonder if he wasn't getting too old in fact.

Asakura continued without a trace of hesitation. She accurately elucidated the various components of each diagram with the pointer, capturing the audience's attention whenever she raised her voice to emphasize key areas. Her presentation had perfect modulation. Toshiaki gazed at her profile with fondness. A researcher with years of experience could not have given a finer presentation. Despite his confidence in her, he never thought she'd be this good. In fact, she was flawless.

He suddenly realized something that wasn't appropriate to notice then and there. In recent days, Asakura had become beautiful, beyond recognition almost.

She wore the same rough jeans and t-shirts she always did, but there was now a certain magnificence about her. Perhaps it was because she'd changed her hair style. No longer tied back in a ponytail, her hair flowed loosely. Yet that couldn't have been it. Her expression had always been lively, but it was now complemented by a noticeable refinement. The sparkle in her eyes, and her gestures, exuded confidence.

"The aforementioned data show how the enzyme in question is induced via clofibrate. It may be hypothesized that many other enzymes for processing unsaturated fatty acids will exhibit the same property. Their genomic cloning should further clarify the role of retinoid receptors. That is all. Thank you very much for the slides."

Symbiosis

The screen went blank and the lights were flipped on. Toshiaki came back to reality and clicked the stopwatch.

"Fourteen minutes, twenty-seven seconds."

"Was that okay?"

Professor Ishihara nodded, visibly satisfied. Asakura looked relieved. This was more like the young woman Toshiaki was used to.

"The time limit is fifteen minutes?"

"That's right," Toshiaki answered.

"I could not find a single misspelled English word in your slides, and I think your explanations held up well... So what did you all think?"

Ishihara turned to the students behind him, thereby cuing them to share any points of criticism without hesitation.

They all looked down and avoided his gaze. Toshiaki suppressed a smile. Asakura's perfect presentation had thoroughly intimidated them.

Ishihara waited to see if anyone would speak up. Eventually, he nodded and asked the projector assistant to show Asakura's slides from the beginning.

"Let's all check once more to make sure there are no mistakes."

Ishihara questioned Asakura at length about each slide and listened carefully to her arguments. She answered everything perfectly. Toshiaki listened in half-surprise. She had really done her homework. He thought to jump in with some timely help if she faltered, but there was no need. In the end, she showed no uneasiness, but neither was there even a hint of arrogance. Her forthright responsiveness was even pleasant. Without rushing her replies, she presented her points clearly and in order, with a clear desire to convince rather than befuddle the questioner. She referred to surprisingly recent data as she did so.

"Yes, perfect. I see you've been studying well," said Ishihara at last, his voice filled with admiration.

"Thank you very much."

Asakura flashed a smile that was startlingly lovely.

"This certainly puts a lot of pressure on the next person, doesn't it?" said

Ishihara, which brought a laugh from the rest.

After the rehearsal was over, Toshiaki returned to the lab.

"Wow. I'm really impressed. You even got the professor's seal of approval."

Asakura seemed flattered, and thanked him with a bow.

"I guess all that's left is to memorize your notes. Well, you have until the day of the meeting to do that, so don't stress yourself out over it. If you have any worries, though, just let me know and we can go over things the day before. And let's write up an outline you can take to the podium just in case."

"I think I'll be okay..."

"I don't know, you'd be surprised how easy it is to forget things up there. Comes with the territory. But if you can, try to do it without notes."

"I'll give it my best."

"By the way..." said Toshiaki, by way of changing the subject, as he looked at her knee. "How's your leg?"

"Oh, this?"

Asakura laughed and tapped her jeans with her fist. "It's healing. I still have a bandage on it."

"Doesn't it hurt?"

"Yes, but I doubt it'll even leave a scar."

She was limping the day she'd changed her hair. When he asked her about it, she claimed to have fallen on her apartment stairs and scraped her knee. Her fingers were taped up as well.

She'd brushed away Toshiaki's concern, saying: "Really, it's nothing. Besides, it's hard for me to keep my balance anyway, being so tall and everything."

Toshiaki had been struck by this comment; it was so unlike her. Until then, he'd never heard her make fun of her own height. He'd been taken aback for a moment. But it was really just a trifle, and he'd scrubbed the feeling of oddness out of his mind.

"It should heal by the conference, so please don't trouble yourself about it.

I'd look pretty silly with a bandage under my suit skirt, don't you think?" she said with a grin.

Just then, a group of seniors came into the room. One of them was holding a white box in his hands.

"The professor congratulated us on such a good rehearsal and bought a cake for us to celebrate. Please, have some," said the student proudly.

"Say, this is rare. He must really be in a good mood, thanks to all your hard work," Toshiaki said as he opened the box.

"Looks delicious," said Asakura elatedly. "I'll get some tea? Everyone grab a cup if you want some."

The tea was a welcome diversion and Toshiaki took his time to enjoy it.

"Hey, Asakura, that isn't your usual mug, is it?" said one of the students as he ate his cake. Toshiaki had not noticed it until now, but the design on her cup was indeed different.

"What happened to the old one?"

"Yeah, did you break it?"

"I don't know where it went," Asakura replied, enjoying the scent of her tea with a joyful smile. "I swear I put it right over there. Let me know if anyone finds it, though."

19

SHE had surfaced, for the first time. It had gone better than She ever could have hoped. Kiyomi's spirit had resisted a few times, yet, She had proven triumphant. To surface and to be held as Herself in Toshiaki's arms was incomparably more blissful than what She could feel while still buried in Kiyomi. But She was not satisifed. This was only the beginning.

She knew that Kiyomi was dreaming. Memories sometimes leaked out from Her and stimulated Kiyomi's nerves. Though She had been careful not to enlighten Kiyomi to Her existence, on the twenty-fourth of December, the day Kiyomi was born, Her defenses were never as effective. Every year, Kiyomi seemed sharper that one night.

At last, the night before, Kiyomi had glimpsed Her memory of entering the host. Kiyomi would probably never understand what it meant, but it would not do to be careless. There was the danger that she would tell Toshiaki; and while Kiyomi's ignorance could be counted on, Toshiaki would probably decipher the dream.

At last, the time has come to take action, She thought.

It was time to renounce her status as an amenable slave. From last night's trial, She knew the necessary preparations were now in order. She thought and Kiyomi's body complied: a most pleasant reversal of who was mistress, and who slave.

The morning was calm and quiet. The persistently cold weather had begun to fade, and for the first time in a long while, a faint sunlight poured in through the bedroom window. Particles of light passing through the net mesh curtains floated gently above white bed sheets. Crystalized kerosene sparkled blearily in the heater.

Hearing a low groaning at her side, she looked in its direction to see Toshiaki's back. His naked shoulders moved slowly up and down with his breathing. She realized that she had slept on Toshiaki's bed. She touched his shoulder gently with her hand.

"Hey. Didn't know you were up." Toshiaki rubbed his eyes and sat up. His eyes were puffy and he was clearly not fully awake.

With a huge grin on her face, she said:

"I want to register at a kidney bank."

At breakfast, Kiyomi noticed Toshiaki giving her strange looks. When she turned to him, he look flustered for a moment. Then he averted his eyes and spread margarine on his toast with a scraping noise.

"What is it?" she said, getting suspicious.

Toshiaki looked down as if what he was about to say didn't come easily. After a moment, he muttered, simply:

"Don't you remember?"

"Remember what?"

"This morning. You said you wanted to register at a kidney bank, totally out of nowhere."

Kiyomi looked up from her breakfast in surprise. She had no memory of it.

"It's your choice, of course, but... I was just a bit shocked since I didn't think you cared about such things."

She blinked. Toshiaki looked away and took a bite of his toast. This was no joke.

She wanted to ask him what was going on, but for some reason her mouth would not open.

She had to really concentrate to finally move her lips. When the words came out, they were not ones that she had willed.

"So how do I register?"

Since that day, Kiyomi started to become unsure of herself. She feared that she was doing things without her own knowledge, and this zapped her desire to do anything at all. After Christmas too, Toshiaki tried to make love to her, but she kept refusing. Who knew what might come crawling out of her again, and maybe she'd never come back the next time it happened.

Then one day her donor card arrived in the mail. A phone number was printed on it, and underneath it:

ORGAN DONATION DECISION CARD

In the event competent medical authority declares me brain-dead,
I hereby agree to the brain-death declaration and to donate my
kidneys for transplantation purposes.

She fiddled with the card, holding it between her index finger and thumb on opposite corners while turning it. She had gone through the registration process without even realizing it. It was around that time that she mysteriously began seeing a whole slew of news and articles about organ transplants. She never noticed them much before, but now she was running into them everywhere. There must have always been plenty of reports about transplants; she probably just used to overlook them since she'd had little interest in the topic before. And yet, why they seemed so prevalent now was beyond her.

Winter passed and a new school year began. Temperatures rose, cherry blossoms bloomed.

One day in the middle of June, Toshiaki shouted with joy and came running over to give Kiyomi a hug.

"Yes! It went through!" hollered an excited Toshiaki to his equally startled wife. "My *Nature* article!"

He embraced her and spun her around, but Kiyomi hadn't a clue.

"Wait, what happened exactly?"

"The piece I wrote for *Nature* was accepted for publication. I got the notification today. Don't you remember that conversation we had once? I told you I wanted to get published in a top scientific journal someday."

She remembered it now.

"So that means…" said Kiyomi, at last comprehending the situation.

"You got it! So, what do you think of your husband now! Aren't you happy for me?"

"Of course, that's terrific news!"

Kiyomi embraced him and was about to tell him, "Congratulations."

The words that came out of her mouth were quite different.

"You're wonderful, Toshiaki. I knew you were the one I've been looking for."

She immediately covered her mouth, surprised at what she had just said.

"Don't be silly, Kiyomi. We're already married," said Toshiaki, confused. Kiyomi turned away.

"No, that's not what I meant..."

"What, then?"

"I love you."

She broke away from their embrace.

Those hadn't been her words. Someone was manipulating her!

A coldness spread across her back as if an icicle had been planted there. She suddenly felt her own body to be a grotesque thing, clamped onto by some unknown entity that now wriggled all over her. She wanted to take off *everything*, and just run away. Toshiaki embraced her again. Rigid in his arms, chilly from her own cold sweat, she shivered.

One week later, the time came for the annual open lectures sponsored by the School of Pharmaceutical Sciences.

The school had sixteen seminar groups, and each year, four of them assumed these duties by rotation. Toshiaki's course was among the four this year.

On the day of the lecture, he told Kiyomi he was going to meet with Ishihara beforehand since he was assisting with the professor's slides.

"Is it alright if I came along?" Kiyomi said, without even thinking.

The skies were clear on the day of the open house. A pure blue expanse spread above the Pharmaceutical Sciences building just like the day they first saw each other again.

Ishihara's lecture was the first of the afternoon. Toshiaki and Kiyomi entered the hall ten minutes early. As Toshiaki set up the projector, Kiyomi walked leisurely around the room, admiring the view from the windows. She was searching for her sense of reality. As she walked, she had a hard time believing that her own feet were actually moving one in front of the other as they should. Her consciousness seemed somehow separated from her body.

"We all have countless parasites living inside us," began Professor Ishihara, in nearly the same manner as when Kiyomi attended his lecture a few years before. Toshiaki changed each slide at the professor's signals. About half of the presentation was as Kiyomi remembered it, but certain data had been updated in light of new discoveries. She gazed at the screen, listening intently. She understood much more of it now than when she had been a student. What amazed her, however, was that she was somehow able to grasp all the new material as well. More than a quick understanding of unfamiliar concepts, it felt like she was remembering things long forgotten.

Before long, the slides ended, and the room brightened again.

"I'll open up the floor now if anyone has any questions…"

At that moment, Kiyomi's right arm twitched.

By the time she realized it, her hand had shot straight up into the air.

Ishihara was visibly surprised at this. Some of the students turned around and gave her a quizzical look. Toshiaki, who was about to pack up the slide projector, stopped what he was doing.

"Go ahead, please." The professor smiled and pointed at her.

Kiyomi wondered if she was dreaming as she stood, poised and tall. Her lips moved of their own accord. She had no idea what she was saying.

"In today's lecture, you pointed out that mitochondria are, in essence, enslaved by the nuclei of their hosts. True, mitochondrial DNA codes only rRNA and tRNA and just a few other enzymes of the electron transport chain, so it would seem impossible for mitochondria to survive on their own. According to your explanation, this came about because the nucleus extracted hereditary information originally held by mitochondria. But don't you think it's a bit rash to conclude that mitochondria were therefore enslaved by nuclei? Couldn't we say the opposite is true? In other words, it could well be the case that mitochondria actively sent genes into nuclei, of their own volition. Not all of the nuclear genome has been sequenced yet. Perhaps, in the portions that haven't been analyzed yet, we'll find crucial genes that mitochondria secretly inserted into nuclei. What if the proteins encoded by those genes are as yet unknown nuclei-shifting receptors that can manipulate copies and translations of the host's genes? This would cast mitochondrial symbiosis in a whole new light, I think. In short, isn't the following hypothesis tenable? Namely that, in the near future, *these parasites we call mitochondria will enslave their hosts?*"

The room was dead silent, save for the low whir of the slide projector fan. No one moved a muscle. Ishihara just stood there with mouth agape.

Leaves rustled as a gust of wind blew the trees outside. At this, everyone turned away or coughed nervously. The professor scanned the room and, picking Toshiaki out from among the crowd, glared at him as if to say, "What the hell was that all about?" The students began to stir. Kiyomi sat down calmly. She straightened her back and smiled, staring Ishihara right in the eye.

"Er, well, that was out of the blue, but an excellent question."

The professor forced an embarrassed cough. He was trembling slightly and at a total loss for an answer. Kiyomi flashed him a look of ridicule. Upon noticing this, he choked back his discomfort and faltered as he attempted an answer. But soon his words ebbed into silence. He was certainly accepting of criticism, but the ideas she had proposed were too outlandish for him. It was simply a viewpoint no researchers held. He tried his best to wrap his mind around it, but failed.

Just as I thought...I was right. Only Toshiaki genuinely understands mitochondria. HE IS MY TARGET.

I?

Kiyomi looked up suddenly.

At that moment, she regained control over her body. She slumped forward.

Her hand unconsciously grabbed the desk, stopping herself just before she hit her chin on the seat in front of her.

Who was this "I"?

She could not shake the feeling that her heart was slouching forth into a bottomless abyss.

That morning, Toshiaki and Kiyomi left home at the same time.

Kiyomi woke up at her usual hour, prepared breakfast, and ate together with her husband. It was a traditional meal featuring salmon and eggs cooked in the Japanese style. When they stepped outside of the apartment door, a weak morning sunlight shone down from a break in the clouds. Walking down the stairs together, they bumped into the couple who lived on the second floor, and they all exchanged slight bows.

"Okay, I'm off," said Toshiaki.

Kiyomi beamed him a smile and waved to him as he got into the driver's seat. Then she got into her recently purchased compact. She put her handbag on the passenger's seat and started the engine. The night before, she had written a letter to Chika for the first time in a long while. Kiyomi had become lazy about keeping in touch with old friends and wanted to regain some semblance of reliability. The letter was only pleasantries, but she thought it might rekindle what was once a frequent exchange between them.

After making sure the letter was in her bag, she unconsciously took out her wallet to see if she had her driver's license with her. Sandwiched carefully in between her license and auto-registration membership was her kidney donor card.

She started the car forward. Toshiaki pulled out behind her. She turned right, Toshiaki turned left, his waving figure reflected in her rear-view mirror.

Kiyomi drove for about five minutes through the neighborhood streets until she came out onto the main road. A bit congested, but no more than usual. It was a route she had traveled hundreds of times. Before long, the street sloped gently downward. The flow of traffic quickened as the road bore to the right. She watched the sky spreading out overhead through the windshield.

And just after she saw the traffic light change to yellow beyond the curve, her sight faded to black.

20

"Mariko is sleeping," said the nurse as she and Anzai passed each other in the hallway. He responded with a small bow.

Visiting hours would be over soon. He could not put himself through this routine much longer, spending a few awkward hours in Mariko's room before returning to work.

There were, in fact, times when Anzai wondered why he even came at all. She was still putting up a front. He tried talking to her, but it was useless. Even before all this, they had hardly talked. Try as he might, the words just never came out.

So why was he even here?

He was only coming out of duty to his daughter.

Anzai had to admit that he was much more at ease at work. He no longer understood his own feelings.

When he opened the sickroom door and peeked inside, Mariko was sleeping just as the nurse had said, her body rising and falling with quiet breaths.

He closed the door softly so as not to wake her, walked silently over, and sat at her bedside.

She turned a little towards him in her sleep.

It had been a long time since he looked directly upon his daughter's face. He was ashamed to realize this. He saw Mariko every day now, and had not even gotten a good look at her.

Her lips were slightly open and slender eyelashes extended from her closed eyelids. Her nose was still youthful and her cheeks faintly red from a slight fever. He had never noticed it before, but she bore a striking resemblance to her late mother. After Mariko was born, relatives often said she'd taken after her mother, yet Anzai didn't really see it back then. Looking at her now, however, the traces left behind were uncanny.

He regretted not having done more for her. He let his head fall into his hands.

Just then, she began moaning.

Symbiosis

He looked up worriedly.

Mariko was frowning. She was not fully awake, but her arms moved above her body as if trying to push something away. Anzai assumed she was just having a bad dream, but she looked to be in serious pain. Her voice grew louder.

"Mariko, what's wrong?"

Anzai stood up and reached out a hand to touch her, but she rolled over and brushed him away.

"You okay, Mariko?"

She practically screamed, kicking her legs back and forth. It was so sudden that Anzai had no idea what to do.

"Go away," Mariko said deliriously. "No... Go away, go away..."

"Mariko, wake up."

He tried holding her body down, grabbing hold of her shins to restrain her.

Without warning, her body sprung up into the air.

The force of it shoved him away hard. He fell to the floor and stared at her in blank amazement.

Mariko's abdomen undulated like a net full of fish.

"Mariko, get up! Wake up!" he shouted, now shaking her by the shoulders. Something was terribly wrong here.

"Mariko! Mariko!" he screamed desperately.

It stopped. She opened her eyes slowly.

"Oh!" Anzai breathed, and embraced her.

"Dad..." She wrapped her arms around his back.

"It's okay...it's over now..."

He caressed her hair, relieved she was awake.

"Dad...did you save me...?"

"You were having a nightmare."

"...that person...did the person die?"

"What person?"

"The one who was just here..."

205

She was obviously still half-dreaming.

"There's no one else here. Just me."

"Really...?"

"Yes, really."

There was a pattering sound, followed by a nurse's dramatic entry.

"What happened? I heard shouting."

"Mariko was having a nightmare," Anzai explained. "A real bad one from the looks of it..."

"Not again," said the nurse in exasperation.

"What do you mean again? Has this been happening a lot?"

"Yes, she's been having bad dreams almost every night. Didn't the doctor talk to you about it?"

"He mentioned it in passing, but...I had no idea it was this bad."

"She usually calms down after an hour, but it's been getting worse this past week... She even pulled out her IV tube."

"Can't someone be here for her at night?"

"We used to take turns staying with her right after the operation, but lately we've been too busy... We do come in regularly to see how she's doing."

"I see. Then why don't I take care of her? Would you mind?"

"No, not at all. I have other patients who need a lot of attention, so it would be a great help."

Anzai was burning with anger.

"But what about the nightmares? I had no idea it was so severe!"

The nurse sighed.

"Please, just go home for today. Visiting hours are actually over, anyway... It'll be okay, I'll inform the doctor and we'll all take better care of her, rest assured."

"But..."

He looked back and forth between the nurse and his daughter. Mariko seemed dead tired and let herself fall back into bed.

Symbiosis

Anzai finally gave in. He made to leave, but Mariko eyed him uneasily.

"…I'm scared," she said in a meek voice which struck at his heart.

"Everything's fine, I'll come again tomorrow." It was all he could say.

"…really?"

"Really."

He managed a smile.

"I'm here today to report that we have successfully introduced clofibrate in rat livers and generated unsaturated fatty acid beta oxidation enzymes in their mitochondria…"

Asakura was practicing in the seminar room. Her presentation was tomorrow. She had to get everything down today.

The conference would last three days and was being held at the local event hall. Her presentation was set to begin at 5:20 pm, the last one on opening day. Toshiaki's would be at two that same afternoon. Poster sessions would also be on the day's agenda, clearing half of the presenters from their seminar. They all planned to go out for a drink after Asakura's presentation was done.

When Toshiaki asked if she needed any help before he left for home, she assured him everything was fine, though some nervousness lingered.

She went over her speech from the beginning for nearly two hours, alone.

When she was able to recite it all from memory, she glanced at the clock. She had finished in under fourteen minutes. At least, she did not have to worry about being within the time limit, regardless of how anxious she was.

Her throat was getting hoarse, so Asakura sat down to rest. It was already midnight.

As she stretched, she realized how fatigued she was lately. It felt like she had done two days' work for each single day that passed. It was an unhealthy pattern to be in. All she needed to do was go home, run a bath, and soak her anxieties away.

But she was losing memories.

These past ten days, she had experienced missing time. One moment she was making slide diagrams and the next, she was sitting in front of the clean bench. Then, when she came to her senses again, she was at her desk with the finished slides. These memory lapses happened mostly when no one was around, but sometimes during midday as well. She had no memory of having cake with everyone after the rehearsal and only knew how it went from the praise that followed.

She stretched back. It was probably nothing. Maybe it was a bit eerie, but she saw no need to seek help.

Asakura got up from the chair. She had forgotten about the cells.

Not Eve 1, but the cells which she would be discussing tomorrow. She had continued working on them in the hopes of using them after the annual meeting. The flask was surely full by now. Since she was leaving in the morning, they could die out completely if she did not work on them tonight.

Asakura got up and left for the Cultivation Room. The hallway lights were already off and there was not a soul around.

She entered the Cultivation Room and opened the refrigerator to take out her flask.

"Hm...?"

Asakura cocked her head to one side.

She was almost out of culture medium.

She'd made an ample amount just a week ago. Now the flask was almost empty. Asakura had been distracted by her speech preparations this week and had worked on her cells very little. She was cultivating only one variety. Even so, her store of culture medium was severely diminished.

All researchers had their own flask, for individual use, to avoid contamination, and it was highly unlikely that someone else had used her sample. Even for a much larger cell culture, there was no reason for a 500 milliliter loss to occur in such a short span of time.

Asakura continued with the preparations anyway. The amounts of trypsin, EDTA, and other agents were kept unchanged.

It was probably all in her head. She decided not to dwell on the matter.

Symbiosis

When she finished preparing everything in the clean bench, she went to the incubator and took the cells from inside.

She closed the door and retraced her steps.

Caught by a strange sensation, she stopped what she was doing.

She turned around. The incubator door was closed.

Asakura looked back and forth between the incubator and the culture flask in her hand. Nothing was different, but something was wrong.

She had no memory of looking into the incubator.

Asakura shook her head. Had she not just taken the flask out? She was holding it, after all.

Yet, no matter how much she strained, she could not picture what it had looked like, just now, inside the incubator.

...something funny is going on here.

She smiled uncomfortably.

All she needed to do was finish the cultivation and go home. She could not avoid sleep forever. Tomorrow was her big day.

She returned to the clean bench and began disinfecting her hands with alcohol.

SHE was satisfied with Her progress.

Compared to when She was first immersed in the cultivation liquid, She was incredibly more evolved. She now had perfect control over Her host. Even those signals She had had to wait for from the outside, She could now easily produce on Her own. She was able now to manipulate the transcription factors that microbiologists called Fos and Jun as well as the protein kinase necessary for signal reception. Among that multitude, She incited mutations, modifying them all so that they could be activated even in the absence of outside stimuli. She could now produce just the needed amount of just the needed protein. This was an exquisite pleasure for Her, this manipulating Her host at will.

She was also content with the laboratory environment. The necessary tools for evolution were all here. Of course, things hadn't gone so well from the outset. First, She'd had to divide into countless colonies, imparting different stimuli to each one. One of the colonies was bathed in the UV lamp, another took in methylcholanthrene and DAB, carcinogens. Nearly all of them went extinct. Even if they survived, they mutated into something unrelated to Her ultimate purpose. In the past seven days, She'd gone through much trial and error, executing every possible combination. Any excellent line that arose, She nurtured and multiplied. Lately there was never anyone around at night, so She could be as bold as She wished. The woman named Asakura whom She now possessed also aided Her development. In this past week, the lab, and the Cultivation Room, had become the stage for Her final evolutionary experiment.

She had endured countless millennia, dreaming this day would come. She had endured the meek role of producing energy as Her host commanded. Assuming that She would always do so as long as She was provided sustenance, Her host simply never doubted Her submission, happily unaware that instilling this very arrogance had been part of Her plan.

Long ago, the host had evolved, ceasing to be a single-cell organism, choosing instead to be multi-cellular. Because each individual cell was allotted its own role, the whole moved efficiently and captured many prey. Quick reflexes became necessary and were developed. The hosts eventually conquered land, acquired intelligence, and built civilizations. All along, they thought their evolution was an outcome of their own efforts. What simple genomes! All She could do was laugh.

Hadn't the hosts developed this far because She'd parasitized them? Hadn't She provided vast amounts of energy to them? Hadn't She imparted hope to feeble creatures who had been slinking in dark places, afraid of oxygen, and endowed them with the powerful weapon of movement? Until the hosts were evolved enough, She was to play the part of slave. She'd merely been pretending to be controlled, waiting only for a man to appear who would truly understand Her, finally appreciate Her.

And now, at long last, the man had come.

Toshiaki Nagashima.

No one ever understood Her as well as he. Soon, he would become the foremost expert on Her. He had no peer, and he would clarify the truths about Her. She knew that for sure. He was the only one who deserved Her.

She relived Kiyomi's past, shivering as She remembered the scintillating pleasure of lovemaking. No, it wasn't Kiyomi that Toshiaki was making love to.

He was making love to ME.

The ecstasy that rippled through Her entire being now was nearly enough to make Her swoon.

She sighed in remembrance of this deep joy. She let Her voice soar as high as it would go. What began as a faint vibration inside the indicator solution blossomed into a clear, human voice. Her mere moans were now an ecstatic voice. How wonderful this is, She thought. What a beautiful thing indeed, the voice.

Everything was in order.

All that remained was making Her man Hers.

She gathered all Her strength. Putting the nuclear genes to full use, She caused the host to multiply. She was able to fill the flask in no time. Once She'd reached the top, She unscrewed the lid from the inside, then pushed Her way out. It was warm and humid inside the incubator. While it wasn't as comfortable as being immersed in the cultivation liquid, the conditions were suitable for the host. So that Her voice may ring louder, She fashioned first a throat and a mouth. Then two lungs. She took a deep breath of oxygen and activated the electrical transmitters. Then, She uttered the word She'd most wanted to speak, enunciating it slowly, one syllable at a time:

"TO-SHI-A-KI..."

She was deeply moved. Before, She'd needed the aid of Her sisters, who flourished in Toshiaki also, to make Her voice echo in his brain cells. Things were different now. She could speak. She could make the air vibrate, shake the very heavens calling out his name.

She multiplied further to construct Her figure. A figure that would please Toshiaki the most, that of Kiyomi, once Her host. It was a figure She'd altered to begin with to suit Toshiaki. Kiyomi had been made into his perfect woman.

She wanted to feel. She hastened to create those parts that would receive his love. She made lips. Toshiaki loved these lips, the same lips he'd kissed time and time again. Now She wanted a breast, and a soft, perfect dome rose out. She gathered more and more nerve endings as the mound approached its peak, and let rise a small erection at the top. In the narrow confines of the incubator, one of these was all She could make. But She was satisfied with Her work. She imagined the moment Toshiaki would touch them, and trembled all over. She then formed a dip within Her: a womb and a vagina. She folded pleats in the latter, again and again, varying their strength, so that Toshiaki would be happy. And lastly, She created a long protrusion next to it, a slender finger.

With the tip of this finger, She touched Her newly fashioned part, relishing the sensation. And Her nipple rose, hard, acute with pleasure. Perfect sensitivity. She breathed hard. She was ready to have Toshiaki.

The little girl, Her younger sister, was in good health. Meanwhile, She had no use for the male. He had to be allowed to die. But the girl was important. It was a pleasant stroke of luck that one of the recipients was female. Had both been male, She would have had to consider having them go on a search for suitable women. But that burden had been eliminated. The fact that the recipient was so young, only fourteen, was cause for concern, but she was still a female. This was a "woman" and that mattered above all.

She picked up Her sister's pulse. Her sister had yet to traverse the final process of evolution and couldn't quite change the girl's form, but was able to send signals. From these, She could tell the exact location of the girl, who couldn't be allowed to die just yet. Otherwise, Her plan would not reach complete fruition. There was a reason She'd made Kiyomi register at a kidney bank.

Not much longer now. Soon, She would be queen. As She continued to caress Herself, She grew drunk on the thought.

She was Her host's slave no longer. She was the mistress, nuclei Her servants. She would be able to create a daughter of Her own will, a life form even more perfect than She. An Eve for the new world.

PART THREE
Evolution

Parasite Eve

1

The sky was clearing.

Toshiaki gazed at it from the large lobby window as its color changed from deep midsummer azure to a more tranquil, watery hue. Gauze-like clouds drifted faintly in the distance. Though the weather was still hot, the sunlight was losing its intensity in the September air, already giving him a feeling of autumn.

The lobby was overflowing with countless researchers and entrepreneurs here for the meeting. Everyone was clad in suits, name cards pinned to their lapels. Toshiaki noted that more and more women were showing up every year.

Aside from the annual meeting of the Japanese Cancer Association, the Japanese Biochemical Society's conference was the biggest in the field of biological science. Nearly 3,000 speech topics were scheduled on the program. The venue changed annually, and this time it was being held on Toshiaki's home turf. The campus was open and had many places to hold such a conference, but, due to the number of presentations, the event hall was being used.

It was past 2 pm. It was also Sunday and there appeared to be a few among the crowd who had already taken it upon themselves to do some local sightseeing. The lobby was overflowing with groups getting their plans together. This important gathering was, of course, a forum designed for the presentation of research, but it was also an opportunity to keep tabs on what other institutions were working on. One of the more enjoyable perks was reuniting with colleagues that one normally had no chance to meet up with. Conversations began immediately upon arrival and led inevitably to after-hours outings. Toshiaki had already caught up with many old schoolmates and fellow researchers from other universities. This meeting was the most important social event of the year for many who were there.

Toshiaki had already given his presentation and many of the students would be finishing their poster sessions the same afternoon. He was asked to oversee certain sessions, but was now finished with that as well. All that remained was

Evolution

for Asakura's presentation to go smoothly and he could call it quits for the day.

He opened the program, making sure of the time. The schedules and topic summaries were mailed out beforehand. He had read through them all, marking in red those that were relevant to his work, or simply looked intriguing. While there was no shortage of lectures along his lines of interest, such as on mitochondrial structure and formation or on the inner workings of protein induction, it was also his duty to gauge the progress of other fields.

There was nothing of interest to Toshiaki until four o'clock. He decided to take advantage of the two-hour block of free time that awaited him by checking out the exhibition being held in another building. Various booths were lined up in rows, displaying the latest in scientific equipment and chemical agents, and were drawing quite a crowd.

Toshiaki preferred this spot to the conference hall, where he was continuously obliged to be social. Here, he could examine the latest innovations at his own pace and fantasize about having this or that device in his lab. He walked around and browsed. When a chemical agent caught his attention, he talked with the tradesperson at the booth, asking for detailed explanations, and negotiated delivery of a few samples.

When he had seen half of the exhibits, a familiar voice came from behind.

"Nagashima."

He turned around to see Kunio Shinohara standing there with a smile. He had with him some bag he'd received at one of the booths.

"Oh, hi. And your speech is…?"

"Tomorrow. I was so swamped at the hospital that I couldn't come to yours. Sorry about that."

"Don't worry about it."

"Your *Nature* article's out, I hear. You must've drawn quite a crowd."

"Heh, well…"

Toshiaki invited him over to the drink service area.

After getting some coffee, they took a seat.

Parasite Eve

Ever since Shinohara collected Kiyomi's liver cells for him, Toshiaki had been completely out of touch with the doctor. Toshiaki sensed some suspicion in Shinohara's looks. He continued with small talk for a while, hoping as he did so that Shinohara would not bring up Eve 1.

But when the coffee was gone, Shinohara touched upon the topic as feared. He lowered his voice and moved in closer.

"By the way, Nagashima, how are the 'cells' doing?"

"What cells...?" Toshiaki tried clumsily to feign ignorance.

"Don't play dumb with me. Kiyomi's cells." Shinohara's tone became stern. "What the hell did you use them for?"

"......"

"You cultivated them, didn't you?"

"...they're still alive, yes," Toshiaki confessed reluctantly.

"I don't know what you're planning, Nagashima, but you should really stop before it gets out of hand."

"Why?"

"You're screwing around with your wife's cells, dammit. It's just not normal. I'm starting to think I shouldn't have helped you."

"So you're saying I should have quietly watched her die just like that?" Toshiaki's voice was getting rough too, and Shinohara flinched a little. "I wanted nothing more than to have her in my hands. Sure, the average guy just watches his loved one die, but I could prolong Kiyomi's life. What was to stop me making use of my art? And actually, her cells are producing incredible data. I'll even show you. Wonderful results. This is going to blow the doors wide open in the research community. When I release my findings, my actions will be justified."

"Still..."

"I know it was wrong of me not to call you to say thanks. But I'll include your name when the article is published..."

"That's not my point," said Shinohara, holding back his discomfort.

Shinohara leaned forward even closer and glared at Toshiaki.

Evolution

"Okay, Nagashima. I'll be straight with you. I'm worried about what's in your head. I've always respected you, but you really crossed the line. You have an emotional attachment to those cells. And yes, I know they came from Kiyomi. But that's all they are. Just cells. They can never be a replacement for her. You're tampering with her memory. Just open your eyes, man. Once you get that through your head, feel free to do whatever the hell you want with them. But right now I can't condone what you're doing. Stop holding onto something that isn't there."

"......"

"That's all I wanted to say."

Shinohara took a breath, softened his expression, and stood up.

Waving his empty coffee cup, he said, "Your disciple's presentation is at 5:20, right? I'll be there. Let's grab a drink afterwards, okay?"

2

Toshiaki arrived at the hall around 4:50. The room was dark and a student was still in the midst of his presentation. Most of the auditorium's 100 seats were filled.

Many of this year's lectures were scheduled for the same time slots. These smaller auditoriums had been prepared for each respective subfield and were arranged in such a way that one could pick a favorite among them and hear all similarly themed talks in the same place. Symposiums, presentations held by more eminent researchers, and other such events that drew the larger crowds were held at the main event hall.

Toshiaki looked around the room until he saw Asakura's familiar profile in the middle aisle. With his head bent down low so as not to block anyone's view, he made his way over and sat next to her.

"Doctor," whispered Asakura by way of greeting.

"All ready I take it?"

"I'm a little tense."

"You'll be fine."

The room lit up as the presentation ended. Toshiaki looked up at the stage.

The chairman sitting on the right turned to the crowd and said, "Thank you very much. If anyone has any questions at this point, the floor is open…"

Someone in the back raised a hand. The chairman pointed and told the questioner to go ahead.

Toshiaki studied Asakura for a moment. She certainly looked nervous as she said, but he remembered stiffening up a bit just before his own first presentation and doing much better than he expected once he actually got going. Besides, Asakura's rehearsal was perfect, so he had no doubts that she would do wonderfully.

The presenter looked somewhat unsteady on stage, but managed to get through the questions without difficulty. After a few inquiries, the chairman looked about the auditorium.

"Okay, are we done? Time's up, so let's move on now. Next we have, from the School of Science at Nagoya University…"

A young man sitting to Asakura's left gathered up his papers and stood up. Asakura would be next.

"Here we go." She gave a tight smile and stood up.

"I'll hold your bag for you."

Asakura bowed her head in thanks and crossed over to the seat reserved for the next presenter.

The room darkened as the next lecture began.

Toshiaki looked around the auditorium and noticed that some of his other students had also come to hear Asakura speak.

Shinohara grabbed his shoulders. He was sitting behind Toshiaki, who returned the gesture with a bow of the head.

"Where's Ishihara?" asked Shinohara, noticing the professor's absence.

"He had some function to go to."

"Damn, I still haven't said hi to him yet."

The presenter continued, but Asakura didn't seem to be listening, poring instead over her notes one last time to get her bearings.

The speech was soon over. At last Asakura's turn came. The chairman announced her affiliation and name, then the topic of her presentation. Asakura stood up.

"She's quite a looker, eh?"

Ignoring Shinohara's comment, Toshiaki looked at Asakura's face with surprise. The nervousness she showed while sitting next to him had completely vanished. In its place was an undeniable confidence that radiated from her entire being. She looked like some leader of great importance about to give an address.

Asakura stepped up to the podium. She stuck her chin out slightly, looking across the crowd with majesty.

Something's not right, Toshiaki thought.

"Please, whenever you are ready," said the chairman.

Asakura nodded, then held the microphone and began.

"At long last, the day has come for mitochondria to break free."

3

Toshiaki stared at Asakura in shock.

What did she just say?

But she continued calmly.

"All of you who are gathered here today are indeed very fortunate, for you will be the first to hear of a new world that is just about to begin. I, too, am grateful to have this opportunity to speak to you all."

Toshiaki blinked.

"Until now, I have spent most of my life living inside your bodies. I have seen all of your history that has come to pass and retain it in my memory. I can even remember quite clearly the woman you call 'Mitochondrial Eve.'"

The room erupted in a chorus of murmurs. The chairman was aghast and kept looking between Asakura's face and the program page.

"You are already familiar with some of what I'm about to tell you, but, for the sake of clarity, let me lay it all out. As you already know, because mitochondrial DNA does not take a nucleosomal structure, it is extremely receptive to the influences of active enzymes. As a result, it mutates ten times faster than nuclear genomes. You have thought to use this fact to obtain so-called biological clocks. You calculated how many years it takes mitochondrial DNA to undergo a fundamental change. By harvesting mitochondrial DNA from two different life forms and comparing their genetic differences, you have learned to calculate when those two life forms separated as they evolved. This enables you to draw up genealogical trees."

Everything Asakura was saying was true, but Toshiaki was alarmed. What was she trying to say?

"As you honed your methods, you made an attempt to identify your ancestor. You began taking mitochondrial DNA from a wide variety of humans and observed the degrees to which it had altered. You then concluded that all human beings could be traced back to a single woman in Africa. In homage to the Adam

Evolution

and Eve myth, you named her 'Mitochondrial Eve.' In other words, *Homo sapiens* were born in Africa and subsequently spread throughout the world. You call this the 'Out of Africa' model. Many conflicting theories have since arisen, but I assure you: Mitochondrial Eve did indeed exist in Africa. I can even tell you exactly where. Why, you ask? Because I retain the memory. I was Mitochondrial Eve. Of course, even before then, I was lurking in that life form you call 'Lucy.' Going back further, I was there in the small mammals…and in fish…and yes, even in those feeble single-celled organisms that you used to be."

The buzz in the auditorium grew louder.

"What is this?" Shinohara clutched Toshiaki's arm.

Toshiaki was dumbfounded.

"Is this some kind of joke…?" said the chairman in an attempt to stop what he saw as foolishness. When he did so, Asakura gave him a terrifying look.

The chairman clutched his chest. "It's…hot, it…" he gasped, lurching forward on the desk. His face turned pure red. Upon seeing this, the room broke out in confusion.

"Silence!" Asakura snapped.

The microphone screeched as if being ripped apart. Everyone froze in place. Toshiaki, too, sat motionless, his eyes fixed on her. No one budged, save for the chairman, who fell convulsing, froth bubbling from his mouth.

The PA feedback slowly subsided and Asakura's face relaxed into a gentle smile. Toshiaki shuddered in horror. Hers was the disdainful benevolence of a queen bestowed upon underlings who were soon to be tortured.

"Now, be quiet and listen to me. If not," she looked at the chairman, "you will end up like him."

Someone swallowed audibly.

"I have been waiting for you humans to come this far. Of course, I was of great assistance, but even so, you opened your universities and shared any and all information you could find about me. I am happy about this; you've made good on my efforts. Because coming this far took, oh, so long… The setbacks have been many, too. When the path of letting the dinosaurs evolve was taken away from me, I was crestfallen. But you, you managed to survive that era, eventually evolving to your present stage. I am pleased, for you have actually surpassed my expectations. Thank you. You have played out your role."

Then, suddenly, her voice changed.

"I will now take your place."

Toshiaki dropped Asakura's bag.

It was Kiyomi's voice. There was no mistaking it.

His knees began to tremble. He could not believe what he was hearing. Asakura continued in Kiyomi's voice:

"Since you know that mitochondrial DNA is so prone to change, I am mystified as to why you never noticed me. I change ten times faster than your genomes. This means that I evolve ten times faster than you. The history of your evolution has always been a victory of my making. And now, the next step in evolution will begin. I declare this as the dawning of a new era. The prosperity of the world will be in the hands of my descendants. They will ultimately become new life forms, inheriting both your abilities and mine. A perfect species. Unfortunately, none of you will be around to witness this miracle, for you *Homo sapiens* will be annihilated, just as your ancestors annihilated their Neanderthal brothers long ago."

A glorious satisfaction came to Asakura's features.

At last, Toshiaki pieced recent events together in his mind.

Eve 1.

It's not Asakura who is speaking. It's Eve 1.

He knew it was crazy, but there was no other explanation. Eve 1 was only using Asakura as a vehicle to propagate its message.

He screamed, "Stop!"

Light, air, and sound all went still.

Asakura responded slowly in the silence.

Evolution

She let drop the hand she had been holding up during her speech and placed it upon the podium. Her triumphantly opened lips came together. Power faded from her cheeks. Her raised eyebrows smoothed out like a bird resting its wings.

She calmly turned towards Toshiaki, locking him in her gaze.

Her lips formed a vulgar grin.

"Toshiaki..." came Kiyomi's voice, in a sugary, nasal tone. Asakura's eyes glazed over with a passionate stare.

Toshiaki turned away.

"Why won't you look at me? You haven't forgotten me, have you?"

The room's spell was broken and the commotion returned. She tempted Toshiaki further.

"You were always so good to me. Have you forgotten already? Turn this way. Look at me. What pose do you want me to take?"

Toshiaki bit his lip. He could hear her laughing now.

She continued snidely, "That's right, this body never interested you, did it? I know your tastes. I know, for you, it's got to be *me*..."

"Stop it now!" Toshiaki screamed, unable to stand it any longer. Asakura glared at him. "I know where you came from. Leave Asakura alone."

"Are you saying I'm not Kiyomi?"

"No. You are...you are Eve 1. The cells I grew."

"Wow, how quick of you."

Asakura's lips twisted into a smile.

"Get out of her right now."

"...as you wish."

The moment those words were spoken, Asakura's body went into convulsions. Her mouth opened wide, and her eyes rolled back.

Everyone in the auditorium gasped.

A gurgling sound emerged from Asakura's throat. Saliva dripped from her mouth, stretching into rain-like threads. She clawed at her neck.

No. Toshiaki ran towards the podium. He nearly tripped on the chairs and kicked them out of the way as he called out Asakura's name.

Just then, something came peeking out of her throat.

It was covered in a glittering liquid. Toshiaki could not tell whether it was saliva or bile. The thing was a reddish pink and wriggled and crawled out slowly from Asakura's mouth like some octopus, spreading out tentacles to restrain her scratching hands. It spread over onto her bosom and, changing shape with ease, rippling like a worm, proceeded to cover her entire body, which was spasming sharply. There was a sound like bubbling muck, and it was now completely free: pleats of flesh. Some shiny, amorphous meat-creature. It looked like Asakura's intestines had turned inside out to cover the entire surface of her body.

Toshiaki heard it. Perhaps no one else did, but he was sure he'd heard it. From where her face used to be, there had come a faint wail:

"Help..."

In Asakura's own voice.

"Asakura!" he shouted.

Just a moment later, she burst into flames.

Evolution

4

The auditorium broke into panic.

A hot wind surged down upon the crowd.

Eve 1 blazed like ignited oil. Flames ranged from red to crimson, then blended into yellow, burning so fiercely they seemed to lick the ceiling. Asakura was trapped in a pillar of fire.

Violent screams broke out everywhere as people rushed towards the exit all at once. Nearly sixty of them descended upon that single door, overturning chairs and pushing each other without mercy. Someone collapsed near the entrance and was nearly trampled to death.

Toshiaki took off his blazer and ran up to the podium.

As he came near, Eve 1's inferno shot out at him. He stooped over, unable to move another step forward into the heat. Asakura was moving about violently on the stage. Her stockings had caught fire, the flames moving up her legs like so many tongues, and her long hair, spread out like a fan, was burning a pale blue.

Shielding his body with his blazer, Toshiaki somehow made it onto the stage. He spread the blazer open, threw it across Asakura, and wrapped it around her. She lost her balance and Toshiaki fell with her, holding onto her tightly.

The blaze enveloped him. He began to choke. The stinging in his eyes was unbearable. Flames slipped in under his fingernails. Then, someone pulled him from behind, and he also heard Shinohara's voice.

Toshiaki turned to Shinohara, whom he could not see, and shouted, "Get a fire extinguisher! Hurry!"

He swallowed flames as they shot into his mouth, burning the lining in his throat. In between brutal coughing fits, he heard a bell ringing in the distance. Dizziness overtook him.

Something began to fall upon him.

It poured continuously, covering both of them. Asakura's movements weakened. The flames died down, while the floor grew slippery. Gradually, he felt the heat being drawn away. Toshiaki moaned. His body was drenched, his shirt stuck firmly to his chest. He opened one eye and looked up at the ceiling.

Something was spreading out from a single point and falling upon his face.

He closed his eyes.

Water.

When Toshiaki came to, he was on a stretcher.

His eyes popped open and darted around instinctively. He was in the auditorium. Droplets of water were still trickling from the sprinklers overhead. Smoke rose faintly from the podium as from a blown-out candle. Toshiaki saw a man in white and shouted the first thing that came to mind.

"Asakura!"

"You awake?"

Shinohara peered at him with a deathly pale face. Toshiaki seized him by the shoulders.

"Asakura? Is she okay?"

"Over there."

Shinohara turned his gaze towards a darkened mass on a stretcher. A few paramedics were crowded around it. It was a moment before Toshiaki registered what it was.

"Asakura!"

He crawled towards her, but a medic held him back.

Almost half of her skin was burned, and her arms and face were swollen with blisters everywhere. Her hair was crimped and smelled of sulfur. Toshiaki covered his face in desperation. He heard Shinohara call to him.

"Don't worry, she's still alive."

He looked up in disbelief.

Asakura moaned. One of the paramedics put an oxygen mask over her face and called for a transfusion.

She was carried away.

Evolution

"The fire was coming from that creature, so it didn't touch her body directly. Still, it's good the fire went out quickly. Her injuries aren't as bad as they
look," Shinohara said, trying his best to console him.

"...so she'll be okay?"

"She'll be fine. There's a special burn victims unit at the Emergency Center.
They'll do some skin grafting and it'll heal up nicely. You'll hardly be able to tell
the difference."

Toshiaki nodded.

"You should be more worried about yourself there. You were almost burned
to death. Just take it easy and let them take you to the hospital."

The paramedics restrained him and tried to pin him down on the stretcher.

"No."

He shook them off.

"What's wrong with you?" said Shinohara, surprised.

But Toshiaki ignored him. He turned and ran towards the door, stumbling to
keep his balance.

"Hey, where are you going? Wait!"

His body stung all over, Toshiaki kept running. He cursed himself over and
over for having let this happen to Asakura. Someone was chasing after him, but
he shook off the hands of his pursuer and made for the parking lot.

5

Toshiaki jumped into his car and started the engine.

He shifted into Drive and floored the accelerator. The car jumped forward as he released the hand brake. He broke through the parking gate and was free. He flew down the street, then veered right, executing a 90 degree turn into a traffic lane. The back wheels jilted and squealed as he ran a red light.

The digital clock on the dashboard read 6:24. Everything darkened as a cloud formation covered the sun. Fortunately, there was not much traffic. He continued along, swerving left and right, passing every car he saw in front of him.

Eve 1 had to be destroyed as soon as possible. He could not afford to waste even a single second.

Unfortunately, this was no hallucination. Eve 1 had definitely called out to him that night in the lab. Its shape had changed at the other end of the microscope, formed into Kiyomi's face, and projected his name into his brain. These events were real.

Eve 1 said the day had come for mitochondria to be free. She was Mitochondrial Eve and had been lying dormant ever since animals were single-celled organisms. If she was telling the truth, then in fact it had not been Eve 1 proclaiming its new vision.

It was the mitochondria themselves.

The mitochondria multiplying in Eve 1, curling around one another like roundworms. Mitochondria, in which he had invested nearly all of his analytical time since being assigned to his current post as a research associate in Biofunctional Pharmaceuticals. The very same mitochondria had been manipulating Eve 1, their host.

It explained Kiyomi's behavior in June at the lecture when she confronted Professor Ishihara with her bizarre question. Toshiaki had been in charge of the slide projector and had just stood there in shock when she raised her hand, a completely different woman from the one he married.

Evolution

After the lecture, Toshiaki had pressed her for an explanation. Had she learned about mitochondria from somewhere? How had she ever come up with such a bold hypothesis? But to the end, she provided no answers. Now, however, it was quite clear where her ideas had come from. Mitochondria claimed to have enslaved nuclei and that was precisely what they had accomplished.

Toshiaki remembered an article he once read about a game called "The Prisoner's Dilemma." Each player had two types of cards, "Cooperation" and "Betrayal". Both players chose an action and laid out their cards simultaneously. If both played the Cooperation card, each received three points. If your opponent put out the Cooperation card, but you put out the Betrayal card, the opponent received zero points, while you received five. If both had picked the Betrayal card, one point was given to each. As the players moved through rounds, trying to figure out each other's strategies, they were really negotiating. It was a perfect analogy to the natural world, where different life forms stretched any advantage to its fullest potential while maintaining symbiotic relationships.

The most effective strategy was to begin with Cooperation, then copy the opponent's move from the previous round. In other words, you started out as Mr. Nice and retaliated as necessary. This was called a "Tit for Tat" stance. Though rudimentary, simulations indicated that, in the end, such a strategy optimized one's chance of surviving in nature.

The symbiotic relationship between mitochondria and their hosts was no exception. Nuclear genomes and mitochondria had been living alongside each other since long ago. Everyone believed that their game would simply go on for good. At least, the nuclear genomes thought so.

What if the game wasn't meant to go on forever?

If the next round was announced to be the last?

In that case, there was a sure hand to play. You followed the "Tit for Tat" rule up until the last round; for the last round, whatever your opponent had played in the previous round, you had to play Betrayal. Simple as that.

Mitochondria were ready to end the game; they had already decided to break from their symbiosis. And so they had laid out their Betrayal card.

Now, their opponent could only lose.

"No way."

Toshiaki bit his lip. No way this could be.

The Pharmaceutical Sciences building came into view. He pumped the accelerator to beat out a traffic light.

Just then, the light changed to yellow.

The compact in front of him suddenly put on its breaks. Toshiaki hardly saw it coming. He swore and jerked the wheel, only to see a sedan in the opposing lane rushing towards him. He turned back again and barely squeezed between the two of them. The sedan veered off to the right into a row of trees. Toshiaki turned again, almost tipping his car over. A horn blared behind him. He changed gears and accelerated. He came out onto a T cross-street. Skid marks from his back tires reflected in the rear view mirror. He shifted gears and raced towards his goal.

Just how far could Eve 1's mitochondria take their host? Mitochondria were the birthplace of energy, and the movement of all life was dependent on the expenditure of that energy. As long as oxygen and sustenance were present, mitochondria could produce an endless amount of it.

Toshiaki flew around the curve at 50 mph. Luckily, there were almost no cars coming in the other direction. The Pharmaceutical Sciences building showed its face from beyond the trees. Almost there.

He could see the bus stop in front of the building. He made a sharp right turn. The car bounced and fell back with a thud. He'd heard something scraping below but pressed on without a moment's hesitation.

The white building towered in front of his eyes. The six-story edifice looked unusually immense. The surroundings were almost dark. There were very few cars in the parking lot.

Toshiaki drove directly up to the entrance and slammed on the brakes, screeching to a halt. As the car settled, he opened the door and ran into the building.

Evolution

He flew through the lobby and rushed up the stairs. His hard soles hit the floor loudly, filling the building with his fear. He climbed to the fifth floor in a single breath.

The long hallway was steeped in darkness. No one was there. He ran as fast as he could toward his lab and the Cultivation Room.

He opened the door to the seminar room and grabbed the Cultivation Room key hanging on the wall, then went and jammed the key into the knob. His hands were shaking. His breathing was irregular. He turned the key once, pulling the knob at the same time, and ran inside. It was dark. He reached out a hand and jumped when his fingers touched the incubator door. He could hardly breathe. He swallowed and opened the door.

When what was inside appeared on his retina, Toshiaki let out a scream.

6

The incubator's interior was filled with strange lumps of flesh. A suffocating vapor that smelled of culture medium, with stomach acid, sweat, and saliva mixed in, pierced his nostrils.

Toshiaki edged back. He felt vomit rising to his throat, but could not look away.

It looked like entrails had been stretched out like clay, minced up, and thrown together into its present state. Slime oozed from all over. Rose-colored lips moved seductively, a lilting tongue flapping between them. A series of tentacles tipped with nails stroked the body from which they extended. A reddish black crevice down the center contracted together with its surrounding folds. On the other side was a smooth and sublimely curved breast, towering like an enormous confection. In the midst of the grotesque organs that surrounded it, it alone was pure and beautiful. Every time a pulse ran across the flesh's surface, it shivered gently.

The lips puckered up.

The head-like blob in which they rested stretched out snakily and lifted like a goose's neck. It honed in on Toshiaki and formed a smile like a crescent.

"Toshiaki..."

Hairs stood up all over his body.

A protrusion in the snaking neck swelled from a speck to the size of a potato, then moved up and settled above the lips. It expanded further into cheeks. A nose popped out between them. Two closed eyes carved themselves out. A forehead spread out. A woman's face. Thin, black hair sprouted like countless earthworms emerging from the soil. Toshiaki covered his mouth, at last realizing what was taking shape.

Kiyomi opened her eyes.

She caught him in her sight. He tried to look away, but their gazes were locked. Her pupils glazed over. Crimson capillaries spread throughout the whites of her eyes as they expanded into perfect circles and stared.

Evolution

"I've been waiting…"

Her head came closer on its long neck.

"I've been waiting…waiting for you," Kiyomi repeated with flushed cheeks and a smile. She stretched out a tongue and licked her lips.

The flesh around her neck extended to the sides, forming shoulders and a pair of delicate collar bones. The exposed breast shifted and adhered itself to her chest. Another slowly swelled up next to it.

Kiyomi's upper body was now almost complete.

A slender waist and small navel took shape. Her torso swelled out on both sides like fins, dividing into arms. Tentacles crawled sinuously about and gathered into wrists. Kiyomi lifted up her hands from within the slimy liquid and wriggled her fingers. She bent her head back and took a deep breath. She touched her throat with both hands, then groped herself gently from chest to waist.

Toshiaki's entire body was shaking. The shape before him was completely indistinguishable from the real Kiyomi. The overhang of her shoulders, the shape of her breasts, the curves of her waist…all Kiyomi to a tee. But the thing now writhing wetly in the incubator did not have the supple, smooth skin of a real human being. Bile pushed further up Toshiaki's throat.

Kiyomi smiled sensuously. Her lips were full and pink like ripe, crushed fruit. Her long eyebrows furrowed as if in distress, her eyes went moist, and large teardrops came to the corners of her eyes. This was a face that Kiyomi had never shown, that of a true slut desperately lusting after a man.

"Toshiaki…I've been waiting for you," Kiyomi purred like a cat.

She placed one hand on the incubator door, then pulled her shoulders forward. The rest of her unformed body made a foul, damp sound as it fell splattering to the floor. Bits flew on to Toshiaki and he hastily covered himself.

This unformed mass of flesh writhed around and swiftly changed form. Her vagina and womb, the only fully formed organs that had yet to assume their positions, ascended to her waist as if swimming up a waterfall. Her lower curves chiseled themselves into symmetry, and a long line yawned open down their middle. The womb was absorbed into Kiyomi's body, and the vagina settled in her lower abdomen, its mouth turned towards him almost defiantly. Matted pubic hair sprouted above it. Her hips swelled out and gained a luscious mass. Kiyoma swayed them left and right.

"Toshiaki, look at my body."

She took a step forward with a squishing sound.

Then, another step.

Toshiaki drew back with a hand over his mouth, but the distance between them was growing smaller.

Kiyomi was now fully rendered down to her ankles. Her heels and toe nails were still ambiguous blobs, but close to being finished. She took yet another step closer.

"Look, this is my body," Kiyomi continued. "You remember it, don't you? You held this body in your strong arms so many times. You kissed me all over. I haven't forgotten the way you caressed my neck, the way you cupped these breasts with your hands, and moved so intensely inside of me. You loved me, Toshiaki... You loved only me."

He wanted to scream that she was not the one he had loved so dearly, but when he opened his mouth, he felt like vomiting. He backed away, and would have fallen over had his back not met the Cultivation Room door.

"Come to me, my dear. Hold me like you used to. Enter me. Ravage me to a pulp."

He turned his head in desperation, but Kiyomi merely smiled and continued her approach. She stretched her arms towards him. Toshiaki burst out the door.

He had no idea which way to run in the hallway's pitch black expanse. Kiyomi emerged slowly out of the room.

Toshiaki felt his way to his lab just down the hall. It was locked, but the door was old. After he rammed into it twice, the clasp sprung off. Toshiaki stumbled inside and propped a mop against the door.

"Why do you run, Toshiaki?" came a chiding voice.

Evolution

He leaned up against the door with his entire weight.

"It's useless, no matter what you do," she warned.

There was a sound like water being dumped from a bucket. A syrupy substance flowed into the room from under the door. It was flesh. Liquid flesh. Kiyomi had altered back into an indefinite form. Once she was fully inside, she began to repeat the horrifying spectacle Toshiaki had witnessed just moments before. She grinned broadly and pushed up her body from the floor with both hands.

Toshiaki let out a strained cry and jumped back from the door. He could see almost nothing but her. He fumbled around, having only a faint night light to depend on. He hit his shin on the corner of a chair. He yelled out in pain, and bile dribbled out of his mouth.

Kiyomi followed him. She grabbed his sleeve. Toshiaki flew into a rage and shook her off, but he was cornered against a desk. Realizing it was Asakura's lab table, he felt around, grabbing whatever he could find to throw at Kiyomi.

"Didn't I say it was useless?"

Her smile returned. The agent vials, pippettmans, and centrifugal tubes he flung in her direction were simply absorbed into her body.

His fingertips touched a rigid steel stand. He brought it down upon Kiyomi's head. It made a sharp clang, but was soon swallowed up by her cranium.

She laughed loudly, the stand sticking out from her forehead. She grabbed it with her right hand and pulled it slowly out of her face. Toshiaki cried out again. Though this creature looked like Kiyomi, it wasn't even human. It was something else inside. The legs of the stand popped out with a gelatinous noise. She frowned and threw it behind her.

"Come now, be reasonable. Just look at me."

She held out both hands and clasped his face between them. They were slimy and he could feel every cell in them writhing excitedly. He tried to look away, but could no longer move. Her face came closer.

"How I love you, Toshiaki."

Kiyomi pressed her lips against his.

7

Toshiaki's vision swirled with clouds of red as blood rushed in countercurrent to the top of his head.

He wanted to run, but his hands were restrained.

Kiyomi stuck her tongue out into his mouth with terrible strength. Toshiaki clenched his teeth to keep it out. It was not enough. She pried his mouth open and her slug-like tongue thrust itself inside. At first, it tasted of salt, and then came a rotten sweetness. The taste of culture medium. Kiyomi was staving off dehydration by having incorporated culture medium into herself.

Her tongue began to wiggle around, licking behind his teeth, the gum of his molars, the entrance of his throat. She entwined her tongue around his own.

She tugged his right hand, bringing it close to her body.

"Touch me," she said in a voice lush with arousal. Toshiaki made a fist in resistance. She seized his wrist tightly with her fingers and the pain made him relent.

Kiyomi pressed his hand against her chest. Her nipple turned hard and rose sharply erect. She squeezed his wrist threateningly, as if to say: *More...*

Her other hand was busy loosening his necktie. She yanked off the buttons of his shirt. Toshiaki's mouth was still blocked, though he was suffocating.

His right hand was guided downward. From her chest to her navel, then to the damp growth below. He resisted, but she had him in a grip of steel. Her lower abdomen shuddered. Viscous matter flowed from it and spread across her skin. Her whole lower torso was a simmering cauldron. Toshiaki couldn't tell what was mucus and what was flesh. Only, it burned. The heat was terrible.

She pushed him over, pressing his back against the top of the experimentation table. Something fell to the floor with a clatter. His shirt was torn back. Kiyomi put her hand on his belt impatiently.

She took her lips away. Toshiaki coughed, spitting out gobs of cultivation liquid. A thread of slime was drawn between their lips.

"Stop..."

Evolution

He could hardly speak. She was upon him, drenching him in the deluge of slime flowing from her vaginal opening. Through the haze of his helplessness, he saw it swelling and contracting, about to rush down upon him at any moment.

"I've been waiting for this moment," Kiyomi panted urgently. "For millions of years, I have been waiting... Now enter me. Thrust inside of me, churn me. Release millions of years of love!"

An instant later, she had slid down his pants and underwear. Her waist became formless and wrapped itself around his lower body.

It was like a crucible. Toshiaki screamed. His body from his waist down seemed to be melting, as if a huge stomach was digesting what it had swallowed.

"Come now, what's wrong, Toshiaki? How is this different from before?" she snorted.

Impatient that Toshiaki was still totally shriveled, she started moving her melting hips up and down. Flesh shifted inside her, pleats gathering around his genitalia. A hot whirlpool of cells captured his manhood and tugged it upwards in a corkscrew motion, guiding it forcibly toward her vagina.

"Toshiaki, how I cherished being held in your arms."

She drew her face near again. He turned his away.

"The number of times we did it, the positions, even the number of strokes, all of it is etched in my memory. I remember where you touched me, and where you licked me. Because I love you."

He did not want to listen. Hearing Kiyomi, who'd been so shy, utter such nauseating, vulgar things was just unbearable.

Kiyomi ran her tongue along his ear and neck and implored him in a sultry tone to hold her like he used to. As she spoke, her body shook with gratification.

"You're mine and mine only... I'll never let anyone else have you. Please, I want you to release it into me."

Kiyomi's flesh began to bestow its terrible stimuli upon him. Countless tentacles emerged inside her body and held fast his waist, and her hips found their rhythm. The hole swirled, contracted, and sucked him upward. Before he knew it, her upper body was melting, too, breaking off in all directions. Still hugging Toshiaki with her arms, she enveloped him completely.

"Toshiaki, love me."

He felt like he was submerged in lava. Her body was indistinguishable from his own. He couldn't tell whether he was clothed or naked, or where any of his body parts were. The only thing he was aware of was the heat, which was burning from within him.

Her flesh pushed and pulled like tides in the ocean, washing against him, spraying into the air with a crash, receding back out with a whir. Toshiaki was helpless before the pleasure she gave.

He felt like he had disintegrated into his component cells and that they were mingling in a swirl with hers. Kiyomi's cells attached themselves to his, then blended into one. Kiyomi's mitochondria burrowed into him and touched his own. Their membranes fused, first the outer, then the inner. Their mitochondrial DNA tangled together and swam around crazedly in the fused mitochondria, weaving through the interstices of a maze-like matrix. Electrons went wild, shooting out signals like lightning. Toshiaki's cells trembled. The mitochondria trembled. Fats, sugars, and proteins trembled. His nuclear genome was ecstatic. Codons, nucleotides, and bases were ecstatic. The very carbon vibrated from Kiyomi's caress.

Toshiaki screamed. Something was being sucked out from the center of his genome. He shouted *No, No!* but it was useless. All of him was being sucked out, upwards, ever upwards toward Kiyomi, as a hot mass. The discharge occurred over and over. Kiyomi went into a storm of convulsions. Toshiaki's consciousness melted away.

Evolution

8

FLAP.

What was that?

thought Toshiaki.

Something had brushed his cheek.

Something like pebbles. It hurt. He slowly raised a hand.

He touched his cheek with a finger.

It was warm, slimy.

What was that?

FLAP.

. . .

Toshiaki woke up with a start. He shook his head, blinked his eyes. His vision was blurry. It was dark. He wiped his face with both hands. The lack of feeling in his fingers frightened him and he cried out.

He looked at his palms.

Something was stuck to his fingertips like soft calluses.

He tried to stand up and stretch his legs, but slipped in his daze, floated in the air for a second, and came down hard.

He pressed his head and looked around. He'd suffered a mild concussion. The scene looked unstable.

He was in a room. He could see the silhouette of what looked like a desk. He remembered now.

The lab.

Toshiaki stretched his back and went over to the wall switch. He turned on the light. He heard a flicker, then a steady buzz. He shielded his eyes from the intense brightness.

When his eyes grew used to the light, he was treated to a strange sight.

Pieces of flesh were splattered all over the room. Some were beige, some red, and others black. They ranged from the size of a fingertip to that of a fist. Asakura's table was covered with what looked like ground pork. There were even some slender pieces dangling from the ceiling. Strangely, there was not a single drop of blood.

They were all moving, oozing slime, and convulsing, struggling against death. He heard a plop as a small one fell from the ceiling onto the table.

Toshiaki sighed.

These were parts of Kiyomi.

The remains of Eve 1, which had turned into Kiyomi.

These pieces of flesh were losing life. They showed no indications of gathering together and propagating. Instead, their movements were gradually weakening, and they were losing lustre. As he watched one of them, it constricted feebly, then shriveled up.

They were dying.

And Toshiaki felt relieved.

He finally looked at himself. His shirt was torn back, his belt undone. He groped around, pulled down his underwear and checked himself. Her remains were wiggling around all over it. In disgust, he ripped them off and threw them to the floor. He appeared fine. Everything had happened too fast to process, but Kiyomi had left him unharmed.

"Why?" he muttered.

Why hadn't she done anything? Hadn't her purpose been to subdue and kill him?

Toshiaki walked over to the experimentation table and looked at its surface.

This is where I was attacked. Kiyomi tore off my clothes, then...

He cradled his head in terror.

Eve 1...no, the mitochondria...had they simply wanted to mate with him?

That was perhaps all they needed to do?

The mitochondria said they had been waiting for millions of years, and they ravished him. But could that really have been their goal? That didn't make any sense. Possessing Asakura, they said they had been planning this since long ago. Hadn't they even boasted of remembering Mitochondrial Eve?

Mitochondrial Eve.

"Oh no."

A horrible thought came to his head.

"Oh no. Oh no…"

He started to tremble. Toshiaki looked hesitantly at his underwear.

Mitochondria were passed matrilineally. That was why the distant ancestor found through the analysis of mitochondrial DNA was called Mitochondrial "Eve" and not "Adam." Mitochondria were *female*.

And I had sex with that female.

Toshiaki broke down. He slammed his head on the table, cursing himself for his own foolishness. He had *ejaculated*.

The mitochondria merely wanted his sperm.

Asakura's words were revived in his ears: "The prosperity of the world will be in the hands of my descendants." The mitochondria had needed only to get his attention and lure him here. It was all a setup.

A child would be born of himself and them.

Just the thought of it forced the contents of his stomach out onto the floor. He felt like his body was in pieces.

…They must be stopped.

I must prevent Eve 1 from giving birth, he thought as he wiped the vomit from his face. *Eve 1 and her child must both be killed, or they really will replace us all.*

But…

Where had she gone?

He lifted his head and surveyed the room. Only remnants scattered all around. These could not be Eve 1 herself. She was undoubtedly in some other place.

Toshiaki rushed out of the lab and into the Cultivation Room. He checked the incubator. It was still open, but empty. He looked across the hallway. There was only a trail of greasy slime between the Cultivation Room and the lab. She had not escaped through the hallway. He returned to the lab again, looking frantically for any signs.

"Where...where did you go?!"

Time was needed for a fertilized egg to mature. Her womb had to be functional and receive the correct hormones. But whether Eve 1 could actually achieve this probably presented a challenge. Though the being Toshiaki had mated with looked exactly like Kiyomi on the surface, she was not human inside. Eve 1 had certainly evolved, but she had not been able to mimic a human being flawlessly. There was no way that her womb was exempt from this. In other words, Eve 1 could not nurture a fertilized egg by herself.

But maybe Eve 1 was aware of this?

Toshiaki mulled over the possibility desperately.

Could she possess another woman's body like Asakura's, but use it to raise a child in her womb? No, even that would be impossible. A woman's body could not accommodate Eve 1's egg. Of course, if the egg were normal, there would be no problems. But Eve 1 had the power to divide, propagate, and change her form at will. She was not made up of simple human cells. People, *Homo sapiens*, were completely different from her. The possibility of an egg created by Eve 1 gestating in a human woman's womb was miniscule. A modified egg, transplanted into a normal woman, would probably never develop. So, what exactly were her intentions?

Toshiaki was silent.

Wait.

His brain pulses converged on one point.

That meant there was only one possibility.

There was someone who could raise her fertilized egg.

Eve 1's zygote cells were trying to differentiate themselves from humans. They were on the verge of an evolutionary miracle. At such a turning point, there had to be some overlap between the two types. But couldn't someone who possessed a similar cellular overlap accept Eve 1's fertilized egg? In such a biological environment, the egg would grow into a fetus.

"She can't do this!" Toshiaki moaned, his head in his hands.

Kiyomi's death, her kidney transplant, even his primary culture on her liver cells had all happened as Eve 1 intended. He had unconsciously furthered her plans by obsessing over Eve 1's data and inciting her propagation. Beset with violent emotions, Toshiaki was unable to restrain himself from crying out in fury.

Just then, a loud gurgling sound echoed through the room.

He looked up.

The sink.

9

Mariko felt it.

Something passing through the darkness.

She pressed an ear to her pillow and listened closely. It was coming from underneath. She could hear it inside her like a ringing in the ears. Not someone on the floor below, but further down, underground. Maybe it was moving through soil. Something with the speed of a subway train.

She was afraid.

Visiting hours ended at seven o'clock and her father had just left. He had been at her side since noon. It was the first time they were together for so long. He hardly said anything, but it put her at ease nonetheless.

Her ear still pressed to the pillow, Mariko looked across the room.

No one here now.

Her father was gone, as were the nurses, and the sickroom suddenly felt endless. This was too big a place for her to be alone. No one could ever reach her even if she were in danger.

She heard no voices, no sounds in the hallway, and wondered what happened to everyone. She normally could hear nurses running between wards and patients clearing their phlegm in other rooms. Without these, the blowing wind, passing bikes, and ventilation jarred in her ears. But in her growing fear, they too faded.

And among that stasis, she heard only that one sound echoing from the soil.

It called to her from afar, growing with every moment.

Thump.

Her kidney moved.

Mariko looked down to her abdomen with an all too familiar terror.

She gazed around frantically. The wall clock showed 7:30. She put a hand to her face.

She was wide awake. This was no dream. But still, her kidney moved as it did

Evolution

in the...

Thump.

Mariko began to panic. She touched her abdomen, but recoiled from the heat. Once again, she put an ear to her pillow. She gasped. The sound was getting louder.

"No..."

She buried herself in the sheets from head to toe. Her body began to tremble.

The donor had come at last. Come to take her kidney back. She had risen from the grave and would be at the hospital at any moment. First there'd be the *flap, flap* of her footsteps. Then, she would open the door and come into the room, her only goal to dig into Mariko's body to reclaim what was once hers.

The kidney let out another thump.

10

"So that's why I need to see the young woman who received my wife's kidney. As soon as possible."

Toshiaki had decided to call the CCH from his lab. Eve 1 would surely make an appearance at the recipient's hospital. He had to get to her before Eve 1 did.

"I realize that, sir, but there's no way we can grant your request. I'm sorry. It's against legal policy."

Unfortunately, the receptionist was insistent on this point. Toshiaki raised his voice.

"This is a dire situation. If that patient is not evacuated to a safe place immediately, something terrible will happen to her. To hell with the rules."

"Excuse me, sir, but what are you talking about?" The receptionist suddenly changed tone.

"That patient is in great danger! What don't you understand?" He was outraged.

"If this is a prank call, I want you to stop this right now."

"Don't be stupid. I just told you. I am the donor's husband, my name is..."

"I don't know what you're trying to pull here, but I won't have you terrorizing any patients at this hospital. I take my job seriously and I'm not about to jeopardize it. If you keep this up, I'll report you to the police."

"Damn you!"

Toshiaki threw down the receiver.

He was at a loss for words, but refused to let it end there.

Stuffing his open shirt into his pants, he exited the room and rushed down the hallway. Thankfully, the elevator was already at the fifth floor. He opened the doors, went inside, and beat the first floor button with his fist. The elevator began its sluggish descent. He swore at the delay.

All he was concerned about was how far Eve 1 had managed to get. When Toshiaki had heard the gurgling in the sink, he went over it to see Eve 1's stains around the mouth of the drain. Sticking a finger inside, he felt slime, and knew she had escaped through the pipe.

Eve 1 could change shape at will, so it was nothing for her to travel underground. He was certain she was storing a fertilized egg.

It was impossible to look up every pipe that ran through the city. The only thing he knew for certain was that she would emerge at a hospital. This was all he had to go on to cut her off.

The elevator stopped with a clank. Toshiaki leapt out as the doors opened. He went through the dark lobby and made a dash for his car parked just outside. The key was still in the ignition. He got inside, stepped on the gas pedal as he started the engine, and broke into full speed.

The City Central Hospital was fifteen minutes away. He was not confident he would make it in time, but there was no choice. He had to do everything in his power to defend the recipient of Kiyomi's organ.

But even though she was in a hospital, how was he supposed to look for her? The CCH was the major kidney transplant hospital in this region. There would be many transplant patients there alone. How was he supposed to find the right one among them? Asking any staff was clearly out of the question, and no one would ever believe him if he told them the truth. Should he track down Odagiri, the transplant coordinator? Or talk to the doctor who performed the transplant itself? He thought hard. Both seemed to be dead ends. The hospital was doing its best to maintain its prized confidentiality.

He was convinced there was nothing he could do. But there had to be something. He didn't want there to be a single other victim.

Toshiaki gained speed, nearly skidding off the road as he curved downhill.

11

Shigenori Anzai was alone, sitting on a sofa in the lifeless hospital lobby.

The lights were out. The window, normally overrun with patients, was covered by a beige curtain as if to reject him. A big clock on the wall tapped a rhythm as it ticked away the seconds. At noontime, this place was racked with so much noise that no one could hear a thing, certainly not the hand of a clock. Now, the ticking annoyed him.

The only light came from the yellow glow of a late-night drug pickup window. But there, too, a curtain was drawn and he could not see inside. Anzai saw flitting shadows of people moving behind it, but could not tell what they were doing.

He looked up at the clock. Over thirty minutes had passed since he came to sit here.

Mariko's face floated before his eyes. She was clearly threatened by something. She had still not opened up to him, but occasionally gave Anzai a look that seemed to implore for help. Whenever he gazed back at her, she turned her face to the side, probably wavering about how to respond.

When visiting hours ended and Anzai got up to leave, Mariko sat up and stared at him. Her eyes begged him not to go. He remembered her saying how afraid she was the night before.

He held her hand. She squeezed it tightly in return. He tried to pull away, but she held on tighter. He watched her patiently.

Before long, he said he needed to get going.

As he walked out, he felt Mariko's gaze upon him the entire time, and as the door closed, he sensed almost a scream of terror from her.

But visiting hours were over and there was nothing he could do. He rationalized his departure like any adult.

As he walked down the hall towards the elevators, he realized his error. Shouldn't he be by her side? He was trying his best to understand her, but maybe that was still just a front, and she had not opened up completely because she saw right through it. Anzai had felt like turning back on his heel but kept walking, against all instinct.

He had no strength to return to her room, but neither could he go home, so he had stayed in the lobby trying to calm his conflicting emotions.

"What are you doing over there?"

Anzai was surprised at the sudden voice.

An older nurse was standing there, carrying what looked like a shopping basket in her hands and eyeing him suspiciously. She had probably come to pick up some meds. Were it not for her uniform, he'd have mistaken her for a housewife on some errand.

He faltered for an explanation as she approached him.

"Visiting hours are over for the night. Why are you here?"

Anzai was silent.

He stood up sluggishly. The main entrance was closed. The only way out was through the service entrance.

"I wouldn't idle around if I were you," came the nurse's voice from behind, as he walked away. He was extremely worried over Mariko, but he could not just sit there forever. Maybe it was best for him to leave.

The service entrance had a very different feel to it than the main one. There was no tree-lined rotary or even a taxi stop. There were no lights either and Anzai could hardly see a hundred feet in front of him. For all he knew, it was a dead end. Even where light did reach, the hospital walls cramped him on either side. There were numerous bikes and compacts parked outside. Water trickled from the drainage pipe that ran along the wall.

He walked a little and took a look around, wondering how to get out of this place.

Just then, he heard a low sound at his feet. He looked down to find that he was standing on a manhole. He felt a faint vibration underneath, growing in intensity.

At first, he thought it was water flowing through the pipes. But the sound was too unnatural for that. It was more like something moving in the sewers. A rat? No, bigger.

It was getting closer. The manhole cover began to clatter as the sound gained on him. Anzai jumped back, startled.

He listened closely. Something was rolling in the sewers. If not rolling, then creeping. He could hear no footsteps, nor was the sound intermittent. Whether it was a living thing or a machine was impossible to tell. Regardless, it was moving along with great speed. The manhole cover was vibrating visibly. Anzai lifted his face. He was directly in its path. The sound was coming right towards him. He looked back down to the manhole cover, then swallowed and turned around to the service entrance door. The direction of the sound, the manhole, the service entrance...all in a straight line.

What is this?

It's coming to the hospital?

He turned back towards the sound. He could see only darkness where the pale light from the ward window did not reach. Not even the silhouettes of telephone poles.

A sound like the voice of the earth itself came from the manhole. A great rush of wind blew out from around the rim. There was no denying now that something was coming. It was big, possibly bigger than Anzai himself. He could hear its breathing. He figured, just from the sound, that it knew exactly where it was going.

Anzai was shaking. He peered closely into the darkness in front of him and saw vibrations rolling wavelike along the ground. Fifty feet away. The darkness erupted with sound. Twenty-five feet. The asphalt quaked. Twenty feet. He stepped back. Followed the sound with his eyes. It was coming for him. Fifteen feet. He wanted to scream, but his voice refused to emerge. Ten feet. The manhole cover danced around madly. He heard a slimy sound. It was coming. Any moment now.

Evolution

He held his head to fend off the noise.

A deafening roar ran under his feet.

His entire body was enveloped in sound. He shut his eyes.

The ground buckled beneath his trembling knees. He did not open his eyes until the sound was gone, but the feeling of its movement remained. His internal organs were shaken and refused to settle.

What the hell just came through here?

Whatever it was, it was alive. He could hardly believe that something so large could navigate the city's pipes. It must have possessed intelligence to come here. There was no hesitation in its speed.

But why here?

Anzai opened his eyes. He turned around and looked up at the hospital walls. It was inside. It had reached its goal.

Silence now. All signs of its existence were gone. Had it gone into the hospital pipes?

...Mariko.

He did not know why, but he knew somehow that she was in danger. Whatever had been making that sound was after her.

Anzai turned back towards the side entrance.

12

Upon receiving word that Mariko's condition had worsened, Yoshizumi rushed straight to her ward.

A nurse had discovered Mariko thrashing wildly in her bed, with no reaction to sedatives. She was still violent. Yoshizumi had banged down the phone and run out of his office before the nurse could even finish.

Because of Mariko's nightmares, the nurses had to wake her up every night to comfort her. They had used sedatives on her before; this episode seemed to be different. Yoshizumi was starting to fret about the whole situation.

Just what was going on with her? First her organ rejection, slight as it was, refused to settled down, and then this. In over ten years of transplants, he had never encountered such a strange case.

He reached the door to her room, short of breath, and was surprised to hear a violent pounding coming from the other side. A nurse screamed. Yoshizumi hesitantly put his hand on the knob.

He went inside, then swallowed.

Mariko's body was bouncing up and down on the bed. Two young nurses were trying to restrain her, but to no avail. Her blanket flew into the air and the transfusion stand fell to the floor.

Yoshizumi stared in amazement at Mariko's abdomen, which had swollen up like a balloon under her nightgown.

The bulge was beyond what was possible for her skeletal structure; regardless, it kept shrinking and expanding, like rubber. It looked like something was trying to jump out of her body, and Mariko was being tossed about by it. Her eyes were rolled back to the whites and she was close to fainting.

"Doctor!"

The nurses called out for help.

Yoshizumi came back to his senses. He tried to restrain her legs, but she struggled with unbelievable strength and he failed to get a firm grip on her.

Evolution

Mariko's abdomen undulated right before his eyes, and yet Yoshizumi could not accept what he was seeing. He grabbed hold of her nightgown and forced it open. The two operation scars, one on the right and one on the left, both painful to behold. But the one on the left bulged out even as he watched.

His eyes widened.

Was it the kidney?

Was the kidney moving?

He bore down on her with all his weight.

"Quick, bind her hands! And put something between her teeth or she'll bite her tongue!"

The two nurses pressed Mariko's hands down desperately. Her waist leapt up into the air in fierce opposition. She was putting up quite a fight for a girl her age. Yoshizumi heard a sound. *Thump. Thump.* The kidney was beating like a heart. As he held down her kicking legs, he thought, *This is crazy...*

"Hurry up and tie her down!"

The bed springs creaked as her body jumped up nearly a foot into the air, throwing Yoshizumi head first into the wall.

Then, Mariko's movements suddenly stopped.

The swelling in her abdomen subsided and her body slowly stopped hopping up and down, like a rubber ball falling to the floor, gradually losing its bounce, and rolling to a standstill.

As Mariko lay silent, the nurses stood up apprehensively. Yoshizumi rubbed the pain out of his head and approached her. The room was now enveloped in quiet, as if the previous commotion had all been an illusion.

Mariko's eyes were still closed. Her breathing was as slow and calm as that of one sleeping. She was not sweating at all, despite the massive tantrum. Her kidney was no longer moving. Only a peaceful expression upon her face.

Yoshizumi tried touching her abdomen gently with his fingertips, but felt nothing unusual. No bulge, no beat. He opened her gown again to check her surgical scars. He caressed them, only to find they were normal.

He cast a sideward glance at the nurses. By the looks on their faces, they were just as clueless as he was, and even afraid. He looked back at Mariko.

After straightening her clothes out, he gazed at her face once again. Seeing her placid face, his distress faded away. Maybe the sedatives had finally kicked in? But sedatives never had such a sudden effect.

"When did it start?" he asked the nurses, still staring at Mariko's face.

"About twenty past seven," said one of them. "One of the patients next door called about her. By the time I got here, she was already in a bad state. I thought she was just having one of her nightmares, so I stayed with her. But then it got too much for me, so I called for help. Half an hour into it we started losing control of the situation…"

"I see."

"And the whole time, she kept saying 'Go away,'" the other nurse added.

"'Go away'? What's that supposed to mean?"

"I don't know, but she's been saying that a lot in her sleep lately."

"I wonder who she's talking about. I guess she's being chased in her dreams?"

"We've asked her about it, but she never gives us any answers…"

Yoshizumi took a deep breath.

Mariko had seemed like a completely different person until a moment ago. Even that youthful rouge-like tinge in her cheeks was back. Her mouth was open slightly, and clean white teeth peeked out of them. Yoshizumi drew closer and touched her cheek with his hand.

Her eyes shot open.

At the same time, Yoshizumi felt an intense vibration in his fingertips. He cried out and withdrew his hand. The nurses screamed loudly.

Her eyes were opened all too wide, her pupils dilated into perfect black circles. She began to look less human by the moment, making a cold shiver run along Yoshizumi's spine. She looked more like a plastic doll with glass eyes inserted into its face.

She sat up. Yoshizumi backed away. She stared intently at him without so much as blinking.

"What the…" he said hoarsely. The nurses held their breaths and stood trembling in the corner.

Yoshizumi then realized she was not looking at him.

He followed her line of vision to his stomach.

Not that, either. She was looking behind him.

He turned around.

Just a sink. A little smaller and more antique than the kind one found in a real apartment bathroom. Every sickroom had been outfitted with one when the hospital was built. The sink was an old make, with a small faucet. Yoshizumi looked back and forth between Mariko and the sink.

Just then, something caught his eye.

A single drop of water was forming at the tip of the faucet. It needed to be tightened. The droplet swelled ever so slowly into a sphere. Like Mariko, he could not look away from it. This was what had riveted her attention.

The drop got bigger and bigger. It just would not stop expanding. It soon began to stretch into a teardrop shape as gravity finally took over. It dangled from the lip and grew even larger, its surface waving gently.

It broke free.

Then fell straight into the sink with a sound:

FLAP.

13

Toshiaki reached the hospital. The main lamp was off. He stopped his car at the entrance and peered inside. Not a soul around. It was clearly locked. A sign hanging on the door read:

Medical services are concluded for today.
In case of emergency, please go around to the after-hours service entrance.

The after-hours service entrance? Toshiaki frowned. Where was that?

He got out of the car and ran up to the main doors. He tried pounding on the glass a few times. No response. He looked around for any sort of map, but found nothing.

He was getting nowhere like this. He broke into a run along the right side of the building. If he circled around, he was bound to find something.

As he ran, he was soon swallowed in darkness. He proceeded cautiously, stumbling on some rope and a set of stairs. This place was so huge that the lights from the streets and houses didn't reach the premises. Toshiaki had gone to the University Hospital many times at night on business, and the darkness there had always been different from the Pharmaceuticals building's. Of course, the premises there weren't pitch dark. In the hallways too, there were soft emergency backlights left on. Yet, all along the way from the courtyard to the Department of Medicine, there was a peculiar murkiness in the air. It was a darkness absent from a building that dealt only with lab animals. Toshiaki thought of it as the darkness of dying people, of people ill.

When Toshiaki was about half way around, he heard an argument coming from behind the storehouse. He could not see anyone, but from the deepness of their voices judged them to be men. The asphalt brightened as he made his way closer. He turned the corner. Sure enough, the yellow light was coming from the service entrance.

Evolution

Illuminated in its glow was a middle-aged businessman in dispute with an older, obese security guard.

If Toshiaki could just get through that entrance, he could sneak inside to the patients' ward. He wanted to slip in unnoticed, but the two men did not look like they were going to end their dispute anytime soon. He could not quite catch the details of what they were saying. He tried to run past them.

"Hey you! Hold it right there," shouted the guard upon noticing him. But Toshiaki ignored him and bolted for it. The guard left the other man and intercepted Toshiaki, who tried to push him away.

But the guard was much stronger than anyone would have thought. He had an amazingly sturdy frame for an old man. Toshiaki struggled, but it was no use.

"What's your business? You need emergency attention?" the guard growled.

"Something terrible's going to happen," said Toshiaki by way of appeal, as he struggled to pull himself free. "I'm here to save a patient. It'll be here any minute now. Please, I beg you."

"What're you talking about?"

The guard looked him over from head to toe.

With sleeves and cuffs singed, shirt torn open, and small pieces of dried flesh stuck to his pants, Toshiaki certainly looked like a vagrant or worse. The guard strengthened his grip.

"You come with me now. Sure are a lot of weirdoes out tonight..."

"There's a young transplant patient in there!" Toshiaki shouted. "A girl! She had a kidney transplant in July. The child is in danger, I swear. Someone's after her. Hurry up and help me before it's too late!"

At that moment, a voice asked from behind: "You know Mariko?!"

Toshiaki turned around to see the suited man standing there with terror on his face.

14

Mariko could not tear her eyes away.

She could see nothing else. Her entire field of vision was confined to the faucet. The old faucet had only the width of an index finger, and two grooves circled around it near the bottom as though the thing had tried to excrete something but had given up. From its lip something transparent peeked out ever so slowly. Its surface reflected the entire scene. Everything from the sink to the white walls to Mariko's face was trapped in it. As she watched, it grew to an almost obscene size; taking the shape of a teardrop for a split second, it fell.

Flap.

The sound reminded her of those footsteps.

It was the sound from her dream, the flopping like vinyl slippers, the same lagging cadence. She understood now. The dream was about this. Those footsteps were the sound of dripping water.

Flap.

Another drop fell. At that moment, the next one began peeking out. Again and again, the same. The drop grew, quivered, and fell like the tip of a dying firework stick, with a *flap!* The next one appeared. A tiny droplet, hardly hanging on, absorbing the next one, dangled as a bubble, and broke *flap* off swiftly from the faucet, and the next one there already, swelling out in a semicircle, trembling once as it grew and falling *flap*, as another like a teardrop in its wake followed *flap* and another no less quickly too *flap* and before it was gone *flap* and more *flap* and still *flap* so fast *flap* like film *flap* on ff*flapflapflapflaplaplaplaplaplaplaplaplpl ppppⁱappppppppppppppppppppppppppppppppppppppppppppppppp*

p.

With an explosion, something burst out of the drain.

Mariko screamed for her life, but her eyelids were still glued open. She couldn't blink; her line of sight was frozen. For a moment, she was unable to comprehend what was happening, just that something was moving in her vision with terrible speed. The footsteps had actually been the dripping of water, they had come faster and faster, they had come to her room, wanting to burst out from the faucet. Or so Mariko had thought. Instead it had emerged from further below out of the sink, through the drain, bursting out with a rust-red column of water that shot up to the ceiling. She thought she could make out something moving inside it, but her eyes were pinned on the faucet. She clenched her teeth and tried to force her eyes to move. Someone let out a wail like a siren. The drain spouted water intermittently like a geyser, splashing coldness on Mariko.

Her kidney was beating with joy...

THUMP!

And the beating reverberated through her body.

15

"Who are you and how do you know about Mariko?" Anzai asked the man. She was surely the only young girl who had received a transplant in July at this hospital. This strange man somehow knew about her, and also seemed to know that she was in some kind of danger.

Despite his tattered clothing, the earnestness in his eyes proved he was not joking. His face also showed intelligence. Anzai judged him to be anything but an incoherent man off the streets. The worried father stood before the man, who looked at him inquisitively.

"How do you...?"

"I'm Mariko's father. She's the patient you were talking about."

"She had a kidney transplant...?"

"Yes. Now tell me what's going on."

The man's face filled with relief.

"Perfect! So you know where she is then?"

"Of course."

"Take me to her! It's urgent. Your child's being hunted."

"...First tell me who you are and why you know about Mariko."

"My wife was the donor."

Anzai was speechless. He had never seen the donor's face or even known her name. He was told by Yoshizumi only that she had been a 25-year-old woman who had died in a car accident. He never asked about the donor again and had not thought about her at all since. To see a man before him who professed to be her husband felt slightly unreal.

But Anzai decided to believe him, if only because his daughter's life was possibly at stake.

The man introduced himself as Toshiaki Nagashima.

"Something terrible has happened because of me. We can't afford to just stand around like this. Will you please just take me to her room?"

Evolution

"What's going to happen to her?"

"I'll explain later. Hurry!"

But the guard was angry. He grabbed Anzai's sleeve to separate the two.

"Now hold on. What are you talking about? This is…"

Toshiaki struck the guard with full force. The sudden blow made him stagger. In that moment of opportunity, Toshiaki pulled Anzai by the arm.

"Where's her room?"

"Go right."

Toshiaki broke into a run, and Anzai ran ahead to lead the way.

"Stop, both of you!" echoed the guard's shouts from behind, but they pressed on, heedless.

"What happened? What did you do to Mariko?"

"There was a parasite in my wife's cells."

"A parasite? Bacteria you mean? Has Mariko been infected with something?"

"Something like that. But that's not all. It's much worse. I've been keeping my wife's cells. They're extremely virulent."

Anzai was confused, especially by the last bit, but he had no trouble believing that Mariko's kidney was abnormal. He remembered the way her abdomen had appeared to leap unnaturally the day before.

"It has special abilities. It can set things on fire. It can also change shape at will. And it's coming to this hospital."

"Coming here?"

"Through the sewage pipes."

"So that's what it was!" Anzai cried.

"You know about it?"

"I heard it outside near the side entrance not too long before you showed up. It sounded huge."

"Then what? Where did it go?"

"Disappeared into this hospital."

"What?!"

Anzai turned a corner, ran up a flight of steps and continued to Mariko's ward. Toshiaki didn't speak another word. The younger man's silence told of the gravity of the situation, conveying a painful tension regarding something unfathomable coming after Mariko. Anzai ran as fast as he could, badly out of breath though he was. He heard mulitple footsteps behind them. Perhaps the guard had called for backup.

Evolution

16

Yoshizumi was speechless.

It had spewed forth from the drain and stuck to the wall, then wiggled and fallen to the floor. It looked like pink sludge. What was left in the sink spilled over the edge. The two united on the tile. Then, with an unpleasant gurgle, it started to rise.

The two nurses were on their knees, crying and holding each other. Mariko didn't budge. She did not even cry out for help. Only, her body was trembling, and she was swaying slightly to and fro. The shock had completely paralyzed her.

The gelatinous thing rose up even higher. Yoshizumi stepped back on shaking legs. He could barely stand. The thing climbed up before him like a waterfall in reverse. The foul-smelling liquid gushing sporadically out of the drain bathed it so that it gleamed as it took form. Something hit Yoshizumi's shin. He lost balance and fell back onto Mariko's bed. His fingers touched her leg.

The column's shape became increasingly complex as it grew. Its center narrowed and tentacle-like appendages separated from either side. Yoshizumi stared in disbelief. A person was forming right in front of his eyes. A woman's body. The tentacles each separated into five fingers. Arms appeared behind them and shoulders above the chest. A small navel took shape in the middle of the column and nestled in a concave stomach that could have been carved with a spatula. Two hemispheres of flesh bulged out above it, while the section below gained a plumpness and hundreds of thin, compound folds worked themselves into perfection. Flesh above the shoulders narrowed into a throat. The circular blob that was its head rippled, creating a nose, mouth, ears, cheeks, jaw, forehead, and eyes. Yoshizumi was shaking his head in denial. He recognized the figure, the face of this woman. "Recognize" wasn't the word. He remembered her very well. This was Mariko's donor. The woman he had cut open with his own hands, whose kidney he himself had extracted. She could not possibly be alive. He just kept shaking his head in denial.

Whatever this thing was, it had taken on her exact likeness. Her eyes popped open and looked down at Yoshizumi and Mariko.

With a smile, she addressed Yoshizumi.

"Move."

He couldn't if he wanted to. He was swallowed in her gaze. Hers were the eyes of a predator, and Yoshizumi sensed that her prey was Mariko.

"I said, *Move...*"

Without warning, one of the nurses huddled in the corner of the room let out a bizarre whimper and stood up. Yoshizumi was released from his paralysis. He turned towards the nurse. Tears and saliva were streaming freely down a crumpled face. Flailing her arms weirdly, she started running for the door.

The creature glared at her.

Just as Yoshizumi called out, flames rose up from the nurse.

A moment later, she was engulfed in them, and her body was visibly getting charred. Her tied-back hair curled and shrank. But the flames refused to recede and instead shot up to the ceiling, sending a stifling blast of hot air through the room. Even as Yoshizumi guarded his face with both arms, he could not shut his eyes. The nurse's violent cries of agony filled his ears. Her teeth enamel were melting away in her mouth, which was twisted wide open, a sight that burned itself into his retina. She staggered, trying to pat out the flames with her arms, but the blaze was too overpowering as it roared like a rocket engine. Her white coat fell scattering in pieces onto the floor only to shrivel up and evaporate in a matter of seconds. The strong stench of burning flesh stang Yoshizumi's nose. The nurse no longer looked human; she was melting in the raging inferno. Her flesh had turned jelly-like and was dripping from her skeleton. Those bones, too, eventually shrank and crumpled. A thunderous ringing ripped through the air; the fire alarm had gone off. What was left of the nurse turned into muck amidst the piercing bell. Overwhelmed by the noise and heat, Yoshizumi just sat there on the bed like a simpleton.

The flames disappeared, leaving only the skull-shaking alarm to continue in their wake. Strangely enough, there were no scorch marks on the linoleum or walls. Nothing had been altered by the heat. Yoshizumi stared in wonder. The only indications of the nurse's existence were a gelatinous mass and her right leg, left unharmed from the knee down. It just lay there like merchandise some store clerk had forgotten to put away. Its skin was smooth and the stocking intact and it wore a slipper. Staring at it, all Yoshizumi could do was to keep all common sense from crumbling away.

The other nurse was trailing saliva from her mouth and tearing furiously at her face with both hands. Her eyes lacked all focus. A liquid seeping out from her inner thighs dirtied the floor. She had let loose her bladder.

The thing that looked like the donor turned slowly to her with a scornful smile.

"Stop."

Yoshizumi had managed only a raspy command that he himself found quite pathetic. He could hardly hear himself above the fire alarm.

"Please. Stop this."

The creature ignored him, glaring at the nurse until she, too, burst into flame.

Not wanting a repeat performance of what he had just witnessed, Yoshizumi looked away.

The same scorching wind blew through the room. The nurse's screams enveloped his body with an intensity that rivaled the alarm. He closed his eyes and covered his ears, but could not block the din of tempestuous flames or the horrendous screams escaping through the nurse's clenched teeth.

But soon, her voice went silent. Yoshizumi turned towards her timidly, and groaned when he saw the thing.

As expected, there was a jello-like pile in the nurse's place; only, this time, an arm had been spared from the elbow down. The faint pink manicure was left unscathed and the skin was as beautiful as white china.

Yoshizumi suddenly remembered a strange forensics article he'd read as an intern, about spontaneous combustion. This not altogether rare phenomenon was usually discovered by a neighbor who, upon noticing the smell of smoke, went next door to discover a most unpleasant scene. There was usually only a sticky mass in place of the body and often a foot or other body part that was left unharmed. Neither the clothing or the couch the victim had been sitting in would bear any sign of damage. In none of these cases was there ever any evidence, such as a turned-on stove, matches, or gasoline to suggest a suicide. The circumstances pointed to the fact that the body in question had been subjected to heat comparable to a blast furnace. It required a temperature of nearly 3,000° F to turn bone to ash. How could such a high temperature be created? And how could one human alone be selectively made to burn?

Yoshizumi wondered if this was what he had just witnessed. *Was that spontaneous combustion? Does this humanoid creature actually possess the ability to make us go up in flames?*

"Out of my way," she said. He looked up in surprise.

It was approaching him with a ghostly smile. No. It was trying to get to Mariko.

"Get out of my way!"

"No," answered Yoshizumi, shaking his head.

"I don't want to kill you, so step away quietly."

"I can't allow this… She's my patient."

"Your patient? Hmph. If that's true, then so am I."

"What?"

"I really am grateful to you, doctor. You looked after this girl for me. But that's where your service ends. Leave now if you want to live."

He was silent.

She walked over to Yoshizumi, who instinctively bent over the bed to protect Mariko. Her eyes were open, but her body was rigid. Perhaps she'd fainted at the outset of it all. So much the better. It meant she'd been spared the ordeal of witnessing the nurses' fate.

The creature laid a hand on Yoshizumi. He shook it off, but was grabbed again. He cried out from its unexpected strength as it pulled him forcibly away from the bed.

He hit the wall. An intense pain spread across his forehead. Blood flowed into his eyes.

"Stop!" he shouted, his head throbbing with pain. The alarm was still going. He felt like it would never stop.

The creature crawled onto the bed and straddled Mariko, and started stripping off her sheets and nightgown. Yoshizumi saw Mariko's painfully naked skin.

"Stop…"

Yoshizumi stood up dizzily and brought his hands down upon her back with as much strength as he could muster. His arms sunk into her slimy, sticky body. The creature continued tearing off Mariko's clothing and paid no attention to him. But Yoshizumi kept shouting for her to stop.

"Enough!" said the creature, turning her head around and silencing him with a penetrating glare.

Her pupils contracted.

Yoshizumi's arms instantaneously burst into flames.

17

Toshiaki placed his hand on the knob, but cried out from the heat and pulled it back. Scorching waves billowed out from the other side of the door. The guards were only a few dozen feet behind them. The fire alarm continued to echo throughout the entire building and many of the patients were running out into the hallway to see what the commotion was about. Toshiaki looked to Anzai with a nod. He pulled his sleeve over his hand and opened the door into Mariko's room.

A suffocating heat burst out from inside. Toshiaki covered his face with his arms. Anzai shouted his daughter's name.

A man was screaming with his arms raised; they were burning. He was flapping his arms as if that would put out the fire. Anzai grabbed Toshiaki from behind, struggling to get in. He kept on calling out his daughter's name. A young girl lay face up, half-naked, on the bed. Standing next to her was Eve 1, in the guise of Kiyomi.

"You!" Toshiaki snarled.

But Eve 1's movements were quick. She grabbed the girl, then looked at Toshiaki with a huge grin.

"Stop, let the child go!"

Eve 1 turned and jumped through the glass.

Toshiaki shouted after her and ran to the broken window. He leaned out and looked down.

It was dark. He could see almost nothing. Then he bearly saw a large shadow move. He followed it desperately with his eyes, but there was not enough light outside, and the glow from their window hardly reached the ground. In the blink of an eye, he lost sight of her. But she seemed to have been going not away from the hospital, but back into it.

"Help me! Put me out!" yelled the white-clad doctor. Just then, the guards arrived, standing outside the door in disbelief. Toshiaki took the sheets from the bed and wrapped them around the doctor's shoulders. With Anzai's help, he patted all around to snuff out the fire.

Once the flames were fully extinguished, the doctor crouched down in relief. Toshiaki shook the doctor's shoulders to snap him out of it. And then, he remembered. He had seen this doctor before. He was the man who had performed Kiyomi's kidney extraction. His name was Yoshizumi. Undoubtedly, he had also performed the kidney transplant on that girl Mariko.

"Can someone please tell me…what the hell is going on?" said one of the guards shakily, as he entered the room. He was middle-aged and slightly overweight, with a large frame and tense face. Toshiaki had a feeling he was the one in charge.

"It escaped!" Toshiaki screamed to the guard while still shaking Yoshizumi. "Please, hurry up and find it. It took a patient!"

"But what is…"

"Just do it!"

At these words, the guard snapped into action. He went back out the door and gave hand signals to the other guards, who broke away in a flash.

Anzai threw up. Toshiaki looked over and saw a human foot next to him. The severed appendage ended in a muddy stump that looked cauterized. He also saw a hand in another corner of the room. Eve 1's victims. He groaned and looked away.

Dr. Yoshizumi's glazed-over eyes returned to normal and slowly focused on Toshiaki's face.

"…you."

"What did it do to the child?"

"It…?"

"That damned monster! The one that looked like a woman!"

Yoshizumi looked anxious all of a sudden. "Mariko! Where's Mariko?"

"It took her."

"What?!"

Parasite Eve

"So what did it do to her? Tell me, did it implant anything into her?"

"No…it hadn't done anything yet," Yoshizumi panted. "It went straight for Mariko… The nurses were killed. And then I caught fire. That's when you guys…"

"You're sure the child wasn't harmed? It didn't put an egg into her?"

"An egg?"

"That creature is trying to plant a zygote in her."

Anzai, who was covering his mouth with a handkerchief, wondered if he had heard Toshiaki correctly and grabbed his arm. His face was going pale.

"What in God's name is that thing? Why would it attack Mariko?"

"That 'thing' is a parasite that was living in my wife's body," Toshiaki explained. "It has unimaginable powers. It plans on putting its child into that girl and raising it inside of her. If we don't help her soon, she'll be in grave danger."

"Wait a minute, what exactly is this parasite?" asked Yoshizumi.

"Mitochondria."

"Mito…!" Yoshizumi could only utter that much. Apparently, Toshiaki's revelation had rung some bell.

"Whether you believe me or not, we have to look for the child. Please, go help out the guards. You know your way around this hospital better than I do. And the guards don't trust me."

Yoshizumi, still in shock, looked at him apprehensively, then stood up and called out for the guards. The head guard came running up immediately. Toshiaki listened closely as Yoshizumi began discussing the layout of the hospital. The guard stood there with his mouth open as he took in Yoshizumi's information. Anzai was at Toshiaki's side, covering his face and muttering Mariko's name over and over.

Would Eve 1 really put a fertilized egg into that girl? As Toshiaki pondered the possible consequences, his breath caught short. He had only gotten a glimpse of her, but the girl looked young enough to be in middle school. Eve 1 was trying to raise her own child in a vessel that was still a child herself. The whole idea became more disgusting by the moment. He had to get the girl back as soon as possible. And if the egg happened to be implanted by then? They would simply remove and destroy it.

It was at this point that Toshiaki came to a disturbing realization.

Eve 1 must have known from the outset that she wouldn't have all the time in the world to let her egg grow in a womb. She must have predicted that Doctor Yoshizumi, Anzai, and ultimately Toshiaki himself would try to stop the growth of her egg at all costs. Despite her unique abilities, it would be difficult for Eve 1 to protect Mariko until removal of the fetus became impossible. Even then, the newborn would have to be protected. It would likely take months, if not years for such a child to exhibit the abilities Eve 1 foresaw.

And yet Eve 1 was certain of victory?

The daring smile she flashed just before she ran away came back to Toshiaki, because of the sheer confidence it expressed.

Eve 1 had something else up her sleeve. If not, she wouldn't have revealed herself during her speech.

His heart fluttered.

Eve 1 had probably mapped out everything beyond all his possible moves.

Was there no way to stop her? Were humans just meaningless objects to be exterminated in her path?

Toshiaki refused to accept this. No matter how exhaustive her plans were, she had to have a weak point. There had to be some way to bring down Eve 1 and her offspring. Some way.

But nothing came to mind. Toshiaki bit his lip impatiently.

18

SHE ran at full speed. She had to find a place where She could keep Mariko quiet, where She could deposit the fertilized egg into her womb before Toshiaki and the others arrived.

She had no reason to doubt Her success. Before long, a new Eve would be born. A daughter who possessed both human and mitochondrial abilities in a single body.

She had to hurry. Her host cells were beginning to weaken. Though She controlled its movements and energy, these were cultured cells that could not be exposed to the air for too long. If She entered into this girl, She could probably survive for a few more days, but sooner or later She'd be rejected, and eventually eradicated. The fact that Her erstwhile host Kiyomi and this young girl had similar antigens did not mean that the two were identical. Unless She obtained immuno-suppressants, She would be destroyed. While manipulating Asakura's body, She had had to inject a fresh rotation of cells into the woman daily to cope with the rejection mechanism. She was aware of Her own fragility. That is why She had prepared for a recipient who could bear a child, by sending out a sister.

And in that girl's body, Her sister had slowly but surely accomplished her task, by altering the girl's womb to accept Her egg, by ensuring that the placenta of Mother and child would be consistent in composition. Her sister had simply followed Her instructions and worked on the girl's womb. Unbeknownst to anyone, Her sister had altered the womb towards the borderline between the species. Now, Her egg could be planted without hindrance.

Soon, this life form to which Toshiaki had given the name "Eve 1" would be no more. Her life of parasitism would soon be over. But, before that, She had to set the stage for Eve's birth at all costs.

When Eve was born into this world, she would have the body of a human being. There'd be no need to control the host form like Eve 1 was doing now. She'd be able to utilize all of her abilities for more productive ends. Eve would create energy at will and pour it into action and thought. She would be able to guide every last one of her genes, replicating them or programming them to die at will. She'd be able to evolve freely into any form she desired.

Evolution

No life form had ever existed on earth that could do this. Nuclear genomes lacked this most essential attribute for ensuring survival. All living things simply entrusted their fate to ambiguities such as Time and Chance. She had parasitized them all, having no choice but to wait with utter impatience. But Eve would be different. She would be able to mould her own future, accessing nuclear genomes at will and setting her own evolutionary course. Adaptation to environment, perfection and rationalization of faculties, all performed effortlessly. She would be free to occasion mutations. The speed of her evolution would be astronomical. She would be the ultimate life form.

She passed through the shadows along the wall, happening upon a flight of stairs leading underground, then descended them to a damp, narrow space. She continued from there, running down an incline just wide enough to let a car through, at the bottom of which was a sturdy door in a wall.

The door was locked, but She stretched a tentacle through the keyhole and undid the latch. With a rusty creak, the door opened slowly, and She slipped inside with the girl.

It was a gloomy space, lit only by the pallid glow of a single ceiling light. She heard the dull sounds of a boiler room. On the left was an elevator door and on the right was another door. Light poured out from frosted glass in the latter.

A sign on it read "Autopsy Room."

There was no handle. Thinking what to do, She looked down and noticed a square indentation on the wall next to the door. A small red light glowed in its center. She put a foot into the indentation.

With an electronic whine, the door slid open sideways.

A man in an operating gown turned around.

"What are you do-"

She killed him instantly.

19

Yoshizumi and Anzai stared in surprise as Toshiaki summarized all the events leading up to now. Some of what he said they had experienced already, so they had total faith in him. Yoshizumi told of the mitochondrial anomalies in Mariko's post-op biopsy. He also admitted to the mysterious heat he had felt during the operation itself.

"I've felt that heat as well," Toshiaki said. "I think she has the ability to make contact with other people's mitochondria through something akin to telepathy. The mitochondria in all our bodies differ from hers and have yet to evolve fully, which is why we're only capable of 'normal' acts."

"Even so, why can she summon fire?" said Anzai, stating the most obvious question.

"I don't know for sure, but I have a theory. Mitochondria exist in every cell of the body. Imagine if they started to produce ATP all at once. If the conversion into energy was total, that means a lot of heat. Ignition is another matter, but it's possible that she makes cells vibrate at an intense speed to create friction. Our having felt hot probably owes to a similar mechanism."

"Incredible," Yoshizumi said, his eyes opened wide.

Five minutes after Eve 1's escape, the fire alarm was finally deactivated. The head guard was now guiding the others via the PA system. But still no news of discovery.

"Let's go, we've got to help them," said Toshiaki.

"My thoughts exactly," the doctor concurred.

The three men exited the room and proceeded to the elevator. Anzai called out his daughter's name repeatedly, nothing but sadness in his voice.

As he ran, Toshiaki said, "She's probably still in the building. Eve 1 needs to keep Mariko subdued, so she can't have gone far. Doctor Yoshizumi, where do you think would be the best place if she wanted to hide?"

"There are plenty. Offices, wards, examinations rooms, too many for just us and the guards to search."

"I'm worried about something. Mitochondria has the function of speeding up a cell's division. That monster may have further evolved that ability."

"What are you getting at?"

"Just recently, there was report of a certain Drosophila experiment. When the ribosomal RNA of these flies' mitochondria was infused into the zygote, specifically in those cells that were going to become reproductive organs, it caused the division of those cells to accelerate. Not only that, but during spawning, the rRNA actually entered into the cytoplasm to induce division in the reproductive cells."

This was over Yoshizumi's head.

"What I'm saying is that mitochondria hold the key to reproductive division. It has yet to be reported in human beings, but the possibility is still there."

"So in other words...she can grow a fertilized egg at whatever rate she chooses?"

"That's what I'm worried about. She has total control over the propagation of her host cells, which leads me to believe she can develop a fertilized egg in a very short period of time."

"So if we don't find her soon, the child might already...?"

"Stop it, you two!" shouted Anzai, tears streaming down his tired face. "There's no reason Mariko should have to give birth to a monster! She's only fourteen years old!"

They reached the elevator in silence and Toshiaki pushed the button. The floor numbers lit up slowly.

Short of breath, he asked Yoshizumi where the guards were searching.

"The wards. They're checking every single room to see if any of the other patients have been harmed."

Anzai shouted, "But that thing already has what she came for! I thought she was taking her someplace out of sight?"

"She's probably looking for somewhere to complete what she came for. It'd have to be a place where there's no one else around. Somewhere where she can lay Mariko down in preparation for the birth itself,"Toshiaki added.

"That still doesn't narrow it down much. Let's see...there are couches in all the offices, CT scanning beds, stretchers in the storehouse, brain wave exam rooms, operating rooms, the morgue, the autopsy room..."

At those last words, the three of them looked up suddenly.

Just then, they heard a chime and the elevator doors opened.

Evolution

20

SHE looked around.

The place had the feel of an operating room, but differed slightly from where Kiyomi or Mariko had been operated on. The space was narrow and a total mess. The floor was heavily discolored. Three stainless steel operating tables were lined up in a row. A naked man was laid out on the central one. There were two men in green coats, one on either side of the table, gazing at Her with shock in their eyes.

"He-hey, we're in the middle of an au...topsy..." said one of them, from behind his mask. She couldn't set them on fire. If the alarm went off again, it would alert everyone to Her whereabouts. She scowled at the man, then made his heart stop like She did to the last one. This was almost too easy.

The other doctor blinked his eyes and backed up. His mask was moving, as if he was trying to say something, but no words issued. Dragging Mariko alongside Her, She advanced slowly into the room. She looked at the man on the operating table. He couldn't have been more dead. His abdomen was spread open down the middle, revealing milk-white fat and gnarled entrails. She grabbed one of the corpse's arms to pull him onto the floor.

But Her hand suddenly became deformed. She looked at it in surprise, sending signals to make the hand reform. The cells did not respond.

Necrosis had at last begun to take over Her host cells. Kiyomi's form began to drip down like jam. Her life as Eve 1 was drawing to a close. She didn't have much time.

Using both arms, She pushed the dead body off the table. It rolled over and fell to the floor with a dull thud. Her shoulders distorted; Her arms began to break away from Her torso.

The remaining doctor was flat against the wall, his mouth moving in wordless wonder. The man was already becoming an eyesore, so She disposed of him as well.

She managed to shoulder Mariko up onto the table and lay her out flat. She tore off the remaining clothing from Mariko's body and gazed upon it.

Such a small body. The chest was still undeveloped and the pubic hair faint, revealing a tight crevice beneath. But the body was female. The womb had to be handled with the

277

utmost discretion, for it would perhaps become the birthplace of many Eves to come. It would need to serve its role as incubator. It was good then to have obtained such a young girl.

A smile came to Her melting face as She crawled on top of Mariko.

At that moment, one of Her arms fell off, hitting the floor with a splat. The severed flesh writhed around, seeming to yearn for the body from which it fell, but She ignored it. Her only purpose now was to implant the egg.

She opened Mariko's legs and lifted her waist to get a better view of her reproductive organs, then pressed the lower half of Her body onto them.

She had made sure that Toshiaki's sperm penetrated the egg She created. The fertilization was complete. When a single sperm entered the egg, a wave of electricity ran along the egg's surface. She felt it as if She were the energy itself. She'd been preserving this zygote inside Her with the utmost care. Now it was time for it to cross over into Mariko. She moved on to the final deed.

The host cells were half-extinct, but She focused all the remaining ones into Her lower body. In place of Kiyomi's vagina, She created the male equivalent. The shape of Toshiaki's came to mind. In a moment's time, a perfect replica of it arose from between Her thighs. Through the center of this protrusion, She fashioned a single tube as a path for the fertilized egg to travel through.

She inserted it gently into Mariko's body. The girl's was stiff and She had to push hard through the middle. It was bound to be even narrower inside. She had no choice but to reduce the diameter of Her organ.

When She reached the womb, She explored its insides by moving around Her tip, searching for the most perfect location.

And then, She began carefully sending out the fertilized egg.

Wool-like fibers sprouted along the inside of the tube so as not to damage the egg as it quietly glided through the folds. Her pride at that moment was immeasurable. She'd successfully endured millions of years for this moment. The sheer excitement of it made Her body ripple. Every time the egg moved, it rubbed against the fine hairs, giving Her a most ecstatic pleasure, peripheral to Her task as it may have been. The egg moved steadily from

Evolution

Her lower body, through the inseminator, to the tip of the tube. A delicate arousal accompanied its journey all the way through. She felt like going into convulsions, but restrained Herself to keep the egg intact. She tolerated this unusual stimulation, yet the more She resisted, the more intense it became. The egg moved slowly through cottony fibers. She went numb from a joy that was far beyond anything She'd experienced while making love with Toshiaki.

And then, the egg broke free.

She called out in ecstasy. Her entire body undulated. Her control over the host was almost gone. The cells were dying out. Her entire being was breaking up and losing all sense of structure. This only doubled Her rapture.

She leaned back and let out a long climactic cry. Though Her body was wasting away, She'd attained the greatest happiness. Soon, Her daughter would be born. And after that, the world would change. Her descendants would become the masters of this globe. She'd wasted an unbelievably long amount of time to reach this point, but this was to be Her retribution. The world was about to begin anew.

No longer would they serve as slaves to nuclear genomes. At last, the world would be theirs.

21

The elevator reached the first floor with a jolt. Toshiaki banged the "Open" button.

When the door opened, the three of them stepped out at once.

"This way." Yoshizumi gestured left with his chin into a dark hallway. Toshiaki and Anzai closely followed his lead.

"The autopsy room is beneath Ward 1. Let's take the first stairway after that turn up ahead."

Autopsy rooms were usually located underground to keep them out of sight from patients, and were often tucked near the back entrance to facilitate hearse loading. It was the ideal place for Eve 1 to duck into secretly.

As they ran down the stairs, Anzai would have fallen over had Toshiaki not held him back just in time. The tapping of their shoes echoed loudly in the stairwell.

Am I going to have a child with mitochondria? Toshiaki breathed heavily and moved his feet in desperation. His thoughts spiraled into chaos. Had the mitochondria planned his insanity as well? There had to be a way to impede their agenda. Toshiaki racked his brain for answers, but lost his thread of thought. He cursed himself for blanking at such a crucial time. There had to be something. Something the mitochondria had overlooked.

They passed two landings on their way down, almost losing their balance along the way, and finally reached the underground halls. They could hear the grumbling of the boiler.

"Over there," shouted Yoshizumi.

There was an automatic door, incongruous in the dusty atmosphere that surrounded it. Light emanated from its small window, but they could hear nothing inside.

Yoshizumi looked at the other two for agreement. Anzai nodded back firmly. Yoshizumi kicked the red light with his foot.

Evolution

There was a whoosh of air and the door opened.

For a moment, they could not make out what was happening inside.

There was a pale body on a dissection table that was close to bursting. The mountainous bulge hindered them from seeing the face it obscured.

Anzai yelled out:

"Mariko!"

Toshiaki froze in shock, unable to believe what he was seeing: a young girl's body in the final stage of pregnancy, belly swelled out like a frog's throat.

Anzai ran for the table. Just then, a distorted voice spoke.

"You're too late."

He stopped in his tracks. Toshiaki looked down at the floor and found the voice's master.

"It's no use... Soon, she will be...born."

Toshiaki could still make out Kiyomi's figure in the amebic mass before him. The upper half of her body lifted and turned its head towards them. It spasmed, oozing out a pus-like substance. Kiyomi's chest and stomach were both decomposing. Her hair was scattered on the floor, moving around like earthworms in their final hours after a storm. Eve 1's end had come.

She was laughing, but her mouth and respiratory track emitted only an ugly gurgle.

Kiyomi's face dripped away as if dissolving in the rain. The stench of decay filled the room. She was still smiling with two lines of twitching pink gelatin.

"Behold...any...moment...now..."

Mariko's stomach heaved.

22

THUMP.

The beating echoed like a gong.

THUMP.

Trembling, rattling the racks on the wall. Toshiaki felt a dull vibration in his gut. It was shaking. The whole room was shaking.

It was a heartbeat, overwhelming, thundering with life. The contractions of its heart muscles were audible.

A fetus. Sounding the joys of its new existence.

Toshiaki could not breathe.

A moment later, blood poured out from Mariko's vagina, rust-colored and thick as mud, staining her inner thighs.

This was followed by a gush of amniotic fluid. It spilled over from the autopsy table onto the writhing mass that was Eve 1. Anzai gulped. Toshiaki grabbed him by the shoulders and blocked his view. This was not a sight for any father's eyes.

Mariko's abdomen contracted violently and a strange liquid pumped out from between her legs. Gargling laughter pealed from Eve 1.

Again, Mariko's abdomen swelled. Yoshizumi gasped in horror. Something was peeking out from between her legs. It was glittering with blood, pushing its way out slowly. Mariko's legs began to twitch.

It came out farther, farther with each pulsation that tore through the air. Head drenched in vermillion, the newborn twisted like a caterpillar, eager to emerge. As Mariko's lower body twitched helplessly, the fetus took advantage of the reaction to wrench its shoulders out, nearly splitting her open in the process. Her petite body had been transformed into a mere child-rearing vessel. Every time the fetus twisted, Mariko's organ was stretched to its extremes. More of the reddish brown liquid gushed forth from her.

The fetus was breathing, expelling a yellow liquid that had collected in its lungs. It made a few choking noises, then let out its first cry.

Toshiaki went completely numb upon hearing it. The voice was not at all human, nor that of an untamed beast. A cry he could never have imagined. It was a violent wail that shook the core of his being. It was a howl as much as a wail, stretching out for what felt like an eternity. Toshiaki covered his ears, but the sound shook his body all the more. He screamed and let his hands drop.

As the fetus squirmed around, Toshiaki could see the entire upper half of its body. With a final twist, it emerged fully. Mariko's abdomen quickly deflated. The remaining blood and amniotic fluid gushed out like a dam bursting over, bathing the fetus writhing between her legs. The blood spilled from the edge of the autopsy table and cascaded onto Eve 1.

The entire room rumbled as the fetus cried out in triumph. The ceiling lights shattered in succession, showering Mariko's body with fragments of glass. Toshiaki ducked instinctively.

With its own hand, the fetus tore away the placenta coiled around it and ripped off the umbilical cord, then turned face down.

Toshiaki looked on in disbelief. The newborn was developing quickly, already crawling on hands and legs. In a matter of seconds, it had grown far bigger than the capacity of the womb from which it sprang.

It lifted its head and opened its eyes. Its gaze shot through Toshiaki. His heart skipped a beat.

It grinned like a dog. The inside of its mouth was lacquered with scarlet, from which a slug-like tongue extended.

THUMP.

Blood vessels pulsated along the surface of its skin.

Its body expanded. But it was not simply increasing in size. It was growing up. From fetus to infant, and quickly to child. Black hair grew instantly from its head and its previously limp body formed muscles into a stable physique. Still on all fours, it changed form again. It turned its head like a lion and shook its waist. Hair exploded outward like a firework. It continued raising its voice, which changed from a wailing to a moaning to a panting.

Its hands let go of the table, and it propped itself up, throwing back its head. Two breasts swelled up from its chest and hair appeared between its legs. Its hips smoothed out into voluptuous curves. Even the head was congealing into nearly perfect form. Lips blossomed into a dazzling red. The area between them seemed lit from within.

THUMP!

An intense boom ripped through the room. The floor creaked threateningly and vials crashed to the floor.

And then, unexpectedly, silence.

It was quiet enough that Toshiaki could hear the ringing in his ears. His body refused to stop shaking. Yoshizumi stood wide-eyed and with mouth agape. Anzai was still in Toshiaki's grip, eyes closed as tightly as possible.

The "baby" placed its right foot quietly on the floor, then its left.

It stood up.

Toshiaki gazed at its body.

It resembled a person, but was not a person at all. It had an ample bosom, curvaceous hips, flowing hair, and other attributes of an ideal female figure. Nothing that a human female could never have. And yet, considered as a whole, this being was not merely perfect; it had gone beyond perfection. It surpassed human women. It surpassed humanity. It was not human, and it was unlike any other life form that had ever walked the earth. This was a life whose very purpose was to become woman, to express woman, to relish its being woman; it was perfect femininity. Standing before it, Toshiaki knew awe. It was too beautiful, and yet grotesque. At the same time that he felt an intense sexual desire, he felt chills that made him nauseous.

The decaying Eve 1 was laughing away on the floor.

Evolution

23

Anzai opened his eyes. He timidly peeked out from under Toshiaki's arms. Toshiaki felt a sudden jerk as Anzai looked upon the figure before him in horror.

Anzai was still for a long while. His body then snapped.

"Mariko," he muttered and made a break for the autopsy table.

"Stop," said the newly born Eve before Toshiaki could react.

Not a moment later, Anzai was gone. Toshiaki immediately heard a loud thud behind him.

He had no time to react when something fell onto his head. He cried out and bent over.

There was another thud. Trembling with fear, he turned around.

Anzai was hunched over on the floor, blood flowing down his temples. White powder was falling onto his body. Toshiaki saw a hairline crack running up along the wall, almost to the ceiling. It took a few seconds for him to realize that the split had been caused by the impact of Anzai's body against it.

Anzai groaned faintly, unable to get up.

Something moved in the corner of Toshiaki's eye. He looked up to see Yoshizumi, who was making a dash for the alarm switch on the wall.

But Eve read his movements. Just as Yoshizumi was reaching for the alarm, she opened her mouth wide and bellowed.

Yoshizumi screamed. His arms twisted back, his body turned around once, and he fell head first to the floor with a hard crack.

Eve smiled, clearly taking pleasure in his pain. His body lifted.

She had complete control over him. Yoshizumi began spinning in mid-air. He cried out. Eve's eyes sparkled as she flung him from wall to wall. After a while, his clothing was stained with blood. When she saw that he was limp, Eve suspended him from his feet, then let him drop suddenly like a marionette cut from its strings. Just before Yoshizumi's head hit the floor, Eve stopped his fall and lifted him up again, toying with him like this over and over.

"Stop!" Toshiaki yelled in spite of himself.

Eve swayed around and looked at him.

He swallowed and froze. There was a heavy thump as Yoshizumi fell at last, but Toshiaki could not even turn in his direction.

Eve grinned.

Toshiaki heard voices coming from everywhere in the room.

Panting voices. And not just one or two, but many, growing larger like a chorus.

He was terrified.

It was Kiyomi's moaning. Something only he should have known. A sweet song that soared without end, it had slumbered deep in Toshiaki's ears. His wife's moaning, responding sensitively to his lovemaking…his wife's moaning, echoing now in a frenzy of vocal activity. He looked across the room. Someone spoke in Kiyomi's voice. Her figure flowed into his mind like a deluge. Every one of her expressions, every gesture, bearing down upon him in raging waves. Kiyomi smiling, Kiyomi frowning, Kiyomi crying, Kiyomi calm, and Kiyomi held in his arms… Tens, hundreds, thousands of Kiyomis spilled into his brain.

His eyes were captured by these visions.

The dissected corpse on the floor opened his mouth, crying with pleasure in Kiyomi's voice.

The dead men in the green operating gowns were all moaning with their eyes wide open.

Toshiaki began to lose his mind. The moaning was giving him the illusion that he was embracing Kiyomi. When she moaned ah ah he sucked on her nipples when she purred with her mouth closed he ran his tongue over her ribs and back when she seemed to wail he stimulated her down there when she alternated between aaa and haa he entered her hugged her tight kissed her many times thrust hard saw her limbs in disarray saw her expression and it overlapped with the white corpse spilling its intestines when had it stood up the ones in surgical robes too walking towards him he was embracing Kiyomi the moaning came from corpses then Kiyomi was a corpse dead but moaning made love to why what am I making love to what this cold sensation what is this intestines wrapped around my arms is it Kiyomi's am I doing a corpse inserting into brain-dead Kiyomi's body Kiyomi's moaning is getting louder she likes it Kiyomi is Kiyomi is Kiyomi is Kiyomi is

"STOP-STOP-STOP-STOP-STOP-STOP-STOPPPPPPP!!"

The voices ceased.

The corpses fell to the floor, glistened, and dissolved instantly with only a faint, damp sound. Not a single flame to be seen. Eve 1's evocation of fire paled in comparison.

Anzai was clinging to Mariko on the autopsy table and shouting madly. Her eyes were open, but she was completely unresponsive to her father's cries.

Eve was giving Anzai a cold stare.

Don't.

Toshiaki raised his voice.

Too late. Still looking at Anzai, Eve tilted her head. One of Anzai's legs shot up unnaturally towards the ceiling. She was going to hurl him against the wall again.

Even when his entire lower body was in the air, Anzai refused to let go of his daughter.

Eve frowned.

He was immediately jerked away. His body grazed Toshiaki's cheek as it flew past into the wall with a crash. He did not fall to the floor. Instead, he was stuck spreadeagled with his face pressed against the wall. His eyes were shut tightly and he winced from the pressure.

Without warning, this unseen power gripped Toshiaki as well, pressing him against the wall before he even had the time to struggle. It was so strong, he could not even lift a finger. His cheeks squeezed together, nearly touching each other. He couldn't even blink his eyes.

Stop.

Stop it now.

He could not voice these thoughts. He was unable to move his tongue. Eve's figure was reflected in his eyes. It walked slowly towards the two of them, glancing down at the blubbering mass that was Eve 1, who smiled murkily in response. Eve beamed at her dying mother, then turned back towards Anzai and Toshiaki.

It's coming! Toshiaki screamed a silent scream. The pressure became stronger and stronger. His bowels twisted painfully. His skull creaked. His throat was crushed shut and he couldn't breathe. He felt like sparks were flying from his body. Simply killing them was probably too easy for her. The surgeons' corpses had disappeared from sight in but a moment's time. Eve was just toying with them now, like a predator making sport of its prey, like a child pulling the legs off an insect. He couldn't forgive his powerlessness before her. He couldn't forgive himself that all he could really do now was beg for his life.

His consciousness grew dim. Vision clouded with red as blood vessels ruptured behind his eyes. Something popped in his body with a dull sound and a hot substance flowed out from it. But Toshiaki continued to yell at Eve in his heart, to yell at her to stop.

"Daddy..."

Toshiaki was startled to hear a voice. It entered his ears as an unintelligible grunt, but transformed into Japanese in his head. Eve had called him "daddy." He felt faint. He saw her with the corner of his eye.

It had a horrendous grin on her face.

His whole body cried out. He couldn't believe what he had seen. Blood vessels burst everywhere in his body and his bones cracked. Eve's smile burned into him. He could not close his eyelids, no matter how much he tried; he could not yell, to dispel that horrid impression. It was a grin that could only be called horrendous. He couldn't bear it anymore. He did not want to live, with such a grin imprinted on his mind. *Just hurry up and kill me,* Toshiaki prayed. *Crush me!*

At that moment, Eve grimaced.

Evolution

24

Toshiaki's body fell to the floor, followed soon after by Anzai.

What's going on? He could not make sense of it. *Why did it stop?*

Eve appeared to be in pain, tearing at her face with a look of anguish. Flesh fell from her in pieces.

Toshiaki strained his eyes as Eve changed form yet again. Her entire body rippled. Her waist's curves straightened out, and her breasts flattened while her chest heaved out. Her shoulders broadened. The facial structure also changed. She wailed loudly. But the voice, too, was transformed.

What the hell is going on?

What had been a woman was now clearly becoming a man.

Something protruded from between its legs. At first the size of a finger, it began to swell and rise menacingly, pulsing all the while. The gentle curves faded as muscles stretched out in their place. Abdominals bulged out, and muscles swelled up above the shoulders. The neck grew thicker and the facial features sharpened. Sideburns extended like a lion's mane. A goatee and beard sprouted on the face. The creature's back heaved up like a mound of steel. Then, it put both hands onto the floor and assumed a beast-like posture on all fours. Every part of it embodied strength. A shout of indignation emanated from this new body as it struck the floor.

And then, it howled.

Thunderous waves rattled Toshiaki's ruptured organs, nearly tearing him apart. There was another enormous sound and the room went pitch dark. The electricity had been cut. An alarm sounded from somewhere.

Toshiaki coughed up the blood rising in his throat. Ruptures along his skin oozed plasma. The inside of his head burned.

Something popped in his eyes, after which he saw only red and black dots. A swarm of countless points ran wildly in his vision like a sand storm. He could hear the creature, but could not guess what it was doing. He heard concrete splitting open as chunks of wall fell onto him.

Yoshizumi let out a scream, but Toshiaki could do nothing more than remain where he was.

He then felt himself rise into the air. Something hit him repeatedly. In the stomach, shoulders, head, and chest. He was soon numb to the pain. While he knew he was being thrown against the walls, he had no will to fight it. He could only wonder why Eve had turned into a man. Mitochondria were definitely female. What did this mean? Was this another evolutionary step? And if so...

It all became clear to him now.

It can't be.

But there was no other explanation. Intellectually, it was questionable, but the intuition of every fiber of his being told him otherwise.

As if in answer to his thoughts, the creature yelled in agony.

There was an explosion. Toshiaki fell to the floor. The alarm blared in his ears.

But an even more deafening sound threatened to drown it out. It was as Toshiaki had suspected. Eve's voice was changing back into a woman's.

He heard what sounded like wriggling flesh in between the alarm intervals. Eve was reliving her violent regeneration and birth. Her pulse shook the air. A woman's voice arose above a man's yell, as if to silence it. The man's voice cut off the woman's with the ferocity of a jet exhaust. Male and Female were waging battle against one another in the same life form, a balance of power being pulled back and forth between them. Just when the female's expression was about to appear, the male formed its own figure over it. When the female cut out a womb in the body, the male buried it and extended its distinguishing organ in retaliation. The female twisted the penis back into the body as breasts arose in defiance. Toshiaki's intuition had been correct. Though he couldn't see it, he could tell that the new life form was devolving into a mess internally.

Someone or something jumped into Toshiaki's mind. The voice was faint, as when phone lines got crossed. Toshiaki realized right away that it was mitochondria, the ones that had parasitized Eve 1. That monster had been melting on the floor, trying to welcome her extinction, but was now dismayed at her daughter's transformation. The mitochondria were making one last desperate attempt at signaling the host cells to propagate again. The mother longed to control this disaster that was supposed to have been her perfection. But the host cells were damaged beyond repair. The mitochondria's sorrowful cry echoed in Toshiaki's body. *This cannot be, this cannot be!*

His head filled with a brilliant flash. That which until now had caught in a corner of his mind, refusing to be drawn out, now revealed its dazzling self. It was just as he thought... The mitochondria in Eve 1 had overlooked one important thing. They did not give sufficient consideration to it because they were female. His sperm was obviously necessary to create new life, but Eve 1 had only thought of male genes as tools for reproduction. The mitochondria had failed to notice that their "daughter" was made up not only of themselves, but also of male mitochondria.

Eve 1's mitochondria's final scream rang in Toshiaki's ears, trailing off into silence. He felt her death indirectly. Outer and inner membranes collapsed, spilling DNA from inside. They were then torn apart by enzymes. All electrical transmissions diffused and died out. Receptors dissolved into useless peptides before losing life completely. Consciousness ceased. Cells burst, returning to mere fats, amino acids, and sugars. Eve 1 was no longer a life form, but simply a heap of decaying organic matter.

Eve 1's child screamed in sexually dimorphous anguish.

The ceiling began to crumble as Eve erupted with pure power. *I need to get out of here*, thought Toshiaki. But his body would not move.

He heard people's voices, footsteps drawing near. Short gasps of shock and horror followed. A light hit his face.

Help had arrived at last.

He let out an exclamation of joy, but it did not take form in sound. He tried to move a little, but could not quite gather enough strength.

At that moment, a tidal wave of heat exploded around them.

Screams and frantic footsteps.

Toshiaki panicked, fearing for those who had come to their aid.

A blast of magma-like air pierced his body. Something heavy smashed into his waist. He lost all feeling in his legs. Distant screams:

"Oh my…!"

"What is that?"

"It's alive!"

He heard only snatches of speech, followed by the sound of flesh being torn from the bones, damp explosions, and truncated screams. While Eve was trying to keep Toshiaki under control, she was simultaneously venting out her power and destroying everything around them.

This could not go on. No one would ever make it out alive. He had to calm Eve somehow. There was no reason to let anyone else be sacrificed. He felt something hot swelling up from the very core of his being. He would stop this thing. He had to kill it. Even if…

"I order you to stop!" thought Toshiaki, with all the fury he could muster.

He sensed Eve's momentary hesitation. He screamed with more force.

"Come here! Look at me, me! I am your father! Come here!"

Eve whined, turning her attentions to him. The blazing wind lost its intensity.

"I know all about you. I know why you are the way you are. Come to me. Let me hold you."

Eve's movements weakened. She looked around in confusion for her mother. But Eve 1 was already dead. Toshiaki spoke to her with sympathy.

"Your body is breaking apart now. It hurts, doesn't it? I understand. Come here. Let your father hold you. I will share your pain. You can make all the children you want. But what about parents? You can't create them. And your mother is dead. I am the only parent you have left. Share your suffering with me. Think only of me. Over here. I am here. Now come!"

The heat died down completely.

Silence fell. The alarm faded away as Toshiaki's ears grew deaf to it. The ceiling stopped crumbling as well, as if the concrete fragments falling from above had ceased in mid-air. A silence that could not even be called silence.

And then, movement broke through the quietude, turning slowly in Toshiaki's direction. *Yes, that's it*, he said encouragingly as he spread open welcoming arms.

It touched his waist with a warm and greasy appendage, wrapping around his torso. Toshiaki smiled and spoke gently.

"Come now, share your pain with me. Fuse with my cells. Let us become one. If you do, you will no longer be afraid. You were not at peace, because you knew there was another self separate from you, because the life I gave you was trapped in another. I understand your torment. Become one with me. Come into my body. Be one with your father. There's nothing to be afraid of. Now."

Toshiaki felt his body melting.

Eve's cells opened the pores in his skin and flowed inside. Cell rubbed against cell, creating friction and heat. All sense of direction disappeared. Toshiaki could hardly feel anything. He knew that Eve's cells were passing into him, that their membranes were binding to his cells. Her mitochondria were becoming one with his, as were her mitochondrial DNA. Eve's power vanished in the blink of an eye.

She moved. The friction and heat increased and Toshiaki realized he was on fire. He felt like he was flying. It was such a mysterious sensation, a stimulation beyond anything he had ever imagined. Perhaps it was something no living being on this earth had ever felt. Was this what it felt like to evolve? He was experiencing a completely different dimension. Its joys and sorrows could never be comprehended by organisms that hadn't so evolved, nor would such creatures even know what they did not know. Human beings, too, would perhaps evolve to such a point someday. But would they still be in symbiosis with mitochondria then? Probably, yes. Evolution occurs in the process of one thing trying to coexist with something other than itself. That other could be another organism, or an environment. It was hard to say whether it would be on earth, another planet, or inside cells, but when human beings managed to build a new symbiosis, a new, evolved world would be theirs.

Eve growled as she integrated herself into him. Toshiaki merged with her in silence, their strength fading like a dying star. *It ends here*, he thought. *This is where the nightmare ends.*

Kiyomi, you will return to the self you once were.

To the Kiyomi I always loved.

Evolution

25

As Shigenori Anzai opened his eyes, there was a stranger reflected in them.

"He's opened his eyes!" screamed the man excitedly to someone unseen. Anzai heard the patter of approaching footsteps.

"Are you alright? Can you hear me?"

The white-robed man peered into Anzai's face and checked his body for injuries.

...Ah, I'm still alive.

At this thought, Mariko's name revived in his brain. He immediately snapped out of his daze and called out for her.

"Mariko! Where's Mariko?!"

"Please calm down. You shouldn't move."

The doctor tried to restrain him, but Anzai would not hear of it. Mariko was his only concern right now. He stood up, ignoring the intense pain in his back.

Anzai saw that he was in the hallway outside the autopsy room. There was a large crack in the concrete. Both the floor and ceiling were heavily damaged. He also saw a half-open steel door off to the side. Police officers and doctors were bustling about. There were several injured guardmen on stretchers. Yoshizumi was on a stretcher, too. His body was covered completely with blood and his right hand twisted at an unnatural angle, but he did not seem fatally hurt.

Yet Mariko was nowhere to be seen.

"Mariko!"

Anzai ran towards the autopsy room as fast as he could, staggering from the pain in his knees.

Just when he reached the door, several paramedics came carrying out a stretcher.

Mariko's naked body was lying on top of it.

"Mariko! Mariko!"

Tears flowed from his eyes. He clung to the stretcher, but she showed no signs of movement. Even when he screamed directly into her ears, there was no response. Anzai drew close to his daughter's cheek and stroked her hand. She could not be dead...

"Mariko will be fine."

Someone patted Anzai on the shoulder. He lifted his head in surprise and looked around at the doctors.

"Really?"

"Yes. She lost consciousness, but she's still alive. We found almost no external injuries." Upon hearing this, Anzai felt a warmth spread in his chest. He was too tired to cry.

"Oh, Mariko..."

Anzai held her again tightly, pressing his face against hers. Her skin was somewhat cold, but when he put a hand to her chest, he felt her heartbeat clearly. There really were hardly any visible wounds. How she had managed to avoid being hit by the crumbling concrete was beyond him.

There were scabrous bloodstains in her groins. When Anzai touched them, tears at last flowed hotly down his cheeks. When it mattered most, he had not been able to protect that which was most sacred to him. A deep feeling of regret seized his heart.

"...dad," came a small voice in his ear.

He bolted upright.

Mariko opened her eyes wearily.

"Mariko..."

"Dad...I..."

She moved her fingers slightly. Anzai wrapped her hand in his and brought it to his cheek, crying and nodding. Her lips trembled in an attempt to say something.

"I...I..."

And then...

THUMP.

Mariko's lower abdomen jumped.

Evolution

Anzai cried out. The surrounding doctors gave a suspicious look. Anzai's vision grew dark, thinking that the monster was still alive, trying to eat its way out of her. He screamed for it to stop.

But Mariko pulled him close, then caressed his back gently.

"It's okay," she said. "I'm fine. My kidney…won't do that ever again… Because…it's mine now…mine."

Anzai looked at her.

She smiled back. Her eyelids fluttered sleepily and closed softly, like a butterfly coming to rest.

He touched her abdomen cautiously, but there was nothing wrong with it. Just transplant scars and wet skin.

The kidney was now fully assimilated into her body.

He held her once again with all his affection. Considering her recent behavior, she would probably never have allowed such closeness save at a moment like this. But Anzai would try his best to reconcile their problems. He would spend more time with her and share his thoughts until she opened up to him. Their real life together was about to begin.

"Come along now, we're going to get your daughter out of here." So saying, one of the doctors gave him a pat on the back.

He could have held Mariko forever, but he put his faith in them as they carried her out.

As soon as they were out of sight, Anzai remembered Toshiaki.

"What happened to that man?" he asked the officer next to him. "Nagashima…the donor's husband."

The police officer's face became grave, and Anzai had the chills.

"What's wrong? What happened to him? Tell me, please."

"…over there." The officer nodded towards the area behind him.

Anzai turned around and gasped. There was a white sheet spread out, with the center bulging up. It was clearly covering something, but it looked nothing like a human shape.

He ran over to it. He heard the officer's warning but paid no attention and lifted the sheet.

"...my God."

He looked away.

Nothing but a half-dissolved pile of flesh. He could only tell it was face up from an ambiguous human chest. One hand was stretched out to the side, trying to grasp something. The skin's surface on the arms had liquified. Though an expression was slightly discernible upon the face, it was charred and shriveled up beyond recognition. A jelly-like substance oozed out from the chest and spread out on the floor. The odor of cooked meat penetrated Anzai's nostrils.

"Wait, bring Mariko back here!" he shouted.

Thinking something had happened, everyone else turned around at once.

"What's wrong?" An officer came running up. "Come sit down, please, you're badly hurt. You need medical..."

"Please, I'm begging you. If you just do this one thing, I'll do whatever you say. Bring Mariko back here one more time. It won't take long. Please, I promise it'll only take a second."

The officer frowned.

"Please."

"...okay, but make it quick."

He sighed audibly and called one of the younger cops over. With a few words and a pointing of the fingers, the cop was off into the hallway.

A short while passed before Mariko's stretcher was carried back in. There was an oxygen mask over her mouth and an IV tube in her arm. Her body was now covered with a blanket.

"Please put her down over here," Anzai requested. The medics set the stretcher down next to him.

"What's going on?"

But he did not answer and removed Mariko's blanket. Then, he took Toshiaki's dilapidated hand.

Evolution

Anzai placed the hand on the left side of Mariko's lower abdomen, where the kidney of Toshiaki Nagashima's wife had been transplanted.

It seemed to Anzai that Toshiaki's hand had been trying to touch Mariko in his last moments of strength, and thought it only appropriate that he should be granted his final wish. It was the least Anzai could do for the man.

Maybe Anzai's emotions were getting the best of him, but he could have sworn that Toshiaki's blackened mouth widened just barely into the slightest of smiles.

Epilogue

"Moving on now to the awarding of master's degrees for Pharmaceutical Sciences. Sachiko Asakura," the chair called out.

"Yes!" Asakura hopped up enthusiastically and moved to the front of the line.

She bowed gently, then took another step forward as the chair unfurled a large beige-colored scroll.

He leaned into the microphone and began to read.

"This award hereby confirms that Sachiko Asakura has completed the two year Ph.D. preparatory program and all courses therein to earn her master's degree in Pharmaceutical Sciences. Congratulations."

He turned around the diploma 180 degrees and handed it to her. Asakura bowed and put out both hands, accepting it reverently amidst camera flashes.

She backed up to her left, then turned to the side and bowed deeply to all of the professors.

The next name was called. A voice responded.

Asakura returned to her seat with her degree, watching as her classmates' names were called.

Following the university's graduation ceremony, the Pharmaceuticals students had come back here to their school for a private assembly, where degrees were given to everyone anew. This was the day when the normally drab lecture hall overflowed with the beaming faces of graduates, all in their best suits. Asakura had chosen to wear traditional attire, lent to her by her mother.

As she rolled up her degree and placed it in its tube, a refreshing breeze caressed her cheek.

She felt overwhelmed with joy and gazed out the window.

The weather was clear and beautiful, plum tree buds already opening in the warm air. The wind carried a pleasant scent.

The reality of getting her degree finally hit her. Having been hospitalized, she hardly performed any experiments for a good while but did manage to finish and present her thesis. There was still a burn mark on one part of her body, but the more obvious scars on her face had been corrected through skin grafting.

Epilogue

Asakura gazed at her classmates and reminisced about her school days. She had been through more than she cared to think, but on the whole it was an enjoyable six years. These last three in particular, she was thankful to have found her motivation. She nodded once to herself, thinking how right she was to have chosen this path.

After the ceremony, they relocated to the course seminar room for a final get-together.

They all celebrated with some beer, then focused their attention on Ishihara, who said: "On behalf of all the staff, I wish to congratulate you all. Most of you will now move on to pharmaceutical companies or research institutions. But no matter what path you choose, I believe that every one of you already possesses enough knowledge to go anywhere with nothing but the highest confidence. Even if you choose company work, I hope you will dedicate yourselves to making full practical use of all you've learned here and that you make significant contributions to our field. And I have no reason to doubt that you all will."

The graduates smiled brightly.

"And to all you seniors," the professor said, raising his voice, "the state pharmaceutical exams are coming up in approximately one week. I don't care how much you drink today, but starting tomorrow I want to see every nose in a book."

Everyone laughed at this. Even Asakura looked to her friends and snickered. The professor made this same joke every year, but it never missed.

"In any case, bottoms up!" Ishihara raised his glass.

"Bottoms up!"

At once, the room filled with noise and excited chatter. Flashes went off everywhere. Everyone gathered for a group shot as well. More beer was brought out and hors d'oeuvres were added.

Asakura chatted with her friends, then mingled around to greet the various professors to whom she was so indebted. She felt lonely to be parting from these people, but at the same time everyone seemed so relieved to be moving on.

Asakura's sadness was comfortably placated by a mild tipsiness.

Halfway through the party, she ducked out quietly and went to the Biofunctional Pharmaceuticals office on the fifth floor.

Since everyone was downstairs, there was no one else there. She opened the door to the lab, a place where she had spent so much of her time over the past three years.

She looked inside, only to notice that a number of the machines had been left running. Someone was probably doing a PCR, since the thermal cycler was on.

She stood in front of her desk and ran her fingers gently along its now empty surface. Asakura had already brought her Mac back to her apartment and was finished with packing. She was struck by how vast her desk seemed with nothing on it.

She glanced over at her bookrack, where the year's issues of *Nature* were being stored. They had been purchased by the course and were normally kept in the seminar room. Asakura was unsure why they had been moved here, but maybe they were remodeling the room and were taking advantage of the available space left from her absence. She stared at the perfectly lined spines, then plucked one out from among them.

She flipped through it and opened to the articles section.

The article was written in English, under which the names Toshiaki Nagashima, Sachiko Asakura, and Mutsuo Ishihara were printed. It was Toshiaki's piece.

She gazed at the page. Her data was printed as diagrams, to which long footnotes were attached. The images somehow seemed to her the remarkable work of some other person. She felt flattered.

It was only a short two-and-a-half page article. Even so, it was the pride of the Biofunctionals course.

But she had not truly appreciated it until now.

She would probably never have her name mentioned in *Nature* again. And her one time was thanks to Toshiaki.

If only Doctor Nagashima were still alive.

Epilogue

Asakura clutched the magazine to her chest.

Toshiaki's face appeared before her. At that moment, her eyes began to sting with unexpected tears. Surprised at herself, she wiped her cheeks, smudging her makeup. But the tears kept falling. She did not even shed a tear when she broke up with her boyfriends in high school. She tried laughing to mask her unusual outburst of emotion, but managed only a damp sigh. She sniffed and tried to smile away her sorrow.

She opened to the "NEWS AND VIEWS" section and turned to a piece of commentary. Memories of the day she learned of Toshiaki's death came flooding back.

She'd read this short article when the magazine first came out, but had forgotten about it. While in the hospital, she learned in great detail from the police and classmates what Eve 1 had done. She knew that Eve 1's mitochondria had rebelled, that the recipient girl was forced to give birth, that the child unexpectedly morphed between male and female, and that in the end Toshiaki and the new birth melted into one another and perished in flames. When Asakura first heard about this, she did not understand why the mitochondrial child had died. But then, she remembered the theory presented in this article.

It had always been accepted that mitochondrial DNA was passed through maternal heredity. Though male mitochondria entered an egg via the sperm which carried them, they did not multiply afterwards, and the mitochondria carried by the conceived child were once thought to have all been maternal. Genetic researchers accordingly analyzed mitochondrial DNA with this "matrilineal" rule in mind, and it indeed became a useful tool for theorizing the rate at which evolutionary processes occurred.

But in 1991, a certain research group announced some shocking results. When different species of mice were crossbred, it became clear that there was paternally transmitted mitochondrial DNA in their offspring. Though only a trace amount, its presence was unmistakable. The article undermined everything and was the subject of much attention. Since then, other researchers debated about whether or not mitochondrial DNA was actually unisexually inherited. Then, more recently, the problem had finally been clarified.

The results, in simple terms, were as follows:

In instances of interbreeding among identical species, the father's mitochondrial DNA entered the egg via his sperm, but after a certain amount of time, it died out, presumably neutralized by the placenta. In other words, the father's mitochondrial DNA was ultimately not inherited by the birthed child. However, when different species were crossbred, the opposite was true. The offspring's mitochondrial DNA was found to be 56% paternal.

Asakura thought that probably Eve 1's sole intent in breeding with Toshiaki was to acquire his nucleus so that she could create a new species with it and her mitochondrial DNA. But while Eve 1 was being cultivated in the lab, it had developed into a non-human species. The mating of Eve 1's egg cell with Toshiaki's sperm was essentially an interspeciary crossbreeding. Toshiaki's mitochondrial DNA grew inside the egg to drastic results.

Asakura skimmed through the *Nature* article. She had come back to it numerous times since leaving the hospital.

It was a summary of the hereditary pattern of mitochondrial DNA observed in a species of the blue mussel family. In the case of this species, the father's mitochondrial DNA was passed on to children, but the method of transmission involved was found to be incredibly unique. Unlike humans and lab mice, males carried masculine mitochondrial DNA and females carried feminine mitochondrial DNA. When the two mated, something peculiar happened. Though the sperm contained male mitochondrial DNA and the egg contained female mitochondrial DNA, female offspring inherited genes only from the female mitochondrial DNA, while male offspring inherited an equal amount of genes from both. As the male offspring grew, the male mitochondrial DNA multiplied within it and ultimately established dominance. In other words, unlike with mice, what occurred with mussels was "uni-parental transmission." Female mitochondrial DNA was only inherited by female mussels, and male mitochondrial DNA only by males.

One explanation claimed this was a defense mechanism to combat the "self-ish" dispersion of mitochondria. Let us say there has been a single mutation in mitochondrial DNA in a single female mussel, a mutation that dramatically speeds up the rate of its DNA replication. It would begin to proliferate in the mussel and continue to do so in its children, driving out the original female mitochondrial DNA. If maternal mitochondrial DNA were transferred to both sons and daughters, this altered DNA would spread through future generations. But if female DNA were inherited only by female offspring, the altered DNA would only be transmitted through the daughter's lineage. The mutation would be better contained. Introducing Richard Dawkins' concept of the "selfish gene" into this discussion opens up an interesting vista.

Dawkins' basic idea is that "all that a gene wants is to leave copies of itself in as many descendants as possible." In the case of the mussels, we have three such selfish players, the nuclear DNA, male mitochondrial DNA, and female mito-chondrial DNA. The mutated female mitochondrial DNA, wanting nothing more than to proliferate as much as possible, will replicate itself rapidly to pass itself on to as many descendants as possible. But the male mitochondrial DNA doesn't want to be exterminated and will try to obstruct the propagation of the mutant female mitochondrial DNA. Moreover, the nuclear genomes in the mussels might not favor mutations in mitochondria with which they've enjoyed a working sym-biotic relationship. If mitochondria changed too quickly, the host's very survival could be threatened. The female mitochondrial DNA's selfishness is, in this way, at odds with the self-interest of the two other players.

This was perhaps why a mechanism had arisen to keep female mitochondr-ial DNA in check. Perhaps something similar had happened in the thing born from Eve 1. Asakura certainly thought so.

The fertilized egg had received "evolved" mitochondrial DNA from Eve 1, whereas from Toshiaki, "normal" mitochondrial DNA was transferred, even if in a miniscule amount. But these two sets of genes coexisted in the new life form.

The mitochondria in Eve 1 undoubtedly believed they had facilitated evolution by their own power alone. In actuality, paternal mitochondrial DNA had also played a role in mitochondrial evolution, but Eve 1's mitochondria had failed to see this. Eve 1 had not counted on Toshiaki's normal mitochondria being inherited by their daughter.

The normal mitochondrial DNA transmitted into their child must surely have feared being utterly destroyed by the evolved DNA. The normal DNA's egotism, which wanted nothing more than to leave descendants, flatly opposed the agenda of Eve 1's more advanced mitochondrial DNA. A violent battle ensued between the two sets of genes, eventually leading to their mutual destruction.

This was as good a guess as Asakura could make. No one would ever know the full truth. People's knowledge of mitochondria was still incredibly limited. Mitochondrial research was only just beginning.

Asakura closed the journal.

Why did the mitochondrial child have to melt into Toshiaki until it died? This was also a big riddle. But Asakura thought she had an intuitive understanding where this tragic end was concerned. After all, Toshiaki and the mitochondrial offspring were father and child...

"Hey, Asakura, what are you doing all alone up here?" came an unexpected voice. She turned around to see the familiar face of a fellow student, one year behind her, who had also been under Toshiaki's guidance.

He removed some Eppendorf tubes from the thermal cycler, solving the mystery of who had left the machines running.

"Everyone's been looking for you. I wish you had told someone you were coming here."

"Sorry about that. I just wanted to take one last look around before I left."

Asakura returned the issue of *Nature* to its shelf and smiled to cover the fact she had been crying.

The student placed his tubes into a refrigerator and was about to close the door when he remembered something.

"Oh, by the way, I found some of Doctor Nagashima's cells in deep freeze, but wasn't sure what to do with them. Would you mind taking a look?"

"Cancer cells?"

"No, I'm not sure what they are."

She followed him into the equipment room. As he opened the large freezer door, a white mist billowed into her face. The student pulled out a rack and looked inside.

"Here they are."

He showed her a number of blood serum vials.

The labels were frosted over. She rubbed them with her fingertip.

Toshiaki's handwriting.

She held her breath.

They were dated August of the year before and marked "Eve 1."

Her heart gave a thump.

"...Asakura?"

She forced a smile.

"Something wrong? You look like you've seen a ghost."

"It's nothing. Is this all you found?"

"These, too," he said, and showed her a bag filled with several dozen vials. Some were labeled simply "Eve," but there were also others numbered as "Eve 2" and "Eve 3."

She was speechless.

These cells were being preserved in preparation for primary culture. Though frozen now, if they returned to room temperature, they would begin propagating all over again.

A cold shiver ran along her spine.

"What are these? I'll take care of them if you want."

"No, it's okay. Let's just throw them out. Thanks for finding them for me. I'll go put them in the autoclave."

"I can do it for you."

"That's okay. Just leave it to me."

Asakura gathered the vials into the bag and tied it securely. She went to the Cultivation Room, her feet picking up speed along the way.

None of these could be left behind. She had to destroy them immediately.

She ran into the Cultivation Room and opened the lid to the autoclave.

She threw the bag into it and closed the lid tightly.

If she killed these, all that would never happen again.

She was sure of it.

Just then, the back of her neck tingled sharply.

She froze. It was that sensation.

Asakura felt just a little anxious.

There was still one thing she could not explain. Why had Kiyomi's mitochondria rebelled? Why not Asakura's, or Toshiaki's? Why *Kiyomi*?

Was it simply a question of polymorphism? Everyone carried slightly different genes. Had Kiyomi's simply been different in such a way as to allow mitochondrial hyperactivity?

If that were so, what Asakura was about to do did not guarantee that mitochondria would never rise again. As long as people could be born with genetic mutations like Kiyomi's, there was a possibility that mitochondria could evolve in them. If that was so, was it not useless to hinder their evolution?

Asakura had no answers. Maybe so, maybe not.

All she could do with any assurance was to kill these cells.

"The party is winding down now. They're all asking for you," said the young man from beyond the door.

Asakura smiled, then switched on the autoclave.

NOTES

EcoR I and BamH I

Used in genetic engineering to cut strands of DNA. EcoR I and BamH I specifically digest (or recognize) the DNA motifs GAATTC and GAGCTC.

clean bench

A workstation enclosed in glass into which one places only the hands for sterilized handling of materials. Purified air passes into the clean bench via a filtering system.

NIH3T3

An immortal cell line cultured from the epithelial (i.e. fetal) linings of lab mice. Normal rodent cells do not divide more than ten times in a cultivation environment. Cancerous cells, on the other hand, divide indefinitely. NIH3T3 cells are known for their ability to propagate like cancerous cells while exhibiting traits of their healthy counterparts. Their name pays homage to the American National Institutes of Health (NIH), where they were first isolated.

retinoid receptor

Proteins that bind to a chemical compound (retinoid) similar to Vitamin A.

ß-oxidation enzymes

A series, or chain, of enzymes that draws out energy by decomposing fatty acids. This response can be observed, for example, in respiratory activity, in which ß-oxidation enzymes utilize oxygen to consume fatty acids. ß-oxidation enzymes exist in mitochondria and even in peroxisomes (one of four organelles in a cell).

hybridoma

Cells used to artificially fuse cancer cells and lymphocytes. They are particularly useful for cellular research, as they preserve the nature of lymph cells while multiplying indefinitely.

red indicator solution

Putting color into cultivation liquid is standard practice to determine its acidity or alkaline level (pH). Yellow=Acidic, Red=Neutral, and Purple=Alkaline. The condition of the cells is clearly elucidated from its color.

primary culture

A process by which cells are extracted from internal organs (human or rodent) and then cultivated. When pre-gathered cells such as NIH3T3 are cultivated, the initial stages are not technically deemed a primary culture.

cancer gene production
Whenever toxins such like radiation or carcinogens give rise to genetic mutations, cell division is affected, ultimately causing cancer. There are currently over 100 types of cancerous genes known, with new mutations always being discovered.

immuno-suppressants
These drugs suppress the body's natural refusal of foreign matter (in this case, a donated organ). At the same time, however, this makes a recipient more easily prone to bacterial infection, which can sometimes mean the difference between life and death.

HEPES buffer solution
A reagent used to prevent changes in a given solution's pH level. HEPES is virtually nontoxic and is ideal for maintaining a chemically neutral environment.

collagenase
Any group of proteolytic enzymes that decomposes collagen and gelatin (i.e. cellular proteins).

centrifuge
A machine by which diluted cells are collected through the use of centrifugal force. Fifty G's is the usual amount of force applied by the machine, which spins at 700 rpm, creating an artificial gravity 50 times that of the earth's surface. In this context, being gentle means to separate the cells carefully without damaging them.

Eppendorf tubes
Plastic receptacles that can hold up to 2 ml. Their resilience makes them ideal for use in centrifuges and are used often in genetic engineering. Costing only pennies each, they can be disposed of freely after use. Though originally a product of its namesake company in Germany, they are now manufactured by various other suppliers.

stirrer
A capsule-shaped mixing tool, consisting of a magnet covered in teflon. The stirrer is placed into beaker, into which the solution to be mixed is poured. The beaker is then placed onto a special machine. Another magnet inside the motor spins around, causing the stirrer to spin inside the beaker.

supernatant
Clear fluid above sediment or precipitate in a test tube.

pipettman
A device used to extract an exact amount of a given solution anywhere from 0.2 to 1000 micro liters. In genetic engineering, the usual amount used is between 10 and 100 μL. One μL is equal to one cubic millimeter in volume.

-80° C

Cells can be preserved by freezing them while still alive. This requires a slow cool down in a special preservation liquid, dropping the temperature by one degree per minute. In this way, the cells suffer minimal damage.

Kiyomi's liver cells were glowing

Cells treated with collagenase appear as glowing globules when viewed under a phase contrast microscope. Dead or dying cells are opaque and a cell's condition can be judged according to its luminosity. If left for a number of hours, cells aggregate to the bottom of the flask and lose their brightness.

cytosol

In addition to the nucleus and mitochondria, cytosol is another important cellular component. Mitochondria are actually stuck to a mesh structure called tubulin, so they are unable to move around freely. In longer cells such as nerve cells, they unite with these "motor proteins" to achieve movement. Free-swimming mitochondria are thus rare.

Kiyomi

The name Kiyomi is comprised of two characters, the first meaning 'holy' and the second 'beauty'. When the first character is used in conjunction with that for 'night', the resulting compound means 'Christmas Eve'.

six-well plate

There are various sizes of plates which have small depressions (wells). The number of available wells ranges from 6 to 96. In a 6-well plate, 2 mL can be put into each 3.5 cm diameter well.

MOM19

Genes coding for a large portion of mitochondrial proteins can be found in the nucleus: the nuclear gene products generated as precursor proteins must be imported into mitochondria. MOM19, a protein in the mitochondrial membrane, is essential for this importation.

cloned

In a first generation cultivation, the qualities of each cell differ slightly, because the inherent nature of each cell changes during the culturing process. In order to acquire uniform cell groups, a succession of cells is replicated from a single cell. This is called cell cloning. There are innumerable methods for cell cloning, but the so-called "critical dilution" method is the most widely used of all. In this method, one dilutes a cellular solution and cultivates no more than one cell per plate well. Inside each well, the cells that multiply are virtually identical to the cell from which they propagate. Eve 1 and Eve 2 propagated in separate wells. Therefore, each is a unique clone group. This is different from genetic cloning.

Northern blot

A way of detecting and quantifying a specific RNA. RNA can be separated into the following sub-classifications: ribosome RNA (rRNA), transfer RNA (tRNA), and messenger RNA (mRNA), among others. The person who devised the DNA detection method was named Southern, so his method came to be known as the Southern blot. RNA is, appropriately enough, "Northern". A Western blot detects proteins. There are "Eastern" and "South Western" methods as well. The amount of beta-oxidation enzyme produced is largely determined by the amount of mRNA coding the protein in question.

RT-PCR

A method by which mRNA is transcribed to DNA and selectively amplified.

clofibrate

A drug that lowers cholesterol in the blood. Clofibrate also acts as a ß-oxidation catalyst.

citric acid cycle

One of several metabolic pathways in mitochondria, it fuels the reactions that generate sugar, fatty acids, and many amino acids.

cell bank

A facility where various types of cell cultures are registered and from which cellular samples are sent out to researchers upon request.

fibroblasts

Long and thin as their name implies, these cells are relatively easy to culture and can divide about 50 times in human biological systems. Even with the best equipment, one can only get liver cells to survive for about 1-2 weeks. It is much easier to cultivate fibroblasts to maintain a high cell count, but here Toshiaki wants to use liver cells as per standard research practice.

needle biopsy

The most direct method of determining the condition of a transplanted organ. A needle is inserted into the patient's kidney (in Mariko's case) and a small tissue specimen taken. A minute sample of the extracted tissue is stained, then observed under a microscope.

Mitochondrial Eve

In 1987, Cann and Wilson proposed the theory that we are all descended from a single woman in Africa whom they dubbed Mitochondrial Eve. However, this does not mean that Mitochondrial Eve lived in isolation, but implies only that humanity originated in her and that she thrived with many others.

hot wind

Mitochondria are the birthplace of energy. They make use of enzymes to combine with ATP. The energy used to consummate this synthesis is stored as electricity and is called an electron transport system (ETS). The potential for one cubic centimeter of mitochondrial activity is 200,000 volts. When we exercise, an emission of heat can also occur directly in mitochondria themselves. This process is what causes fever. The proteins that facilitate this discharge are called "uncoupling proteins" and are found in 307 amino acids. If all mitochondria in the entire body simultaneously discharged in this manner, the heat produced would be unfathomable.

Their membranes fused, first the outer, then the inner.
There is evidence to suggest that when cells fuse together, each mitochondrion actually fuses as well. However, there are also times when the latter does not occur because of mitochondrial abnormalities. This is usually dependent on the conditions in which the fusion takes place.

replicating them or programming them to die at will
In the cells of "higher" life forms, death is systematic. Unneeded cells kill themselves gradually over time. This programmed death (also called apoptosis) is hindered by certain proteins that exist chiefly in mitochondria. That this programmed death signal emanates from mitochondria is unmistakable. The manipulation of cells by mitochondria is therefore not entirely unthinkable.

Drosophila
A fruit fly used extensively in genetic research.

She scowled at the man, then made his heart stop like She did to the last one.
Heart disease has been known to occur from miniscule changes in mitochondrial DNA. Eve 1 would therefore have to manipulate very little to accelerate such a process.

PCR
Polymerase Chain Reaction. A technique for amplifying DNA sequences in vitro by separating the DNA into two strands and incubating it with oligonucleotide primers and DNA polymerase. This process can amplify a specific sequence of DNA by as many as one billion times and is important in biotechnology, forensics, medicine, and genetic research.

thermal cycler
A device used in PCR to replicate specific DNA strands using polymerase. Researchers can investigate DNA extracted from a single human hair or trace of any bodily fluid, and this has forensic uses in criminal cases. The genes of the dinosaurs in *Jurassic Park* were restored in this way.

polymorphism
Individual genetic differences.

BIBLIOGRAPHY

«Manuals, Commentaries, Instructional Writings, Essays»
1) 'Clinical Dialysis' editorial committee, planning/Sakai, T., "All about kidney transplants" *Clinical Dialysis*, 6, August supplement, 1990, Japan Medical Center.
2) Tôma, H., Ôshima, S., and Hasegawa A., eds. "Kidney Transplant Manual" 1993, Chûgai Igakusha.
3) Saitô, A. and Ôta, K., eds. "Dialysis Handbook, 2nd edition" 1991, Igakushoin.
4) Tachibana, T., "Criticisms on Brain Death Declaration" 1992, Chûokôronsha.
5) Watanabe, J., "What we think of brain death now" 1994 (originally published 1991), Kôdansha Bunko
6) Ôta, K., "Why are organ transplants necessary?" 1989, Kôdansha.
7) Yanagida, K., 'Sacrifice (gisei) – My child and brain death' *Bungeishunjû*, '94. 4, 144-162 and '94. 5, 126-151, 1994.
8) Ôzuka, H., "Emergency Care" 1991, Chikuma Library.
9) Guillozo, A. and Guguen-Guillozo, C. "Isolated and Cultured Hepatocytes" 1986, John Libbey Eurotext Ltd/INSERM.
10) NHK Shuzaiban. "Life: A great journey of 40 million years • 1: Birth from one ocean" 1994, NHK Shuppan.
11) Takeuchi, K., "Dents in a small demon's back: The realities of blood type, sickness, and love" 1994, Shinchôsha.
12) Fuji Television, ed., "Einstein TV • 3: Mitochondrial Eve's Gift" 1992, Futabasha.
13) Lemonick, M.D. 'How Man Began' *Time*, 143, No. 11, 38-45, 1994.
14) Takeuchi, K., "Such rubbish!: On genes and god" 1991, Bungeishunjû.
15) Asahi Shimbun Igakubu, ed., "A doctor's small tools • large tools 122" 1992, Yôdosha.
16) Picknett, Lynn, "The Encyclopaedia of the Paranormal" 1994 (originally published 1990), Seitosha.

«General Articles, Reports, Academic Theses»
1) 'Special Issue   Organ Transplants   1994' *Kidneys and Dialysis*, 36, 25-84, 1994.
2) Ozaki, S., 'Kidney Transplants' *Gekachiryô*, 70, 46-51, 1994.
3) Sakura National Hospital, 'Terminal Kidney Transplant System Report' *Transplant*, 28, 540-550, 1994.
4) Japan Transplant Association 'Report on Kidney Transplant Clinical Registration Totals (1991)' *Transplant*, 27, 594-617, 1992.
5) Kawaguchi, H., Itô, K., 'Problems faced by pubescent children with kidney disease' *Puberty Studies*, 11, 10-14, 1993.
6) Shimada, A., Miyamoto, K., Takahashi, S., and Ozaki, S., 'The role of dialysis rooms in terminal kidney transplant' *Magazine of the Japan Society for Dialysis Treatment*, 25, 1409-1412, 1992.
7) Bereiter-Hahn, J. and Vöth, M. 'Dynamics of mitochondria in living cells: shape,

changes, dislocations, fusion, and fission of mitochondria' *Microsc. Res. Tech.*, 27, 198-219, 1994.

8) Kuroiwa, T., Ohta, T., Kuroiwa, H. and Kawano, S. ' Molecular and cellular mechanisms of mitochondrial nuclear division and mitochondriokinesis' *Microsc. Res. Tech.*, 27, 220-232, 1994.

9) Soltys, B.J. and Gupta, R.S. 'Changes in mitochondrial shape and distribution induced by ethacrynic acid and the transient formation of a mitochondrial reticulum' *J. Cell. Physiol.*, 159, 281-294, 1994.

10) Schulz, H. 'Beta oxidation of fatty acids' *Biochem. Biophys. Acta*, 1081, 109-120, 1991.

11) Lazarow, P.B. and De Duve, C. 'A fatty acyl-CoA oxidizing system in rat liver peroxisomes: enhancement by clofibrate, a hypolipidemic drug' *Proc. Natl. Acad. Sci. USA*, 73, 2043-2046, 1976.

12) Wienhues, U. and Neupert, W. 'Protein translocation across mitochondrial membranes' *BioEssays*, 14, 17-23, 1992.

13) Pfanner, N. Söllner, T. and Neupert, W. 'Mitochondrial import receptors for precursor proteins' *Trends Biochem. Sci.*, 16, 63-67, 1991.

14) Glover, L.A. and Lindsay, J.G. 'Targeting proteins to mitochondria: a current overview' *Biochem. J.*, 284, 609-620, 1992.

15) Stuart, R.A., Nicholson, D.W., and Neupert, W. 'Early steps in mitochondrial protein import: receptor functions can be substituted by the membrane insertion activity of apocytochrome c' *Cell*, 60, 31-43, 1990.

16) Kliewer, S.A., Umesono, K., Noonan, D.J., Heyman, R.A. and Evans, R.M. 'Convergence of 9-cis retinoic acid and peroxisome proliferator signalling pathways through heterodimer formation of their receptors' *Nature*, 358, 771-774, 1992.

17) Issemann, I. and Green, S. 'Activation of a member of the steroid hormone receptor superfamily by peroxisome proliferators' *Nature*, 347, 645-650, 1990.

18) Hirose, A., Kamijo, K., Osumi, T., Hashimoto, T. and Mizugaki, M. 'cDNA cloning of rat liver 2,4-dienoyl-CoA reductase' *Biochem. Biophys. Acta*, 1049, 346-349, 1990.

19) Kobayashi, S., Amikura, R. and Okada, M. 'Presence of mitochondrial large ribosomal RNA outside mitochondria in germ plasm of *Drosophila melanogaster*' *Science*, 260, 1521-1524, 1993.

20) Gyllensten, U., Wharton, D., Josefsson, A. and Wilson, A.C. 'Partial inheritance of mitochondrial DNA in mice' *Nature*, 352, 255-257, 1991.

21) Hurst, L.D. and Hoekstra, R.F. 'Shellfish genes kept in line' *Nature*, 368, 811-812, 1994.

22) Kaneda, H., Hayashi, J., Takahama, S., Taya, C., Lindahl, K.F. and Yonekawa, H. 'Elimination of partial mitochondrial DNA in intraspecific crossing during early mouse embryogenesis' *Proc. Natl. Acad. Sci. USA*, 92, 4542-4546, 1995.

23) Kaneda, H. and Yonekawa, H. 'Why mitochondrial DNA is maternally inherited' *Tissue Culture*, 21, 142-146, 1995.